BENDERS

D M SMITH

COTTONWOOD BOOKS PUBLISHING
DURANGO COLORADO

BENDERS

This is a work of fiction. Unless otherwise indicated, all the names, characters, businesses, places, events, and incidents in this book are either the product of the author's imagination or used in a fictitious manner. Any resemblance to actual persons, living or dead, or actual events is purely coincidental.

ISBN 979-8-9864687-0-9
LCCN: 2022913544 (print)

bendersnovels.com

For Carolyn. Thanks for believing in me.

BENDERS

PROLOGUE

That night Ellie lay awake for hours, staring up at the intricate tangle of shadows cast onto the ceiling by the limbs of the cottonwood tree that grew just outside her bedroom. She felt trapped within that pattern, lost at the center of a complex maze whose path shifted erratically with every breeze, making it impossible for her to escape. But it was not mere shadows keeping her awake so late.

Since that afternoon, her mind had been in turmoil, the scene of a struggle where what she had once believed true waged a fierce battle against what she now feared was possible. The further removed from that earlier moment of revelation she became, the less certain she was of its truth, but she was convinced enough that she had been gripped by a gut-churning dread ever since.

She heard her sister shift in bed at the far end of the room. Maybe Sam was still awake, too. If so, should she say something? Say what, exactly? The ideas bouncing around her brain sounded crazy even to her. Her thoughts were clear enough inside her head, but the vocabulary she needed to express them stubbornly eluded her. She soon realized she wouldn't be able to rely on words alone, and just before drifting off to sleep, she had one last thought—*Tomorrow I'll show her the pictures.*

1

FOUR DAYS EARLIER

Six minutes passed following the last bell of the day before Ellie finally exited through the doorway of her American History class-room. Distracted by her frustration over running late, she burst into the hallway without looking and nearly collided with fellow junior Jordan Baker.

"*Geez!* Try getting your face out of the books and, like, pay attention to what's going on around you for half a second!"

Ellie knew this sentiment was common among her peers and no longer considered it worth getting angry over. "Sorry, Jordan, I...."

Annoyed, the girl flashed Ellie her palm. "Don't care!" she snapped, then stormed off.

Ellie looked across the hall to where her older sister Sam leaned against her locker, waiting as she often did so they could walk home together. A witness to the awkward encounter, Sam was trying—and mostly failing—to suppress a grin.

Ellie was not nearly so amused. "*See!?* That is exactly why I avoid these people as much as possible!"

Sam stopped resisting and let the smile come, but she remained silent as the two fell into step and joined the daily exodus to freedom. Ellie took a deep breath, trying to regain a sense of calm following her near-miss. She waggled a tightly rolled stack of paper in front of her as she apologized for the second time in half as many minutes.

"Sorry you had to wait. I was trying to get some help with my term paper. Mrs. Comnena said my first draft was a little 'dry,' whatever that's supposed to mean. I stuck around to ask her about it, but it seemed like she and Dylan were going to take forever, so I bailed. I mean, seriously—if there's *anyone* who could use some help!"

"What's your topic again?" Sam said.

"Child labor laws in the early twentieth century."

"*Hmm....* It's very likely she has a point. For *my* term paper, I wrote about Jackie Kennedy's impact on U.S. fashion during her time as First Lady."

"Like I could forget. For week after week, it was 'Dior' this and 'Chanel' that."

"Mock if you must, but the world just lost a genius, you know."

Ellie knew Sam was referring to the recent death of famous clothing designer Hubert de Givenchy. "I do know. So sad. I sent you a card—didn't you get it?"

"*Thppt!*"

"Or were you referring to Stephen Hawking? He was an *actual* genius. Seriously—this town is *full* of geniuses! How you can possibly compare a glorified seamst—what do you call a male seamstress? A *seamster?*—is that a word?—compare *him* to...."

"This town is full of *nerds!*"

"This town" was Los Alamos, New Mexico. Perched high atop the rugged, colorful cliffs of the Pajarito Plateau and guarded on its west by the Jemez Mountains, its geographic isolation had made it the perfect place for the U.S. Army Corps of Engineers to hide the most secret part of the clandestine Manhattan Project. In the early 1940s, scientists worked here at a fevered pace to beat Nazi Germany in the race to develop an atomic weapon. Seventy-five years later, Los Alamos was no longer the nation's best-kept secret but was world-famous as a leading center of scientific research and technological development. The city proudly boasted that its population comprised one of the country's highest concentrations of doctorate-level college graduates.

Even though a limited amount of work remained focused on testing and maintaining the country's nuclear arsenal, the facility's largest employer was now Los Alamos Biotechnologies, which was universally referred to as "the LAB." Its sprawling campus was made up of over a dozen separate facilities where more than a thousand scientists, technicians, and support staff explored widely differing areas of research. Ellie and Sam's parents had been lured to the town years earlier by the unique job opportunities, and both held research positions in separate divisions at the LAB.

The school was Los Alamos High. It was widely recognized for its academic rigor and consistently ranked as one of the country's best secondary educational institutions, facts generally underappreciated by its attendees. The students' parents, many of whom held at least one PhD degree in a hard-science field, insisted the district recruit only the best educators to fill the school's highly coveted teaching slots. As a result, LA High graduates could usually count on attending whichever university they chose.

"Nerds *rule!*" Ellie shot back. "This town wouldn't even exist if it weren't for nerds. Your *boyfriend's* a nerd."

"Ryan is *not* a nerd!"

"He's getting straight A's in Calc Two and AP Physics—that's gotta mean something. Oh, and *Apple Watch?!*"

"He's on the swim team. And the track team. *And* he wrestled freshman year."

Ellie snorted. "Yeah, like *those* aren't nerd sports! Okay, so he's in the nerd closet. No, wait—I've got it! He's like a nerd Tootsie Pop—a thin layer of crunchy macho on the outside, but all chewy nerdiness in the middle!"

"Are you calling Ryan a sucker?"

"He's dating you, isn't he?"

Sam saw too late how she'd set herself up for the jab. "*Oops!* Ha! Good one."

Anyone unfamiliar with the Henderson sisters could easily mistake their back-and-forth banter for serious bickering, but to them it was merely a rhetorical sparring game, a verbal form of fencing, and all in fun. Cleverness was the measure of it, and each readily acknowledged when the other scored a point.

"'Cause you're a nerd, too," Ellie continued. "Only what's in your closet is *way* more trendy."

"*Not* a nerd."

Ellie snorted. "Right! You're a *fashion* nerd! Remember when you got all excited because you thought that Jupiter probe was named after *Oleg Cassini?*"

Sam affected a sigh. "What can I say? I was young. And besides, what's wrong with wanting to look nice? Especially being stuck out here in the boonies."

"What's the point if there's no one to look nice for?"

"Well, I *have* someone."

As if in on their game, Ryan appeared from around a corner ahead of them. He stood slightly taller than the students around him and was easily recognizable by his sandy hair, which he kept styled in a way that always made Ellie think of David Beckham. Spotting them, he stopped and waited in place rather than fight the oncoming flow.

"Speaking of suckers...."

"*Shush,*" Sam hissed.

"Hello, ladies," Ryan said, sounding far too smooth for Ellie's tastes.

"Hello, Tootsie-Nerd!" Ellie chirped.

Instantly recognizing that he was coming in on the middle of something, Ryan let the odd greeting slide. He had long ago grown used to feeling more than a little adrift whenever he was in their company.

"Ignore the child," Sam said.

Ryan dropped in behind them, and together they headed toward the lobby. "You know, the 'sister act' you two have going is way funnier than the movie."

"Wow," Ellie said. "*That's* going back a ways."

"Yes, but you can never go wrong with a classic."

Sam and Ryan loved movies and watched three or four every week as the demands of study and sports allowed. They enjoyed the 'classics,' in both the usual sense and as the term applied to those more recent films that had so far stood the test of time, and they could quote at length from their favorites. Both were cinematic omnivores, and as long as a movie was generally considered good or, occasionally, utterly terrible, they'd sit through it. Sam was equally as willing to settle in front of *Blade Runner, Arrival,* or the latest *Star Wars* offering as he was to sit through *Lost in Paris* or *The Devil Wears Prada*.

"It's 'prAna,' actually," Ellie had observed at the time, a sly allusion to the fact that although Sam's sartorial preferences didn't lean toward Prada or Christian Dior—or Oleg Cassini, for that matter—she nonetheless wouldn't be caught dead on even the most remote hiking trail in anything "less" than Columbia, and then only as a last resort.

"What's in your queue this week?" Ellie said.

"I dunno. What've we got, Sam?"

"There's *Young Frankenstein, Eternal Sunshine, Upstream Color*—which I don't know anything about...."

Ryan held up a finger. "My pick," he interjected.

'...and the original *Solaris*. I think that's it for now."

Ellie's taste in movies was more selective, but occasionally she allowed herself to be persuaded to sit in on a good science-fiction film, one where the emphasis was squarely on the science. She had enjoyed *The Martian* and the much older *Andromeda Strain*, and from what she knew of *Solaris*, she suspected she might like it, too.

Once they reached the lobby, Ryan steered them out of the flow of exiting students and into a corner at the end of a row of glass trophy cases where they could talk without getting trampled. "I've got a swim team thing to go to. Coach wants to schedule some extra practices now that it looks like we could go to the finals. Albuquerque—woo-hoo!" He pumped his fist in the air, but it was a sarcastic gesture. "Anyway, shouldn't take too long—catch up with you later?"

"You know where I'll be," Sam said.

"Hey, when you see him, remind A-Ron about Friday." He leaned forward and planted the briefest of kisses on the tip of her nose.

A warning voice sounded from near the school's main doorway where Mr. Telford, the shop teacher, manned his usual end-of-the-day post. "Mr. Collins, classes may be over, but you're still on school grounds!"

"Yeah, yeah," Ryan muttered, not bothering to give the speaker so much as a glance. He winked at Sam and left, heading back up the hallway they had just come down.

As he dodged and weaved his way against the oncoming flow of stragglers, they could see the rolled-up crown of his New York Yankees baseball cap, its brim tucked into the waistband of his jeans, bobbing against the small of his back. This way of carrying his hat indoors was a habit instilled in him by his father, a retired Marine Lieutenant Colonel who now ran security operations for the LAB.

Sam called down the hall after him. "Bye!"

"*Bye!*" Ellie echoed Sam in the exaggerated, breathless tones of the most tragically love-struck. She looked at Sam and fluttered her eyelashes. "Isn't he *so* dreamy?"

"Oh, just... *zip it!*"

In truth, Ellie genuinely liked Ryan. She knew the ladies'-man persona he sometimes affected was not a reflection of his true personality, and while she might find him annoying at times, she couldn't imagine a better match for Sam.

When Ellie and Sam exited through a set of deeply recessed glass doors, they spotted Aaron Siskin leaning against a thick cement wall in the coolness of the entry's shade. Even in the deep shadow, his short, spiky hair, so blond it was practically white, seemed to glow. Like Sam and Ryan, Aaron was a senior, even though only a few months older than Ellie. Unlike them, he did not try to conceal his enthusiasm for learning, especially as it pertained to any device, gadget, or gizmo, new or old. Nor did he attempt to deny his position on the nerd spectrum.

The vivid purple backpack sagging heavily from his shoulders displayed a large, equally vivid green button near the top that announced, "I Grok Spock." With his pale hair, vibrant pack, and a pair of large, round, wire-rim glasses that often rode slightly askew on his nose, he was never hard to pick out of a crowd.

Seeing them come through the doors, he kicked off the wall and trotted over to join them.

"Hey," he said.

"Hey," Ellie said back.

Aaron used his middle finger to settle his glasses into place. Had the lenses been smaller, Ellie might have been reminded of those worn by a certain storybook wizard. In conjunction with his shock of white hair, however, they most often made her think of Hedwig, the wizard's messenger owl, instead.

"We're a bit late," Sam said, "because *someone* was getting help learning to write an essay like an actual human instead of an AI bot."

"Really?" Although Ellie and Aaron spoke in unison, they were asking entirely different questions. She meant *is* that *the problem?* He wondered *why would she want to do* that?

"You two are so cute."

Aaron gave Ellie a puzzled look, but she could only shrug in reply.

"Are we still on for Friday?" he said.

"I almost forgot!" Sam said. "We are. Ten o'clock at the far end of Rim. Are you two going to pedal out together?"

"He mentioned getting our lunches at the co-op, so I guess we'll do that first, then meet you at the trailhead. Do you know what the weather's supposed to be like?"

Sam pulled her iPhone from her back pocket and depressed the home button until she got a beep. "Siri, what's the weather for Friday, please?"

Ellie glanced at Aaron and rolled her eyes. He grinned back.

"Here's what I've found," Siri said.

"Thank you."

Ellie laughed. "Siri's not listening anymore, you know. And besides —*app?!*"

"Make fun now, but when the AIs go nuts and take over—*and they will*—they'll remember which of us were nice to them right from the beginning." She turned to Aaron. "Sunny and seventy-four."

He squinted hard at her, intensely concerned. "So your ultimate defense strategy against the rise of Skynet is, what, *politeness?*" This he truly wanted to know. More than anyone in their tight-knit foursome, Aaron viewed the theoretical *singularity* as a more or less eventual given and was prepared to be genuinely dismayed if that were her entire plan.

"That and being as annoyingly irrational as possible," Ellie said. "Messes with their logic circuits."

Sam furrowed her brow and scolded them in mock outrage. "That's it! After the take-over, you two are on your own! I am *so* not helping either of you!"

"Maybe they'll hire me to write their press releases or something," Ellie said. She held up her paper baton. "I can submit this as a writing sample when I apply for the job."

Aaron stopped at the base of one of the two pedestrian overpasses that bridged Diamond Drive, the four-lane road that separated the high school and university campuses. "Hey, uh, I've got work to do on my science fair project. See you guys tomorrow?"

"We'll be here," Ellie said.

"Where else would we be?" Sam muttered.

They watched him start up the tall, metal stairs. Seeing the cluster of academic buildings across the street, Ellie sighed. "I guess you'll all be over there next year. And I'll still be here. *All alone,*" she added, sounding as whiny and self-pitying as she could manage.

Sam's reply was unsympathetic. "Poor you." They turned away from the overpass and continued walking home. "I was kidding with the 'AI bot' thing, by the way. Your writing is fine, although it can be a bit, um...."

"'*Dry?*'"

Sam shrugged. "I was going to say 'succinct.' Do you want me to take a look at your paper?"

"No. At least not yet. I'll have you look at the next draft, maybe. But thanks."

"Don't sweat it too much. In the end, she's looking for proper citation of sources, correct grammar and spelling, and logical flow, not flowery prose. You'll do fine."

"Well, I have all of those things. I can footnote with the best of 'em. It's obvious she's looking for something more on the 'flowery prose' side. Something… I don't know… *moister?*"

Sam chuckled. "So the day it's due, dunk it in your coffee and hand it in dripping!" Ellie smiled as she imagined her teacher's expression if she presented her with a sopping wet essay. Sam placed a hand on her shoulder. "Trust me—you'll do fine."

Ellie resisted the urge to remind Sam that merely doing "fine" on any school assignment was not now, had never been, and would never be an acceptable option. Rather than retread old, familiar ground, she changed the subject. "Are you guys gonna watch a movie later?"

"I think so. Probably. Wanna join?"

Ellie shook her head and again waggled the rolled-up essay in front of her. "No, I better take another crack at this."

Later that evening, Ellie worked alone in the bedroom. The sun had set while she studied, and now the room's only light came from the screen of her MacBook. She was dressed for bed, which by late May meant simply an extra-long tee shirt that reached almost to her knees. Pragmatic by nature, she chose most of her clothing based solely on utility, but she enjoyed using her extensive collection of nightshirts to show off her sharp, intellectual wit. This one was dark blue and bore a white line drawing of a cat in a box, below which the caption read:

Schrödinger's cat is

☑Alive ☑Dead

She sat at her small desk, plowing steadily through the day's homework. She had completed her calculus problems and American Lit assignment in forty-five minutes and was finally free to return her attention to her problematic history essay. On the glowing screen in front of her, a Firefox browser window displayed the results of a Google search for the word *dry*. She was not ignorant of the word's meaning in this context but hoped the exercise would give her a fuller understanding of precisely what her paper lacked. She muttered to herself as she read through the list of synonyms.

"*Simple, basic, straightforward*—those are good things, right? No, wait! *I have an idea*—let's do research, then make the report as murky as possible!" She continued reading down the list. "*Emotionless, stiff, wooden*—okay, that's not so good, but it's a history paper, not a romance novel."

Speaking of romance, her concentration was broken yet again by another outburst from the living room. Sam and Ryan were boisterously enjoying whichever movie they had picked for the night, and judging by the frequent fits of hysterical laughter that echoed down the hall and slipped in under the bedroom door, Ellie guessed it was either one of the best comedies ever

made or one of the worst dramas. Spitefully, she hoped it was the latter. She
rolled her eyes and tried to ignore the frequent interruptions.

Scanning the monitor a second time, her gaze was drawn again to the
two synonyms that bothered her most—*unexciting; dull.* That didn't sound
good at all. Although she preferred clean, concise writing, she loathed the
idea of turning in a dull, unexciting paper, whatever the topic.

She picked up her first draft and tried to uncurl it. She rolled the stack in
the opposite direction, then dragged the pages over the desk's edge at an
angle. When the essay would again lay nearly flat, she flipped over the title
page and reviewed her first few sentences:

In the early part of the twentieth century, there were few laws in place to
protect young workers in the U.S. from exploitation—or even outright
abuse—at the hands of mill, mine, and factory owners. Early attempts at
regulating child labor, such as the Keating-Owen act of 1916[1] or the
Revenue Act of 1919[2], for example, were determined to be unconstitu-
tional, as were state laws aimed at restricting workweeks to no more than
sixty hours. These judgments reflected the strongly pro-industry attitude
within the federal government. There was also a prevailing social belief
that allowing children to work not only helped keep them out of trouble
but enabled them to provide additional income for the poorest families.[3]

The underlying problem was rooted in the previous century, in the
consistently negative legal decisions rendered toward efforts of
employees to act collectively on their own behalf—to unionize, in other
words....

It was dry, all right. Arid, in fact. Downright Saharan, if she were being
completely honest. She sighed heavily.

"I'm doomed!"

Setting the paper aside for now, she tugged her stack of library books
toward her. She slid a thin, large-format volume called *The Bread and Roses
Strike—Two Months in Lawrence, Massachusetts* from the middle of the pile and
studied it. She had learned the basics of the millworkers' strike in Lawrence
in a few of the other books she had checked out, but had so far chosen not

to devote her limited time to reading an entire book, slender though it was, that dealt with but a single episode in a long movement.

Tonight, though, something about the faces in the cover photograph captured her imagination. She closed her laptop, clicked on her bedside lamp, and flipped forward from the back cover until she found the last numbered page. There were only a hundred and thirty-three pages, many of which she knew were mainly photographs. Figuring she could get through it by the time the movie ended and Sam came in wanting to go to sleep, she propped her pillows against the wall, shimmied up onto her high bed, and began to read.

2
_____

"What the..?" Ellie woke up disoriented. She was sitting mostly upright but listing so far to the left that her head nearly touched the wall alongside her bed. Once her mind started to clear, she realized that she must have nodded off while reading.

As she straightened herself up, she reflexively touched a hand to the front of her nightshirt and was relieved to find she hadn't been drooling in her sleep—Sam could have fun for days tormenting her about something like that. Her book sat on her desk beside her, but she had no memory of putting it there, nor could she recall how much progress she had made before dozing off. She was in the middle of an intense, full-body, moan-inducing yawn when Sam reentered their room, hair wet from the shower.

"*Ahhhn-yahhh!*"

Sam grinned. "And a good morning to you, too."

"Morning." Ellie's response came out as a croak, and she cleared her throat before continuing. "Did I put my book away last night, or did you do that?"

"Ha! You were so deeply out that I literally watched to make sure you were still breathing. I pried the book out of your hands, but apart from grabbing your ankles and yanking, I didn't know what to do with you. I figured you'd wake up at some point and, you know, fix yourself. Guess not, huh?" Sam pointed at Ellie's book. "I did mark your page, though."

"Ooh! Thanks!" Ellie picked the book up from the nightstand and opened it where a tiny scrap of paper poked out from the top. She checked the page number and scanned the text to find the last section she remembered reading, a paragraph halfway down page 125. "*Wow!* I almost made it through the whole thing." She still made no effort to rise. "How was the movie?"

"It was *Young Frankenstein,*" which Sam pronounced as *frahnkensteen,* "so it was hilarious!" Recalling the film, she laughed. Then her expression became serious. "You know, you've only got about twenty-five minutes to get ready."

"*Really?!*" Ellie's eyes snapped to the ancient, hand-me-down electric clock on the small nightstand beside Sam's bed and read seven forty-eight. "*Aaagh!*" She jumped out of bed and darted across the hall to the bathroom.

During the walk to school, Ellie consumed the blueberry bran muffin she had grabbed on her way out the door, washing bites of it down with coffee Sam had brewed for her while she rushed to get showered and dressed. Their daily route covered three-quarters of a mile, and she had always found the twenty-minute walk provided just enough time to make the mental adjustment from home mode to school mode in the mornings, then back again each afternoon.

The first half involved hiking along a short part of the extensive trail system that threaded through Pueblo Canyon, the deep ravine that divided the plateau into smaller mesas and Los Alamos into distinct residential, commercial, and research areas. Over the years, previous owners of their house had maintained an unsanctioned spur that led from the far end of their back yard to the 'official' trail in the ravine below. Since most of the year was suitably warm and dry, they used the trail nearly every day. On the occasions when it was dangerously icy, snow-covered, or simply too muddy, they hitched a ride with one of their parents, biked, or, in a worst-case scenario, rode the bus. Biking took less time, but Ellie enjoyed hiking through the wooded canyon and chose the trail whenever possible.

"Thanks for this," she said, raising the mug in Sam's direction.

"No problem. You know, if that book you were reading last night was on how to cure insomnia, I'd say the author was on to something."

Ellie laughed through a mouthful of muffin, swallowed. "*Ha!* It's about a labor strike that happened in Massachusetts in 1912."

"Yep—that'd do it!"

"You'd think. It was pretty interesting, though, as far as I can remember. A young girl got hurt in a mill accident there, and the workers used her story to get public support on their side when they went on strike. I was reading it to see if I could use any details in it to improve my paper."

"And?"

"And... I don't know. It's a research paper, right? Who cares if it's just a bunch of facts and figures—that's sorta the point, isn't it?"

"You might feel a little different if you had to read thirty of them."

"If you mean Mrs. Comnena, then I say if she doesn't want to *read* a bunch of essays, she shouldn't *assign* a bunch of essays. All I'm concerned about is getting a good grade."

"And that's part of your problem."

"Meaning?"

"Meaning it sounds like your focus is entirely on getting the 'A,' not on writing the best paper you can. Why did you decide on the topic you picked?"

"For one thing, I figured I could find a lot of information on it pretty quickly. And because...."

Sam knew at once where Ellie was headed and didn't need to let her finish. "Because you thought it would be easy, in other words." She pressed her for a more personal reason for picking her subject. "What I meant was, why were you interested in it to start with? What about it grabbed you?"

"*Grabbed* me? Hundred-year-old *labor laws?* Not much!"

"There you go. It's hard to write about something with emotion if you don't care about it. I know you know this, but I'll say it anyway. Teachers—most teachers, at any rate—*want* to give good grades. They'd like nothing more than to stand every day in front of classrooms full of bright, motivated students, each of them eager to learn."

Thinking of a select few of her classmates in particular, Ellie rolled her eyes. "Yeah, well... good luck with that."

"I didn't say it was reasonable, but I don't believe you can even *be* a teacher if you aren't basically optimistic."

"And what's that got to do with my paper?"

"I had her last year, right? So believe me when I say she hates it when people try to coast. She can tell whether or not you care about your subject, and if you don't care, why should she? My advice? Find something about child labor laws that truly interests you, or else pick another topic."

"Oh, come on! It's not like you were really interested in *haute couture*. You're not going to major in fashion design or anything."

"No, you're right. But just because clothing design isn't a career option, that doesn't mean I'm not interested. Following what's going on in Paris, New York, Tokyo? Okay, I admit that's mostly just me trying to feel a little less cut off from the rest of the world while we're stuck living up here on this rock, but I genuinely do enjoy it. So no, I don't plan to work for Zara, but that doesn't mean I can't drool over that pleated, palm-print miniskirt they have, even if it *is* mostly orange. But when it came to writing my paper, I could take *that* kind of interest in fashion and apply it to something else, like Jackie Kennedy in the sixties. Does that make sense? But mostly? Wearing nice clothes makes me feel good, and I'm not the only one who gets a little lift out of it, if you know what I mean."

Ellie chose to pretend she didn't and returned instead to the topic at hand. "All of that's easy for you to say—you *enjoy* this stuff!"

It was true. Sam delighted in every essay, book report, short story, or poetry assignment her teachers threw at her. She had even worked on the high school newspaper during her freshman and sophomore years, eventually stopping only when it started taking up too much of what might otherwise have been "Ryan time." Then, almost as soon as she'd quit, she'd begun keeping an online diary—*journal*, Ellie reminded herself—simply because she missed the process.

"And I can't start over," Ellie grumbled. "It's *way* too late!"

"Well, then…." Sam didn't bother filling in the blanks.

Ellie blew out a long, defeated breath. "I hate writing!"

-"That's funny, because I can see you putting out a *huge* best-seller one day."

The lilt in Sam's tone made Ellie suspect a trap, but she couldn't see it. Even so she responded cautiously. "Really?"

"Absolutely! It will be over a thousand pages long and be called *Things My Sister Taught Me.*"

Ellie rolled her eyes. "Har har. I guess I could come up with one or *maybe* two things." She made a dramatic show of giving the matter serious consideration. "Nope, just one, and I can't remember what it is."

"'Har har' yourself. Still, think about what I said."

Which she did. She spent most of her study hall period and all of American History going back through the *Bread and Roses* book, taking notes on the injured girl, her family, and how the strike had gained some important, if ultimately short-lived, workplace improvements for the millworkers. The girl, whose name Ellie now knew was Carmela, was one of the hundreds of children smuggled out of Lawrence to other cities like New York, Philadelphia, and Boston. This was done partly to keep them well-fed and out of danger, but also so that they could spread the word about the hardships they faced working in the unsafe mills.

Fearing bad publicity, the mill owners sought to prevent the children from leaving Lawrence. They went so far as to hire private security firms like the Pinkerton Agency to stop them from boarding the trains meant to carry them out of town. Carmela spent several days in strangers' homes before finally getting the opportunity to tell her story to a Congressional committee in Washington, D.C., that was drafting laws to improve workplace conditions.

To her surprise, Ellie found she was developing a deep respect for this young girl who had lived so long ago, and she wondered if she could have made the same tough decisions had she been in her place. Los Alamos might feel isolated—she couldn't argue with Sam about that—but her life there was as idyllic as it could be. It was hard to imagine having to work at such a dangerous job at so young an age. It was even harder to picture leaving her parents behind to avoid the threat posed by some goon squad hired by that very same company.

Although she wrote exclusively on her MacBook, she stuck to her old-school habit of recording notes on index cards. It was a technique her mom had taught her years ago, and she had come to appreciate how simply rearranging the cards could give her a whole new insight into her subject. She printed the relevant bits of information on the front of the card and recorded the bibliographical details on the back. As she slowly worked her way through the book, her pile of cards grew steadily taller.

When the end-of-day bell finally rang, she tidied her stack of notes, bound them with a rubber band, and slipped them, her computer, and various library books into her backpack. She did not expect to see Sam when she left the classroom. Ryan had the first of the swim team's extra practices after school, and she would almost certainly be in the bleachers, cheering him on. She did find Aaron waiting in the same place he had been on the previous afternoon, and they walked slowly toward the street together.

"How's the science fair project coming along?" she said.

"Meh... I am not, as they say, 'feeling it' this year. Everything I *can* do is hokey and has been done a thousand times before, and anything I'd *like* to do is way beyond what I could possibly pull off. You know, without petawatt lasers or access to a CRISPR lab."

"So making a rechargeable battery out of a rutabaga and a box of Froot Loops is out?"

Aaron snorted. "Please—that is so third grade! I do have one idea, though. You've heard of the bacteria that eat plastic?"

She was only now realizing she wasn't even entirely sure what a rutabaga was, but this sounded at least somewhat familiar. She nodded. "Uh-huh."

He heard the uncertainty in her voice and gave her a brief primer. "Researchers working in landfills discovered that a few bacteria species were feeding on some common plastics. Since then, they've been trying to find ways to use them to break down trash that otherwise would be around after even the roaches have gone. Plastic is wonderful for lots of things, but *shopping bags?!* You put your groceries in the bag, you put the bag in the car, then you put the groceries away and put the bag in the trash."

Ellie opened her mouth to protest, but he waved a hand to cut her off.

"I know, I know—not you guys, but most people do. They've used it for fifteen minutes, and then it goes off to sit in a landfill for the next millennium or so.

"So these bacteria that can digest plastic, or certain components of certain plastics, to be precise...."

"And when are you ever not?" she said.

Aaron smiled at what, to him, was the ultimate compliment. "Anyway, they could be really helpful. But the flip side is this—think about how much of what we use every day is made of plastic, and imagine if suddenly these plastic-eating critters started to spread out everywhere. Or maybe their eating habits evolved. You could be going down the road at sixty miles per hour, and all of a sudden, a third of your car starts falling apart!"

"*Seriously?!* They could do that?"

"Well, no, probably not. At least, not without some help. At the moment, they're trapped where they are by requiring a highly specific environment. But these are bacteria, right? Not terribly hard to modify if someone wanted to."

"*Hmm*.... A potential bioweapon that rids the landscape of plastic. I confess I'm having mixed feelings about that. And your project idea?" she said, trying to nudge him back on track.

"I was able to get a small culture sample shipped to me—or to Mom at her lab at the LAB, actually—but I haven't been able to get the sample to replicate to the point I have enough to do anything with. I was hoping I could demonstrate some additive that could be used in plastic products that were meant to be 'permanent,' something that the little guys wouldn't like, which would prevent those things from being broken down. A sort of safeguard. But if the bacteria won't do their part, I won't have enough to work with."

"They're not 'feeling it' either, huh?"

"Evidently not."

"How's *her* project coming along, by the way? Your mom's energy-from-algae thing."

"Great! She's supposed to go to Washington next month to give presentations to NASA, JPL. SpaceX is looking at her work for its own Mars plans, and some clean-energy start-up people are interested, too."

"That is so cool!"

"Yeah, Mom's great! Her work could literally save the world. Or, at least be a big part of doing that, anyway."

Whenever he talked about his mother, the usually reserved Aaron became more animated and even seemed to glow with pride. Ellie liked seeing him happy that way, but she switched the topic back to his project.

"You said something about controlling your plastic-eating microbes?"

"*Huh?* Oh, yeah. Why?"

"I was wondering if there might be something doing that to them now, something to do with how you're trying to get them to grow, maybe? Let's see...." She used her fingers to tick off some of the environmental conditions she knew it was necessary to control for when growing bacteria. "You've got the growth medium, humidity, temperature...."

Aaron stopped in his tracks and ran the list through his mind for several seconds. She imagined that an intricate set of gears had been set in motion behind his round eyeglasses. Suddenly, he knocked the heel of his hand against his forehead.

"*Idiot!*" Ellie blinked at him, startled. "Not you—you're brilliant! I, uh, I gotta go!" And without further elaboration, he turned and started toward the overpass at a slow jog, his purple pack bouncing heavily on his back. At the base of the stairs, he called to her over his shoulder.

"See you tomorrow!"

As he bounded up the metal treads, the fingers of her partially raised right hand curled in a half-hearted wave. "See ya," she called back, although by this time she was talking only to herself. She watched until he reached the steps at the far end, sighed, then turned and headed for home alone.

Ellie spent the rest of the afternoon and evening at her desk. She started with her calculus homework and spent an enjoyable thirty minutes determining the dimensions of the strongest rectangular beam that could be cut from a cylindrical log, optimizing the size of a conical paper cup, and proving that a square has the largest area of all rectangles with a given perimeter. Assignment complete, she quickly scanned the next lesson, a habit she found made it much easier to follow along during class the next day. As one of only a few juniors in the senior-level course, she was extra careful never to appear lost during the lecture. After dinner, during which she got to hear all about the amazing aquatic prowess of one Mr. Ryan

Collins, she returned to the bedroom to review the Spanish subjunctive for half an hour before finally resuming work on her American History paper.

She left her books and note cards in her backpack and instead opened her laptop. She began by running searches for *lawrence strike 1912, american woolen company,* and *international workers of the world* in separate tabs. The number of hits listed for the Lawrence strike search surprised her, but she quickly concluded that this was mainly due to the many articles written in 2012, the strike's centenary year. Skimming through a sample of these articles, she was struck by the number of references to children. As cheap and ideally-sized workers, they were critical to the profitable operation of the mills. They were a vital source of additional money for their families. They were also crucial to the ultimate success of the Lawrence strike.

Reporters wrote stories that described the deplorable conditions faced by the young millworkers, and these gained support for the strikers throughout the northeast. Some of these were the same children who, along with Carmela, shared their stories with members of Congress. Articles about the union organizers who helped with the strike, mainly men and women from the International Workers of the World, explained that placing so much emphasis on the children's plight was a calculated ploy that had originated with them.

She clicked on the *american woolen company* tab and opened the Wikipedia link to read about the mill's early history. From there, she moved on to a brief biography of the man who had run it and several other mills in the northeastern U.S., William Wood. She clicked on the "Images" option above the search results and began browsing a succession of old, black-and-white photos of grim, brick buildings. What particularly caught her interest were the numerous depictions of women and young children tending endless rows of complicated and somehow menacing-looking machinery.

Many of the women in the photos were dressed in long, flowing skirts and frilly blouses, and their hair was pulled up into what she considered an unnecessarily elaborate style. One look at the machines was all it took to understand why they'd want their hair tied back, but the women in many of the photos also seemed too nicely dressed for factory work. Had that simply been the fashion back then? Whether that was the case or not, she guessed it was most likely that these photos had been staged, perhaps meant for use in a company brochure or to be handed out to members of the press. After all, it's not like reporters or photographers would be allowed to wander around the factory floor at will, would they?

Bleary-eyed from reading the articles and staring at grainy, low-contrast photos, she brought up Google Maps and scrolled her way east until she found Lawrence, Massachusetts. She zoomed in on the city and centered the Merrimack River on the screen. Situated along a canal on the river's north side was a rectangular outline labeled "Washington Mill Lofts." Washington Mills had been part of Wood's American Woolen Company.

There it is, she thought.

She clicked into Street View, and suddenly there *she* was, too, standing on a sidewalk along the canal on a cloudy summer afternoon, looking up at the mill's enormous brick and glass façade. She rotated the view to the right and clicked her way down the sidewalk until she reached a bridge. With one more click, she was abruptly transported to the bridge's opposite end, standing on the road between the Washington and Pacific Mills. Large signs mounted on their exteriors advertised apartment vacancies—at some point, both buildings had been converted to residences.

Curious, she opened a new tab and typed in *washington mill lofts*. She found the company's website, selected "Photos & Tours," and began browsing a slideshow of images. Some photos were of high-ceilinged apartments with arched windows set into brick walls that overlooked the canal. Others showed the lobby area or apartment floor plans. She clicked on a thumbnail to enlarge a photo of a living room furnished in a contemporary style. The room featured a concrete floor, a wooden plank ceiling, and was dominated at one end by a pair of the tall, iron-framed windows she had seen from the outside in Google Street View. She knew next to nothing about the formal principles of interior design, but even to her untrained eye, the contrast of old and new seemed to work. *They look pretty nice,* she thought, and immediately felt a twinge of guilt. *People suffered in these places for years, and now they're apartments?* It didn't feel entirely right.

"Wow," she muttered.

"'Wow' what?"

"*Aaagh!*" Ellie jumped, startled by the unexpected voice behind her. She spun around on her chair to discover Sam sitting on her bed, her iPhone resting in her lap. Ellie figured she was either texting with Ryan or updating her online diary but couldn't tell which. Whatever Sam was doing, she looked comfy and settled in, like she had been sitting there for some time.

"I didn't hear you come in!" That was unsurprising. Her sister could be scarily quiet—like ninja-assassin quiet—when she wanted to be. Ellie glanced again at the phone and decided to play the odds. "What's Mr. Collins have to say?"

"*Hmm?*" Sam followed Ellie's gaze to her lap. "Oh. No, I was writing down something Missy Fergusson said in AP Bio today. She meant to ask if a certain anti-parasitic drug worked on multiple organisms, but what she actually said—from the back of the room and loud enough for *everyone* to hear —was...."

Ellie gasped. "*No, she didn't!*"

Sam nodded, grinning gleefully as she delivered the punchline to her story. "Uh-huh... 'would they be good for multiple *orgasms?*' Everyone in class totally cracked up, and Missy's face turned a shade of red I didn't even think was possible. Mr. Zenker was cool, though. He looked at her for a second, like he was trying to figure out if she meant good for *preventing* them or for *causing* them, then he simply said he wasn't aware of any such studies and went on to the next topic. Not something I ever want to forget."

Ellie was still laughing. "I bet *she* sure won't! She's lucky there are only a few weeks of school left, or she'd *never* live it down."

"Yeah, well, *maybe* it's luck. I'm just saying—it seems like getting off easy is kinda her thing! So, what were you 'wowing' about?"

"Well, nothing *that* exciting. I was looking at pictures of some old textile mills back east. Some of them are still standing, but they've changed a lot in a hundred years."

Their mom, passing by on her way down the hall, leaned in through the open door and gave them a wry smile. "Get back to me in a hundred years, and we'll see how well *you're* holding up!"

"Hi, Mom," they said in unison.

"Don't stay up all night, you two," she said, then was gone.

"G'night, Mom," they said.

"So why 'wow?'" Sam said.

"I don't know. It just struck me that these mills.... I mean, people worked and suffered, and some even *died* there. People who were struggling to be treated as actual human beings and not just as lines on some company's balance sheet. Now it's a hundred years later, and people see those places only as trendy lofts, but the truth is they're...." She trailed off, not sure exactly what she thought they were.

"*Hallowed ground?*"

"Something like that, I guess."

"Remember our conversation from this morning?"

"Yeah...?"

"I think you may be getting close." Without further explanation, Sam returned her attention to her phone.

Nearly an hour later, Ellie heard Sam close the book she'd been reading, click off her bedside lamp, and slide under her covers. She did not stay up all night, but she did spend a little time re-reading parts of the *Bread and Roses* book, particularly the section describing the tense period leading up to the strike. She found it impossible to believe that conditions like those described by the millworkers had even existed in this country, let alone that they had been legal.

There were many photos interspersed with the text. A couple of them showed scenes of a speech given the day the workers voted to end the strike. Others depicted various views of the crowd of workers bundled up against the sharp bite of a New England winter morning. The people in the pictures, all dressed like extras in a BBC period drama, looked a little strange to her, and the grainy quality of the black-and-white photos did nothing but heighten her sense of separation between her world and that of the strikers.

She noticed a photo of a family at the lower right corner of one page—a man, a woman, and their daughter. The girl wore a flower on her coat, which Ellie found especially interesting given that it had been mid-March when the photo was taken. The caption read, "Genarro, Camella, and Carmela Teoli just moments after the vote that ended the two-month-long 'Bread and Roses' strike." The names sounded familiar, but she couldn't immediately place them. She flipped past several more pages before she remembered—

Carmela was the girl injured in the factory accident, one of the children who had been sent to Washington.

She turned back to the photo and peered closely at Carmela's face. *So that's her.* She was impressed by how the girl's calm, confident expression made her appear even more self-assured than her parents. It was the look of someone who had passed through harsh trials and emerged stronger, her spirit unbroken. Then Ellie remembered something else. *In this picture, she's only fourteen!*

After she set the book on her desk and turned off her own bedside lamp, she lay awake a while longer, thinking about giant mills, small children, and the slow, plodding pace of progress.

3

E llie was up early and had finished in the bathroom before Sam even made it out of bed. When she returned to their bedroom, she carried a steaming mug of coffee in each hand. After scooting back to sit upright against her headboard, Sam extended her arms in front of her and made clutching "gimme" motions with her fingers. Ellie gave her a bright smile and passed her a mug.

"My turn."

"My sister—the saint!" Sam said, canonizing her on the spot. She lifted the cup to her face and breathed in the aroma before taking a small sip.

"Ahh, s'aint nuthin'," Ellie said and smiled at her pun.

"Somebody's in a chipper mood this morning."

"I think I get it! About the paper, I mean. I think I know how to make it better."

"Congratulations. Did you work on it very long last night?"

"No, I turned in shortly after you did. I thought about it for a while, though, once I laid down. I'm going to pitch most of what I've done and stick with what happened in Lawrence. The strike there." She paused to take a long drink from her mug. "If I try to cover as much time as I was planning, I won't be able to put in enough details to make it—I don't know—*personal*, I guess. But if I focus mainly on Lawrence, I can do it."

"So what you're saying is…."

Ellie raised her mug toward Sam. "That my older sister is indeed very wise and offers excellent advice."

Sam lifted her own mug. "I'll drink to that." She took another quick sip before placing the coffee on her nightstand and sliding out of bed. "Just remember this when you write that book!" She smiled, then headed across the hall to take a shower.

Forty-five minutes later, they were at the mid-point of their walk to school. As soon as they stepped onto the narrow, steel and wood footbridge that spanned the wash at the lowest point on the route, they were loudly scolded by a pair of Steller's jays that swooped and dived at them repeatedly, evidently protecting a nearby fledgling. By the time they reached its far end, the jays had stopped their defensive display.

"The mornings are starting to warm up," Sam said. Living at an elevation of over seven thousand feet, they were accustomed to waking to cool mornings even when the afternoon high might top ninety degrees. Now that they were well into spring, the sun rose earlier each morning, and the day heated up a little more quickly.

"Yeah, it's nice. And everybody's lilacs are blooming. The smell's pretty intense on the way home."

Ellie went abruptly quiet then, and the silence stretched out for over a minute. They were nearing the small playground at the far end of the trail when Sam finally nudged her to share the thought that had made her go silent.

"Yes?"

Ellie shook her head in frustration. "People are so—*stupid!*"

"Umm, I thought this town was full of geniuses."

"Yeah, well, sometimes I wonder about some of *them*, too. But I was thinking of the mill owners and almost everyone else in the northeastern cities. Every time a new group of immigrants came over to the U.S., everybody would hate on them. The Irish, Germans, Italians…. People thought every Italian was an anarchist or part of the Mafia. Wouldn't even rent them apartments in a lot of places. And the Irish were all 'belligerent drunks.'

These were people doing the dirtiest, most dangerous jobs there were, and everyone was like, 'Go home—we don't want you!' And it's not like they weren't immigrants themselves. It hardly seems any better there than it was in the south, and that was *horrible!* The only people everybody back then seemed to have something against…."

"Let me guess," Sam interjected.

" …were the Jews, yeah."

"'The more things don't change, the more they stay exactly the same,' as Grandma used to say."

"She still does, probably. But yeah, it's not like it's all that different today except now it's Latin-Americans and Middle-Easterners we're supposed to be afraid of." She sighed.

"Is that part of the new angle on your paper?"

"Absolutely *not!* I'm sticking with the whole 'less-is-more' approach. All of *that* stuff could be a paper on its own."

Sam commended her in a formal, ritualistic tone. "You have found the path of wisdom, young *kohai*."

Ellie executed a minute bow without breaking stride and replied with equal solemnity. "Thank you, *senpai*."

They both laughed.

"I've often wondered how much easier Ryan's anime phase would have been to get through if they offered Japanese at school."

Ellie tried to sound sympathetic. "We each have our struggles." *Oh, yeah,* she thought, *he's so not a nerd!*

They were crossing the street that bordered school grounds when Sam abruptly remembered an afternoon appointment. "Hey, before I forget, I'm getting my hair cut after school, so don't hang around waiting for me." She laughed. "I'm just having her tidy up the ends, but I told Ryan I'm having it all whacked off for the summer job this year. I think he's freaked."

Ellie found she was in complete agreement with Ryan on this one. For as long as she could remember, her sister's hair had hung to the middle of her back, and the image of her with short hair seemed fundamentally wrong. Knowing beyond any doubt that Sam would never commit such an act, she let the thought pass without comment.

"Okay. I'm sure Aaron will be around."

"Oh, I'm sure he will be."

Ellie gave her a quizzical look, but that was all Sam had to say on the matter.

The day crept by at an unusually slow pace. Also unusual was the frustrating sense of impatience Ellie felt about getting to history where she could finally write! She found the unfamiliar sensation unsettling.

Maybe I'm coming down with something.

Once she finally got to class and opened her MacBook, she attacked her essay with enthusiasm. With the new direction held clearly in her mind, words and sentences—even whole paragraphs—seemed to flow from her fingertips directly onto the glowing screen. She was so completely absorbed in her work and excited by her considerable progress that she was startled when the final bell rang. She loudly protested the interruption without thinking.

"What?! *No!*"

The outburst earned her an assortment of looks from her classmates, running the whole gamut from concern to contempt. She thought she saw Mrs. Comnena hide a smile behind her hand before deciding there was something important to look for in her desk. The same passion for learning that often alienated her from her fellow students served only to endear her to teachers, but either way, she could do quite happily without all the judgment.

Whatever! she thought and flopped her laptop closed.

Aaron was not waiting in his usual spot when she exited the building. Puzzled by his absence and feeling oddly let down, she lingered outside the doors, wondering if he had been held up after class. When she finally thought to check her phone, she found he'd sent a message soon after the bell had rung.

Aaron—Need to get home and check on bact. More later. CUT

She tapped out a one-letter response:

Ellie—K

She set off for home, that vague sense of disappointment suffusing her mood. Minutes later, she came to an especially luxuriant lilac bush near where the asphalt ended and the trail into the canyon began, its blossom-laden branches spilling over a low, chain-link fence to block nearly half of the sidewalk. She cast a furtive glance toward the house to make sure no one was watching, then stripped off three large clusters of flowers, raised her little bouquet to her face, and drew in a deep breath. For a moment she simply stood there, eyes closed, savoring the heady scent. Lilacs grew well in the region's arid climate and were common in yards throughout town. Over the years, the distinctive fragrance had become synonymous with spring, and today it helped lift her out of her funk. When she reopened her eyes, she was suddenly aware of how truly fine an afternoon it was, and she resolved to enjoy the rest of her walk home as much as she could.

She ignored the shortcut that led directly to their house and instead followed a much longer trail that would eventually bring her out of the canyon at a sidewalk in a different part of her neighborhood. Along the way, she stopped to observe half a dozen Abert's squirrels leaping through the pine trees. Elegantly furred in dark gray and white, their black ear tufts obvious even from a distance, these were the first new animals she had learned to recognize after her family moved to New Mexico. She heard the raucous calls of numerous ravens, and once she had to do a quick, little hop-step to avoid trampling a smooth green snake stretched out in a patch of sunshine in the middle of the trail. When she squatted for a closer look, she saw its scales were so vibrant that she assumed it must have recently molted. Nearly getting stomped on did not seem to have bothered it in the slightest, and this, too, cheered her. She considered shooing it out of the center of the trail—strictly for its own good—but she'd long made it a point to disturb her fellow creatures as little as possible, even the slithery ones. At that point, she noticed her lilacs, in contrast to her improving mood, were beginning to wilt. And so, leaving the snake to bask in peace, she set a brisk pace for home.

Back at her house, she headed straight for the kitchen to tend to her sad-looking bouquet. She filled a heavy tumbler nearly to the top with cool water, lowered the flowers into it, and made a silent wish that they would perk back up rather than continue dying. She placed the tumbler on the counter peninsula that divided the kitchen from the small dining area and studied the drooping blossoms. She was not optimistic.

After she had climbed out of Pueblo Canyon's cellular dead zone, her phone had pinged repeatedly, alerting her to a series of long, rambling messages from Aaron. They all seemed related to his science fair issues, complete with pictures, so she'd decided to wait until she was home to read them. With her flowers tended to, she pulled her phone from her pocket and cradled it close to her face.

Aaron guessed that his bacteria problem had something to do with sunlight that, at a certain time of day, bounced off the window of an RV parked in the driveway next door and blazed directly into the makeshift incubator containing his cultures. The heat—or maybe it was the ultraviolet —was just enough to kill a portion of the cultures each day, and after more than a week of this cycle, he wasn't sure they were going to make it.

She was so engrossed in trying to make sense of it all that she was only dimly aware of the distant sound of a door closing followed by soft footsteps in another part of the house. A moment later, she felt a pair of hands clasp her loosely on her sides, slide down and around her waist, and come to rest with gentle pressure low on the front of her hips. Every muscle went rigid with surprise, and for a second, she was unable to move or speak. Then a soft puff of warm air tickled the back of her neck.

"Love the haircut," Ryan said, his mouth mere millimeters from her ear. His voice was pitched somewhere between a whisper and a purr. "Sorta Lily Collins circa, say, three or four years ago? *Very* sexy!"

Sexy?! That broke her paralysis. Her body jerked forward, knocking into the counter hard enough to send water sloshing from the flowers' improvised vase. She whirled around to face him, shuddering as a brief, intense spasm rippled through her entire body, just as if she had walked through an unseen spiderweb in the back yard.

"*Eww!* What the hell, Ryan?!"

"*Wha...?!*" He looked totally and genuinely surprised.

"Are you two having fun?" It was Sam, standing in the kitchen doorway, hand on hip. Ellie couldn't tell whether she had been in their bedroom all along or had come into the house right behind Ryan, but it was clear she had witnessed at least part of their encounter.

Ellie scoffed at the suggestion. "Not even a teeny, tiny bit!"

"Exactly why, *Mister Collins*, were you molesting my sister?"

Calling Ryan "Mister Collins," complete with the slow, Agent Smith-style delivery, was a holdover from watching *The Matrix* years ago. It had started as a meaningless, jokey interjection, but over time it had become the equivalent of their parents' use of their full names when they were in deep trouble. Knowing this, he instantly went into defensive mode. Spinning to face her, he found it was now his turn to be speechless.

"I—no, I—I wasn't…." he stammered.

"He was *so!*" Ellie did not hesitate to add to Ryan's discomfort, even though she was already sure he had made an honest mistake. "I thought he was about to stick his tongue in my ear!"

"Really?" Sam asked in a tone that said, *do tell!*

"No, really, I was molesting *you*." He realized at once how completely wrong that sounded. "I mean—I thought she was *you*." Having regained some of his composure, he tried to go on the offensive and adopted an accusatory tone. "You said you were getting your hair cut this afternoon!"

"So I did. Do you like it?" She slipped her hand under her hair, lifted it up and outward, and allowed the strands to slide down between her fingers.

Understanding he was right back to playing defense, he squinted at her, scrutinizing her hair as she stepped toward him. If it were any shorter at all than it had been that morning, he couldn't see the difference, but he was now terrified of committing a second unforgivable sin mere seconds after the first. He took a chance and tried hard to sound confident.

"Yeah, it looks *great!*"

"He said *my* hair was 'sexy,'" Ellie pointed out, still doing her best to be as unhelpful as possible.

"So, 'great,'" Sam said, "but not 'sexy?'"

Sweat beaded on Ryan's forehead and made his palms feel clammy, but he resisted the urge to wipe his hands on his jeans. "No! No! Yours is sexy, too!" He winced, hearing the mistake even as he spoke it.

"'Too?' Meaning you think Ellie is sexy?"

"No!" His voice was reduced almost to a squeak. "That's not.... *You're* sexy, Ellie is... is...."

Ellie bounded past him to stand shoulder to shoulder beside Sam. "Practically her twin!" she chirped.

She knew what he was seeing—two girls born a year apart but almost physically identical. Same five-foot, six-inch height. Bodies similarly toned from years of gym periods spent on the soccer field and by summers pedaling around the plateau. Same golden brown hair, same dark eyes set in identically oval faces with warm, olive undertones—features passed on to them by their mother from her Italian ancestors.

Indeed, the two of them were practically famous in school for how much alike they looked. After Ellie joined Sam in high school and their classmates started referring to them as the "Henderson clones," she'd used a pair of scissors to hack her long hair off bluntly at the level of her chin. Shortly after, her mom insisted she have it more professionally cut, and she had kept it in its present style, somewhere between a pixie and a bob, ever since. To a casual glance, there was little else to set them apart.

"She's right, Ryan," Sam said, the intensity of her gaze daring him to contradict her. "Either we're both sexy, or neither of us is."

He was smart enough to recognize a no-win situation when he was neck-deep in one. He hung his head in defeat and looked quite miserable.

"*Umm...* I'm sorry?"

Sam turned to look at Ellie and smiled. "You good?"

"I'm good," she said, smiling back. "He's kinda easy, though."

Sam turned around and headed toward the living room. "Come on, you goof," she said, calling back to him over her shoulder.

Ryan, having finally realized that they had been toying with him all along, looked relieved but thoroughly wrung out. He wiped the side of his hand across his damp brow. "I *hate* it when you do that," he muttered, even though Sam was already out of earshot. He appeared on the verge of saying something more to Ellie, but noting her irritated expression and tightly crossed arms, he wisely decided against digging his hole any deeper.

"*Goof!*" she repeated, stuck out her tongue, then stormed passed him and out through the screen door.

She was already regretting her childish display even before her feet reached the far edge of the patio. From where she stopped in the middle of the back yard she could hear Sam's fading voice saying, *Seriously—did you think I would actually...* and she wondered how she had finished that question. *Cut it so ridiculously short? Do* that *to my hair?*

Pondering that question made her even more irritated, only this time with Sam. *They are* so *welcome to each other!* She thought again that love, relationships, and all the associated nonsense was just that—*nonsense!* Then she wondered, oblivious to any contradiction, what Aaron was doing at that moment.

That evening she sat alone at her desk, trying unsuccessfully to concentrate on her history essay. Her computer had long since given up on her and was back in sleep mode, its tiny power indicator light slowly dimming and brightening in the rhythm of deep, relaxed breathing. She knew she was right about the need for an almost total rewrite and was acutely aware of how little time she had to accomplish the task. During class, she had nearly completed an entirely new skeleton for her essay. But now that it was time to put some meat on those bones, to add all the "touchy-feely" elements her original draft had lacked, she was again stuck. She knew what she needed to do—she just wasn't sure how to do it.

Although annoying, writer's block was not her biggest problem. She was still rattled following her earlier encounter with Ryan. She was convinced he had genuinely mistaken her for Sam, and she didn't take his actions personally. But in the seconds before she had understood what was happening, while she was feeling the warm, intimate touch of his palms on her hips, her body had responded in a way that was *intensely* personal. She wouldn't *let* her mind focus on *that*.

Until that afternoon, she had never thought that Ryan viewed her as anything more than a minor inconvenience, someone whose presence he often had to tolerate to be around Sam. Now, however, she had to consider the possibility that somewhere in the deep recesses of whatever passed for an adolescent male's brain, he thought that she, too, was attractive. *No, 'sexy,'* she amended, and felt her stomach churn in a decidedly unsexy way.

To make matters worse, Ryan was still there. He and Sam were watching another movie. It was a quiet one. There was no gunfire, no big explosions or chase-scene tire squeals. Based on the occasional snippets of dialogue that filtered down to the bedroom, which she thought could've been Russian, she assumed it was *Solaris*. She remembered it had been on their list of upcoming titles and wondered again if she would enjoy it. *Lady Bird*, *Coco*, *Young Frankenstein*, and now *Solaris*? What would be next, *Casablanca*? Or would it be *Annihilation*? With them, there was no sure way to predict.

It was pretty amazing, she knew, this ability to watch anything at any time. She remembered joining them a year ago for *Hunt for the Wilderpeople*, an indie movie she had thoroughly enjoyed and one she knew would never in a hundred years have come to their small, quadruplex movie theater. Yet they could call it up anytime they wanted, anywhere they happened to be.

In an abrupt mental change of direction, she wondered if theirs was the first truly 'post-generational' generation. Technology allowed them to enjoy the latest movies, music, and books with merely a few taps on a screen, but they were not limited to the music and films of today. People were now able, in an unprecedented way, to appreciate the very best each preceding generation had produced with the same ease with which they could experience the most up-to-the-minute hits. Sam and Ryan's eclectic movie-viewing practice certainly seemed to be proof of that hypothesis. But how much of that was due to a shift in attitudes generally, and how much was it the unique result of living in such a small, relatively isolated town, one that out of necessity had incredible Internet bandwidth? Or maybe it was simply because those two were just plain strange.

No, she assured herself, her thoughts veering back again. She did not secretly like Ryan. Not in *that* way, anyway. He was nice enough, sure, and far more intelligent than he usually gave anyone reason to suspect, but he was always looking for the joke. He never seemed to take anything seriously, although she admitted she didn't know what he was like when he and Sam were alone. And there was *another* place she wouldn't let her mind go.

Still, when he touched her, her insides had done that... that *thing*. For a second, she could feel his hands sliding along her ribs before coming to rest low on her belly, the feathery brush of his breath on her neck.... She shuddered again, the way she had in the kitchen.

"*Grr!*" she said, and stabbed her MacBook's space bar, rudely bringing the device out of its slumber. She opened her history paper, stripped the rubber band off her stack of note cards, and forced herself to start writing.

4

Ellie woke Friday morning feeling intensely cranky. Her fitful sleep had been filled with dreams of the most wildly inappropriate sort, ones in which Ryan.... No, she couldn't bear to remember! Sam asked her what was wrong, but there was no way—absolutely no way at all, *ever*—that she was going to tell her, of all people, what had gotten her so out of sorts. Long accustomed to her sister's mercurial nature, Sam soon gave up and let her stew. Instead of dwelling on Ellie's grumpiness, she occupied herself with the task of making sandwiches for the day's planned outing.

This was one of the rare days they were out of school due to a teachers' planning session, made rarer still by coming so late in the school year. They had decided to take advantage of the perfect, late-spring weather to spend as much of the day as possible outside. They met at the east end of Rim Trail and locked their bicycles to a sturdy rack at the edge of the parking lot. The small pack Ryan clutched by its top handle contained water, sandwiches, and other snacks for him and Aaron. Ellie, too, carried a daypack loaded with similar provisions for her and Sam.

In recent years, it had become a semi-regular routine for them to hike away from town into the surrounding forest or desert, discover whatever was there, and have lunch somewhere along the way. Sometimes they would hike north, skirting the eastern edge of the town. Other times they explored the slopes of the Jemez mountains to the west. On most outings, they were rewarded with nothing more than a gorgeous view and a glimpse of some local wildlife. Now and then, however, they would discover an old rancher's homestead, long-abandoned and crumbling, or perhaps a much older Ancestral Puebloan ruin. They could pass an entire afternoon there, imagining how life in the area would have been a hundred or even a thousand years ago. Sam might resent their isolation from the "real world," but even she couldn't deny the beauty of the region's landscape, especially at this time of year, when the various green hues of the sage, rabbitbrush, and desert grasses stood in vibrant contrast to the orange and yellow sandstone that made up the plateau.

Today they had chosen to head south. Their route would take them along the eastern edge of the Pajarito Plateau, an area deeply cut by multiple east-west running, steep-sided arroyos. Some were relatively shallow washes, no more than thirty or forty feet deep, but others were deep enough to call true canyons. The land they were preparing to hike through was technically every bit as restricted as the rest of the LAB research campus, but aside from a small, isolated nuclear research lab near the start of their path, this section of the plateau was deserted. They had long ago stopped worrying about encountering anyone so far from the central part of the facility. That it was so little traveled was part of the area's allure, and some of their favorite days had been spent there, knowing that they were the only four people for miles in any direction. Ryan had best summed up their attitude when he asked on one of their earliest incursions, "What are they going to do—arrest us for criminal picnicking?"

Ryan placed his pack on the ground next to Ellie's and spread the top open wide. "Tell you what—I'll trade you our sandwiches for your waters."

Right! she thought, resenting the offer's implication. *Like they're all that heavy!* But before she could give her eyes an exasperated roll, it occurred to her that he might be trying to make up for the previous day's transgression, and she managed to contain her irritation.

"Okay... here."

She held up the two liter-sized Nalgene bottles from the main compartment—a third she left in a side pocket—and swapped them for the two deli sandwiches. They were wraps, actually, so large and densely packed that they hardly weighed less than the water.

Aaron pointed at her pack. "You have the camera in there?"

He meant the small digital camera Ellie's grandmother had given her two years ago, even though she had never expressed any enthusiasm for the hobby. After Aaron had shown uncharacteristic interest in the gift, she'd offered to let him use it whenever he wanted. Since then, he had taken it on all of their hikes, its sleek, blue plastic shell dangling from his wrist by a thin strap. He insisted that she keep it at her house, however, for some reason unwilling to assume full-time possession.

"Yep!" she said. "You know, you should think about emptying the card. It's almost full."

Her comment came out sharper than she had intended, and she looked up at him to soften the effect of it with a smile. But he was looking away from her, gazing out across the expanse of the first canyon. She decided to leave the camera in the pack—if he decided he needed it, she would dig it out then.

They walked west along the level, paved trail for almost two hundred yards until they found the one spot along the cliff that offered a safe path to the canyon floor a hundred feet below. On their first exploration of this area, they had hiked directly up the wash's opposite side, attempting a shortcut across the next section of the plateau. Once they reached its far edge, however, they were thwarted by a long expanse of sheer sandstone walls that offered no way down. Lesson learned, from then on they stayed at the canyon's bottom.

After hiking around the end of the finger-like projection, they turned back to the west and made their way up a second wash. Before going far, a tangle of dead juniper and piñon trees forced them to make a short, difficult detour up one of its steep sides. The snag was a stark reminder that although the gullies that drained the plateau were dry most of the year, during the summer they could become death traps almost without warning. Run-off from the seasonal monsoon rains scoured them with muddy torrents carrying soil, dislodged rocks and boulders, and even uprooted trees, such as the ones that now forced them to leave the usually clear path on the canyon's floor. The grinding effect of such a flash flood in one of the longer, deeper canyons could reduce an unlucky hiker to a widely dispersed residue of shredded cloth and splintered bone.

It seldom rained in late May, and today their sole cause for concern was the research lab perched at the tip of the next mesa. Getting past the remote facility required them to cross the long, narrow access road connecting it to the main LAB complex. The challenge was making it unseen across a wide stretch of open ground that offered not a single place to hide. To minimize the chance of detection, they made it a point to pass through the area during the middle of work shifts, when the fewest number of cars would be heading in or out. Although they had never been seen, it was the one place they risked detection, and everybody felt more at ease once they were out of sight on the far canyon's floor.

In their favor, the tree line on the road's north side gave them a safe place to check for oncoming vehicles before sprinting across the open area. Also, once they reached the road, a large drainage culvert provided a way to pass under rather than over it. The tunnel's far end deposited them into a deep drainage ditch that continued to minimize their exposure as they dropped into the next wash. They paused at the edge of the trees, assured themselves the road was clear, then made a hasty scramble for the culvert. Within minutes, they were safely at the bottom of the third wash.

Ellie's dark mood had not brightened in the least as she began trailing Sam and Ryan up the steep, opposite slope. Despite knowing it was completely absurd, she was even irritated by their *clothes*. She and Aaron wore simple outfits of blue jeans and plain tees. In contrast, Ryan was clad in the latest Arc'teryx synthetic hiking pants and a plaid Kühl shirt over a muted, yellowish tee. And, of course, his Yankees cap. Sam wore a matched outfit from "Patagucci," an ensemble consisting of a string-necked top and plum-colored shorts. Following Sam up the steep incline gave Ellie more time than she would ever have wanted for the up-close viewing of those shorts, and that she was forced to admit—although she would never do so out loud, not even at gunpoint—that they really did make her sister's rear end look good only made her more irritated.

What a pair!

She glanced back to see if Aaron had likewise taken notice of the view, but when their eyes met he merely offered her a bland smile. Then the sun glinted off his large, round lenses, briefly obscuring the eyes behind them, and once again, she couldn't help but be reminded of Hedwig the owl. She smiled back, though more at her private joke than in response to his expression.

Ellie didn't understand why she felt so peevish, but she knew one thing —her state of mind wouldn't improve if she remained in the rear, forced to endure watching Sam and Ryan chattering inanely into each other's ears. When they reached the top of the ravine, she strode out ahead of the others in what she thought was an unexplored direction. Her hiking companions exchanged bemused looks as she briskly passed by them to take the lead, but no one said a word. Sam gave a helpless *what are you going to do?* shrug before they dropped into line behind her.

An hour later they were still hiking, making their way southeast across another finger-like projection of sandstone. The goal was to find a new spot where they could hang their feet over the edge and enjoy their picnic lunch. Focused on the physical demands of the hike and distracted by the spare beauty of the evergreen and Gambel oak forest, Ellie soon began to feel more like her usual self. She set a steady pace, leading them across another wash to an area that was new to them. Although where they stood was still technically a "Restricted Area" and therefore off-limits to anyone without a security clearance, a valid pass, and a *very* good reason for being there, the closest people were miles away, and they weren't worried about being caught. She had just decided to turn east and make for the nearest edge of the mesa when Ryan pointed out a small, wooden shack nestled in a clearing under a stand of ponderosa pines fifty yards away. Instead of turning left, she veered toward it so they could investigate.

When they got close, they were forced to walk around the trunk of a massive, fallen ponderosa. It was well over two feet thick at its base, and judging from the rust-colored needles still clinging to its limbs, it hadn't been down more than a year or two. The lower end was free of branches for twenty feet, and it had come to rest almost perfectly horizontal.

Ryan flapped a hand at it. "Looks like a good place to have lunch."

Ellie's response was a distracted, *"Mmm."* Her attention was directed entirely at the building before them.

At first, the structure seemed like nothing more than yet another long-abandoned cabin, probably built by the area's early European settlers. They had come across a similar one north of town at the end of the previous summer and had spent the whole afternoon in temporary residence, trying to visualize an existence vastly more isolated than their own. This new find was roughly the same size and appeared about as old, but its sides were covered in rough, silver-gray shakes rather than having been built from logs.

Now that they were standing close to it, they began noticing more differences. The forest had encroached right up to the walls of last year's discovery—there was even a young tree growing up through a gap in the roof—but around this shack, the ground was virtually barren out to a distance of ten or twelve yards. And although its surface looked old and weather-beaten, this cabin was otherwise in almost perfect shape.

"Kinda makes you rethink *weird*, doesn't it?" Ryan said.

After their first brief study of the building, Sam and Ryan walked back to the fallen ponderosa and sat. He set his small daypack near his feet, removed the water bottles and a bag of chips, then they snacked while talking softly. Ellie peered at the curious structure a minute longer, then joined them at the makeshift picnic bench.

Watching Aaron slowly wander over, Ellie took the sandwiches out of her pack—lunch meat and sliced cheese with a little lettuce for her and Sam, each nestled in a wax paper sandwich bag. The wraps from the co-op were swathed in shiny cellophane. She peered at it for a moment, wondering if Aaron's bacteria would find it palatable. She passed the sandwiches around, making sure Sam got the one with mustard, and placed the sliced apple and two tangerines they had brought on top of her pack. She placed her own sandwich beside her on the log, picked up her water bottle, and unscrewed the cap. Alternating between bites of sandwich and occasional sips of water, she tuned out the others' small talk and focused on the shack.

Who cleared out all the plants around it? Why would anybody do that?

Leaving her bottle on the ground but taking her sandwich with her, she stood and began a slow walk around the building, orbiting it from the perimeter of the barren area. She wasn't looking for anything in particular, just seeing what there was to see. She realized that her first impression had been wrong and that the space around the building was not truly barren. Many stalks and stems protruded from the ground, some almost two feet high, but they were all leafless and brown. All but one. In all of that wide, de-vegetated zone around the building, there was a single, incongruously lush bush. It was growing directly against the south end of the west-facing wall.

"*Hmm....*" She thought that was odd, but she decided to come back to it. For now, she continued her overall inspection.

A moment later, Aaron joined her, likewise compelled to investigate the odd building further. He stood in the vicinity of the bush but was looking away from the shack, out into the woods. He shuffled from side to side a few times as if he were trying to see something hidden by distant trees.

Ellie passed behind him and began a second slow circuit around the building. This time she was close enough to touch it. She found herself agreeing with Ryan's initial assessment—it was undeniably weird. She guessed it was twenty feet on each side, give or take a foot, and at least fifteen feet high at the tip of its peaked roof. The wood-shingle exterior was dry and chalky, extremely rough, and had that unique shade of dull silver-gray, dotted liberally with scaly, multi-colored growths of lichen that usually signified great age. In that respect, it was precisely what they expected to find in these woods.

Except it wasn't. It appeared old, yes, but it was not dilapidated. Instead, Ellie got the sense that it was extremely solid, as if the wood were merely a disguise concealing a massive block of concrete beneath. Rapping on the wall produced a thud so muted she might as well have been tapping on a granite boulder. There were no gaps in the wood with sunlight streaming through, no gaping windows, no half-open door inviting her to lean in and take a peek around. In fact, now that she thought about it....

"Hey—there's no door! And these shutters? I bet there aren't windows behind them. They don't have hinges."

"Come over here and look at this." Aaron motioned for her to join him where he had stood almost since joining her in the clearing. "Stand here and put your shoulder up against mine," he said.

Behind them, Ryan chuckled. "Good one! High marks for originality, you old smoothie."

"Ignore him," she muttered, wondering as she stepped close to Aaron's side where he was going with this. Behind her, she could hear Sam saying something in a low voice. She sounded irked, and although Ellie couldn't hear everything she said, she thought she caught the word "ass."

You tell him, Sis!

"What is it, Aaron?"

"I dunno, maybe nothing. Look that direction, but not at anything in particular." He pointed into the forest along a line that would lead almost directly toward the occupied area of the research campus. "Just sort of take in the whole scene."

She followed the tip of his finger out into the trees. The forest and its sparse undergrowth receded into the distance, but she didn't see anything of note. She let her focus drift, not allowing it to rest on any one thing. It was clear he expected her to see something, but what?

"How about…. Here, come this way." He gripped her upper arm and guided her to the spot where he had been standing, one short step nearer to the corner of the building. "Try again."

"I'm sorry, Aaron, but I don't…." She broke off when she suddenly saw it. "Wait, are you talking about that faint line through the trees? Almost like a path?" That slight shift in position was all it took to reveal an alignment of elements in the scene that didn't look entirely natural. It was barely noticeable, though, and she wasn't sure it was more than a random occurrence.

"Yes!" he said. "Like an old trail, or possibly a recent one someone made and then tried to cover up."

Drawn by the excitement in their voices, Sam and Ryan left the log and joined them.

"What's up?" Ryan said.

"Stand behind me and look out through the trees." Ellie pointed down the faint suggestion of a path. "Do you see there's sort of a straight line there?"

Ryan was half a head taller than her, and it was easy for him to follow the direction of her finger from that position. However, as soon as he stood behind her, she felt an uncomfortable crawling sensation start between her shoulder blades.

Too soon! She quickly stepped aside and tugged Sam over to take her place in front of him.

"Right through there," she said, pointing again for Sam's benefit.

"Yeah," Ryan said. He drew the word out, starting on a hesitant note but finishing with conviction. "Yeah! It goes for maybe a hundred and fifty yards. Then it fizzles out. Like I said—sorta redefines 'weird.'"

Sam scoffed. "So, it's a path? There are paths all through these woods. We followed a path to get here."

Ellie found her sister's contrariness irritating. "Fifty different ones, all deer trails, and they weren't perfectly straight for more than six feet at a time!"

Sam refused to concede the point. "So why would there be a path to an old shack in the woods, anyway? Besides… it doesn't even look used."

"Ladies, ladies, please."

Ryan's unctuous tone annoyed Ellie even more, and she couldn't stop herself from snapping at him. "*What?!*"

"What else do you see here? What else is off in this little tableau? And by 'off,' I mean a bit too much *on*."

He smiled at her, but it was the smug smile of the proverbial cat who had eaten the canary. He had figured out something important, and it irritated her that he had beaten her to it. Frustrated, she puffed out a loud breath and turned back toward the line through the trees.

"I don't know. What?" She noticed Aaron was studying the woods again, too.

"Look…." Ryan paused for effect, "…closer."

She stood shoulder to shoulder beside Aaron once more, peering intently into the distance. *No, not the distance—"closer."* She mentally extended the path's trajectory right up to her toes, but she saw no obvious answer to Ryan's riddle. She realized the shack was closer to her than the path, so she turned around and focused on it, feeling like she almost had the solution.

Directly in front of her, pressed up against the shack's wall, was the anomaly she had noticed earlier, the silvery green shrub she was pretty sure was buffaloberry. It was three feet wide, three feet tall, and grew to a depth of two feet from the shake siding. But that's all she saw—just a bush.

She turned around and again picked out the path. How had Ryan put it— a bit too much *on*? All at once, she had it. If the cut through the trees ran directly toward her, it also pointed straight at the oddly situated bush. The bush was directly *on* the path! She spun back around and crouched, plunged her hands deep into the shrub, and spread its branches wide. What she revealed surprised everyone.

No, not everyone, she thought. She twisted her head around to see Ryan smiling down at her as if pleased that she had successfully solved a puzzle of his own devising. "You *knew* this was here?!"

His smile got even wider. "No, but once I realized what the 'path' actually is, I figured it had to be."

Sam crouched and peered over Ellie's shoulder into the depths of the bush. "But what *is* it?"

It was a metal box, twelve inches on a side and five deep, and in contrast to the rest of the structure, it looked very new. It was attached to the wall a few inches above the ground and was painted the exact hue of the buffaloberry's leaves.

Aaron dropped down beside Sam to look over Ellie's other shoulder. He recognized the object at once. "It's a service entry. Check below it."

Ellie ducked her head as low as she could and tried to see underneath the box. It was deeply shaded, but she thought she could make out a vague shape. She swept her right hand between the box and the ground.

Seeing this, Sam squealed and shot to her feet, flapping her hands in front of her. "*Eww! Spiders!*"

Ellie encountered something in the dark gap, but it wasn't a spider. It felt like a pipe, four inches across, coming out of the ground and entering the bottom of the box.

She glanced over her shoulder at Aaron.

"Conduit," he said.

She nodded in understanding. As she pulled her arms out of the shrub, she noticed it felt strange, its slender limbs unnaturally rigid. She peered closely at the plant and ran her palm over its glossy leaves, but she saw nothing out of sorts. It seemed to be just a regular buffaloberry bush.

"That," Ryan said, indicating the cut through the trees, "is a utility trench. Well, *was* a trench. You remember we had to have the power re-run from the street into our house last fall? It looked exactly like that after they tried to fix the landscaping they'd dug up. Except, of course, this one's a lot longer."

Ryan's explanation made Ellie feel better. He hadn't really figured anything out—he had just seen it before.

"*Hmm....*" Aaron said as he stood up. "Somebody cut a trench through the woods and ran electricity, maybe water—who knows?—to this ancient-looking cabin. *Weird* is right." He looked westward through the forest, trying to picture their location relative to the broader landscape. "If that's coming all the way from the LAB, it has to be at least three, three and a half miles long. More, if it's not very straight."

"So," Sam said, "we have what looks like a trail but isn't, bringing power to what looks like an old, abandoned cabin, which also isn't." She nodded, finally willing to concede the point. "Okay, I admit it is a little strange."

"*Weird,*" corrected three voices in unison, and even Sam had to laugh.

"It still might be a trail," Aaron said. They were once again sitting on the fallen tree, eating their lunches and trying to unravel the puzzle in front of them. "I mean, if you were coming here from the LAB, the way they'd choose to run the power would presumably be the shortest route, and that's also how the path would run. Maybe they don't use it very often. Or else they do something to cover their tracks after they go back."

"Yeah, maybe," Sam said. "But why come very often to an old shack way out here with no windows and no way in? What would be the point of coming at all?"

They all chewed on that puzzle while they chewed on their lunches. Ellie picked her water bottle up off her sandwich bag, took a sip, then quickly set it down again before the nearly weightless wrapper could blow away. *That is the essential question, isn't it?* She ignored the continuing discussion. Why was the building here to begin with? What was its "point?" She turned the question over in her mind.

Okay, back up… What's the purpose of any building? Shelter? Storage? No, at the most basic level, a building separates the outside from an inside. If you can't get to the inside, there's no point in making it.

There had to be a way in. She ruled out an underground entrance at once. If they could still see the minor disturbance to the ground where the power line had been run, any excavation on a scale sufficient to construct a tunnel large enough for people to use would be too obvious to miss. And besides, if they had dug a tunnel that large, they simply would have used it for running the power, too. No—there had to be a door.

She studied the shack and tried to picture what it would look like if it were a normal cabin. She imagined herself coming up on the building along the line of the utility trench. *Where would the door be?*

She rose from the log, the remaining quarter of her sandwich in hand, and walked around to the side of the building closest to the trail. She figured that was where the door would go, in the middle of that wall. She thought of secret passages behind bookcases opened by cleverly hidden latches. She took a bite of her sandwich. She visualized high-security entrances at banks or out at the LAB, doors equipped with key card readers and number pads.

Deep in thought, she was barely aware that the others were now standing a few yards behind her, watching. She took another bite and chewed it slowly. She thought about science fiction computers with facial recognition cameras, retina or DNA scanners, or other exotic, biometric devices. She studied the rough wooden boards, and the earlier sense that the ancient-looking façade was but a cunning sham came back to her.

She stepped up close to the exact spot on the wall where she imagined the door would be. Acting solely on intuition, she raised her hand to a point two feet right of center and slightly below shoulder height, and pressed firmly near the top of one of the rough-hewn shingles. At first nothing happened, but thinking she felt a slight movement, she maintained steady pressure on the spot. A moment later she heard a faint click as a section of shingles under her hand moved inward, then slid sideways to reveal a shiny metal and glass panel.

Ellie was not especially surprised. She'd taken the presence of a door as a given, and basic logic said that if there was a door, there had to be a way to open it. Some kind of control *had* to be there, and there it was—it was as simple as that. Still, she was gratified when she turned around to face three identical expressions of amazement.

"My work here is done," she said, then popped the final corner of her sandwich into her mouth.

5

Sam, Ryan, and Aaron rushed to Ellie's side to get a better look at the device she had revealed. The contrast between its sleek, high-tech surface and the rough, organic texture of the surrounding wall was so stark it seemed almost alien. It was eight inches wide by eleven inches high, with a dark, glass circle roughly seven inches across set into the polished steel face, offset toward the bottom. A keypad was centered above the glass circle, slightly rounded in outline, which displayed the digits zero through nine, a *back* arrow at the lower left position, and an *enter* key in the other bottom corner. A small, square LED glowing green on the *enter* key indicated that the panel had power.

"Palm scanner," Aaron said.

"You don't often see those on nineteenth-century wooden shacks," Ryan said. "Not even around here."

"No. No, you don't."

"What *is* this thing?" Sam's voice was barely more than a whisper.

Ellie turned and slowly scanned the woods around them, suddenly sure she'd see surveillance cameras hidden in the trees. When she failed to spot any, that worried her even more.

What secret was so dangerous that they couldn't risk a video record?

She refocused on the discussion regarding the control panel. Aaron was responding to something Ryan had said.

"Yeah, but even if it would accept one of our palm prints—and it wouldn't—there's still the number code. If it's four digits, that's ten thousand possibilities, a hundred thousand for five digits, and my guess is you get just three tries. Maybe only two."

"That doesn't sound promising," Ellie said.

"The odds...." Ryan said and looked at her expectantly.

When it came to conjuring up movie references appropriate to a given occasion, she couldn't begin to compete with him and Sam, but she had this one down cold. "'Not in our favor,' yeah." This earned her a smile and a congratulatory thumbs-up.

Aaron continued squinting intensely at the panel, deep in thought. Sam, meanwhile, had become alarmed by where the conversation was heading.

"Wait a minute—what are you guys talking about?! We are *not* breaking in there!"

"No," Ryan said, his voice laced with exaggerated disappointment. "It certainly doesn't seem like it,"

"I'm serious! Security from the LAB would be here in minutes! We'd be arrested and thrown in prison, our parents would lose their jobs... not to mention I'd never be able to show my face in school again. You guys are *nuts!*"

Ellie's irritation came out as an exasperated huff. "In case you weren't listening, there's both a palm scanner *and* a passcode that we don't even know the length of, so stop worrying. There's absolutely no way we can get in there."

"Actually," Aaron said, "there is one thing we might try."

Ryan clapped him between the shoulder blades hard enough to knock his glasses out of place. "A-Ron, coming through in the clutch!" Aaron nudged his glasses back into position with the tip of his middle finger.

"Really?" Ellie said. "What is it?"

"No! We are *not* doing this!" The pitch of Sam's voice had risen into a range Ellie knew well, one that made having to add *and that's final* unnecessary.

Aaron's eyes darted from Ellie to Sam and back to Ellie.

"I, uh… I mean, it probably won't work."

"Come on. Out with it," Ryan said, then saw Sam glaring at him. "I just want to know what he's got. It doesn't mean we'll try it." She crossed her arms and glared harder.

"Okay," Aaron began. "Remember the science fair freshman year?"

"Well," Ryan said, "it's not like you'd let us forget."

Along with the numerous football, basketball, track, and swimming trophies the school teams had won over the years, all of which were on prominent display inside enormous glass cases in the school's lobby, a large wooden plaque mounted on the wall nearby listed every year's science fair winner. Each name was engraved on a small brass plate screwed to the plaque. One plate read, "2015—Aaron Siskin."

Aaron blushed, coughed self-consciously, then continued. "So, when I was trying to come up with a project that year, one topic I considered was something to do with biometric devices. You know—fingerprint readers, retina scanners, voice recognition. Those sorts of things. I read a ton of articles about all kinds of cool tech, and it was all of it interesting stuff, but in the end, I couldn't figure out what to do with it. You know, as a project. Anyway, one of the web pages I found had to do with manufacturing and testing scanners like this one. It wasn't a public page—I think it was part of a promo piece or something—but I found it through the site map and was able to link…."

Ryan, all too aware that when the talk turned to tech, the normally taciturn Aaron could blather to beat the best of them, twirled an index finger in the air. *Fast-forward to the good part*, he meant.

"Yeah. Okay." Aaron took a moment to organize his thoughts. "So, say you have a fairly large company, and you're making, testing, and installing a lot of these things." He pointed at the scanner. "Having to create hand scans of all your engineers and give them all codes, and then have all of those scans and codes be in every device would be a huge pain, right? But then so would be having to limit a given unit's entire production process to a single tech or two. And what happens when they hire someone new?

"This page said that this company's way around that problem was what they called the 'white glove test mode.' All the techs wear these special, lint-free nylon gloves during assembly and testing, see, to keep the electronics free from contamination. Their solution was to make each unit respond to a scan of any hand in a white glove, regardless of specific outline or size, by automatically going into a test mode. That way, any technician can work on any device, even if his or her scan isn't in that particular unit. There was a short video clip of a couple of different techs doing demonstrations, and one thing I noticed was that when they put in the code, it was the same each time—different scanners, different techs, but the same code.

"The other thing I remember noticing is this." He pointed at the keypad. "See the way the buttons taper in at the corners? And the way the power light is part of the 'Enter' button? That matches what I saw in the video. This scanner was made by that company, so...."

"So you know the code!" Ryan said, eager to bring Aaron's rambling story to an end.

"Umm... *maybe.*"

"But you said you saw them enter the numbers," Ellie said.

Aaron scrunched up his face and waggled his head to say *not really.* "I saw the way their hands moved. Top, down, right, left. But I couldn't actually see their fingers hitting the keys. Getting the exact code would be a... say, a very well-educated guess. *And,* to be totally clear, this only works if someone screwed up and forgot to disable the test mode."

"Wait," Ellie said. "I'm not following. Are you saying we *can* get in, or we *can't?*"

"I'm saying that instead of being one in ten thousand or a hundred thousand, the odds might be more like...." He thought for a moment. "One in six?"

Sam turned a gloating smile on Ryan. "But unlucky for you, nobody thought to bring any white nylon gloves along, so 'oh, well,'" she said, her tone breezy. "As you know, orange is so not my color."

"Relax," Ryan said. "The whole LAB complex is considered federal property, even this far out."

She looked confused. "I know! What's that got to do...?"

"Federal prison jumpsuits are green, not orange."

She scowled and slapped his arm. "I hate you," she said, although without much conviction.

Ryan tracked her departure as she stomped back to their picnic log and sat down, fuming. "Whoops! I think a one-in-six chance is probably *way* better than I can hope for any time soon."

"She's not wrong, you know," Aaron said. "If we manage to get in and *do* get caught, what Sam said is the best-case scenario. There's no way of knowing what's hidden in here or what someone might do to keep it a secret."

Ellie thought that argument only made learning what was inside even more vital. "But that's the point, isn't it? There are no signs, no guards, no... freakin'... *door!* Just a shack in the middle of nowhere, one somebody cut through miles of rock to run power to. If this were a legit project, even a shady one, it'd be over at the LAB behind fences and razor wire. The more I think about it, the worse this feels. I want to know what's in there."

A deep sigh from Sam drew everyone's attention to where she sat, elbows on knees, face buried in her palms. She straightened to look back at them.

"I *really* hate to say it, but she's right. There isn't a single good reason for this to be stuck way out here like this." She walked back to join them at the scanner panel. "Even if we can't figure out who built it, we should at least try to find out what it is."

"Alrighty then," Ryan said as if that settled the matter.

Ellie waited for Aaron to explain what came next, but he remained immobile, eyebrows raised, waiting for her to give the go-ahead. She was surprised that the final decision seemed to be up to her. She hesitated for a second, then gave him a single nod.

"Let's try. If you can open the door, we'll take a quick look at what's inside. If it turns out to be something bad, we'll figure out how to let somebody know. Does that work for everybody?"

She got three nods in response.

"Sounds just like a plan," Ryan said.

"Okay," Ellie said. "Let's give it a shot."

"In that case," Aaron said, "I'm going to need your sandwich bag."

"Okay," Ellie said automatically, then realized he had lost her. "*Huh?*"

"The wax paper thingy your sandwich was in. Actually, bring me both of them." He held a hand up and waggled it in the air, exactly as if that explained something.

"Okay, hang on." Still clueless, she began walking to where they had left their daypacks beside the fallen tree. She retrieved her baggie from under her water bottle, then started groping around inside her daypack for Sam's. As she tilted the pack onto its side, something fell out and grazed the front of her thigh on its way to the ground. She looked down and saw it was her camera. Aaron, watching her as she collected the wrappers, saw her pick the camera up and move to put it back in her pack.

"Hey, wait! That reminds me—I wanted to get a group shot today. I forgot at graduation. Can you balance that on the log and set the timer?"

"Sure."

She located the second sandwich bag, slipped both into her rear pocket, then crouched behind the log to set up the camera. As she worked to position it, Aaron posed Sam and Ryan at the end of the shack, their arms wrapped around each other's waists. Aaron moved to stand against Ryan's shoulder and let Ellie know where he wanted her while she continued trying to align the camera on the bark's irregular surface.

"Make sure you leave a little extra room on the right for you."

It took her several more tries at different places on the trunk to find a spot that would support the camera steadily at the correct angle. She made sure the timer was set for ten seconds and pushed the button.

"Okay... Nine... eight... seven...." she said, trotting over to join the group. Stepping over the log slowed her return, and she made it into position with only two seconds to spare. As a result, her pose felt awkward. She placed her hand on Aaron's back, leaned toward him, and smiled at the camera just as she heard a faint *click* as it captured the scene.

She walked back to the log and retrieved the camera. On her way to rejoin the group, she pressed the 'play' button to bring the picture up on the display. She thought it was pretty good, even though her hastily struck pose did make it look like she was photobombing the others. She handed the camera to Aaron to let him judge the image for himself.

"Thanks," he said, and, apparently satisfied, he switched the camera off and slipped it into his pants pocket. "Got those bags?"

She passed him the two wax paper envelopes. "Here. But I don't...."

"Glove," he interrupted. "Or at least as close as we can get."

They all watched as he slid one bag into the other, then slipped his right hand in. The shape of his hand was clear, but the double layer of translucent paper obscured all of its surface details. He held his hand up, palm facing him. Using his other hand, he pushed in on the areas between his fingers, doing all he could to make the resulting shape look as glove-like as possible. Lastly, he pulled the corners of the open end of the bags around his wrist. When he was finished, he studied the results of his efforts. The wax paper, tucked as tightly against his hand as he could manage, barely extended beyond the heel of his palm.

"Good thing you have those dinky little hands, dude," Ryan said.

"Please," Aaron said, trying to sound indignant. "I prefer to think of them as 'presidential.'" Their nervous laughter dissipated some of the tension. "Okay, then." He took a deep breath, let it out with a loud puff. "Here goes."

He turned toward the scanner, but then he froze and closed his eyes. Ellie was sure he was seeing the online video replay on the insides of his eyelids. Ten seconds ticked by. Twenty.

"Okay," he said again. He placed his wrapped hand on the glass surface of the scanner. Almost instantly, it was surrounded by a red outline.

"That can't be good," Ryan said.

Aaron raised his left index finger in a *wait-for-it* gesture, and sure enough, the red outline turned green. He lifted his hand from the scanner, then used his other to enter a code into the keypad. "Two, eight, six, four," he said as he tapped each of the numerals, the code appearing across the middle of the palm scanner as he typed. When he was done, the whole scanner flashed red twice, then it went dark.

"Well, that *certainly* can't be good," Ryan said.

Ellie tried to sound more positive. "But on the plus side, now our odds are one in five."

"Yeah, but we might have just one try left," Aaron said. He closed his eyes again, longer this time. Finally, his eyes snapped open. "*Ha!* I think I got it! Of the four- and five-number combinations, only six fit the pattern of hand motions I remember. Maybe two, five, six, four, but probably not. Not enough 'down.' I also ruled out six-digit codes because, first of all, *why?* and because, again, the hand motions wouldn't quite match. Like Ellie said, that means we're left with the four five-digit codes and the other four-digit one."

"Yeah, so which one is it?" Ryan said.

"In the video, they interviewed the head of the tech department. Part of it was shot on the shop floor, the other part in his office. He was sitting with his elbows on his desk, hands kind of tented up in front of him. I remember thinking, 'cufflinks—spiffy guy.' Little *cross* cufflinks. He was a devout something, apparently. Catholic, maybe?"

"And how does that help us?" Sam said.

"When it comes to codes, some people are number people—birthdays, anniversaries, old phone numbers, et cetera. To guess their passwords, you have to know something about them.

"Others are pattern people. They relate better to shapes. They're a little easier to guess because all people tend to use the same basic patterns. Still, it helps to know at least a little bit about the person if you don't have the option of incrementally working your way through all the possibilities."

He placed his hand once again on the scanner. "I'm assuming this guy, an administrator and not a tech, was a pattern person. So I say we throw out all the five-digit combos," the scanner outline changed to green, "and go with the other four-digit code that makes," he started punching in numbers, "the sign... of... the... cross!"

As soon as he entered the second code—2064—the scanner flashed green twice. At the same time, a low, solid-sounding *clunk* came from the side of the building. A rectangular outline appeared around a section of the rough wall as it separated itself from the building and swung partially open. They were in!

"Dude, that was the most awesome thing I have ever seen! And trust me, that's saying something." Ryan aimed a suggestive waggle of his eyebrows at Sam.

She grinned and gave him a playful nudge with her shoulder. "*Shush!*"

Aaron beamed at this unexpected compliment. "Let's see what we've got."

Ryan and Aaron grabbed the outer edge of the door and pulled. It swung smoothly and silently on large, complexly articulated hinges. Ellie estimated it to be twenty inches thick, and the width tapered from four feet wide on the outside to a little over three on the inside so that it seated into its opening like a bathtub plug into a drain. Seeing the door's edge confirmed

Ellie's guess about the shingles—they were nothing more than a thin veneer disguising a material that was considerably more contemporary.

"It's like you'd imagine a vault door to be," Aaron said. "Looks like it weighs a ton, and maybe it does, but once you get it going, it just glides."

When they had created an opening wide enough to look through, all four crowded forward and peered inside. Their eyes, adjusted to the forest's bright, dappled sunlight, couldn't make out anything within the dim interior beyond the first few feet. Aside from finding out that the floor inside the shack was more than a foot and a half higher than the ground outside it, they knew little more than they did before they got the door open.

"No alarms on this end, anyway," Sam said. "Let's get in and get out of here." Now that they had successfully defeated the lock, she wanted to be away as soon as possible.

Ryan pulled on the door again until the opening was barely big enough for them to squeeze through.

"Remember—five minutes!" Sam said.

"Five minutes," Ellie agreed. "Promise."

Ellie stepped inside first, followed by Sam, Aaron, then Ryan. She stopped two steps inside the door and looked around the room, giving her eyes time to adjust to the gloom. The difference between the building's rustic-hunting-shack exterior and its slick, cleanroom-like interior could not have been greater. They were in a square space twelve feet on a side and eight feet high. The walls and ceiling were covered in rectangular panels, arranged horizontally on the walls, each two by three feet and separated by barely discernible seams. The room was dark, but less so than Ellie expected it to be. It was faintly lit by a dim glow she guessed came directly from the panels themselves. She rotated slowly, scrutinizing every square inch. The only discontinuity on the smooth surfaces surrounding them was on the inside of the recessed door. One of its panels was contoured to accommodate a lever-style handle that would open it from the inside. She now noticed that panels like those on the walls also covered the floor, but these were dull, light grey instead of white. Other than that….

"It's *empty!*"

6

Ryan cast his eyes around the dim, featureless space. "Okay, I'll see your 'weird' and raise you one 'bizarre.'"

"It was *your* 'weird,'" Aaron pointed out, "so technically, you're raising against yourself. Even *I* know that's not right."

Ryan ignored him. He remained near the door as the others began to fan out around the room. "I kept trying to imagine what was in here. 'Nothing' didn't even make the list. This should be a very boring five minutes."

"Sometimes boring is just what you want," Sam said.

Ellie noticed they were speaking in hushed voices, each hyper-aware of intruding into a place where they absolutely were not supposed to be. She also noticed that the door was still hanging open behind them, a giant, gaping mouth shouting, *Hey, they're in here!* to anyone walking by.

"Close the door," she said, discovering that she, too, found it impossible to raise her voice above a whisper.

"But don't lock it," Sam added.

Ryan grasped the handle, leaned back, and got the door moving. It swung silently until it was fully seated into the wall. They heard another loud clunk when the door handle jerked itself out of his grip and snapped into a vertical orientation. This was followed by the unmistakable sound of heavy latches sealing the opening shut.

Sam gave him an exasperated look. "I said *don't* lock it!"

He raised his hands in a *don't look at* me *gesture*, but before he could say anything in his defense, several new things began happening at once. The first was that the room suddenly brightened to a normal, classroom-level of illumination, and it became clear that the light was, in fact, coming from the wall and ceiling panels. The utter flatness of that light made it difficult to focus on the surrounding surfaces, and the room now seemed much larger than before.

At the same time, a red, hexagonal outline appeared in the middle of the floor. It flashed in time with a pulsing alarm, a sound which, like the light, came from all around them. Aaron was standing at almost dead-center within the shape. He hastily cleared the area and joined Ellie and Sam along the wall opposite the door, and the alarm went silent. A second later, they heard another mechanical clunk, followed by a loud, high-pitched whine as a portion of the ceiling, nearly four and a half feet long on each of its six sides, began to descend.

Fascinated by the transformation of the space before them, Ellie barely heard the series of urgent-sounding beeps coming from the wall at their backs. She glanced over her shoulder just as the two middle panels in the row third up from the floor thrust out several inches. Startled by the sudden movement, Sam let out a sharp squeak.

Unsure what would happen next, they retreated to the room's far side. The tops of the panels shifted downward, and their lower edges moved out from the wall until they came to rest just shy of being horizontal. Once locked into place, bright images appeared on their previously plain white surfaces.

The whine stopped when the hexagonal platform impacted the floor with a deep, resonant *whump*. The middle of the room was now occupied by an array of six identical stations facing outward from a central column. Each station was dominated by a black, crudely rendered chair, executed in materials that made Ellie think of exercise machines at a gym. The chamber, which had conveyed an illusion of vastness fifteen seconds before, now seemed very crowded.

Peering over the backs of the chairs, Ellie saw that the newly repositioned panels looked like a touch-sensitive control center. The left side presented arrays of readouts, buttons, and sliders. The right showed a version of the opening image from Google Earth, a familiar blue and white planet slowly revolving in a field of pure black.

Aaron ignored the panels and focused on the chairs. He stepped to the nearest station and began examining it, starting at its top and working his way down. "Now that's more like it!"

"Yeah, but more like what?" Ellie said. Tacitly acknowledging that Aaron knew more about gadgets than she did, she stayed back and let him examine the device without distraction.

"We should go," Sam said. "Now!"

"Nope. You agreed to five minutes." Ryan held his left arm up and tapped a pale band of untanned skin around his wrist where his Apple Watch usually rode. "This says we still have four."

Unamused, Sam rolled her eyes.

Aaron spoke without pausing in his examination of the chair. "Three miles through the woods? Even if someone's already on their way, we're okay for a while yet."

Ellie noted the strip of pale skin encircling Ryan's wrist. "By the way, what *did* happen to your watch?" She kept her eyes on Aaron as he peered closely at the seat's back, then moved on to study the armrests.

"In my defense, let me first remind you that I am a senior this year," Ryan said.

Ellie gave him a quizzical look, not seeing the relevance, and Sam's attempt to clarify didn't help much.

"He's claiming he had a 'senior moment,'" she said.

"I dove into the pool and did four laps before realizing I still had it on."

"I thought they were waterproof," Ellie said.

"The new ones are, yeah, but that was Dad's old original model. Those ones… not so much. It's on my dresser, drying out in a bowl of rice."

"Ah! Well, good luck with that," she said, then returned her attention to Aaron's inspection. More interested in the control panel, Ryan walked around the chairs to get a better look, Sam close on his heels.

"What are we looking at?" Ellie said. "Any ideas?"

"Each of these stations," Aaron said, indicating the spartan seats, "has multiple, um, 'connections,' I guess you'd say. Or maybe 'contacts' is better." He pointed to multiple pairs of gleaming metal studs attached to the chair's frame. "But starting at the top, there's this bike helmet sort of thing."

Ellie agreed that the device did look a little like a cyclist's helmet. One of the sleek, racing ones. It was attached to a post at the very top of the seat-back by an adjustable support that allowed it to slide up and down, presumably to accommodate users of different heights.

Aaron pointed inside the helmet. "See those?"

At least a dozen more metal studs dotted the inner surface of the helmet. These were interconnected, network fashion, by fine wires that came together to form a cable and exited through the helmet's back, made a small loop, and plugged into a port on the large, central column. The loop's apparent purpose was to give the helmet's support a limited degree of back-and-forth movement.

A sudden motion drew her focus beyond the helmet to where Ryan was trying to make sense of the long display panel. His efforts were hindered by the fact that each time he attempted to work the controls, Sam slapped at his hand. Ellie rolled her eyes and returned her attention to Aaron.

He pointed at the midline of the backrest. "These all appear to be the same types of contacts."

She leaned close for a better look. Eight pairs of studs ran along either side of a contoured metal bar that ran from the top of the seat's back down to the bottom pad. The two pairs at both the top and bottom of the support were spaced more tightly than the pairs in the middle, creating one tight cluster of four at the lower end of the spine and another at the base of the skull. She saw no other studs on the body of the chair.

"And out here, we have these," Aaron said.

Near the end of each of the chair's arms, where one's wrists would rest, was yet another pair of studs. These were smaller and more tightly spaced than the others. Attached to the arms just past the studs was a shallow, circular container filled with what looked like some kind of gel. The substance was a dingy, pale beige and looked to be over a centimeter deep. Ellie suspected it would be tacky to the touch, but she refrained from testing her hypothesis. The devices resembled nothing so much as a pair of oversized metal Petri dishes filled with translucent agar, and she wondered what function they could possibly serve.

She leaned in so that her nose was only a few inches from one of the circular dishes. Through the distorting effect of the gel, she thought she could make out a fine pattern of what looked like wires or tiny tubes on the bottom of the depression. It looked similar to a printed circuit board, although it lacked the characteristic green color. She also noticed a faint, organic odor that might have been unpleasant had it been more pronounced. This close to the chair, she saw a new detail, a small hole, directly between the two wrist studs. She pointed it out to Aaron.

"Did you see this?" she said. "These holes?"

He peered over her shoulder and nodded. "Yeah. Some kind of socket, maybe? I can't see contacts down inside it, though."

He directed her attention downward, and they both crouched at the chair's base. Two metal rods supported a pair of footrests. They were like those on a wheelchair, except these were fitted with toe cages similar to the type Ellie had seen on some bicycle pedals. Grasping one of the footrests, she discovered they could be pivoted up and out to the sides. She assumed this was to make getting in and out of the seat easier.

"Yeah," Aaron said. "I guess they don't want your feet going anywhere."

"So, what's all this mean?"

"I dunno."

"And the pads are…?"

The seats were fitted with three pads, each about an inch thick, one covering the seat's bottom and another on either side of the rows of studs running along its back. She placed her hand on the lower pad and leaned her weight onto it. It felt cool, like memory foam. She pulled her hand back and watched the depression it left gradually fill in and disappear.

"Just pads, as far as I can tell," he said.

They stood and together regarded the contraption for a long, silent moment. Although the core of the device, the central column, and the platform on which everything sat seemed to have been built to purpose, the chairs, footrests, helmets, and gel pad components all had an unrefined, almost flimsy appearance that made them seem like prototypes forced into service before their time in R and D was up.

"Is it me, or does it all look a little...." Aaron trailed off.

"Improvised?" she suggested.

He shrugged. "Maybe it's still a work in progress."

They moved around the room to join Sam and Ryan at the control panel. "What've you guys got?" Aaron said.

Sam pointed at the left half of the six-foot-long display. "This is obviously those," she said, gesturing toward the chairs behind them. The display showed a minimalist representation of the chairs arrayed in two rows of three. Above each graphic was a numeral from one to six, and below was a single word in green—NOMINAL. There was an input area to the right of the chair icons. SELECT was followed by the numerals one through six. Below that glowed two words—INITIALIZE, in green, and CANCEL, in red.

Ryan picked up the explanation from there. "And on this side? Well, what's weirder than 'weird?'" He swiped his index finger across the surface of the display and set the Earth spinning. "You can zoom in to any spot."

To demonstrate, he touched the screen with his middle finger and thumb pinched together, bringing the rotating globe to a stop at a random spot in the vast expanse of the Pacific Ocean. As he spread his digits apart, the image of Earth grew to fill the entire screen, then continued to expand until it was centered on the Hawaiian Islands. The map was made up of satellite imagery, with all cities, roads, and major natural features outlined and labeled.

"So, why is that weirder than weird?" Aaron said.

"Because when you zoom *way* in...." Ryan spread his fingers again. "This happens."

Once the magnification reached a certain level, when Honolulu filled the display area, a red crosshair appeared, centered on the right side of the map display. The left half offered a new input area that overlaid the map image against a hazy white background. There were two columns of text. The left column consisted of three clocks or timers labeled CURRENT TIME, START DELAY, and MISSION. The top one gave the time as 18:29:32Z and was steadily ticking forward. The other two clocks read -00:00:10 and 00:00:00, respectively.

The second column was labeled TARGET and showed a set of latitude and longitude figures. When Ryan placed his finger on the crosshair and dragged it around the map, the coordinate values changed. Ellie noticed that the crosshair would occasionally flash green, then instantly revert to red. Below the coordinate values, the screen read, AUTO OPTIMIZE: Yes

The following line said TIME. Below were two sliders, and to the right of the sliders was the current setting. It read 22 July 2006 — 08:30Z. Ellie put her finger on the top slider and moved it to the right. Nothing happened. She tried sliding left. As she did so, the year changed, rolling swiftly backward until it stopped at 1903 and wouldn't go any earlier. As she slid her finger back to the right, the year value moved forward again. She paused at 1941 but left her finger on the screen. After a second, the slider flashed twice. When she moved her finger again, the month and day values changed. She stopped on December 7. She assumed the other slider adjusted the time of day.

"'A date which will live in infamy!'" Ryan said this in what Ellie assumed was meant to be Roosevelt's voice, although it sounded as much like Teddy as Franklin. Or even Eleanor, for that matter.

The final line was simply one word—CONFIRM—rendered in red and pulsing slowly.

She turned away from the panel and looked around the room, assimilating all the details. Looking down between her feet, she noticed that each floor panel had a slight irregularity, barely discernible, near the edge of one of its short sides. Crouching, she found these to be small, shallow dimples. She pressed one gently with an index finger and felt it move. She pushed harder until she heard a click, and when she pulled her hand away, the dimple popped up from the panel's surface to become the knob on a tiny handle. It looked like one of her parent's golf tees. She pulled, and the panel tilted up on hinges along its opposite edge to reveal a tightly packed arrangement of four dark, rectangular boxes, each connected to its neighbors by cables thicker than her pinky. Their surfaces were unmarked save for a "+" and a "-" near the terminals, and where "GraphMax—10,000Ah" was stamped in white at the center of each box. The cables from the visible boxes extended into the areas covered by neighboring panels.

Aaron, peering over her shoulder, let out a low whistle. "Batteries," he said. "If those are behind every panel, there is a huge—I mean a *huge*—amount of energy stored beneath this floor. And inside the walls, too, I think. Did you notice how much smaller this room is compared to the outside? Here, let me see that panel."

Ellie moved out of the way, letting him take the handle as he knelt in her place. She watched him move the free end up and down a few inches, judging its weight, then he gave it a couple of taps with his fingernail and listened to the sound. Finally, he lowered the panel into place and pushed the handle back into its surface.

"*Hmm....*" he said to himself.

"But that trench outside says it's on the grid," Ryan said. "Why all the batteries?"

"Backup?" Ellie said.

"That's a *lot* of backup!"

Sam jabbed her thumb at the wall behind her. "These panels on the walls, are they all, like, TVs or displays of some kind?"

Aaron nodded. "That's my guess. OLED film over a non-metallic backing. Feels like some kind of ceramic. And based on these two," he indicated the control panels, "you could probably put any image you wanted on them."

"If that's the case...." Ryan tilted his head back and aimed his voice toward the center of the room. This time he spoke with the accent of a television starship captain addressing his vessel's central data core. "Computer, show the area surrounding this room on the internal walls." A second passed, then another, but nothing happened. "Oh, well. I figured it was worth...."

A collective gasp filled the small space when, all at once, they seemed to be standing back outside. The white walls and ceiling now projected live, ultra-high-resolution video images of the surrounding forest. The six chairs were still there, as was the control console, which now appeared to float in mid-air. Beyond it, they could see their packs leaning against the fallen tree. Overhead, filtering through the sparse branches of the ponderosas, the sun appeared to shine on them from the area around the hole left by the descended central section. A pair of ravens skimmed over the treetops, heading south toward Cochiti Pueblo.

"...a shot," he finally finished.

Sam laughed in delight. "Hey! Look down!"

Even the floor panels were in on the joke, displaying an image of pine duff, fallen twigs, and lichen-covered rocks that blended seamlessly into the walls. This made it feel like they were standing at ground level, and Ellie found the illusion of having suddenly dropped more than a foot disorienting.

"This... amazing!" It was all Aaron could manage.

"Hologram?" Ryan said.

Aaron swayed from side to side as he studied the forest image. "No. No parallax," he said. "Regular old hi-def two-d."

"There is nothing 'regular' about any of this," Sam said.

Ellie, who had been trying to make all the observable pieces fit a single, coherent concept, felt them suddenly click into place. "Guys—I think I know what this is!"

7

"I mmersive *virtual reality chamber*—that's a mouthful. But then what's with all the fancy technology if the walls can produce the illusion of open space?" Ryan indicated the chairs and control panel with a sweep of his arm.

"I don't know," Ellie said. "Maybe it can be, like, 'either-or.' There aren't any visors on the headpieces, though, so maybe the visual part comes from the walls and the rest works through the chairs." She looked at Aaron to see if he had any technical objection to her idea.

"For that to work, the walls would have to display a unique image to each person, but... focused pixels?" He shrugged. "Theoretically possible, sure."

"Okay, so maybe they only use the screens when they're designing the virtual spaces. But these chairs? Look at them. All those metal studs are in places where we have lots of nerves. Maybe they're the way you interact with the virtual space. If I'm right, these goopy-looking hand pads can probably pick up the slightest twitches and convert them into normal motions in the simulation."

"That's a whole lot of 'maybes!'" Sam said.

But Aaron was quick to support Ellie's interpretation. "No, that all makes sense. One of the biggest problems with VR systems today is figuring out how to perform the training tasks—or whatever you're doing—in the virtual world without needing the same amount of space in the real world. They've tried treadmills and giant touchpad kinds of things, but they don't feel natural. But if whoever built this has figured out a way to, ah, I don't know, 'hijack,' let's say, the nerve impulses going back and forth between your muscles and your motor cortex, that would be the perfect solution. In that case, it could feel like you were walking around a city, climbing a mountain, or even running at full speed, but you wouldn't be moving at all."

"So," Ryan said, "whoever sits in these chairs would all be in the same virtual space?"

Ellie and Aaron looked at each other. He shrugged again.

"I would assume so," she said. "Why else would all the chairs be wired together like that?" That was a guess, she admitted, but it felt right.

"But that's not all." Aaron picked up on her speculation and took it a step further. "With this kind of set-up and the degree of nerve interactivity needed to make it work, you'd probably feel everything!"

"What do you mean 'everything?'" Ryan said.

"Like… *everything!* How rough tree bark feels, grains of sand under your feet, the wind blowing on your face, heat, cold—things current VR can't begin to do. At its best, there'd be no way you could tell you weren't actually… well, wherever you seemed to be."

"Then what's all this for?" Sam said, pointing at the console still appearing to hover on the far side of the room. Then she shifted the angle of her finger to indicate the wall's forest image. "And that's kind of annoying now."

Ryan raised his index finger in an *I've got this* gesture. "Computer," he said, then realized he wasn't sure how to phrase the request. "Uh… return to normal interior lighting."

"*Please,*" Sam said.

"Please," he echoed.

A second later, the panels reverted to their original, blank state.

"That's *so* much better," she said. "But like I said, what's with the map and stuff?"

Ellie realized Sam was no longer intent on getting them out as quickly as possible. Fifteen minutes had passed since they hacked their way in, and nobody had arrived to haul them away in manacles. Now she was as curious as the rest of them.

"To know that for sure," Aaron said, "we'd have to know what this room was intended for. NASA astronauts rehearse complex missions in VR simulators. Top athletes sometimes use it for learning specific tracks, like bobsled or slalom. Architects, interior designers, surgeons—lots of people use it for very different reasons."

"The military uses it for training, especially for infil/exfil ops," Ryan said, then nodded for Aaron to continue.

"Yeah, right. There are definitely military uses. Consumer VR tech, though—the stuff made for the rest of us—is mostly for entertainment. 3D movies, video games, virtual sports, that sort of thing. There are also other, ah, 'erotic' applications." His face reddened as he delivered this last tidbit.

"Ohh, do tell!" Ryan said.

Sam jabbed her elbow at his ribs, but he dodged it easily. "So, what's that say about all this," she said.

Aaron paused to think. "It's possible it's meant to be a way to experience different locations at different times. It's one thing to read a history book, but another to live the actual history, right?"

"True," Ryan said, "but it wouldn't be the 'actual history,' just a recreation. It would be like getting up on stage in the middle of a play. Think about it—if you could interact with the people around you, you'd be altering the way things happened."

"That would depend entirely on how it's programmed. Perhaps you can only observe. But by using a super-advanced AI interface, for example, it might be possible to...."

Live the actual history. Now there's *a thought.* Ellie once more tuned out the conversation and never heard Aaron's ideas on the role of artificial intelligence in creating an interactive virtual world. She thought about the dismal review the first version of her American History research paper had received. Her revised draft centered on the so-called 'Bread and Roses' strike and particularly on Carmela, the young girl who had been central to its success.

Suddenly excited by the possibility, she wondered how good a simulation it would be. *How cool to see the town as it was when she was there!*

She felt she already understood the right half of the control panel. She zoomed out until the continental U.S. was visible and used a finger to slide the map to the left. Once she had reached the eastern seaboard, she gradually zoomed her way back in until she was centered on Lawrence, Massachusetts. The city was smaller than she expected, and the surrounding area appeared to be a dense, hardwood forest. Next, she focused on the first slider under TIME. She slid her finger to the left, and the year moved backward until it reached 1912. Then she fine-tuned the date to March 14 and noticed with only mild surprise that the urbanized area on the map now looked even smaller.

Of course—it would *work that way!* The display was not merely a map, but a simulator in its own right. It showed the world as it was on the date selected, and a moment ago she had been looking at the Lawrence of 1941. She used the other slider to set the time to 14:00z.

She stared at the pulsing red crosshair symbol. No matter where she moved it around the map of Lawrence, it obstinately stayed red. Wherever she stopped, a new text field appeared on the screen next to her finger—

INPUT: Override Authorization Code

Well, I am fresh out of those today. She frowned, thinking that her experiment had just reached its end. Then she noticed the Auto Optimize option again. She pressed Yes, and after a brief hesitation, the crosshair symbol shifted slightly northwest of Lawrence, stopped on an area the map indicated was covered in forest, and switched to solid green.

As she turned her attention to the other half of the display, she was distantly aware of Aaron explaining the concept of nerve induction. She hoped he could keep them focused on him while she made sense of the controls. *That's it. Keep them busy a little longer.*

She studied the representations of the chairs, then twisted her neck around to peer over her shoulder at the actual items. She noticed for the first time that the metal frame of each backrest was etched with an identifying numeral. The seat closest to her, the one facing the control panel, displayed a '1.' The chair to its left was number two. As she turned back to the display, she heard Aaron say something about 'subjective time.' *Just a few more seconds.*

She quickly scanned the panel, and then she had it. *So simple!* She tapped the chair icons numbered from one through four to the right of SELECT, then touched INITIALIZE. Instantly, the low, heavy *chunk* of a large circuit breaker switch engaging sounded from deep within the array of chairs. That noise was followed immediately by a low, resonant hum she seemed to feel as much as hear, then the room was otherwise silent. For a moment, anyway.

Sam looked around to confront Ellie, sounding cross. *"What did you just do?!"*

"Tell me you don't want to try it out," Ellie said.

"I *don't* want to try it out!"

"You sure? Not even a little?"

"Well...."

"*Ha!* Knew it! What about you guys?"

Ryan looked at Sam while he answered, trying to gauge the actual depth of her opposition. "Uh, I don't know, Ellie. How do we know it's safe?"

"What do you have in mind?" Aaron wanted some specifics before making his decision. He pointed at the control panel behind her. "You think you've got that all figured out?"

"Easy-peasy," she said. "You pick a time and place, turn on the chairs, then press go. I picked one of the places I'm writing about for my U.S. History class, a mill town in Massachusetts." Studying their faces, she saw emotions ranging from eagerness to apprehension. "Come on, guys, it's a simulator... how dangerous could it be?"

"The second-most famous of last words, right after, 'Hey, guys, watch this!'" Ryan said.

Ellie viewed the comment, coming from Ryan, not as true opposition to the idea but merely as a joke. Sam, though, chose to take his statement at face value.

"Exactly!" she said. "After all, it only plugs directly into your *brain!*" She pointed at the nearest headpiece with its gleaming silver contacts.

"Aaron?" She sensed he was her best shot at winning over an ally. "Five minutes, just to see what it's like. What do you say?"

Sam cut in before he could answer. "You said five minutes before, and we've already been in here what... *ten?*"

"Sounds pretty close," she said, silently willing Aaron and Ryan not to contradict her. She thought it had been at least twice that long,

"I've done the Oculus thing," Aaron said. "I'd love to see how this compares." He considered her proposal for no more than a second. "For five minutes? I'm in."

"Sam?" Ellie knew Ryan would go whichever way she decided. She also knew Sam would assume he wanted to try it out and would consequently feel like she was being put in the position of playing the spoiler. That would certainly explain the glare Sam was now giving her.

"Ellie, I...." she began, but Ellie interrupted.

"Pretty please? I'll do all our laundry for a month!"

Sam glanced to Ryan for guidance. He managed to keep his face nearly expressionless, which Ellie found impressive given the circumstances. He said nothing, only gave Sam an indifferent, one-shoulder shrug. *It's no big thing—you choose,* was what that shrug said. Ellie knew the shrug was lying. Sam knew, too. She glared again at Ellie, irritated by having been so manipulated. "All right, *fine!* But that's it this time—five minutes!" She held up her hand, palm outward, fingers splayed wide.

"Woo-hoo!" Aaron said. Behind Sam's back, Ryan made a single fist-pumping motion and mouthed a silent, *Yes!*

"Okay, Miss Smarty-Pants," Sam said. "What do we do?"

"Each chair has a number on the backrest below the helmet. Find numbers two, three, and four, and sit in one of them—Aaron will help you get set up. Once everybody's in place, I'll hit the button and sit in chair number one."

"I'll take two," Aaron said, talking fast. "Sam, you sit here in number three, and we'll get you situated." Ellie knew he was trying to hurry things along before Sam could have second thoughts and change her mind.

Sam sat and slid against the backrest. Aaron used his foot to flip the two footrests in from the sides. She placed her feet in position, snugging them up into the toe cages. When she pressed down, small tabs at the bottom of each metal plate slid up to meet her heels.

"Okay, now we slide this down." Aaron adjusted the headpiece until it was nestled securely on her head. He checked the connection where the wire harness entered the headpiece, found it was tight, and nodded to himself.

"And now your hands...."

She laid her palms onto the tacky-looking substance in the circular containers.

"Ooh, that feels gross! But it's warm—you'd think it'd be cold." The gel quickly conformed to the shape of her palm until her hand was partially embedded below its surface.

"Relax and keep your hands flat like that," he said. "You okay?"

She nodded. "Mm-hmm." She squirmed against the seatback. "I can feel those bumps moving on my back!"

A flicker drew Ellie's attention to a change in the data on the left-hand control panel. With Sam seated, the display offered a new set of readings below the icon of chair number three. Pulse and respiration rates were stated numerically, and an ECG-like graphic spiked with every heartbeat. Then a new reading appeared. This number was a fraction labeled BP. Her first thought was that the gel pads did much more than she initially assumed. Or were there perhaps other devices at work, ones they hadn't yet discovered?

Additional details of Sam's vital functions continued to appear on the display. The largest of the new readouts showed a pattern of multiple, overlapping sine waves that expanded and contracted, each according to its unique rhythm. *Brain function?* Other bits of data were more straightforward. She saw numbers with the labels hydration, blood oxygen, and electrolytes, but she had no idea if the values were good or bad. She also noticed that another symbol had appeared directly below the '3' that indicated Sam's chair. It was a familiar icon composed of a circle with a plus sign descending from the center of its lower arc. Somehow the chair knew Sam was female.

Aaron looked at Ryan, who had silently observed while he got Sam prepared. "You good to go?"

"Yeah, yeah. I got it." Ryan took his seat and got himself ready.

Ellie motioned for Aaron to come close to her and whispered in his ear. "Did you notice that?" She pointed at the monitor display.

"Wow," he said, keeping his voice low. "Seems like overkill. You sure about this?"

"Mm-hmm. You? Say the word, and I'll hit the cancel button."

He didn't hesitate. "Oh, I'm all in!" He sat and began adjusting the gear.

As Ellie rechecked each of her settings, she spoke over her shoulder in a bright, sing-song imitation of an airline flight attendant. "Ladies and gentlemen, this—um—'shack' is ready to depart. Please keep your seatbelts securely fastened throughout the flight, and remember—remain seated until we've come to a complete stop! Okay, then… ten seconds." She tapped the execute button and saw the start delay clock start counting backward from ten.

She immediately sat down and pulled the headpiece on, wiggling it until it felt properly seated on her head. She deftly tipped the footrests into position, slipped her toes into the cages, and leaned back. Despite Sam's comment, she was surprised by how warm the gel pads felt when she laid her hands on them. They really did look like they would be cold. Watching with fascination as her hands settled into the semi-firm substance, she wondered if the heat was necessary to make the gel soft, and regretted not touching it earlier when the device was off. At the same time, she could feel the studs along her back moving on either side of her spine, adjusting their positions to achieve even pressure at every point of contact.

As she waited for whatever was about to happen, she realized she hadn't needed to be so hasty to get into position, and she wished she had taken a few seconds to scan the rest of the display. She tried raising her head enough to peer over the edge of the control panel, but the headpiece had locked firmly into place. Then, as she relaxed against the seatback, she felt the bands within the headpiece tighten. The sensation was like having her blood pressure taken on her skull. The force of the studs against her scalp increased until it became uncomfortable, but stopped short of being painful. She heard someone start to cry out, either in surprise or in pain, but the sound abruptly cut off. She tried to ask if everyone was okay, only then understanding why the cry had been so short—she couldn't move a muscle, not even to speak. She tried to lift first one arm, then the other, but neither would so much as budge. She felt panic rising in her mind.

This can't be right!

Fighting to remain calm, she drew in a deep breath. To her enormous relief, she discovered she could still breathe on command. She remembered Aaron saying that the studs possibly hi-jacked their nerve impulses, and the thought allowed her to relax a little. Maybe this *was* the way it was supposed to work.

Ellie had barely enough time to wonder what would happen next, then everything went black.

8

Ellie found it impossible to tell how long she drifted in that darkness. She had lost all sense of time. The word itself was now meaningless, a nonsensical sound devoid of any denotation. Eons passed with every heartbeat while seconds stretched into centuries. She had likewise lost any concept of her own body. She felt tiny, a dust mote adrift in deepest space.

In contrast, her awareness exploded outward, expanding at an ever-increasing rate until she felt it encompassing all of existence. She sensed alien worlds circling distant stars, undiscovered galaxies, and the inscrutable dark matter that dominated all else. She was the universe, the universe was her, and she possessed all of its secrets. It was a state of being she never could have imagined, and she knew she would never find the words to describe it.

She was no longer gripped by that mind-freezing panic, nor even the slightest hint of fear. For as long as this new state of being continued, the entirety of her experience was reduced to a single emotion, one that transcended happiness or even joy. It was a moment—or a millennium—of pure, perfect contentment.

Then, departing as abruptly as it had arrived, the feeling was gone. For a single second, her heart ached, unable to bear the magnitude of the loss.

The next second she was beyond any hope of recalling more than the faintest impression of the most profound experience of her life. She could only remember a brief moment, immediately before the blackness had taken her under, when she had felt like she was falling. The sensation, which had lasted only for an instant, made her feel as if the shack had tilted over the edge of the plateau and was tumbling head over heels into a bottomless arroyo.

Her normal awareness returned swiftly, leaving her feeling decidedly less content. She still sat rigidly immobile on the chair, but now it was by choice. A nauseating wave of vertigo rolled through her, and she feared the slightest movement would cause her to be violently sick. But even without trying to move, she sensed her body was back under her control. She also knew that it was not actually dark now but seemed that way only because she kept her eyes clamped tightly shut against that sickening wave. She forced herself to draw in slow, deep breaths and then exhale just as slowly. Her senses were fully back now, and she heard soft groans from the others. Evidently, they'd all been affected the same way.

She kept her eyes closed even after regaining full consciousness, letting the nausea subside. A minute later she felt only slightly better but was eager for her first glimpse of Lawrence in 1912. She forced her eyelids open only to find that she was surrounded by the same four blank walls.

"*Huh!*" She looked down at her hands and carefully eased them out of the gel, starting with the heels of her palms and finishing with her fingertips. They came out cleanly with no sign of residue. The gel's surface leveled out much like the memory foam in the seat pads had, and a second later it was smooth and pristine.

Ryan spoke next, sounding every bit as queasy as she felt. "Yeah. 'Huh!' is right. I have to say—I did not see that coming."

Ellie didn't know whether he was referring to how the chairs had seized control of them, the bizarre, out-of-body interlude and subsequent nausea, or the utter lack of change to the space around them. No matter how he meant it, she had to agree.

"Definitely should have taken the blue pill," Sam groaned. "What *was* that?"

Ellie turned to her left and saw Aaron slumped forward in his chair as far as the helmet bracket would allow him to go. She couldn't tell if he was conscious or not. A sudden surge of concern instantly displaced the last trace of queasiness. She yanked her helmet off, kicked the footrests aside, and scrambled from her chair.

"*Aaron!*" She leaned low over him. "Aaron, are you okay?"

He managed a feeble nod and a weak "thumbs-up" gesture. "I'm fine. I'm trying not to throw up all over the fancy technology."

Ellie kneeled to look up at his face. He didn't seem any paler than usual, so she relaxed.

Sam was unimpressed. "Not *too* fancy. This stupid thing doesn't seem to work. Or else this is an exquisite simulation of the room we were already in. *Whee*, this is fun!" Her voice was laced with a double dose of sarcasm.

"Computer," Ryan said, "show us the outside again."

Either still too queasy to quibble or simply beyond caring, Sam didn't bother to correct his brusque command. After the same three-second pause, the walls and floors again displayed a woodland scene.

"*Ha!*" Ryan said. "Look at that!"

"Whoa...." Aaron said, sitting upright for a better view.

The forest now surrounding them was not one that could be found anywhere in New Mexico. Gone were the towering ponderosa pines and scrubby piñons and junipers of the Pajarito Plateau. In their place stood a stately deciduous forest dominated by a mix of bare oaks and maples with a dark green understory of rhododendrons and holly trees spreading beneath. The brilliantly sunny sky of minutes before was now a cold, leaden gray. Ellie knew this to be the forested area selected by the map program when she pressed Auto Optimize. It appeared something was working after all, just not how they expected.

Sam and Ryan rose from their seats and stepped closer to the wall to study their new surroundings. Still kneeling in front of Aaron, Ellie spoke softly.

"Can you stand?"

"Oh, I'm fine now," he said, and he did sound better. "Whatever that was, I think I'm over it." He reached up and slid off the helmet, then rubbed at the reddened indentations where the contacts had pressed into his scalp.

Whether in response to him removing his headpiece or merely by coincidence, the forest scene disappeared, and the room abruptly resumed its flatly illuminated appearance. At the same time, a series of loud clicks came from the opposite side of the room before a tightly spaced group of four wall panels swung partially open. The surface of each open panel displayed a numeral, one through four, rendered in pale gray. Sam and Ryan stepped over to investigate.

"So… these are like the numbers on our chairs?" Sam said.

Ryan pulled the one marked with a 4 completely open, revealing a variety of clear plastic bags stuffed with dark objects. He withdrew two of the shiny parcels and held them up for the others to see.

"I hate getting clothes as presents," he said. Then, catching himself, he turned to Sam and quickly added, "Except from you, of course."

Ellie approached the wall and pulled a similar package from cubbyhole number one. As Ryan had said, they were articles of clothing vacuum-sealed in heavy, reusable plastic storage bags. The one she held contained a dress. The next package she pulled out was thicker and looked like it held a winter coat. Flipping through the remaining bags, she saw additional outfits, assorted outerwear, and, at the rear of the compartment, a pair of shoes or possibly a kind of lightweight boot. Each bag had a small pouch displaying a label that described the outfit it contained. The label on the bag with the dress read "Teacher." Curious about the rest of her options, she sorted through the other bags in the compartment, stopping when she found one that said "Millworker."

Perfect! She pulled out the shoes, the bag containing the heavy coat, and the millworker's clothes from the bin. She noticed Ryan was still examining his packages.

"You have boy clothes?"

He nodded. "Looks like."

In light of the costumes and their apparent need to change into them, Ellie was forced to acknowledge the obvious. "I, uh…." She cleared her throat. "This is going to take longer than five minutes."

Sam snorted. "Like *that's* a surprise!" Leaning in to investigate the contents of her bin, she examined the bags from various angles, peering with interest through the tough plastic. "Okay, so this is a costume party?"

"Maybe it's like...." Aaron started off sounding confident but quickly ran out of steam. "No, I have no idea."

"Well, 'When in Rome....'" Sam said, excited to try on the mystery outfits.

"Or Lawrence, as the case may be," Ellie said. "We're clearly meant to put this stuff on." She shrugged. "Why not?"

They regarded one another for a few uncomfortable moments, clutching their chosen packages to their chests.

"It's not like there are changing rooms," Ryan finally said.

"Look, you two stay here," Ellie said. "Sam and I will go over there." She pointed past the array of chairs. "Besides, it's not like we'll have to get completely naked."

Ellie and Sam retreated to the relative privacy of the room's opposite side, and everyone began unpacking their outfits. Each time someone broke a seal, they heard a quiet *whoosh* as air rushed in to fill the expanding bag. After pulling the tightly compressed items from their bags, they gave each a vigorous shake to restore some of its normal loft.

Although Sam had selected a costume labeled Shopkeeper/Service, the two female outfits were nearly identical, both consisting of ankle-length woolen dresses, cotton blouses, and long, heavy, woolen stockings. They differed mainly in that Sam's dress was a rich, deep blue, obviously used but otherwise in good condition, while Ellie's was a washed-out, no-color gray and had been patched and mended in numerous places. The repairs had been made with care, though, as if the wearer knew the dress would have to last much longer, despite its tattered state.

Ellie pulled an unfamiliar item from the bag and held it up, eyeing it doubtfully. It was a wide, lacy band with four straps dangling from it. She held it out in front of her. "What's this?"

Sam recognized it at once. "Garter belt. To hold your stockings up."

"Well, *that's* not happening!" She tossed the strange contraption back into the bag.

"I think these blouses will hide our tops, but you may have to lose those pants."

"We'll see," she said, hoping Sam was wrong. She pulled the blouse on, and, sure enough, the high, Victorian collar buttoned well above the neck of her t-shirt. Next, she pulled on the long stockings and worked their tops up under her pant legs, hoping that once she rolled up the pants, friction alone would keep them from pooling around her ankles.

Sam, meanwhile, had pulled her garter belt on over her shorts and was attaching the tops of the stockings to the straps. Ellie, watching from the corner of her eye, thought the thing looked ridiculous but kept her opinion to herself. Finally, they pulled the dresses over their heads and worked them down into place. Ellie tried to fasten the row of buttons that ran up her back, but no matter how hard she tried, she could not reach more than the top two.

"Here, let me," Sam said.

Ellie spun around, and while Sam buttoned her dress, she studied the control panel. The map showed a green crosshair surrounded by forest. The mission timer read 4:14:09 and was ticking steadily down. Ellie had no time to wonder what that meant before Sam was finished.

"Okay. Now do me," Sam said.

It took Ellie just seconds to return the favor, and Sam called out to the boys just as Ellie fastened her final button.

"You guys decent over there?"

"We're, uh, *dressed*," Ryan said.

Curious to see what had provoked his enigmatic tone, Sam and Ellie moved around from behind the chairs. They started laughing at once.

"Yeah... I'm not sure how *decent* we look," Aaron said.

Ryan's Worker/Tradesman outfit consisted of long woolen trousers, a dark shirt made from some other heavy material, and a double-breasted jacket. A visored cap perched atop his head at a rakish angle. He held the fingers of his right hand tucked into what Ellie guessed was a watch pocket, looking for all the world like he was posing for a turn-of-the-century photograph.

But it was Aaron's costume that caused the most amusement. He wore a long-sleeve, chambray shirt covered by patched overalls that reached only to mid-calf—the clothes of a farmhand. Standing there bare-footed, he seemed to have just stepped out of a Whitman or Whittier poem, minus a basket of strawberries and maybe a straw hat. Then there were the glasses, which, despite the rest of his costume, still made Ellie think of snowy owls.

"I know—major high-waters," he said. The overalls would have been even shorter had they fit correctly, but they seemed to have been intended for someone an inch or two taller. "I wasn't sure I could pull off the 'business owner' look, though."

"You two look wonderful," Sam exclaimed. "And what do you think of our *couture?*" She placed her hands on her hips and made a quick spin.

Ryan appraised her look and grinned. "The snake's suspenders, my dear! The bee's knees, the cat's...."

"I can see your pant legs," Aaron interrupted, pointing toward Ellie's feet.

"Well, let's check out these shoes," Ellie said.

Like the dresses, the women's shoes were of a type—high, narrowly fitted leather boots secured by dark laces threaded through ten or twelve pairs of eyelets. Ellie glanced over to see what type of footwear Aaron and Ryan had been provided. Their pairs were likewise basically identical to each other and similar to her own, although theirs were shorter and looked sturdier, made of thicker leather with heavier soles and more rounded toes.

Aaron had already pulled on his stockings, the tops of which disappeared up into his overalls. She noticed a slight bulge around his ankles and realized he had put his hiking socks on first and put the stockings on over them. That was probably a good idea if, like the clothes, his shoes were half a size too big.

She held one of her shoes up to the bottom of her foot to double-check the fit, then snugged her feet into them. She laced them up tight, then rolled her pant legs up until they were no longer visible below the hem of her dress. She looked down at her costume and wished there were a mirror in the room. She figured she could get "Computer" to give her a look at herself, but would have felt foolish asking.

"March in Massachusetts," she said. "Let's hope this stuff is warm enough." She saw Sam pull a wide-brimmed hat onto her head and position it by feel. It was showy, not at all Ellie's style. "I think I'll pass on a hat."

"Nonsense," Sam said. "I saw one in here that...." She reached into her compartment and examined the labels on a few of the smallest packages until she found the one she wanted. "Here it is!" She handed it to Ellie. "That one will totally work on you."

Ellie looked at the tag. *Cloche; wool; gray.* She opened the flap and pulled out what was, to her surprise, a very plain, perfectly acceptable hat. It was similar in its general shape to a stocking cap, but was more structured and less stretchy. "Thanks!" While Ryan and Aaron folded their pants and set them and any other clothing they were leaving behind on their chairs, Ellie emptied her final package and gave the long, woolen coat a hard shake. She shrugged into the coat and pulled her hat down firmly onto her head.

They were now all in full costume, and Ellie was delighted by the effect. "Wow! We look exactly like the people in all the pictures I've been staring at for the last few weeks. I wonder if I had set it to July if the clothes would be different."

"We'd probably be leaving the heavy coats behind, is all," Sam said. "Workers didn't have a ton of fashion choices back then. We might be wearing cotton dresses instead of this wool."

"You would have died!" Ryan teased her.

Sam pointed her nose into the air and spoke in a breathy accent that was, *apropos* of nothing, straight out of Dixie. "I would have been the mill owner's daughter. It would have been all fashion, all the time." She reached up and tweaked the position of Ryan's paperboy hat. "That's better." She lowered her hand and examined the details of his jacket. "This stuff is really *good!* Edwardian right down to the buttons, hand-hemmed—I'm impressed!" She looked up to catch Ryan and Aaron exchanging amused looks. *"What?!"*

"It's not like any of it's *real*," Ryan reminded her.

She fixed him with an icy stare and spoke with equally cold precision. "I know that, *Mister Collins.* I was simply noting that, for a simulation, the level of detail far exceeds what one would expect."

"Ah. Well, then, you are absolutely correct." The stare continued. "As always," he finally added. Sam, ever gracious in victory, flashed him a wide smile.

Eager to change the subject, Ryan turned to Aaron, who had donned his wool coat and cap. "Is *that* the hat you got?" he said. Aaron's hat was similar to his own but had a three-inch-wide strip that descended from the sides of the inner band and wrapped around its back and sides.

Aaron seemed confused by the implied criticism of his headwear. *"Huh?!* I like it. It has this cool ear thingy."

"Later, you and I are going to have a long talk about what's 'cool,'" Ryan promised him.

"I believe that is called an Ainsley cap," Sam said. "Very fashionable in its day."

Aaron gave Ryan a smug smile.

Ellie was impatient to do something more than play dress-up. "Are we ready?"

"I guess," Sam said.

Aaron double-checked all four bins for any other potentially useful items. Finding nothing, he closed them and turned to face the others. "I'm good."

"Let's do this," Ryan said.

He moved to the door and pulled down on the handle. It rotated halfway, then locked at a forty-five-degree angle. The sound of sudden motion behind them caused everyone to jump. They watched the chairs and control panels retract into their concealed positions. At the same time, a panel to the left of the door popped out from the wall and slid sideways to reveal a palm scanner identical to the one they had used to get in. The scanner portion of the glass was outlined in red, and across its middle, it said—

CREATE ENTRY CODE: Yes No

Ryan looked at Ellie, then Aaron, who had suddenly gone pale. For him, this was something of an accomplishment. "What?" he said, his brow knitted in concern. "Still feeling it?"

"No, it's not that. It's.... I never thought to bring the wax paper. We could've gotten stuck outside."

Ran scoffed. "Yeah. 'Virtually' stuck, anyway." He sounded unconcerned by what Aaron considered a potentially disastrous near miss. "So, do we do this?"

"Go ahead," Ellie said and nodded to Aaron.

He placed his hand on the scanner. After a moment, the light changed to green, and he keyed in the same four-digit code he had used before—2064. The panel flashed green twice, then returned to its previous state.

CREATE ENTRY CODE: Yes No

"Let me put one in," Ellie said. She repeated the process but finished by entering 1912 as her personal access code. Once again, the scanner asked its question.

"Do you guys wanna...?" She pointed at the scanner.

Sam shook her head, but Ryan stepped up to the device. "Sure, why not?"

Ellie pressed Yes again. Ryan thought for a second before placing his hand on the glass, then entered 1138 when prompted. This time Ellie chose No when the question reappeared on the screen. The face of the scanner went dark, and the wall panel shifted back into place.

Then the room showed them yet another trick. All the panels changed to mimic the inside of a rustic, wooden shack, complete with warped floorboards and tightly sealed shutters outside the virtual "windows." What they knew to be a flat ceiling now appeared to be peaked, with rough-hewn planks overlaying square-cut roof beams.

"*Okay*...." Ellie said, stretching the word out as she swept her gaze around the room. "Try the door again."

Ryan pulled the handle, and this time it pivoted smoothly down to horizontal, and the door clunked slightly open. He gave it a nudge with his shoulder and created a narrow gap.

Ellie remained in place while Sam, Ryan, and Aaron slipped outside through the partially open door. Standing alone in the silence, she thought she could feel—maybe through the thin soles of her antique shoes or perhaps thrumming through the air itself—a faint vibration. She thought about what Aaron had said regarding the tremendous amount of power that must be under the floor, but when she knelt to place her fingertips on the simulated pine boards beneath her feet, the sensation disappeared. *Or maybe it's my imagination.*

Ellie hopped down into a small clearing surrounded by a dense grove of bare hardwood trees. It was a crisp, late-winter morning, just as the images on the wall had shown, but filled with a loamy smell that reminded her of their old home in Virginia. It was a rich, earthy fragrance that no video panel could begin to convey. She heard a small creek bubbling not far away, out of sight but clearly audible, and a smattering of bird song from overhead. The ground was covered by a thick blanket of dull, nearly colorless leaves, still damp from a recent rain- or snowfall, and they made little sound as they spread out and investigated their new surroundings.

"*Whoo—chilly!*" Sam said. "You weren't kidding about the temperature! I wish *I* had some pants on under this dress."

"It's early. It'll warm up later on," Ellie said.

"Let's hope," Ryan said. "But right now it makes me wish I had a 'cool' hat, too."

Aaron was too engrossed in his thoughts to notice the dig. He was staring at the shack, studying it intently, his head slightly cocked to one side. "Maybe it's like the holodeck arch on *Next Generation*. Like we have to come here to stop the simulation or control anything."

Ellie considered this and could not think of a better explanation for the building's continuing presence within the virtual environment. "Could be. We ready?" she said again. This time everyone nodded.

Ryan returned to the shack and put his shoulder to the door, but Aaron stopped him as he was about to swing it shut.

"*Wait, wait, wait!*" he said.

Watching him leap back into the shack, Ellie wondered what he could have forgotten. Sam took advantage of the momentary lull in the action to raise herself onto tiptoes and plant a brief kiss on Ryan's lips. He grinned at her as she dropped back onto her heels.

"What was that for?"

She gave him a kittenish smile. "Just testing out the whole 'nerve induction' thing. I give it an A-plus."

"Yeah, me too. I definitely felt *that!*"

Then Aaron was back, holding Ellie's little camera high as he dropped down from the door. "I have no idea what this will do here in VR Land, but I'd hate to miss the chance to find out."

9

Ryan shoved the door closed and they heard the deep *clunk* of the locking mechanism. Ellie examined the surface of the shack closely, but despite knowing precisely where the wall ended and the door began, she couldn't detect the slightest seam.

Ryan turned away from the door, twirled his hand over his head twice, his index and middle fingers extended, then pointed out into the forest. Ellie recognized it as an imitation of a military hand signal. Lieutenant Collins was leading the way.

"All right, team, let's move out!" he said, and started walking away from the shack.

The dense forest stretched away from them in every direction, and there was no path to guide their way. Out of habit formed by summers spent hiking the trackless mesas around Los Alamos, Ellie kept glancing over her shoulder, trying to spot a large rock or a distinctively malformed tree—anything that would help them find their way back. To her dismay, the scene looked the same in every direction.

Based on the display panel's map, she figured they had to walk south and a little east for roughly two miles to find Lawrence. At this early hour, that would mean heading toward the sun. Although it was impossible to be sure of its location behind the low ceiling of thick, gray clouds, she thought the sky seemed somewhat brighter to their right.

"Actually, guys, I think we need to go this way," she said, veering diagonally toward the brighter patch of sky.

"Corporal Henderson will navigate," Ryan said, relinquishing the lead to Ellie.

Aaron came up alongside Ellie's left shoulder. "This way to go where, exactly?"

"Exactly to Lawrence Common."

"And we are going there why?"

"To see a speech by a guy named William Haywood. He was a union leader who helped organize the strike."

"Why are...?" Sam began.

"Strike?" Aaron said at the same time.

"You'd better back up some," Ryan said. "The town is called 'Lawrence Common'?"

"The town—it's a pretty big city, actually—is Lawrence, Massachusetts. Lawrence Common is a park in the middle of it, sort of like the plaza in Santa Fe. In 1912, Lawrence had a population of 85,000 people, almost half of them immigrants, nearly all of whom came here to work at the mills. There were twelve of them—mills, I mean—and all together they had about 32,000 employees."

"Mills. What, like sawmills?"

"Textile mills. They carded wool here, made it into yarn, and then fabric. They also processed cotton brought up from the south. The important thing is that they were horrible places to work. The workweek was as long as sixty hours, and the machines were extremely dangerous. One book I read said that a third of the people hired by the mills died before they were twenty-five years old."

"That's *brutal*," Aaron said.

"The worst of it was that young kids worked at the mills, too. You needed to be at least fourteen to get a job there, but some families were so desperate for money that they sent their children to the mills as soon as they looked old enough to pass. For a couple of dollars, you could buy forged papers that added a year or two onto a kid's age."

"So, you had thirteen- or even twelve-year-olds working sixty-hour weeks?" Sam sounded appalled.

"Technically, women and children were limited to 'only' fifty-six hours, but...." She shrugged. "It was a pretty big deal when a new law took effect in January that reduced that number to fifty-four. The problem was that the mill owners both sped up the machines *and* reduced the monthly wages to compensate. Finally, in February, there was a big strike for that and other reasons."

"Like what other reasons?" Sam said.

"Like the machines were basically death traps, and it was the kids who were doing some of the most dangerous work. Because they were quicker and had smaller hands than adults, they were often used as spinners and doffers, which sometimes meant they had to climb up onto the machines to change bobbins. If they weren't quick enough, the machines would start back up with a hand still inside, or their clothes would get caught and pull them in. Many—*too* many—kids got killed in the mills, but even more got badly hurt. One of them was a girl named Carmela Teoli, whose family had come over from Italy. She dropped out of school and went into the mills when she was thirteen after her father paid a guy four dollars for a fake immigration document that made her out to be fourteen."

"Four dollars seems cheap," Ryan said.

"Now, yeah, but back then, that was about three days' wages. Most people made around eight to nine dollars a week."

"That's like...." Aaron quickly did the math in his head. "Fourteen cents an hour!"

"All for the privilege of breathing in lint all day and the possibility of getting maimed by the machines that were also, day by day, slowly making you deaf. Some places even made you pay for drinking water or ice!"

"So, what happened to Carmela?" Sam said.

"She had been working there only a few weeks when a spinning machine snagged some of her hair and ripped a patch of scalp off her head!" Ellie said, an angry glint in her eye. "She spent the next seven months in the hospital recovering at first from the original injury, then from the infections that came later. The mill she worked for, Washington, did pay her hospital bills but not any lost wages. Her father ended up getting arrested over the forged papers. And the guy he had gotten them from? *He worked for the same mill!"*

They came out of the trees at the edge of a dirt road. Ellie turned right and the rest followed without comment, so caught up in her story that they didn't even think to question the direction. Almost at once, they came to a narrow bridge spanning a stream, which Ellie assumed was the source of the sound of running water she had heard while standing outside the shack. Their feet were loud on the bridge's loose, wooden planks, and she waited until they were across before continuing her story.

"Because of her injury—which I gather was kinda gross—Carmela's story became pretty well known. Even outside of Lawrence. Reporters came from other cities to interview her. After the strike started, she was chosen, along with about a dozen other kids, to go to Washington to testify to a Congressional committee that was writing new labor laws. While there, she got to meet President Taft and the First Lady.

"The mills were bad enough, but most of the workers lived in apartments that were no better than slums, ate mostly beans, bread, and molasses, and were very, *very* lucky if they didn't get TB. Much of the housing was owned by the mills, so the employees were giving a third of their money back to the same people who were exploiting them."

A cluster of wooden homes just beyond the bridge marked the edge of a small town. Ellie studied each house they passed as they continued along the road.

"Carmela's family was a little better off. Her father—his name was Genarro—came to America a few years before the rest of the family. He managed to put together enough money to buy a house outside of Lawrence in a town called Methuen, which I think is where we are now. He had been a farmer in Italy, and his plan was to start a small vegetable farm and eventually quit working in the mills. I know he made some extra money selling homemade wine on the side, but I don't know if he was ever able to get the farm thing going. If you see a place with fire damage, let me know. There was a fire at their house a month or so back, probably set by someone working for the mill owners. They would've done almost anything to stop the workers from walking off the job."

"So, we're back to the strike," Aaron said.

"Which seems to have been inevitable," Sam said. "The mill owners sound like some *really* nice guys."

Ryan waggled his eyebrows at her. "It's enough to make you want to give up wearing clothes."

Ignoring Ryan's comment, Ellie went on. "When the mills cut their pay, the workers voted to strike. Some people from the Industrial Workers of the World, like William Haywood and Elizabeth Gurley Flynn, came to help organize the strike. Soon after, more than 20,000 people walked off the job. The IWW hadn't been around long, but they provided a lot of help to the strikers. They advised them on strategy and provided money to replace part of their lost wages. Another thing they did was send a lot of the workers' kids to sympathetic families in New York and Philadelphia, people who supported the union. This was partly to keep them safe and make sure they were fed, but also so they could spread the word about how bad conditions were in Lawrence. It was never proved, but the fire at the Teoli house was likely part of an effort to keep Carmela's family quiet. Her seven-year-old brother, Anthony, died in the fire. This happened the day after her father was beaten so badly he ended up in the hospital for five days."

"Well," Ryan said. "I can certainly see why you picked this place to visit. It sounds delightful."

"Actually, today is a good day. The workers will vote to end the strike after the mill owners agreed a few days ago to meet their demands. They won a fifteen percent raise, an increase in overtime pay, and a promise that the mill owners would not retaliate against the strikers, which was, of course, practically everyone. If we make it to the park in time, we'll be able to see Haywood's speech and the final vote."

Following Ellie's explanation, they walked on in silence. They did not pass any burned houses, and although they did see a few people on the streets, no one did more than give a curt nod or a slight tip of his hat. Methuen didn't end so much as merge with the edge of Lawrence, but where the buildings thinned a little at the margin, the ground began sloping downward, and about a mile away, they could see tall smokestacks protruding from the cluster of brick buildings that formed the industrial core of Methuen's vastly larger neighbor. The road they were on pointed directly in that direction. The farther they walked, the more people they saw, all converging from side streets onto the main road at the town's edge. Whatever was going to happen at the park, they weren't too late to see it.

"I've been thinking about all of... this," Aaron said, and he swept his arms out to include the whole of their surroundings.

"Do share," Ryan said.

"If we're in some kind of super-detailed simulation, what's with the clothes?"

"Yeah!" Sam said. "I thought there'd be a flicker or something, and then we'd suddenly be here, right in the middle of things. That we'd just see each other as people from this time."

"Maybe it's a part of getting into character?" Ryan said.

Aaron considered this. Not having a better idea, he merely shrugged.

"That's an interesting thought," Sam said. "Remember the paper I did for psych? It was all on the effect wearing costumes and masks has on people's behavior. Putting on a costume can be like putting on a whole new personality. With masks, it's even more so because of the sense of anonymity that comes from having your face covered."

Ellie remembered a bit of conversation she'd heard while working to figure out the shack's controls. "Aaron, what were you saying earlier about how we perceive time?"

"That lots of different things affect the way time seems to pass. Your mood, for one, like if you're feeling anxious or excited. Whether you're busy and distracted or bored and watching the clock. Some drugs can change the way people sense time. Where it gets especially odd, though, is in dreams. Dreams usually last around half an hour or so, but have you ever had a dream where it felt like you were experiencing days or even years?" Everyone nodded. "So, what I was saying was that with normal VR systems, everything is in real-time. Whatever you're doing—playing a game, rehearsing a mission, training for the Olympics—it takes as long as it takes. But if we're currently in some kind of dream-like state, as I strongly suspect we are, then what we're experiencing could all be happening within just a few minutes, a few *seconds*, even, of 'real-time.'"

"So, wouldn't that mean that we're getting *all* of this through the chair's nerve interface, even the visual part?" Ellie said.

"My guess is you were right about the wall screens being used just for designing or previewing the different environments."

"So, and tell me if I've got this wrong, you're saying we could be in here for what seems like hours, but that only a few minutes would go by, you know, *out there?*" Ryan said.

"That's the theory, anyway."

"That's good," Sam said, "because if I had to spend an actual couple of hours in these shoes, my feet would fall off!"

"*Hmm....*" Ryan said. "Maybe that's why they built that thing out in the middle of nowhere."

Ellie turned and squinted up at him, not seeing his point. "What do you mean?"

"I've been trying to figure out why they put it way out in the woods like that. Exactly what about it were they trying to hide? But what if the way it creates its interface with... well, with *us*, for example... is considered unethical or something? Like editing human DNA or cloning people. Or maybe it's just not, you know, 'FDA approved.'"

"That, or maybe they're just super serious about protecting their intellectual property," Aaron said. He tilted his head back and drew in a deep breath through his nose. "I mean, you can even *smell the air!* You could charge almost any amount for this kind of experience. But only if no one else can offer it."

Ellie pursed her lips and waggled her head uncertainly as she considered both of their guesses. She sensed the real reason was something else entirely, but that was as much as her intuition had to say on the matter.

They had gradually become part of a larger group heading toward the city, and something in their tone or the content of their conversation was drawing suspicious looks from those nearest them. Although the road was becoming ever more crowded, Ellie felt like she and the rest of her group were walking in a bubble of space that kept them separated from everyone around them. Suddenly, a car approached from ahead. It was older than any she had ever seen outside of a museum, with a fabric top and large, spoked wheels. The crowd split down the middle and moved toward the edges of the road to let it pass.

With her group now packed closely together, Ellie spoke to them in a whisper. "You know, maybe this is not the time to talk about that. We should be trying to blend in, and I bet we're the only ones out here who don't have an Italian, or Irish, or *whatever* accent." The car drove by and everyone began merging back toward the center of the lane. "The last thing we want is for these people to think we're spying on them for the mills or something, so let's drop it for now, okay?"

Aaron nodded and went quiet. Ryan, on the other hand, aimed a friendly smile and a casual wave at a young man coming up from behind on their left. "Hey, kid! How're you doin'? How 'bout them Yankees?" The boy eyed him skeptically, then sped up and passed them by without a word. Ryan looked at Ellie. "They had the Yankees back then, didn't they? This is supposed to be 1912, right?" He thought for a second. "Oops, my bad. Not until next year. "

Ellie rolled her eyes. Suddenly self-conscious, she lowered her head and tried to study the people surrounding her without being obvious. She realized that the four of them really did stand out quite noticeably from everyone else on the road, despite their period clothing. That was spot on. But while the women all wore their hair pinned up under their hats and bonnets, Sam's hair spilled around her face and down the back of her dress. Worse still was her own short bob, which was not disguised in the least by her odd little cloche. Aaron looked like an albino compared to the swarthy men in the crowd, a fact made all the stranger by his outdoor laborer outfit. But more fundamentally, they each had a just-off-the-assembly-line freshness that contrasted sharply with the weathered, beaten-down faces peering suspiciously back at them.

She saw quite a few children on the road with their parents and assumed most of them worked together in the mills. That meant they were mostly in their mid to late teens, but when she looked into their eyes, they seemed much older. A feeling of guilt washed over her. She was worried about not getting a good grade on a history paper—the kids around her were worried they wouldn't make it to their next birthdays!

Despite the unmistakable signs of hardship, she detected quiet excitement in the air. Everyone, regardless of age, seemed energized by the upcoming event, aware of its importance, and eager to be a part of the upcoming vote. It was the spirit of hopeful people on their way to take care of serious business. She reminded herself that although she already knew the outcome of the vote, these people did not. She guessed they would each be feeling a mix of optimism and dread over a decision that would—for better or worse—have a major impact on their lives.

When they first left the shack, Ellie had been worried that they might have trouble finding the park. The closer they got, the more apparent it became that all they needed to do was follow the thousands of people, all streaming in the same direction. Indeed, as the crowd got thicker, it became impossible to do anything else. The crowd also made it difficult to observe her surroundings in detail. She was aware of walking past seemingly endless blocks of somber brick or wood structures lining both sides of the streets, and she guessed many of these were tenements for the millworkers. Signs above the ground-floor entrances indicated many of the spaces below them were businesses, but she couldn't see into them.

She began to work her way to her left, hoping she'd feel less confined at the throng's outer edge. She glanced over her shoulder to make sure the others were following. Soon the four of them were positioned to the side of the crowd, and she could more easily study the shops along the street. As they passed one of the storefronts, she saw a young girl inside, probably about her own age. She stood alone behind the store's long counter, staring incuriously through the large, multi-paned window as the crowd swarmed past. She was a shopkeeper's daughter, not a millworker. The events playing out in the streets were a part of her world only so far as the strikers were potential customers, ones who had been going without regular paychecks for two months. She wore a bright green hat, and Ellie was struck by how cheery it seemed in this otherwise drab city. No one else in the crowd appeared to so much as notice the girl, and a second later she was gone from view.

With startling suddenness, they burst out of the narrow street into an open space the size of several city blocks. After crossing a wider street, they found themselves at the edge of a mud- and slush-covered field dotted with bare trees. They could see an octagonal wooden bandstand in the distance, and it was toward this structure that the crowd was heading. Ellie pointed across the open space toward the large gazebo.

"That's where we need to go."

10

"Gee, you think?" Ellie ignored Sam's snarky remark, too wrapped up in the scene unfolding before her to care. People streamed into the park from all directions, and already a large crowd surrounded the bandstand. They rejoined the flow, and when they were within fifty yards of the structure, Ellie stopped and looked around. She spotted a large tree off to their right that looked like it might give her a view over the crowd, and she led them to it across the brown, mushy lawn. Once there, she stepped in front of Ryan.

"Can you give me a boost onto that branch?"

He glanced down at her feet and grimaced. "Umm… you're a bit muddy, actually."

She scowled and was about to make a snarky comment of her own when Aaron stepped in between them.

"Here, let me," he said. "I might blend in a little better with some dirt on me."

She smiled to herself, having had nearly the same thought just minutes before. He positioned himself below the low, stout-looking limb, crouched, and laced his fingers in front of him.

"We can get a lot closer, you know." Sam pointed to a gap of more than thirty feet between them and the back of the crowd.

"I know," Ellie said. She placed a foot on Aaron's joined hands and braced her own hands on the trunk of the tree. "Ready?" He nodded and she stepped up. He let out a quiet *oomph* as he took her weight, then stood upright and let her shimmy back onto the branch. As soon as her weight left his hands, he stepped away from her dangling feet and wiped them on the legs of his overalls. Ellie, now safely seated, finally finished answering Sam.

"But I want to watch the crowd, not be lost in the middle of it. Besides, there are going to be over fifteen thousand people here. We'll probably end up in the thick of things anyway."

"Fifteen thou...? What, is it Saturday?" Ryan said.

"Thursday, but everyone's, you know, on strike?"

"Oh, yeah," he said. "*Duh.*"

No sooner had Ellie settled into place than the rough, unyielding wood began digging into the backs of her thighs. Stretching one arm over her head, she used the branch above her to keep from falling while she rocked from side to side and used the other hand to tuck her dress under her legs as additional padding.

Below her, Sam hugged herself, clasping her arms tightly across her chest against the cold. During their walk through the city's center, packed into the middle of the dense crowd, they had felt warmer, almost comfortable. Standing apart in the middle of the park, exposed to the light breeze, the day's chill was more evident.

Sam stomped her feet on the soft ground. "Is this going to happen soon? I'm freezing my knickers off." She turned her back to Ryan and pressed up against him. He opened his coat and wrapped it around her, pulling her close to share his warmth.

Ellie scanned their surroundings from her higher vantage point. "I think so. There aren't as many people coming in now, and I see some activity around the bandstand."

She noticed that most of the workers were packed tightly around the wooden structure. Its lower section was covered in cedar shakes up to the level of the platform's railing. Eight posts supported a peaked roof covered in dark green shingles. She could easily imagine a small band playing there on a warm summer evening, people reclining on blankets spread out on the grass, and little kids playing hide-and-seek among the trees.

Both in the middle of the crowd and around its perimeter, she spotted what she took to be newspaper journalists, many of whom bore large, clumsy-looking cameras. Occasionally one would stand still, raise one of the boxy contraptions to eye level, and peer for a moment at its back. Next, he'd lower it and do something with the back that she couldn't make out from her distance, briefly raise the camera, presumably to take the photo, then lower it again and fiddle with the back some more before moving on.

After a few minutes, she could feel her feet going to sleep. Once more gripping the branch above her for stability, she scooted close to the trunk, wrapped her arm around it, and carefully stood up. Now able to use the higher limb as a handrail, she sidled back to her original spot above the rest of the group. This, at last, was the view she'd been hoping for.

Ellie didn't notice any signal, but suddenly three men climbed the stairs and entered the bandstand. One of them approached the railing and prepared to address the crowd of workers. She realized that when picking a place to perch, she should have paid more attention to the orientation of the podium. The speaker was facing ninety degrees to their left, and she could only catch a part of what was said. Sounds from more of those obsolete cars sputtering noisily around the park's perimeter made hearing him even harder. He made a brief statement, then backed away to make room for a second man, and she recognized the stout figure and stern expression of William Haywood as he stepped up to the railing.

"I guess PA systems weren't around yet," Ryan said.

"They're around," Aaron said, "but there weren't very many in 1912." He removed his cap and folded the ear flaps up, hoping that would allow him to hear a little better.

Ellie could hear Haywood only slightly more clearly than the first man, but she had read through the speech multiple times and had even used a few excerpts in her paper. Once he reached a section she recognized she could follow along easily enough, and from her perch, she relayed a condensed version of his speech. "He's commending the strikers, calling them the 'heart and soul of the working class,' praising them for their bravery in standing against the mill owners in such a peaceful way. You know, there were only two deaths during the two months of the strike. Plus Anthony, I guess. One was a woman shot by police, although they tried to pin it on the strike organizers, and another was a striker stabbed by someone in the militia. Now he's recognizing the sacrifices they made during the strike, talking about the importance of being unified, and congratulating them on their victory. Like I said, the mill owners conceded to every demand." She paused, trying to pick up where he was in his delivery. "Okay, he's getting ready to call for the official vote to end the strike."

Despite already knowing what the results would be, she felt her heart pounding in anticipation of the next few moments. She scanned the crowd, trying to imagine how much more intensely those people were feeling that same sense of hope and excitement. A group of three people standing not more than twenty feet to the left caught her attention. One was a man, broad across the shoulders and tall, easily over six feet. He looked to be in his late forties, but she backed off a few years to account for the hardships that went along with mill life. The woman beside him was younger and considerably shorter.

The third person, almost certainly the couple's daughter, was the one who had initially caught Ellie's eye. She was thin, a little over five feet tall, and unlike most of the crowd, she was not hanging on every word coming from the stage. Instead, she silently observed the people around her as if she, like Ellie herself, were trying to capture and remember every detail of the day's events. She radiated an air of relaxed self-confidence that Ellie, for reasons she couldn't explain, found strangely familiar. Then the girl looked in Ellie's direction, and the shock of sudden recognition hit her so hard that she nearly fell out of the tree. She was even wearing the flower!

"No freakin' way!"

The others tilted their heads back to look up at her.

"What?" Sam said.

"Look over there." She nodded toward the girl and her family. "See those three standing a little off by themselves? That's Carmela, the girl I told you about. And those are her parents, Camella and Genarro."

"Are you sure?"

If the Teolis noticed the sudden, intense scrutiny, they didn't show it. Considering the tumultuous events of recent months, Ellie figured they had grown accustomed to getting a little extra attention.

"Totally!"

On stage, Haywood had finished reciting the list of concessions the mill owners had made and was calling for the vote.

"On the matter to end the strike and accept these terms, all in favor?"

The phrase was echoed from random places throughout the crowd. "All in favor?"

All around them, hands shot into the air, more than fifteen thousand of them, and a thunderous cry of fifteen thousand *ayes* filled the Common.

"All those opposed?" Haywood said. This was again repeated around the park. They heard a few feeble *nays*, but Ellie found it hard to believe these were from legitimate strikers.

"The ayes carry! I hereby declare this strike over!" Haywood announced, and the entire park erupted in cheers.

Ellie dropped down from the tree. Her hat flew off her head on her way to the ground, but Ryan snagged it with a one-handed catch that saved it from landing in the mud. He held it out to her.

"Thanks," she said. Instead of replacing it on her head, she bunched it tightly in one hand. "Come on!"

Ellie set off toward Carmela and her family, walking fast. She passed a pair of reporters along the way, one of whom carried a version of the bulky cameras she had seen in use during the speech. The Teolis were already making for the park's edge when she caught up to them, Sam and the boys close behind her.

"Carmela! Carmela!" The young girl and her parents stopped and turned around. Ellie saw suspicion, maybe even a little fear, on the faces of Genarro and Camella, but Carmela merely looked curious.

"Yes?" she said. "Can I help you?" Her voice, lightly accented by her native Italian, made Ellie smile.

"Um, not exactly. My name is Ellie. We haven't met, but I've read a lot about you, and I just wanted to tell you how incredibly brave I think you are." She looked up at the girl's parents. "Mr. and Mrs. Teoli, I hope you realize how amazing your daughter is."

"Sì," Genarro said. He wrapped an arm around Camella's waist and pulled her close to him. "Yes, we do. *Brillante*. Her mother and I are very proud of her." His speech was more heavily accented than his daughter's.

"I also wanted to say...." But Ellie faltered, not knowing what that was.

She took a deep breath and pressed on. "Look, what happened here today is not the end. It will take a long time to fix things completely, but whatever happens next, never doubt that this was a very important step along the way."

"Thank you," Carmela said. She took a half-step forward, her hand extended as if to place it on Ellie's arm.

Ellie closed the remaining gap between them and wrapped the younger girl in her arms. "No," she said, whispering into her ear. "Thank *you.*"

Carmela went rigid at the initial contact, but after a second, she relaxed and touched her hands softly to Ellie's back.

"Yeah, she's a hugger," Ryan said.

"Sorry." Ellie stepped back and used a knuckle to wipe away the tears gathering in the corners of her eyes. The blossom on Carmela's dress, a purple crocus, was now thoroughly crumpled. Ellie pointed at it and laughed self-consciously. "Whoops! I smooshed your flower."

"It's okay," Carmela said. "We have many more."

"Good luck to all of you," Ellie said. She waved to the trio and took another step back.

The three Teolis nodded in unison, then turned and resumed making their way out of the park. Ellie thought of all the other things she could have said. That almost everything accomplished today would be undone within a few years. That Carmela would lose her husband at forty-seven and her eyesight from diabetes by sixty-four. She sighed—it was all so sad. She could overhear their conversation as they left, but the smattering of Italian her grandmother had taught her years ago did not allow her to understand more than a few stray words.

"*Quella ragazza era molto strana,*" Genarro said.

"*Sì, molto,*" Camella said.

"A *little,* maybe, but I liked her," Carmela said, then glanced over her shoulder one final time. Whatever came next was lost in the noise of the crowd.

Ellie, her eyes still brimming with tears, suddenly felt depressed and oddly limp, as if most of the air had gone out of her. She started to wipe her eyes with whatever she held in her hand, then realized it was her hat. She used her other hand to punch it out to its original shape and pulled it back onto her head.

Ryan saw the sad look on her face. "You know I'm not the kind of guy to make fun of somebody's name. Right, A-Ron? But her mom's sounds a lot like what you call an appendage at the end of a camel's foot. Don'tcha think?" He nudged her side with his elbow. "Huh? Huh?"

She peered up at him, saw his mischievous grin, then finally interpreted his meaning. She couldn't help but snort out a short laugh at the crude reference. "You're a pig!" She wiped her eyes with her sleeves.

He wrapped an arm around her shoulders and gave her a comforting squeeze. "Possibly," he said, "but you're smiling again." He looked into her red and puffy eyes. "Well, sort of."

"Where to now?" Aaron said. "Or should we just head back?"

"I want to see the mill, too," Ellie said. "It's only a few blocks away. Is that okay?"

"Do you know which way to go?" Sam said.

Ellie had been looking at Google Maps images of the city so much recently that she felt she could move there and drive for Uber, and now that they were in the park, she felt more oriented to her surroundings. She nodded and pointed in the direction from which they had just come. "Yep, that way. Then we make one turn, and it's three blocks straight to the canal."

Sam gestured for Ellie to take the lead, and they began making their way across the sloppy ground.

11

E llie led them toward the park's southeast corner, matching their pace to that of the departing workers. When they reached the street, they turned right. As Ellie had said, a large, brick building dominated the view three blocks ahead. They kept walking until only a dozen or so yards lay between them and the mill's seemingly endless façade. The enormous structure, along with several others nearly identical to it, stood on a long island separated from the bank by a narrow canal.

Ryan let out a soft whistle. "Man, that is a whole lot of bricks all in one place!"

Ellie pointed at the water streaming through the canal. "There's a dam up the river that sends water through here. Originally, all the mills were strictly water-powered. As you can see, though," and she waved her hand at the numerous smokestacks piercing the skyline, "steam power has been added to most of them to help keep up with demand. Let's cross over."

Short metal bridges spanned the dark canal to either side of where they stood. Looking left they saw a six-story tower rising from the corner of the building, topped by an American flag. Ellie thought that was where the main entrance would be.

"C'mon. This way," she said, leading them away from the tower and toward an older version of the bridge she had used on Google Maps. They paused in the middle of the short span and looked over its edge at the murky water flowing below them.

"*Eww!* That can't be the way that's supposed to smell," Sam said.

"But all the three-eyed catfish you can eat!" As usual, Ryan was trying to find the bright side, but Ellie wasn't sure the even catfish of the three-eyed variety could survive for long in that foul soup.

Abruptly, Aaron slapped his palm against his forehead. "Oh, *man!*"

"What is it?" Ellie said, concerned.

"We just sat there through that whole speech, and I totally forgot about the camera. Hang on...." He extracted it from his pocket and switched it on. "You guys lean against the railing there. No, go that way a bit. I want to get the mill in the background."

He crossed the bridge and positioned the camera on a narrow iron railing, his attempt to frame the shot hindered by his inability to see the camera's rear-facing screen. After lining it up as best he could, he pushed the button to start the timer, then trotted over to join the group. He had barely made it into position when a horse pulling a heavy cartload of cloth scraps rounded the corner of the mill and headed toward them at a brisk pace. He started across the bridge to stop the timer, but Ellie grabbed him by the back of his jacket.

"Wait—you'll get trampled! You can just set it again."

But as soon as the horse stepped onto the bridge, she knew there would be no second try. The entire structure shuddered under the pounding of its hooves, and the camera began to dance on the vibrating rail. Then the wagon rolled in front of them, blocking the camera from view. When the cart was gone, so was the camera. All four rushed to the other side and peered into the opaque water. They were in time to see one last bubble rise to the surface, marking the precise spot where the camera had gone under.

"I'm sorry. I'll get you a new one," Aaron said. "You know... someday."

She laid her hand on his back, feeling an inexplicable need to comfort him over the loss of *her* camera. "You used it way more than I ever did. I wish I could have seen that picture, though. It would have been great for my paper! Oh, well. Come on. Act natural, like you belong here, and nobody should bother us."

She led them across the bridge, and once back on firm footing, they passed directly below one end of the massive, five-story brick structure.

"This place is huge!" Sam said.

"This is Washington Mills," Ellie explained, "one of eight that are part of the American Woolen Company, all owned by a guy named William Wood. It's even bigger than it seems. That building," she said, pointing to a lower brick building in front of them, "and that taller one behind it are all connected to this one at the far end. It looks like a giant capital 'E' from above."

"Seriously?" Ryan said.

"Yep, this is all one factory. Largest in the world, in fact."

"No, I meant the guy's actual name is 'Willy Wood'?"

She rolled her eyes. "C'mon... let's find a way in."

They rounded the end of the building and found a doorway close to the corner on the wall facing the middle building. They stopped and looked around, making double sure they were as alone as they seemed. Aside from the driver of that cartload of rags, now several minutes gone, there was no sign of anyone.

Ellie stood on tiptoe and peered in through the nearest window. "Good—it looks empty." She stepped away from the building a few paces and tilted her head back, but standing so near to the base of the wall, she couldn't see in through any of the upper-story windows. "Let's check out that door. If it's open, we'll take a peek inside. You won't believe the machinery!"

As they walked toward the door, Ellie noticed Sam and Aaron glancing around nervously, their heads swiveling back and forth like they were watching the Olympic ping pong finals. It was the exact opposite of acting naturally.

"Will you two stop that!" she hissed. "Just relax."

She pulled on the handle and the large wooden door swung outward easily. She poked her head in through the opening, and, finding the floor empty for as far as she could see, she slipped inside the cavernous space.

"Come on," she said. "The coast is clear."

They stepped inside and walked forward until they were halfway across the factory floor, standing between two narrowly-spaced rows of complicated metal contraptions set at right angles to the room's central aisle. A large shaft ran the length of the space, suspended from thick, wooden joists. Perpendicular to this main shaft, smaller shafts sprouted at regular intervals. These ran above each row of machines, and from them, wide leather belts dropped down to power the individual workstations. The heavy odor of machine oil, harsh and irritating, permeated the room. Ellie noticed a slight haze that she guessed was due to fine particles of fabric that probably never completely left the air.

"These look like carding machines," she said. "They were used to prepare the raw wool for spinning into thread. Women and older children ran these. It's quiet right now, but if these were all running, the clattering would be pretty intense. Imagine being surrounded by that for ten hours a day, six days a week. And the dust, the rapid, non-stop pace of it all, and, in the summertime, the heat and humidity.... It would have been nearly unbearable."

"But people were coming from all over the world to work here?" Sam said.

"Just Europe for the most part... Italy, Ireland, Portugal, Hungary...." Ellie's eyes were on Aaron as he stepped carefully into a narrow aisle between two rows of machines. He leaned in close at a couple of places, peering into the depths of the complicated arrangement of wheels, gears, belts, and levers. His fascination with mechanical contraptions drew him in, but some other instinct caused him to keep his hands clasped loosely behind his back as if he feared leaving fingerprints behind. Or fingers.

"Makes you wonder what their lives were like back home if this was a step up," Ryan said.

"I think that in Europe at that time, you were stuck in whatever class you were born into. If you were a farmer or some other kind of laborer, that's what your son would be... your grandson. Your daughter would end up the wife of a farmer or whatever. Coming to America meant maybe they'd have a different future. *You* might still be stuck at the bottom, but your kids would have a real chance at something better. Despite places like this—well, mostly *because* of them, actually—this truly was the 'land of opportunity.'"

Finished with his inspection, Aaron stood straight and walked back to rejoin the group. "I'm impressed," he said. "It's like Sam said about the clothes—everything's *very* detailed. There are more machines upstairs?"

She nodded. "All the way up. Five stories."

"Can we...?"

Ellie looked at Sam and raised her eyebrows.

Sam sighed heavily. "Sure. Why not?"

They continued along the central aisle to where a wide stairway separated the room they were in from a nearly identical, although perhaps even larger, one. They paused to peer for a moment at a similar arrangement of machines before climbing the stairs to the next level.

"How did school work if kids were starting here at fourteen?" Sam said as they stepped onto the next floor. "They couldn't put in sixty hours a week at a mill and still be going to classes."

Ellie could only shrug. That detail had not come up in her research. "I assume not all of them did. But I guess if the family desperately needed the money, they dropped out and went to work."

They turned right and stepped onto another vast production area deeper inside the enormous building. It was identical to the room downstairs except for the machines themselves. Aaron strode ahead along the central aisle, eager to check them out. A third of the way down the floor, he ducked into one of the side aisles for a closer look and vanished from sight. From where he had disappeared, they immediately heard a sharp cry of surprise, then a loud, solid *clunk* followed by an even louder shout. This second outburst expressed not surprise so much as pain and anger. Aaron abruptly reappeared, hurriedly backing out into the main aisle. He was trying to keep a safe distance away from a very large man brandishing a very large wrench in one hand while rubbing the back of his head with the other. When the man finally spoke, his voice was thunderous.

"What're you doing sneakin' up on me, boy?!" he said. "I nearly brained myself!"

Momentarily too stunned to move, the others watched as Aaron retreated down the main aisle while the big man continued to advance, repeatedly jabbing the wrench at him. Then they heard loud footsteps coming up on them fast from behind just before another, even louder shout filled the room. Ellie spun around and saw a second man striding toward them, older and not as large as the first. He carried a bundle of wide leather straps tucked under his left arm and gripped an intimidatingly large hammer in his right.

"What in the bloody hell is going on out here?!" the man demanded. "Teague?"

"This slum rat snuck up behind me with my head in the machine, and I nearly cracked it open when I started."

This answer seemed to confuse the older man more. "You're supposed to be workin' on the line shaft. What were you doin' with yer fool head in the works?"

Teague's bluster lost some of its steam as he was now forced to admit a mistake. "I—I dropped my spanner into it and had to fish it out."

Listening to the exchange between the two men, Ellie noticed they shared the same, almost musical accent. She caught Aaron's eye and made a subtle gesture for him to rejoin them. He gave Teague a sidelong glance to be sure he was still distracted, then eased his way up the aisle to stand at her side. They watched as the exchange between the two men continued.

"So, not only do you frighten like a little girl out after dark, but you're clumsy, as well? Be certain you go over that one before we spin it up—make sure you didn't knock somethin' out o' true." Finished for the moment with Teague, he redirected his attention to the odd foursome trespassing in his domain. "Now then—who are you lot, and why should I not be calling the police to haul you off?" He shifted his piercing gaze from one face to the next.

Ellie had no idea what to say, finding the notion of being dressed down by a computer-generated shop foreman in a long-closed factory thoroughly disconcerting. She opened her mouth, unsure what would come out, but was spared having to answer when Sam stepped toward the man. Smiling sweetly, she extended her arm and offered him her hand, palm down.

"My name is Samantha. Samantha Wood. This is my sister Ellie. I'm sorry if we startled your man, Mr...."

At the mention of the name *Wood*, the man's aggressive attitude evaporated, replaced at once by an air of polite deference. He accepted her hand, awkwardly taking her fingers into his calloused palm, gave them a light squeeze, then released his grip.

"'Thomas,' Miss. And this gobdaw is Teague Larkin."

"Miss," Teague said and politely removed his cap.

"Well, it is a pleasure to meet you both. As I said, I'm sorry if we gave you a start, but you needn't pay us any mind. We just arrived from New York to visit my uncle and thought we'd enjoy a stroll around your magnificent mill while he's finishing up some business. We heard you from outside and decided to come in and see what was happening."

"My apologies, Miss Wood, but you do look more like the strikers in the streets than the boss's nieces, although it's clear you've got a bit of spit and polish about you beneath those rags you have on, beggin' yer pardon."

Sam looked at Ellie, Ryan, and Aaron, then down at her own dress as if assessing their outfits for the first time. "Too true, I'm afraid. But Uncle William felt it might be safer, what with all the recent unpleasantness in town, if we didn't stand out too much. Do you think we overdid it, Mr. Thomas?" She gave him a coy smile and set her dress swaying with a seductive twist of her hips.

Mr. Thomas' face reddened. He coughed once, swallowed nervously, and quickly changed the subject. "And who are these gentlemen with you?"

"Friends of ours along for the visit. This is Ryan Collins...."

Ryan took a step forward and offered his hand. "Mr. Thomas." He gave the man a nod as they shook.

A warning thought flashed through Ellie's mind as she suddenly remembered her conversation with Sam the previous morning. Before Sam could continue with the introductions, she indicated Aaron with a sweep of her arm.

"And this is, uh...." Finding her mind had gone completely blank, she blurted out the first name that popped into her head. "Hedwig... um... Potter!" She was relieved when Aaron, although he stared at her through narrowed eyes, just went with it.

"Hi," he said, but instead of coming forward to exchange handshakes, he merely gave Mr. Thomas a polite wave from where he stood. Then he turned to face Teague. "Sorry."

In response, Teague spat on the floor, turned on his heel, and disappeared between rows of machines to check for damage caused by the dropped wrench.

"'Uh-Hedwig-um-Potter,' eh?" Mr. Thomas said. "So you're close then, are you?"

Ellie heard the note of suspicion in his voice. "It's just that we, um, usually call him...."

"Mr. Thomas," Sam said, trying to distract the man's attention away from Ellie and whatever was suddenly up with her, "can you explain what you and Mr. Larkin are working on? I'm sure it's most fascinating."

But Mr. Thomas continued to subject Ellie to a penetrating stare. She endured his scrutiny coolly and returned as bland an expression as she could muster, trying to project only innocent thoughts. Finally, he pulled his gaze away and looked at Sam.

"Yes, Miss Wood. You see the drive belts that drop down from the countershafts along the ceiling?" She nodded. "Teague and I were checking the tension of each of those belts. They stretch and loosen over time, and if they get too loose, they can slip off the pulleys. If that happens, the machine stops. Or the belt can jam and snap, and that can be real bad if someone gets hit. After a while, the belts wear out altogether and need replacing. We had just finished putting a new belt on this one here when you and your friends showed up." He slapped his hand against the side of the tall iron machine.

"These are spinning machines," Ellie said.

"Tha's right, Miss," Mr. Thomas said.

Ellie explained their function to Ryan and Aaron. "They use these guys to spin the carded wool from downstairs into thread. As the thread is wound up on spools, the people working these machines, 'doffers,'" she made the air-quote gesture, "run up and down the line exchanging the full spools for empty cores."

They silently studied the equipment. Each machine had two sides, and each side was fitted with as many as thirty spindles for spools. A single worker would stand between two machines and thus be faced with sixty spools to monitor.

"Mr. Thomas, how old are the workers who run these machines?"

Following Ellie's concise explanation of the spinners, he seemed to regard her more favorably. "We like to use the younger ones up here, Miss," he said. "It helps to have hands that are wee an' quick when changin' the spools. We get 'em as young as fourteen. After a year or two, they can move downstairs to the carding room or start over on the looms. Beggin' your pardon, Miss Wood, but we need to test these belts. Stay or go as you like, but we'd like to get back to work so we can finish up and go home." He gazed out through the windows that faced the Common. "Sounds like we'll be back up an' running on the morrow."

"Monday, actually," Ellie said.

"Do you say so?" He sounded dubious.

"Yeah, I'm pretty sure...." She felt Sam place her hand on her shoulder and give it a short, firm squeeze. She got the message and closed her mouth.

"We won't keep you any longer," Sam said, "but we will stay and watch for a few more minutes if that's okay."

"As I said, stay or go. It's up to you. But if you stay, please stand back from the machines while they're coming up to speed." He indicated the stairwell with a nod.

Sam held out her hand again. "Thank you, Mr. Thomas. You have been very gracious."

"Miss Wood," he said. He gave her hand another tentative squeeze, then turned away and bellowed to Teague, who had quietly disappeared.

"Okay, Teague, let's get 'er rolling!"

Wherever he had gone, Teague evidently heard the order. A second later, the shafts above their heads began to rotate.

"Let's get out of their way, guys," Ellie said.

The four of them backed away toward the stairs, all the while keeping their attention fixed on the machinery coming to life before them. As the spinners picked up speed, the room quickly filled with sound.

"All the way now," Mr. Thomas shouted again. This time his cry was much louder, and Ellie guessed he had been put in charge as much for the volume he could achieve as for any other reason.

The shafts sped up, as did the spinners, and the noise crescendoed to a cacophony of hums, whirs, clacks, and thumps. Without warning, the belt connecting a drive shaft to a spinner halfway down the line snapped and flew violently across the aisle between the banks of machines. Sam let out a startled shriek and clutched at Ryan's jacket as the four of them, reacting in perfect unison, all took an involuntary step backward.

"*Damn!*" Ryan said. The belt slammed into the neighboring spinner with such force that there could be no doubt that had anyone been passing through that area, he—or more likely a very young *she*—would have been seriously wounded at the absolute least.

Mr. Thomas called to his unseen assistant. "Kill it, Teague! You damned fool! You overtightened the belt on number twelve. Get in here and get a new one up. Come on now—I don't want to be here all day!" He stormed down the aisle to retrieve the ruined belt, rolling it up over his arm like a fire hose.

"Guess the show's over," Ellie said. "Thanks, guys. This will help me out a lot!"

They started down the stairs toward the door they had come in. When they reached the landing at mid-flight, Ryan moved close to Sam and slipped his arm around her waist. He shook his head and grinned at her with admiration.

"Wood's nieces! You're amazing, you know that?"

"Thanks!" She flashed him a bright smile, pleased by the compliment.

"This is pretty cool," Aaron said. "Imagine all the power it took to run these machines, and it was basically free."

"For the most part," Ellie agreed. "At least earlier on. But like I said, by now they were burning a lot of coal, too. You'd see the smoke if the mills weren't all closed."

After traversing the entire length of the carding room a second time, they exited into the relative brightness of the overcast day. For a moment, they stood still, soaking up impressions of their surroundings and admiring the incredible level of reality of the virtual world.

12

I t was Ryan who finally broke the silence. "It's clear you're not going to say anything unless someone asks, so what was with the 'Hedwig' thing?"

Ellie looked at Aaron and felt her face grow hot. She was sure it was already beet red and heading fast toward boiled lobster. He peered back, blinking at her through his big, round lenses in a most unhelpfully owlish way.

"I, um… okay. I'm sorry, Aaron, I *really* am. I didn't mean anything…." She stopped stammering long enough to collect her thoughts. "One of the things I read recently is that right around this time, there was a lot of especially nasty anti-Semitism. I have no clue about those two, obviously, but I thought it best if you weren't, you know, 'Aaron Siskin' right then. But then my brain dropped into neutral, and I couldn't come up with another name, so I just went with…." She shrugged, trailing off.

Ryan erupted in laughter. "I *totally* see it!" he said, staring at Aaron. "I can't believe I never thought of that myself."

"I got it," Aaron said. "I mean, I understood then what you were doing. I never knew until that second that I remind you of an owl, that's all."

"And a *girl* owl, at that," Sam added.

"*Huh?*" Ellie gave Sam a bewildered look. "Wait—you mean Hedwig is a *girl's* name?" Had she known that back when she'd read the books? This many years on, she couldn't remember.

Ryan noticed her consternation and laughed again.

Aaron's face was still devoid of any readable expression, but Ellie had heard the rebuke in his voice and felt wretched.

"They're, um… very wise." She hung her head and peered up at him from under her brows. "Forgive me?"

Aaron continued staring silently at her for a long, uncomfortable moment. He finally nodded, but he looked no less sullen.

"You know what's funny?" Ryan said, still chuckling. "I'm pretty sure both those guys were Irish. Teague *definitely* was. There's no doubt they would have thought you said *Erin*, as in *e-r-i-n*. It's pretty much as Irish a name as you can have." Then he laughed again. "'Hedwig'—good one!"

Sam took that moment to announce that she'd had enough. "I'm done! Let's get back to the shack and end this thing."

"Yeah, okay," Ellie said. She slowly turned through one complete revolution, a final attempt to memorize every detail of the scene before her—the enormous mill building and its towering stack, the gritty texture of the soot-grimed bricks, the dull grey of the sky overhead, even the crunch of gravel beneath her shoes. "Thanks again. You guys are great."

They recrossed the canal and began zigzagging through the city blocks until they reached the park's southwest corner. Ellie noticed a man across the street, dressed much like Ryan, leaning against a lamppost and smoking a cigarette. Their eyes met for a moment, and she had the impression that he was waiting for them. Then he dropped the butt, crushed it with his toe, and hustled away.

They passed many people along their route, but fewer than they might have expected. Sam noticed this and pointed it out.

"Not exactly a bustling city."

Aaron had one explanation. "Limiting the number of non-interactive characters reduces the processing power needed to pull something like this off. I doubt there was anything like fifteen thousand people in the park earlier. It just had to look like it from our perspective."

Ellie had a different opinion on the matter. "The mills are about to start back up. People are at home celebrating their win and getting ready to go back to work."

"Interesting," Ryan said. "That would mean simulating not behavior but motivation. If you did that, then behavior might be automatic. It's like with the CG fighters in those big battle scenes in *Lord of the Rings*. Instead of writing specific commands for thousands of individual virtual orcs, elves, and so on, they gave them each basic motivating instructions. A kind of conditional logic. Each character would then 'decide' on its own either to attack, defend, or retreat based on what was going on around it."

Aaron picked up on Ryan's train of thought. "So instead of complete, preset scripts for every person, you'd write a comprehensive set of *if/then* statements. If we go into a store, the shopkeeper greets us, asks how he can help...."

Ryan interrupted, highjacking Aaron's line of thought. "And if we asked to see the latest iPhone, he'd say, 'I've no time for your tomfoolery, young whippersnapper! Now, get outta my store, the lot of you! Go on, now, before I call Constable McNally!'"

"Well, for one example, I guess," Aaron said. "My point was that he'd respond to *whatever* we said based on his programmed 'desire' to sell us something rather than by going through a set routine."

"I was thinking about something like that on our way into town," Ellie said. She turned to Sam. "Remember when we went to Colonial Williamsburg? The people wearing the costumes there—the characters, I guess you'd call them—they were all talking like people from the eighteenth century, but they didn't react if you mentioned something like cars or computers. It's like they pretended not to hear anything like that. But the people on the road with us this morning *weren't* ignoring us. They were giving us the hairy eyeball just because we were acting a little different from them. I thought that was interesting."

"The 'hairy *what*,' now?" Ryan's question was ignored.

"As impressive as this is, it isn't anything like what I expected," Sam said, indicating their surroundings with a sweep of her arm. "I always thought of virtual reality as an escape to some other, perfect world, or maybe into some fantasy where you could fly or something. This place, though...."

It's cold and gray and so realistic it's almost... *boring?* That's not exactly what I'm trying to say, but...."

"*Mundane,*" Aaron said. "It's like it's just a place. It's cool that it's Lawrence, Massachusetts, in 1912 and all, but it's just Lawrence, Massachusetts, in 1912, you know? Maybe if it were Athens in 450 BCE, it might be different."

"Why?" Sam said. "What happened there then?"

"The clepsydra was invented around then, for one thing. And I'm sure they were fighting the Persians. They were *always* fighting the Persians. But what I was getting at is that maybe all of this—as good as it is—is too familiar. There's nothing here to really *wow* us. If we went there—here, I mean, the real one in our time—a lot of it would probably look the same. Except for these clothes and the almost complete lack of auto traffic, that is. That mill might be offices, but I bet it's still there."

Ellie nodded. "*Ha!* So close! I checked—it's lofts."

Aaron spread his arms, palms up, as if to say *there you go*.

Whatever the explanation, Ellie was thankful for the lack of people on their return walk—it was easier to take in their surroundings. She made a point to look into the same store she'd noticed earlier, but the shopgirl with the green hat had been replaced by a severe-looking, older woman who wore her hair pinned up in a tight bun.

The absence of tightly packed bodies also made it easier to experience the many other scents of the city. A sharp, slightly sweet odor she knew to be coal smoke was everywhere, and it formed the background for the other aromas. As they passed from one tenement to the next, they were treated to fragrances of cuisines from across Europe. For a while, they inhaled the herbal tang of a marinara, which was replaced half a block further on by the earthier aroma of a goulash. She knew the regular diet of most of the mill workers was meager, but perhaps today's vote was cause enough to make this evening's meal a special one.

They soon put Lawrence behind them and re-entered Methuen from the south, continuing to stick to the same streets they had used a few hours earlier. Sam didn't want to take a different way back and risk getting lost, but Ellie thought that kind of worrying was unnecessary. This environment couldn't go on indefinitely—how lost could they get?

They saw minor celebrations on the front porches or in the back yards of several houses they passed, but the festivities seemed muted. It was as if the excitement of winning was competing with the sober reality of knowing that now they had to go back to work, and what little merriment they witnessed was subdued. A pair of men standing on a corner watched as they walked by. One was considerably younger than the other, and Ellie thought they might be father and son. She gave them a nod, but they only stared back at her, their faces blank.

A block later, they had just rounded a curve toward the far end of town, no more than a quarter-mile from where they had emerged from the woods, when they saw four men standing in a row across the street in front of them. They weren't big men, not like Teague, but they were solidly built from years of physical labor. The baseball bats two of the men carried looked solid, too, enough to make up for any lack of stature on the part of the men.

Ryan spoke from the corner of his mouth. "Let's slow down a little, see if we can figure out what's going on here." Then he laughed at the suggestion. "Yeah, right! You said it—it's just a simulation. What's the worst that can happen?"

Ellie reached over, gripped a bit of skin on the back of his hand between her thumb and forefinger, and gave it a sharp twist.

"*Ow!*" He yelped in pain and jerked his hand away.

"Exactly! Remember what you said about famous last words? Don't do anything stupid."

Ryan vigorously massaged the spot Ellie had pinched. "Stupid? *Moi?*"

Sam snorted. "Yeah… *toi.*"

Ellie studied the line of rough-looking men. Most of them looked calm, waiting impassively for them to draw near. All except the one on the left. He was roughly her age, she guessed, give or take a year. Still more boy than man, really. And it was clear he was highly agitated. Sweat beaded on his face despite the day's chill, and he shifted his weight from one foot to the other as if the final choice between fight or flight remained up in the air. She desperately wished he weren't one of the two men with a bat. He held it low in front of him, one hand wrapped tightly around the grip, the other grasping a spot three-quarters of the way up the barrel, and bounced it nervously against his thighs. His eyes darted from one member of her group to another, each time lingering longest on Ryan.

That's good, she thought. *He might be scared, but he's certainly not dumb.*

The other "armed" man, standing at the opposite end of the line, was older and seemed more relaxed. He held his bat loosely in one hand, letting its business end rest casually on his right shoulder. It could be a threat, or he might merely be waiting to ask if they wanted to shag a few flies. The face of the man positioned at the left of center was one she recognized—he was the smoker they had seen lurking outside the park on their way back from the mill.

Sam twisted her head around and saw that the two men they had passed at the last corner had entered the street and were coming up on them from behind. "Hey, guys? We're sorta surrounded."

Retreat no longer an option, they continued walking toward the men in front of them. Behind this human barricade, a man and woman appeared from around a building at the intersection. When they caught sight of the tense knot of people in the street, they did a quick about-face and disappeared back the way they had come.

A subtle hand signal from Ryan brought them to a stop a few feet from the line of men. Ellie hoped he would keep any of his "how about those Yankees" wisecracks to himself, but it was one of the men behind them who spoke first.

"*Angelo, sei sicuro che questi siano quelli giusti?*"

"*Sì.* They're the ones," the older man in front of them growled.

"*Ma sono solo bambini!*" another voice said.

"Children cannot be spies?"

"*Spies?!*" Ellie gasped. She realized they were suddenly facing the exact situation that had so worried her earlier. Alarmed, she took a step forward. "No, no, no—listen to me! We're *not* spies! We're not here to cause you any trouble. We're only trying to get home." She tried to speak reasonably, hoping to prevent the situation from escalating, but knew her words were coming out too aggressively. She tried harder to sound calm. "We just need to get out of town...."

She raised her hand, intending only to point in the general direction of the shack. The nervous boy, a coiled spring already wound far too tight, interpreted her sudden movement as a threat. Twisting to his right, he drew back his bat. Maintaining his two-handed grip, he raised it up and away from his body.

Ryan roughly shouldered Ellie aside, causing her to stumble. He extended his arms out in front of him and yelled. *"No! Stop!"*

Ellie knew that the kid had already identified Ryan as the biggest threat and that his getting involved was precisely the wrong move, but it was too late to prevent the inevitable consequences. She managed to stay on her feet and turned back just in time to see the end of the bat strike Ryan directly in the center of his chest. Instantly, without uttering a sound, he collapsed onto the street.

"Ryan!" Sam cried, and dropped to kneel at his side.

The boy raised his bat again, only this time grasping it as if he were swinging an ax into an oak log.

"Wait!" Ellie cried, leaping sideways to stand between the raised bat and her sister.

Before the boy could bring the bat down for a second blow, the smoking man gripped his upper arm and jerked him back. The older man, the one who had mentioned spies, shouted something in Italian. It was a rapid-fire string of syllables Ellie couldn't begin to differentiate, but it was clear that the kid understood. He lowered his bat, rested its tip on the street, and stood there looking abashed.

Ellie glanced behind her and saw Sam frantically palpating the side of Ryan's neck in search of a pulse, then watched her place her ear against his chest. Sam looked up, her eyes wide with fear. "Oh, my God, Ellie! His heart's stopped!"

Hearing this, several of the men took a step back, including the older man with the bat. The second of the younger men, the one standing behind them, crossed himself and ran off. Apparently, being an accessory to manslaughter was not on his to-do list for the day.

"Wait!" Ellie cried again. She pointed at the man who was obviously in charge of the mob. "He called you *Angelo*, is that right? Your name is Angelo?" The man stared back at her, emotionless, his eyes like ice. "It is, isn't it? You're Angelo Rocco?"

The other men exchanged uncertain glances, then looked to Angelo for instructions. She could tell they were wondering how she knew his name if she wasn't a spy. She tried hard to recall every detail she had read about Carmela and her family's time here during the strike. Since no one was actively taking swings at them, she risked another backward glance and saw that Aaron had joined Sam on the ground beside Ryan. He sized up the situation at once and did not sound optimistic.

"*Commotio cordis.* I'm not sure CPR is going to be enough."

"It has to be—it's all I've got!" Her first-aid training had overridden her momentary panic, and her voice, frantic seconds ago, sounded calmer and more self-assured. She began unfastening the buttons on Ryan's coat as quickly as possible.

Aaron helped Sam spread the heavy wool jacket, then leaned away while she tore the cotton shirt open, sending its buttons flying and revealing a mustard-colored tee beneath that announced: "Han shot first!" Ellie spared another split second for half an eye roll before turning back to face the men.

"Just… *listen!*" She knew she sounded like she was begging now, but that might be what it took to save them. "I know we don't look like millworkers, and we're not, okay? But we're not spies for Wood or any of the other owners. Or the Pinkertons, or for anyone else! We're on *your* side, I swear!" She paused, inhaled deeply, and tried to calm her voice. "I know about you, Angelo. You've worked with Genarro for years. You helped him get Carmela safely to the train when she needed to get out of town, right? You're a good man, Angelo. A good friend to the Teolis. I know you think you're protecting them, but trust me—Genarro would not want you to do this."

The men around her, at least the ones who understood English, looked more uncertain by the second. Behind her, she could hear Sam softly grunting as she performed chest compressions, heard two loud puffs as she forced air into Ryan's inert lungs. Angelo's men observed this seemingly bizarre behavior with intense interest.

"When we went over to Carmela and her parents at the park, it wasn't to threaten them, okay? I swear! I only wanted to tell her what a brave thing she had done, that she and her parents should be proud. We didn't mean them any harm."

Angelo considered this a moment before speaking. "How do you know about Carmela?"

"A lot of people know about her. She's kinda famous. In certain circles, anyway. You know about the newspaper stories? And what she did in Washington?"

Angelo nodded. "And me? You heard of me, too?"

She sensed an undercurrent of suspicion in the man's question. Or else he was just curious to know if he was also famous. She chose her words carefully. "You're... part of her story."

Angelo looked at her for a moment, then uttered a soft, self-deprecating laugh. "*Abbastanza buono.*"

When Ellie finally saw his shoulders drop and his fists unclench, she exhaled a deep, shuddering breath. She heard a low groan, followed by a series of hoarse gasps, coming from the ground behind her. Looking over her shoulder, she saw Ryan with his eyes wide open. He was still lying flat on his back, but now he was gulping in loud, rasping breaths.

With Ryan breathing on his own again, the emotional Sam instantly returned. She collapsed on top of him, weeping loudly. "Oh, Ryan!" she repeated. Now Angelo's men were all focused solely on the boy who appeared to have come back to life before their eyes.

Ellie turned back to face Angelo. "Are we okay here?" she said. "Are we good?"

"*Ehi!*" Angelo barked, drawing the attention of his men. "*Basta!*" As he said this, he brought his hands up in front of him, one above the other, palms down. Then he quickly drew his arms in a short, outwardly slashing motion. He jerked his head in the direction from which Ellie's group had come, and what remained of the tiny mob began walking that way. Seconds later, only Angelo remained. He removed his cap and held it tucked in the crook of his left arm.

"*Per'dónami, signorina.* When I saw you talking to them in the park, the Teolis, I thought maybe you do threaten them, and so I had some men follow you."

Ellie understood at once. Anyone following would have seen them enter the mill, then come out again twenty minutes later without a fuss. It's no wonder they had been suspicious. But even so....

"If you were watching, then you must have seen us hug."

Angelo scoffed at this, and his reply was bitter. "Did Judas not betray

Jesus with a kiss?" He quickly waved his hand as if to erase his harsh comment, then continued in a gentler tone. *"Mi dispiace.* The Teolis have suffered many threats and worse since the strike began, and not always from the expected places."

"I know," Ellie said. "I'm so sorry about little Anthony."

Angelo seemed touched by the sincerity in her voice. *"Sì. Bastardi!"* He spat the word out and quickly sketched a cross on his chest. "I see now I should have talked to Genarro first, but...." he shrugged. "I believe you. As you say, 'we're good.'" He extended his large, rough hand, and she shook it. "I am sorry, too. About your friend there. That was not meant to happen."

Ellie glanced behind her, then back at Angelo. "Eh, he's tough," she said, flapping a hand dismissively in Ryan's direction. "They're still going to need your help, you know. The strike is over, but the danger is not. Take good care of them."

Angelo nodded solemnly, then turned to follow his men. After a few paces, he stopped and turned around, a quizzical expression wrinkling his face. "Who is Han?"

Ellie smiled. "If you're still around in—what is it, sixty-five years?—you'll find out."

He considered this a moment, shrugged again, and resumed walking away, muttering what sounded like *strana.*

I'm definitely going to look that word up.

Ellie turned and dropped to her knees beside Sam, still noisily covering Ryan's face with kisses. She took his hand and was gratified to feel warmth and vitality in his grip.

"Uhhh, Sam?" Ryan groaned. "Why are we making out in the middle of the street?"

Sam sat back on her heels. *"Making out!?* I just revived you, you jerk, after *she* got you *killed!"* She jabbed an accusatory finger at Ellie.

"Wait a minute! *I* got him killed? I didn't have anything to do with those guys being here! I *certainly* didn't ask him to jump in and save the 'damsel in distress!'"

"True, but we wouldn't even be here if you hadn't made us try that thing out."

Ellie was incredulous. "Made you?! *Made* you?! I didn't *make* you anything. You were all for it right up until…."

A weak croak from Ryan stopped her in mid-rant. "Ladies? Can I get up now?"

Aaron got their attention with a soft cough. "We're, um… starting to draw a crowd." He nodded toward the nearest intersection. Following the break-up of Angelo's *ad hoc* gang of enforcers, people were beginning to reappear along the road, many of them peering curiously at the four strangers crouched in the middle of their street.

"Are you okay to stand?" Ellie said.

"I guess we'll see. I think maybe I was only 'mostly dead.'"

After a brief struggle involving Ellie and Sam pulling from the front and Aaron lifting from behind, they got Ryan to his feet. He stood unsteadily, his arms draped over Aaron and Sam's shoulders for support. Ellie noticed Angelo had paused at the end of the block, and he stood there now, watching them. He seemed to be waiting to make sure Ryan was okay, and she found she liked him for that, despite the attack. She gave him a wave, just a quick flick of her wrist, then watched him disappear around the corner.

Not until he was out of sight did anyone speak, and then it was Ryan, sounding confused. "I know I was a little out of it, but I swear I heard someone saying something about… *pink curtains?* That can't be right."

"*Huh?!*" It took Ellie a second to realize what he meant. "Oh! I'll explain later."

With Ellie leading the way and Sam and Aaron helping Ryan stay on his feet, they slowly made their way through the rest of the town while suffering nothing worse than a few judgmental stares. Ellie decided she couldn't blame them. *I guess it does look like he's had a few too many.*

They eventually left the last house in town behind them and recrossed the bridge. Ellie found where they had emerged from the trees hours earlier and veered off the road.

"You guys okay?"

Aaron puffed out a breathy, "Yeah!"

Sam didn't look at Ellie, but she gave her a short nod.

"Ryan?" Ellie said.

"Peachy."

She thought he sounded decidedly un-peachy. Although Sam's anger seemed to have exhausted itself, Ellie knew she hadn't heard the last from her. Right now, though, all her focus was on getting them all safely back. She tried to picture the shape of their path after they left the shack that morning and curved southeast toward the town, then tried to imagine it backward. She felt confident they were covering pretty much the same ground.

"Where *is* it?" Sam said.

"Not much farther, I think," Ellie said, although she thought they should already be there.

"You *think?!*"

"Should have brought some bread along," Aaron said, still puffing. "You know, to leave a trail of crumbs."

Ellie was immensely relieved when she finally spotted the small wooden structure less than five minutes later. As they drew nearer, however, she felt a sense of unease prickle along the nape of her neck. The shack looked just as it had a few hours earlier, and the creek and various songbirds still provided the gray surroundings a cheery soundtrack, but she felt as though the rough, mossy building had taken on a sinister air.

"Get a grip," she muttered to herself.

"What's that?" Sam said.

Ellie shook her head and refocused on the small wooden structure. The feeling, whatever it had been, was gone. "Nothing. Let's get back in there and… you know… whatever."

"Now *that* sounds almost, kinda, sorta like a plan," Ryan said. His voice was still weak and reedy, but Ellie figured so would hers be if she'd just been thwacked with a bat.

Ellie searched the shack's side for the correct shingle, found it, and pushed. For a second, she was convinced she would find nothing but unyielding wood, but to her relief the cedar-covered panel quickly slid aside to display the palm scanner. She placed her hand on the pad, waited for the green flashes of recognition, then tapped *1912* into the keypad. When the door cracked partially open, she reached into the gap and pulled. Instead of the door opening, she went down on her rump. She rose and tried again, but her feet could not find enough purchase on the damp forest floor.

"You're going to have to let go of him and help me, Aaron. These stupid shoes keep slipping on the leaves."

Aaron helped Sam guide Ryan to the side of the cabin and prepared to ease him into a sitting position.

"It's okay. I can stand," Ryan assured them, but as soon as Aaron released his grip on his arm, he teetered unsteadily, then slumped back against the wall.

"Okay, so I can lean." Sam stayed with him, her arm around his waist just in case he started to slip, and Aaron joined Ellie at the door.

"Ready?" Ellie said.

He nodded. "Go."

With both of them pulling on the door, they quickly opened it wide enough to enter. Sam led Ryan to the door and, with Aaron giving him a boost from behind, helped him up the high step.

Once inside, Ellie grabbed onto the door handle, leaned back, and pulled as hard as she could. It swung slowly but smoothly into place, seating into the surrounding wall with a dull thud and triggering the room's transformation. When the process had finished, Sam and Aaron guided Ryan to his seat and eased him onto it. Meanwhile, Ellie went to check the control panel.

"*Holy crapoli!*"

"Oh, good," Ryan said. "You picked up some more Italian on our little vacay."

Ellie ignored the comment. "I don't know how important this is, but the mission clock only has about eight and a half minutes left on it. Let's get these clothes off and get back into the seats." She and Sam quickly unbuttoned each other's dresses, and they all began shedding their costumes.

Ellie stuffed the various items back into the vacuum bags as she undressed. After sealing the bags' edges, she folded them over on themselves and knelt on them one at a time, squeezing out as much air as she could through their one-way valves. She finished first and moved around the chairs to assist Sam and Aaron. She held her hands out toward them. "Here —I'll take care of your stuff while you guys help Ryan."

Ryan was fumbling gamely at the buttons on his jacket, but his fingers were weak and uncoordinated, refusing to perform the simple task. Aaron helped Sam get him out of his antique clothing while Ellie repacked everything into bags and returned all of it to the wall cubbies. They had to get him standing again to make the switch with his pants, but he managed to stay upright with little need for assistance. Sam slipped his Yankees cap's brim into the waistband of his shorts before pulling the Kühl shirt onto his shoulders, and he was ready to go. Ellie returned the final bag to its compartment and closed the door just as Sam and Aaron lowered Ryan back onto his chair. Sam placed the helmet on his head, checked that his hands and feet were where they needed to be, then turned to Ellie.

"How're we doing for time?"

Ellie glanced at the display. "Great! Almost two and a half minutes to spare."

"What does that even mean?" Ryan said. "I mean… *seriously!*"

Instead of taking his seat, Aaron stood at its base as if transfixed, staring at it the way he had stared into the forest when he had first noticed the path of the utility trench. Seeing this, Sam peered quizzically at him, perplexed.

"What is it?"

"Assuming that we're already sitting there, I was trying to see if I could, you know, *see* myself."

"*Just sit!*" Ellie hissed, exasperated, and waited while they took their places. "Get ready. I'm going to hit the return button… now!"

She tapped the screen with under two minutes remaining, then sat back on her chair and pulled the helmet device onto her head. She placed her palms on the gel pads, snugged her feet into the toe cages, then closed her eyes. She braced herself, wondering if the transition back to the "real world" would feel as bad as the earlier experience.

Seconds later….

13

M oans of misery once more filled the shack's dark interior, and this time, it really was dark. They could barely see their own hands as they peeled them out of the gel and removed their helmets. The ceiling panels provided only faint illumination, and the walls none at all.

"I thought it was bad the *first* time!" Aaron croaked.

"Let's stay in the chairs for a few seconds," Ellie said. "It passed pretty quickly before."

"At least we haven't just eaten this time," Aaron said.

But Sam, either unaffected by the VR side effects or too concerned about Ryan to notice, was already rising. Her footrests clacked loudly when she kicked them aside and sprang from her seat. She crouched in front of Ryan and tried to study his face, but found it impossible in the weak light. "Hey," she said gently. "How're you doing?"

He slowly peeled his hands off the sticky pads, clenched and unclenched them a few times, then cautiously touched one hand to his chest. Surprised by the lack of pain, he smiled at her. "Hey! I actually feel a *lot* better! Except for the whole wanting-to-puke-my-guts-out thing. You aren't kidding, Double-A. That was *much* worse. Computer, show the outside again." He held his hand up before Sam could say anything and added, "Please."

As Ellie waited for something to happen, she thought she could see a little better than before, but couldn't tell if the room was getting brighter or if her eyes were merely adjusting to the darkness. After ten seconds, the walls remained blank. Then a flicker on the control panel caught her eye and she saw a message had appeared. She stood up to read it, but the text was barely bright enough to make out.

"'Power level critical,' it says. 'Non-essential functions temporarily off-line.' I guess we wore it out. Wait—now it says, 'Re-establishing power connection.'"

The wall panels switched on a second later, the ceiling brightened, and suddenly the light was intense enough to make them all squint.

"*Are we done now?!*" As though it had found a fresh power source of its own, Sam's irritation was back. "Can we *please* get out of this thing?" Standing up straight, she pulled the helmet from Ryan's head and repeated his request. "Computer, may we see the outside, please?"

"Hey, that's *my* thing!" Ryan said.

Guess he's feeling better, Ellie thought, but she also noted he still hadn't made any effort to get out of his chair.

Already the panels displayed the familiar clearing in the ponderosa pine forest. Ellie saw their packs leaning against the fallen tree where they had left them hours earlier. Behind her, Sam puffed out a huge sigh of relief.

"Oh, thank God!" Sam extended a hand to Ryan and helped him stand.

"One more sec," Ellie said. Still standing beside the control panel, she motioned for Aaron to join her. "Look at this." She pointed to the clock readout labeled CURRENT-ZULU, hardly able to believe what it said.

Not hours *earlier*, she thought. *Not even* minutes!

"What is it," Aaron said.

Ellie tapped the time display. "Looks like you were right about the whole 'subjective time' thing. When I hit the button at the beginning, that said eighteen forty-two. We've been back what, two, three minutes? Look at the time."

"18:45:21 and counting," he said. "*Whoa....*"

"Yeah," she agreed. "'Whoa' is right!"

"But that would mean the last four hours happened in absolutely no time at all!" Sam said.

"Whoa...." Ryan said, swaying slightly. "That means... that means we can still watch *Big Bang* tonight! No, wait... today's Friday, isn't it?" He exhaled a theatrically loud, disappointed sigh.

Ellie rolled her eyes. *Yep, he's definitely feeling better.*

She turned to see Sam monitoring Ryan closely, ready to rush in if he decided to keel over, but he looked steady enough for now. Ellie made a final examination of the room to make sure they weren't leaving anything behind. She could pick out a few faint smudges on the floor, but the room was otherwise pristine.

"Should we wipe it down?" Aaron said. "You know, for prints?"

She wasn't sure if he meant the suggestion seriously, but after considering the idea for a moment, she shook her head. "No, let's just go." She suddenly felt exhausted and wanted nothing more than a hot shower, a warm meal, and a cool pillow under her head. Then she remembered it was still barely past lunchtime and had to stifle a sudden urge to whimper. *Oh, great!*

Ryan grasped the lever on the inside of the door and tugged. It had barely budged when he let go to clutch at the center of his chest. He turned away from the door, wincing.

"*Oww!* That *hurt!*" He pulled up on the hem of the Star Wars tee he wore under the open Kühl shirt, exposing his chest. Ellie saw no sign of injury. There was no bruise, no abrasion—not even the slightest reddening.

"It doesn't hurt to touch it, but it didn't like me pulling on that thing." He scowled and pointed at the door.

"I got it," Aaron said. He stepped forward, gripped the handle, and found it moved easily. The door opened a crack, and the seats and control panel began to retract.

"Show-off!" Ryan said.

Sam was first through the door. She stopped just outside to help Ryan make the long step down, then guided him away from the shack. Aaron and Ellie exited, put their shoulders against the door, and shoved hard until it slid home and they heard its lock engage.

Aaron looked at her and smiled. "Well, we did that!"

She smiled back. "Yes. That we did."

Sam called to them from the picnic tree, sounding more worried now than angry. "Guys, we *really* need to get Ryan home."

He sat hunched over on the log, hands on his knees, leaning the weight of his upper body onto his legs. Out in the natural daylight, his face looked pale. "Yeah. I used up my one burst of energy getting this far."

"Here, drink the rest of this," Sam said, offering him a half-empty water bottle. He drained it, then passed it back.

"I'll take your pack," Aaron said. "You done with those other bottles?"

Sam put the empties into the pack, then Aaron closed it and swung it onto his shoulders.

"There's more when you want it," Ellie said. "Are you going to need help?"

"Maybe getting up from here. I think I'll be okay once we're moving, as long as we take it slow. But first things first—where's my hat?"

"You're sitting on it," Sam said.

"Am I?" He reached behind his back and found his hat tucked into his waistband. He tugged it free and looked at it. "*Hmm...* I do *not* remember doing that." Sam looked at Ellie and shook her head while Ryan carefully aligned his cap on his head. "Okay. *Now* we can go."

He held his arms out in front of himself. Ellie and Sam each took a hand and carefully pulled him to his feet. "*Wheee!*" he said, swaying slightly. Ellie stared at him, wide-eyed with worry. "Head rush," he explained. "I don't suppose we have any of those oranges left, do we?" he said.

Ellie nodded and rummaged through her pack for the remaining tangerine. She held it up for him to see. "Yep. Got it."

"We still have that snack mix in here, too," Aaron said, giving the pack a shake. "The salt might help."

"*Ugh!* No, thanks! I'll stick with the fruit."

As they began walking back toward the trailhead, Ellie peeled the tangerine and passed segments to Ryan one by one as, at first tentatively but with increasing enthusiasm, he gradually consumed them. The sugar seemed to help, and soon they were making slow but steady progress. For a long while, they were quiet, each searching for some means of expressing what they had just experienced. Aaron took the first stab at it.

"Thinking about that is *very* disorienting. It's like waking up from an especially vivid dream, one so real you have to work very hard to convince yourself it didn't happen."

"Tell that to my chest," Ryan said. "I must have tensed up and majorly pulled something in there because it feels like I actually got thumped! But now that I mention it? I feel much better now than I did even fifteen minutes ago."

"How do you feel otherwise," Sam said.

"Tired. Weak all over. Kinda like that first day you're starting to feel better after having the flu. Nothing a good night's sleep won't fix, probably."

They were still plodding along slowly when Ryan spotted a ponderosa sapling that had made it to a height of seven or eight feet before dying. All that remained was the slender central shaft. He pointed it out to Aaron.

"Can you check that out? See if it'll make a good walking stick?"

Aaron went to the dead tree, knocked off the few remaining spindly branches, and gripped its slender trunk tightly with both hands. By tilting it back and forth, gradually increasing the distance on each swing, he eventually broke it off at ground level, leaving the roots behind. Holding it upside down and angled away from his body, he brought his foot down hard near its spindly top. It snapped at a weak spot a third of the way back from the tip, leaving a staff roughly five feet long. On his way back to the others, he used his hands to wipe as much residual dirt as he could from the parts that had been in the ground.

"That's as good as it's going to get," he said.

Ryan took the staff, and, holding it by its thicker end, he stabbed the ground several times, harder on each successive jab, testing its strength. When he failed to break it, he nodded to Aaron. "Thanks. This is perfect."

As Ryan got more comfortable relying on the staff for support, they made more rapid progress. Ellie thought he looked like a well-groomed Gandolf making his way through the forest of Fangorn—if Gandalf had been a Yankees fan. Now and again, he would pause for a few moments, grip the top with both hands, and lean his weight on it until he felt rested enough to continue. They hiked quietly for another long stretch until Ryan broke the silence.

"Not to come across as an effete fop...."

"Is there another kind?" Aaron interjected.

"*Touché, mon ami.* Anyway, it was hard not to notice a general disregard for personal hygiene there on the streets of Lawrence. I know it was a simulation, so accuracy is up for debate, but I can't imagine what it would have smelled like in one of those mills in the middle of July."

"I'm not sure that was entirely about bathing," Sam said. "I think it had more to do with laundry. Would they have had enough soap saved up to last the entire two months they were on strike? And can you imagine washing all those heavy wool coats and stuff in the middle of winter? It was probably stinky clothes more than stinky people."

"Our clothes didn't smell at all," Aaron said. "Maybe *that's* the reason they were giving us funny looks."

"Yeah," Ryan said. "You mean that 'hairy eyebrow' thing."

"*Ball,*" Ellie said.

"No…. No, I'd remember if *you* said 'hairy ball.'"

An hour later, they were again at the nuclear lab access road. Sam and Ryan waited inside the north end of the culvert until Ellie and Aaron reached the tree line a hundred yards away. When Aaron whistled to let them know the coast was clear, they dashed across the open expanse as fast as Ryan could run. Seeing how quickly they covered the distance, Ellie would never have guessed he had been hurt. But when they reached her position just behind the first row of trees, Ryan was thoroughly winded from the exertion. Even so, they had successfully made it once again.

They moved deeper into the trees and rested briefly before moving on. After carefully picking their way past the snag again, they stopped in a small patch of shade at the bottom of the final ravine to give Ryan the chance to gather his strength before starting the last big climb. Ellie, who had hardly said a word since they started the hike out, stood apart from the group, appearing to be intensely interested in the tops of her shoes.

Sam called to her from where she sat beside Ryan. "Hey. You okay, El?"

Ellie continued staring at her feet, unable to face them.

"What's up, Buttercup?" Ryan said. "Leave your tongue in Lawrence?"

When she finally raised her head to look at them, her eyes were red-rimmed and damp. "I'm sorry, guys. I *really* am. Turning that thing on was impulsive, and selfish, and so… so *stupid!* Ryan, I… I feel *terrible.* I never thought…."

With obvious effort, Ryan stood and walked over to stand before her. He placed his hand on her shoulder and gave it a soft squeeze. "Hey—no harm, no foul, okay? Not *too* much harm. Besides, I was the one who thought it was such a great idea to try to block a baseball bat with my chest. Of course, had I known at the time that you were on a first-name basis with the gang leader, I would have let you try the diplomatic approach first. Hey," he said. He cupped the fingers of his right hand under her chin and gently tilted her head back. "Look at me." She reluctantly raised her gaze to meet his. "You and me? We're good, okay?"

She nodded. "Okay. Thanks." Enormously relieved, she wrapped him in a tight hug. As soon as her arms encircled him, she felt his entire body stiffen.

"*Oof!*" he said, his teeth clenched in a grimace of pain. She let go at once and stepped back.

"Sorry! Sorry! I forgot!"

He leaned forward and whispered in her ear. "It's okay. You may have to give Sam a day or two, though. I'm pretty sure she still believes you nearly got me killed."

"'*Nearly?!*'" Sam was annoyed by his obtuseness. "Your *heart* stopped, Ryan! That's the very definition of being dead."

Ellie was well acquainted with that angry tone and knew hoping to be forgiven after only a *week* or two was being overly optimistic.

Ryan whispered in her ear again. "Seriously—how does she do that?"

She couldn't help but smile at him. "Haven't you figured it out? Bat-like hearing is one of the Henderson women's superpowers. Get used to it."

"There was no way to know how, uh, 'interactive' that thing would be," Aaron said.

Ellie took his words of support as a sign he was no longer upset with her over the "owl" thing. "Yeah, I know, but I still feel terrible. Sam...."

"Don't waste any breath apologizing to me. And just you remember—if you don't get an 'A' on that paper, you... are... dead!"

14

E llie woke the following morning to find herself alone. She had been alone when she went to sleep the night before, too. After they made it home yesterday, Sam showered, put on fresh clothes, then left to check on Ryan. Ellie had tried to talk to her, but Sam wouldn't listen. She'd held up a hand, said, "Just... *don't!*" and stormed from the house without another word.

When Ellie sat up, she saw that Sam's bed was unmade. She must have come in late and gone out again early without saying a word. Ellie exhaled a long, dispirited sigh. She still felt miserable about what had happened the day before but knew Sam would continue to be angry with her until the emotion had burned itself out. There was nothing she could do except wait, and then—maybe—they could have the conversation necessary to move them beyond Sam's lingering hard feelings and return their relationship to normal. Meanwhile, she would write.

She had spent much of the night dreaming about everything she had witnessed in the simulator's version of Lawrence. Snapshot images flickered through her mind like her MacBook's screensaver playing photos on a random loop. She saw the many families on the road leading out of Methuen, the sooty brick buildings lining their path through the city, and relived the calling of the vote as she watched from her perch in the tree. In her dream, she noticed details she had not been aware of at the time—the knots of tense-looking men that stood outside the crowd at the Common, for instance, who kept the strikers under constant observation. She saw the girl in the green hat more than once, a scene that repeated like the chorus of a song, and now it reminded her of something Sam had said while they were changing clothes, something about it being "all fashion, all the time."

It's more likely you would have been that shopgirl, your one prized possession that bright green hat. You probably would have worn it into your old age, a bittersweet reminder of your dreams from youth.

In that instant, the abstract world of the strikers she had read about in her library books, with their grainy, black-and-white photographs, merged with the sights, sounds, and scents she had experienced in the virtual Lawrence. Combined, they formed a real place in her mind, one she could finally relate to. Every person they had encountered had been somebody's sister, brother, father, or mother. They all had plans for themselves, dreams for their children, and little hope of making any of them come true. All at once, Ellie not only understood the uncertainty and the anguish the workers had lived through, she could *feel* it. Her block was gone!

She opened her laptop and began to type.

Feeling tight all over, Ellie leaned back against the wall and stretched. To her surprise, the clock in the corner of her screen said it was already eleven-fifteen. She had been writing for over three hours without so much as a cup of coffee since dinner the night before. She was pleased by her progress and regretted having to stop, but she could no longer ignore her stomach's constant rumbling.

She set the laptop aside and swung her legs over the edge of her bed, wondering why she had never heard anyone moving around the house. Then she remembered—her parents had taken off early to run some household errands and do some shopping out of town. With Sam also gone, she would likely have the house to herself for at least another hour, maybe two. Still wearing nothing but her nightshirt, she left the bedroom to get something to eat.

When she entered the kitchen, she discovered she wasn't as alone as she'd thought. On the outer windowsill above the sink, her fur pressing in through the screen, crouched a large, orange cat. Seeing Ellie walking toward her, she sat up and launched into a series of loud, plaintive *meows*. Ellie stood at the sink and rubbed the cat's haunch through the screen.

"Good morning, Sunshine," she said, echoing the phrase that had given the cat its name.

Sunshine had made her first appearance in early spring. Crossing the patio as they left for school, Ellie and Sam spotted her basking in a patch of light alongside the house. "Well, good morning, Sunshine!" Sam said. It seemed so appropriate that it became her name on the spot.

One of her names, anyway. By talking to their neighbors over the next few weeks, they learned that Sunshine made a meandering circuit through the surrounding blocks, surviving on whatever wildlife she could catch, supplemented by handouts from other households. Who knew what those others called her? One of their more conscientious neighbors had taken her to a nearby vet to be spayed. One feral cat could wreak a heap of havoc on the local wildlife, but at least this one wouldn't be producing any more. Despite her itinerate lifestyle, Sunshine seemed healthy, friendly, and relaxed—even playful—when she dropped by to visit. But she was not, strictly speaking, their cat.

"Not even loosely speaking," their father said when he discovered they had begun feeding her. "I'm never going through another sob scene like we had with Mr. Pib."

Mr. Pib—a.k.a. The Pibster and, more recently, Notorious PIB— was the tuxedo cat they had brought with them when they moved to Los Alamos from their previous home in northern Virginia. The *Pib* in Mr. Pib was an acronym for Puss-in-Boots, and he had sported the markings to warrant the name. Neither of the girls could clearly remember a time Mr. Pib had not been a part of the household, and both took it hard when the vet made it clear the previous fall that the time had come to put their ailing pet to sleep. The appearance of Sunshine a few months later lifted their spirits, and they both enjoyed having even a part-time cat again. But in light of their father's lack of enthusiasm, they handled feeding time with all the diligence of spies making a dead drop.

"Hang on just one second. I'll be right out."

Sunshine replied with an impatient *yowl*.

Ellie filled the electric kettle with filtered water from the fridge and switched it on. Next, she dropped a paper filter into a ceramic pour-over cone and set it on a large mug. As the final step, she scooped coffee beans out of a bag from the co-op, ran them through the grinder, and tipped the grounds into the filter.

Squatting low, she opened the cupboard below the sink and reached in deep to pull out a small box of Purina Cat Chow secreted against the back of the cabinet behind spare rolls of paper towels. She poured a quarter cup of it into a small, blue bowl. Hearing the distinctive tinkle of kibble on stoneware, Sunshine began to turn tight, seemingly impossible circles on the narrow windowsill, her whiny meows becoming more insistent. Ellie grabbed a banana for herself, then pushed through the screen door to deliver breakfast.

"Best human on the planet, huh?" She bent to place the bowl on the brick patio, and Sunshine's nose was in it before it reached the ground.

Picking the sunniest seat at the round, metal mesh table, Ellie sat and propped her feet on a neighboring chair. She peeled the banana and began nibbling at it while the cat greedily devoured her food. After what seemed an eternity, the welcome rumble of the kettle coming to a boil drifted out through the window above Ellie's head.

"Coffee, Sunshine! I'll be right back." She sprang up and went into the house to prepare a late breakfast. By the time she returned to the back yard bearing a large, steaming mug and a bowl of cinnamon granola, the kibble was gone and Sunshine sat nearby performing her usual post-feeding cleaning ritual. Ellie resumed her seat, sliced the remainder of her banana into her cereal with the side of her spoon, and enjoyed that unique feeling of tranquility that only came from watching a cat.

While she ate, her mind drifted back to the previous afternoon. After Sam had left the house in a huff, Ellie tried to block out her sense of guilt by unloading her day pack and washing the water bottles. She made sure all the pack's many pockets were empty before replacing it in the closet, realizing only then that Aaron had never returned her camera. She meant to text him about it but had forgotten. She made a mental note to follow up on that later. The possibility occurred to her that, amid all the upset over Ryan, the camera had somehow ended up in *his* pack. Aaron had been the one to carry it back, she now remembered, so maybe he had put it in there. She'd have to ask Sam when she got home.

After draining the final drops of milk from her bowl, she walked across the spacious lawn and stretched out on one of the wooden lounge chairs. A large cottonwood tree shaded the upper third of her body, but she could feel the sun's soothing warmth on her stomach and legs. She closed her eyes and let out a deep, contented sigh as she luxuriated in her silent solitude. A few minutes later, Sunshine climbed onto her belly, laid down, and started gently kneading a spot at the base of her ribs. Ellie found the cat's weight comforting, and she relaxed even more.

"Let's do this the whole rest of the day," she mumbled, eyes still closed. Soon they were both deeply asleep.

Ellie snapped awake with a start and was momentarily confused to find herself in the back yard but dressed for bed. Then she remembered having coffee and feeding Sunshine. She scanned the yard and was disappointed when she didn't see the cat anywhere. As her head cleared, she noticed that the sun had barely moved and realized only a few minutes had passed. She suddenly felt vulnerable dozing outside in nothing but her nightshirt and wondered what had awakened her. She looked around again, paying close attention to the top of the vine-covered wooden fence that ran the length of each side of the yard and the few windows visible beyond it. Finally convinced she was still as alone as before, she rose from the lounge chair, gathered her dishes from the table, Sunshine's bowl from the patio, and went back inside.

Standing at the kitchen sink, her hands washing the dishes without any conscious direction, her thoughts returned to her paper. She had taken her break while describing the strikers' vote in Lawrence Common. The fact that she could actually "remember" the events, insofar as she was willing to accept the simulation's accuracy, was vaguely disconcerting. She wondered if her knowledge of the strike, based on her recent studies, had influenced how the shack had recreated the events for them. The experience still felt utterly genuine, and she had to remind herself she hadn't *really* seen the drive belt in the factory fly across the room, hadn't *really* witnessed Ryan getting whacked by a kid with a baseball bat.

She transferred the clean dishes from the washer to the cupboards, then toweled her breakfast dishes dry and put those away, too. She used a damp sponge to take a perfunctory stab at cleaning the countertop, dropped it into the drainer, and headed back to her room.

Glancing at Sam's clock as she entered, she saw it was barely past twelve-thirty. *Excellent!* With any luck, she still had at least another hour to herself. She considered showering but decided to wait. Instead, she shifted her laptop from her bed to her desk and sat on the wooden chair. She tapped the space bar and while the screen flickered back to life, she pulled the *Bread and Roses* book out of the middle of the pile of references stacked on the floor against her bed.

Resuming her line of thought from the kitchen, she marveled again at how precisely the scenes they had witnessed in the simulator matched the photos in the books she had been poring over for the past few weeks. Had somebody created that environment using actual period photography? If you could pick literally any place on any day of any year for the shack to recreate, that quickly became a seemingly impossible amount of scanning and input. Maybe they had designed a single cast of background characters but gave them different clothes and hairstyles to match the specific times and places. Or perhaps the range of experiences was more limited than the control panel suggested.

She flipped through the book and found the section covering the end of the strike and the big vote at the park. She studied the various photographs, of which there was a surprising number. *I guess it's not too surprising, considering all the press we saw wandering around there.*

Catching herself "remembering" yet again, she experienced a mix of amusement and frustration. She looked at the pictures of William Haywood making his speech, noting that photos of the event had been taken from at least two different angles. It seemed she was right about there having been more than one paper covering the story.

One of the pictures filled the page's entire width. Even though it was taken at some distance from the gazebo, the details were sharp enough for her to recognize Haywood's face, captured in right profile, as he announced the official vote results to the crowd. Then she saw something in the photo that made her laugh. There was a figure in the background she hadn't noticed before, someone watching the speech from a low branch in a tree. Judging from the angle of the shot, she figured it was almost where she had been in the simulation.

"That is so cool! Great minds *do* think alike, I guess."

She turned the page and began scanning the next set of pictures. There were several shots of the crowd's jubilant reaction to the vote. One captured Haywood descending from the gazebo. Another showed a man and woman locked in a tight embrace. Tears were streaming down the man's face. The last one....

"Wait a second...."

What she saw in the last photo baffled her. She flipped another page forward, then back a few. She had been spending so much time looking at this book recently that she thought she knew by heart every single picture and where it was, yet the image in the lower right corner of page one-nineteen didn't look familiar. Or at least not *entirely* familiar.

She turned back to the photo and looked at it again. She expected to see a picture of Genarro, Camella, and Carmela Teoli all looking uncomfortable as they posed for a photographer on their way out of the park. They were there, all three of them, and dressed exactly how she remembered. However, the image differed from her expectations in a very significant way, and that difference made the hair on the back of her neck stand on end.

Puzzled by the discrepancy, she leaned forward for a closer look. Something seriously strange was setting off all kinds of alarm bells in her head, but what? Had the photo been in color, she might have understood more quickly. She continued staring until recognition finally set in, and then she felt as though her veins had filled with ice water.

"No freakin' way!"

She flopped back in her chair and stared blankly through the window blinds as recent events replayed themselves in her mind. Experiencing this flashback in the context of these new observations, supposed facts took on new definitions, and at least one nagging question suddenly had an answer. When she could no longer deny the obvious, logical conclusion, she was filled with a feeling that was equal parts wonder and dread.

"No. Freakin'. Way."

That night Ellie lay awake for hours, staring up at the intricate tangle of shadows cast onto the ceiling by the limbs of the cottonwood tree that grew just outside her bedroom. She felt trapped within that pattern, lost at the center of a complex maze whose path shifted erratically with every breeze, making it impossible for her to escape. But it was not mere shadows keeping her awake so late.

Since that afternoon, her mind had been in turmoil, the scene of a struggle where what she had once believed true waged a fierce battle against what she now feared was possible. The further removed from that earlier moment of revelation she became, the less certain she was of its truth, but she was convinced enough that she had been gripped by a gut-churning dread ever since.

She heard her sister shift at the far end of the room. Maybe Sam was still awake, too. If so, should she say something? Say what, exactly? The ideas bouncing around her brain sounded crazy even to her.

When Sam had returned in the middle of the afternoon, she'd told Ellie that she completely agreed that her actions had been impulsive, reckless, selfish, and yes, *stupid*. She said she'd also decided that Ellie had managed to make herself feel bad enough on her own, so although she was still mad at her, she was past the point of needing to inflict further punishment. Since then, Ellie had decided it was best to avoid any reference to the previous day's adventure, but now she felt an overwhelming need to talk about it. Reaching a decision at last, she spoke quietly into the darkness.

"Something's been bothering me."

"I can tell. What is it?"

"It's...." she began, but all that followed was a long silence. She could sense Sam waiting patiently at the opposite side of the room for her to continue. "It's... I don't know how to *say* it. You know... so that it doesn't sound totally insane."

She rolled onto her side and propped herself up on her elbow to peer across the dark space between their beds. Sam was lit well enough from the same street light responsible for creating the shadow maze on the ceiling that Ellie could look her in the eyes as she went on.

"Is there an opposite of *déjà vu*? An experience that should feel familiar but doesn't?"

Sam shook her head, not following what Ellie was trying to say. "Where is all this coming from?"

"When I was working on my paper earlier, I saw something in one of the books that wasn't what I remember seeing before. And believe me, I know them forward and backward at this point!"

"What do you mean by 'before?' Before when?"

"Just *before*. When I was last reading it. Before yesterday."

"You mean, like, Thursday there was one thing, and today it was different?"

"That's exactly what I'm saying."

"Something written in the book was different." Sam was making sure she understood. "And you didn't imagine it."

"Yes! I mean, no, I didn't imagine it. Something was definitely different," Ellie reaffirmed. "And not just different—*impossible*."

Sam shook her head. "You aren't making any sense."

"What happened yesterday?"

"Seriously?" Sam scoffed. "I'd think that a little thing like, you know, Ryan *dying* might stick in your mind for more than a day!"

"Yes, I remember that. Obviously. But what I'm asking is what *actually* happened? We—okay, *I*—assumed that shack was a virtual reality device of some kind, but that's all it was—an assumption. But what if it's something, I don't know... *else?*"

Even though Sam heard the distress in her sister's voice, she couldn't keep her skepticism out of her reply. "Else as in.... Wait! Are you suggesting that what we did in that room had something to do with what you say you saw in your book? That's nuts!"

Ellie was stung by Sam's tone. She sighed loudly, slid her arm out from under her, and flopped back onto her pillow. She spent several minutes silently staring at the ceiling before Sam spoke again.

"I'm sorry, El. I didn't mean it to sound that way." The silence continued. "Ellie? Come on, tell me what's bothering you. Please?"

"No, you're right. It *is* nuts. Let's just talk about it later, okay?"

"Sure, whatever. We'll talk about it tomorrow."

Ellie remained awake for a long time, trying to make sense of what she believed she had discovered. Her thoughts were clear enough inside her head, but the vocabulary she needed to express them stubbornly eluded her. She soon realized she wouldn't be able to rely on words alone, and just before drifting off to sleep, she had one last thought—*Tomorrow I'll show her the pictures.*

15

When Ellie opened her eyes the following morning, she was disappointed to discover she was alone once again. She had hoped Sam would hang around until they had a chance to talk. She slipped on a pair of ankle socks and left her room to search for her elsewhere in the house. She found her parents, as she nearly always did on warm Sunday mornings, sitting at the table on the back patio. They each had a coffee mug close at hand, and a plate set between them was loaded with slices of hearty, whole-grain bread and an assortment of spreads. A third chair held an untidy stack of read and yet-to-be-read sections of the day's newspaper. She stood at the sink and watched them through the screen for several minutes, wondering how they would react if she told them what she believed about the device she, Sam, and the others had discovered out in the forest. Aside from thinking she was completely wacko, that is.

Sam was not in the living room, either. Was she already out with Ryan? Ellie considered texting but decided she didn't want to intrude and risk making Sam mad at her all over again.

Still feeling let down, she opted instead for a shower. After picking out clothes for the day, she crossed the hall to the bathroom. When she hung her nightshirt on a hook on the back of the door, she noticed a tiny coffee stain below the MANH(A)TTAN logo emblazoned across its chest, and took a second to dab some shampoo onto the spot before stepping under the spray.

When Ellie returned to the bedroom freshly scrubbed and dressed, Sam was waiting. Her earlier absence was immediately explained by two large to-go cups of coffee and two *very* large blueberry muffins, all from the Atomic City Café. Ellie looked at the goodies, then at Sam, and smiled uncertainly.

"What's the occasion?"

"I got the feeling we were looking at a pretty heavy discussion this morning. You were still dead to the world when I got up, so I decided to go get us some treats. Wanna go out back?"

"Mom and Dad are out there. I'd rather talk to you alone."

"Not anymore, they're not. They just left. They're walking into town."

"Oh, okay. Yeah, that's fine then. Maybe Sunshine will come by again. Did I tell you she was here yesterday?"

They each picked up a cup and a muffin and filed out to the table. Ellie was about to sit when she suddenly remembered something.

"*Oops!* Be right back!" She dashed into the house and returned half a minute later with a pair of books tucked under her arm. She leaned them against one of the legs of her chair where they wouldn't be a distraction until she needed them.

Sam, meanwhile, had peeled the paper liner from her muffin and was flattening it into a makeshift plate. She looked up from her work as Ellie took her seat. "So—what was on your mind last night?"

Ellie was quiet for a minute while she organized her thoughts. "Would you say I'm fairly rational?"

"Often to the point of being annoyingly so, yes."

This opinion was not news to Ellie, so she pressed on. "And reasonably intelligent?"

Sam grinned. "Are we feeling a little underappreciated this morning?"

"I'm not fishing for compliments, okay? I just...."

Sam interrupted her quickly. "Sorry! Yes. You are one of the smartest people I know. Definitely in the top five."

"Top *five?! Who...?!* Nope—never mind." She genuinely wanted to know who else was on Sam's list but was determined not to get sidetracked. "So, if

I were to tell you that I had discovered there really isn't such a thing as gravity but that the Earth just sucks, you'd at least hear me out?"

Sam managed to swallow her coffee before laughing. "I can't say I'd be all that surprised, but yeah, I'd listen."

Ellie hesitated again before moving on.

"So once again, what happened on Friday? And by that I mean, what do you believe *truly* happened?"

Now it was Sam's turn to be silent while she pondered the question. Ellie kept her eyes on her sister's face, trying to anticipate her answer. When it came, it was much as she expected.

"I believe what you guys said at the time—that the shack is some kind of super… duper… virtual-reality room that can create the illusion of being in different places at different times in the past. Why? Isn't that what you think?"

"But does that explain *everything*? You wondered about the clothes—does it explain them?" She pulled off a big chunk of muffin and popped it into her mouth. She had thoroughly chewed it and swallowed before Sam responded.

"I guess that would depend on what whoever built it was planning to use it for. Like Aaron said. Maybe it only seems strange because we don't know everything about it."

"Maybe. That is a possibility, but to me, it sounds more like a simple rationalization than a reasonable explanation."

Sam bristled at that. "Look, why don't you come right out and tell me what you think instead of asking all these questions?"

"Sorry. I'm not trying to annoy you or to imply anything. I'm trying to get you to see the problem in a certain way, that's all."

"Great! Fine! But I don't have the foggiest idea what the 'problem' is!"

Ellie responded softly, trying to diffuse the growing tension. "Okay, okay —fair enough."

She reached beside her chair and brought the books up onto her lap. She looked at each of the two covers before choosing one. She flipped through its pages while she started explaining what was on her mind.

"Remember I said I saw something in one of my books that looked off to me?"

"Yeah, you said something seemed different from what you remembered."

"Correct." She placed the selected book on the table. "Here, look at the picture in the bottom right corner. Recognize them?"

Sam studied Ellie's expression for a moment as if making sure she wasn't playing a joke on her before looking down at the photo. Shocked to realize she actually *did* know who the people were, her body stiffened. "It's *them!* The people you talked to—the Leonis."

"The *Teolis*, actually, but yes, it's them. This is the image I remember seeing last week while I was working on my paper. But—this is not the book I was reading." She closed the book and pushed it to one side.

"So... why does it matter that a picture in a different book is different from the picture in your book? I don't get it."

"Because *this* is the one I was using."

The book she placed beside the first one appeared identical in every way. Then Sam noticed a design at the cover's upper right corner. It was printed to resemble a medallion, a gold circle with zigzag edges. The words inside it read, "100th Anniversary Edition."

"Okay, now I *really* don't get it!"

"The first book is older, from, like, 1987 or something. They're both from the library, but I originally checked this one out because it's the more recent edition. And if we open this one to the same page...." She opened the book randomly in the middle, then thumbed back a few pages at a time until she reached the same spread of photos.

"What do you see now?"

Sam glanced down. "There are other people in the picture with them." She looked up from the page. "So, they used a different picture in the newer book. What's the biggie?"

"But they didn't. That's the point. If you had asked me before yesterday afternoon to describe the photo in the lower right corner of page one-nine-teen, I would have described the picture in *this* book," she said, slapping the cover of the older edition with her palm. "I was totally surprised to see *that* photo yesterday." She pointed at the newer book.

"Isn't it possible you looked at the other book and remembered that picture?"

Ellie was shaking her head even before Sam finished the question. "Nope —never even opened it. Not until yesterday when I went and got it out of the library. *After* I saw *this* picture." Again she pointed to the image in the open book.

Sam frowned in frustration, still unable to see the point Ellie was trying to make. "Pictures in books don't change."

"I have one last question."

Sam sighed. "Let's have it."

"Okay. So, who are those other people in the picture?"

"How could I possibly know *that?!*" Sam was back to sounding exasperated.

"Humor me, all right? Just look at them and tell me honestly what you think you see."

Ellie knew Sam had to see what she herself had seen with as little prompting as possible. Ellie remained silent as Sam leaned in for a closer look. She drew in slow, deep breaths as she tried to stay calm, all the while experiencing a case of intense, whole-body jitters that made her want to jump out of her skin.

Sam looked up at Ellie for a second, clearly bewildered, then resumed her study of the photo. Ellie followed the minute movements of her head as she carefully examined first one figure, then moved on to the next.

After a moment, Sam began shaking her head, her brain trying to deny what her eyes plainly saw. When she at last spoke, her voice sounded flat and distant, as if she were talking in her sleep.

"But... that can't *be!*"

16

Ellie sat alone at a metal picnic table in Ashley Pond Park, an expanse of neatly trimmed grass near the edge of the commercial part of town. In the middle of the nearby pond, the spray from an aerator created a rainbow that danced erratically amid the wind-tossed droplets. As she watched Sam, Ryan, and Aaron walk toward her, she felt her stomach knot with the sudden fear that she was about to make a complete fool of herself, that particular dread piling itself on top of a more generalized anxiety she was already barely keeping at bay.

After Sam had seen the second altered photo, the one of the distant figure in the tree, she'd hit Ellie with a barrage of questions she could not even begin to answer. Sam desperately wanted to deny the truth of the evidence her own eyes presented her while at the same time seeking an explanation for it. Ellie had argued they were more likely to come up with those answers by bringing Aaron and Ryan into the conversation, and Sam eventually agreed to get the group together so Ellie could run through everything again. Via a flurry of texts, they had arranged to meet ninety minutes later, and that time was now up.

Ellie studied the others as they took seats at the table. To her great relief, Aaron seemed to be back in his usual, easygoing mood. She was glad for that, although she now found it even harder not to call him "Hedwig" in the privacy of her thoughts, despite having resolved not to.

Ryan still looked pale, and his motions lacked their usual lanky fluidity, as if he were concerned the slightest wrong move would rekindle the flames of yesterday's pain. He occasionally reached up to rub absently at the spot on his chest where the bat had struck him. She shook her head to clear it of a flashback to the sight of him lying motionless on the road through Methuen. She was nervous enough about sharing what she was about to say —she didn't need that image in her mind.

Ellie pulled her books close to her while the others waited in expectant silence on the table's opposite side. She looked at each member of the little group. Sam had agreed to let her make her presentation without comment but was withholding a final decision on whether she thought Ellie's theory was correct. She seemed open to accepting the idea, but Ellie sensed she could still go either way if no one else supported her interpretation of the evidence. She knew Ryan would listen, but he would also be a smart-ass whenever the opportunity arose. Aaron was the one she needed to win over. If he agreed with her, he could help Ryan see it, and that would take care of Sam, too. But of the three of them, Aaron was the one she most minded looking foolish in front of should they decide her idea was as crazy as Sam thought.

"My sister thinks I'm, in her words, 'squirrel-stash nuts,'" she said. Sam rolled her eyes but, as promised, kept her mouth closed. "I can't completely rule that out, and that's why I wanted to show you guys this. To get your opinions."

"I'm with Sam, as far as you being nuts," Ryan said, "but show us what you've got."

He flashed a conspiratorial smile in Sam's direction, made a "crazy face" complete with crossed eyes and a lolling tongue, but she ignored him.

"*Anyway*... somebody said if you can't explain something to a five-year-old, you don't understand it yourself, so I've been sitting here for the last twenty minutes trying to come up with the most straightforward way to explain what I think is going on. In the end, though, I think it's easiest just to tell you the same way I told Sam.

"I brought a couple of books I checked out last week for my term paper.

Well, one I checked out weeks ago, and the other one I got just yesterday."
She held up one of the two *The Bread and Roses Strike—Two Months in Lawrence, Massachusetts* books. "This is all about that 1912 millworkers' strike in Lawrence."

"Six," Aaron said.

"Huh? No, *twelve*."

"Einstein said it, and it was a six-year-old," he clarified.

"Let the record show not only is Ellie crazy, but she misquotes Einstein," Ryan said. He wielded his fist like a judge's gavel, pounding it solidly onto the table.

"Just shush," Sam hissed at him. "Listen!"

Surprised by her stern reaction, he raised his hands in a gesture of surrender.

"Anyway...." Ellie said again, unexpectedly feeling warmed by her sister's demonstration of support. "What I want to show you is right here." She opened the volume to where a slip of paper marked a spot and turned the book around for them to see. "The copyright date on this book is 1987, but forget that for now. Here—look at this." She pointed at a paragraph marked by an arrow drawn on a sticky note. They leaned forward and read:

> Carmela's testimony helped bring an end to a two-month strike after President Taft called the Massachusetts governor and requested he apply pressure on the mill owners to settle. Carmela, pictured here with her mother and father immediately following the vote, was among the estimated 15,000 workers who gathered on Lawrence Common this morning to make history.

Aaron completed the section of text first, then he looked up at Ellie. She held up a finger until Ryan finished reading, then nodded for him to ask his question.

"This is what you told us before—in the shack," he said. "What are we supposed to be seeing?"

Ellie slid a fingernail under the loose edge of the sticky note and peeled it from the page to reveal a black-and-white photograph roughly four inches by five. Aaron and Ryan—Sam, too, although she had already seen Ellie's 'evidence'—leaned over the book and studied the photo. The faces in the picture weren't difficult to make out—the photo was plenty big, and the large negative had captured a sharp image. After only a brief examination, everyone recognized the members of the Teoli family. Behind them was the gazebo, sufficiently far enough away to be out of focus, along with several small clusters of strikers on their way out of the park.

"Hey, that's *them*," Ryan said, unknowingly echoing Sam.

Aaron read the caption. "'Genarro, Camella, and Carmela Teoli moments after the vote that ended the two-month 'Bread and Roses' strike.'"

"Isn't it amazing, I mean absolutely, totally, *incredibly* amazing how precisely it matches what we saw on Friday?" Ellie said. They studied her face, looking for the deeper point she seemed to be trying to make. She leaned forward and pointed at several specific parts of the picture. "The people and their dress, the weather—somebody did an *excellent* job recreating all that, wouldn't you say?"

"Um, yeah, I'd say so," Aaron said. Ryan merely shrugged. They still couldn't see her point.

"Okay, a few things. But first, look at this picture." She turned forward a page and pointed to the photo of William Haywood on the bandstand. "See anything unusual in the trees in the background?"

"Like what?" Aaron said.

"Like a lost kite, a sniper, a roosting dragon... anything at all."

Both shook their heads.

"Not a thing," Ryan said. "Just bare branches."

"Right. Now look here, at the first photo I showed you," she said, turning back a page. She placed her finger near two indistinct figures in the background, one large and male, one smaller and wearing a dress. "Notice how they're positioned. See how they're holding hands but that she's trailing behind like he's walking a little too fast for her?" They nodded without looking up from the page. "And here," she said as she placed her finger on Carmela. "It's small, I know, but look at the flower she's wearing. It could be the first crocus blossom in the city, probably from one of Genarro's greenhouses. See how it's in perfect shape?"

"Okay, so?" Aaron said.

"So look at this."

She brought the other book up onto the table and let them see the cover, nearly identical to the first, though perhaps a little less worn.

"*The Bread and Roses Strike...* It's the same book," Ryan said.

"Yes and no. When I was checking books out from the library, I noticed there were two copies of this one on the shelf. I picked this one because it's newer. It was printed in 2012 for the strike's centennial." She pointed to the little *100th Anniversary Edition* medallion on the cover's upper corner. "So I thought there might be stuff in here that wasn't in the earlier edition." She could see traces of impatience with her little show-and-tell starting to creep into their expressions. She raised a hand in a placating gesture. "Stick with me another second. Trust me—it'll be worth it."

She placed the newer book between them, laying it on top of the first.

"Open it to one-nineteen," she said. Aaron flipped through the second book until he found the right page. A yellow sticky note covered a photo here, too.

"Okay, now read that same paragraph."

Carmela's testimony helped bring an end to a two-month strike after President Taft called the Massachusetts governor and requested he apply pressure on the mill owners to settle. Carmela and her family, pictured here with four unidentified fellow strikers, were among the estimated 15,000 workers who gathered in Lawrence Common this morning to make history.

"It's different," Aaron said.

She reached out and pulled the yellow Post-It from the page. "Now, look at the photo."

In it, a group of people stood in the park with the bandstand out of focus in the background. The Teolis were only part of that group, but they looked much the same as they did in the other book. For this photo, the photographer had positioned them to the left side of the frame, rather than at the center, to make room for additional people. The Teolis were being addressed by a young girl standing with her back to the camera. Another young girl and a boy about the same age stood in partial profile near the right edge of the frame. A seventh figure, standing in front of the righthand pair, had been captured while turning his head, making him less sharp than the other subjects. What mattered was that the photographer had caught the side of the boy's face. He was wearing large, wire-rimmed glasses, and his short-cut blond hair protruded below the turned-up band of a dark, woolen Ainsley cap.

Aaron recognized the boy at once. "*Hey!* That's *me!*" He pulled the book closer to him and stabbed his finger at the caption where it read, *Genarro, Camella, and Carmela Teoli, along with four unidentified others, moments after the vote that ended the two-month 'Bread and Roses' strike.*

Ryan laughed, amused by the idea. "Yeah, it's just like we were really there!"

Aaron was transfixed by the photo and leaned even closer for a better look.

"No, man," he said. "That's *definitely* me. And *you* are there," he said, picking out Sam in the picture, "and *you*, and...."

"Give me that, Dorothy!" Ryan yanked the book toward him. Sam remained quiet, sticking to her agreement to let the boys see the evidence first and allow them to form their own opinions. They'd discuss whatever conclusions they came to later.

"Look at my pants," Aaron said. "You can see where I wiped the mud off my hands after I boosted Ellie into the tree."

"*Your pants*—that could be anyone." Ryan was still being contrary, but now his voice was tinged with doubt. Ellie took that as a good sign. "That does look like that goofy-ass hat you were wearing, though."

"No—wait!" Aaron said. His eyes went wide as a remembered image entered his mind. "I *saw* a guy with the camera when we turned and left. I looked over and there he was, slinking around behind us with this big, boxy thing. I didn't realize he was taking a picture, though."

Ryan scowled at him. "Yeah, right."

"No, I *did!* He...."

Ellie didn't think Ryan could have sounded any more skeptical, and she was starting to lose hope. When Aaron began to protest, she cut in, feeling an urgent need to back him up. She leaned forward and placed a hand on her chest.

"It's true, Ryan. I saw them, too. When we were walking over from the tree. There was a reporter and the guy who must've taken this. And see these two?" She drew their attention back to the book, pointing at a pair of people in the background, the man walking with the girl trailing slightly behind him. "And here?" She indicated several other distant figures whose postures and positions were identical in both books.

"All those details are the same, but look at this." She placed her finger below the flower on Carmela's coat. If the girl standing with her back to the camera had been positioned even an inch further to the right, she would have blocked the camera's view of the flower. However, it was plainly visible, and its condition was decidedly not perfect. One of the petals was folded down, and the whole thing looked like it had been lightly stepped on.

Next, Ellie pointed to the girl whose back was turned. Her cropped hair was very much out of style for 1912. "What about her, Ryan? Do you like her hair? Would you say it's... *sexy?*" Unaware of Ryan's recent faux pas, Aaron gave her a quizzical look. She pretended not to notice.

Ryan leaned so close to the book that his chin practically touched the page as he peered intently at the image. He looked from the girl to the boy in glasses, then to the couple near the edge of the picture, then back to the girl. He could not deny the obvious any longer. He sat up and pushed the book away from him in a feeble gesture of rejection. However, when he looked up at Ellie, he realized he was staring at the same hairstyle.

"What the *hell?!*" he said.

"Now do you get the thing about the flower?"

Aaron pulled the book close to him for another look. "That's easy. You smashed her flower when you hugged her. My first thought was 'different edition, different photo,' but you're right—it *should* be the same photo— same place, same people in the background—except, 'hello,' there *we* are."

"It's not *us*, dude. It can't be," Ryan said. His color, which had been steadily improving the longer he sat there, was now a queasy shade of green.

"Look at that other photo," Ellie said. "Go back a page…. There—the one taken during the speech. See anything interesting in the trees now?"

Aaron looked at the other photo and scanned the area above the people in the crowd. Just to the left of center, he spotted the small but unmistakable image of a person standing on the lowest branch of one of the distant trees. He leaned forward to examine the tiny figure, then looked up at her, his expression radiating delight.

"Wait! Is that...?"

Ellie tapped her chest again and smiled. "Uh-huh, *me!* I think it is."

Ryan pulled the book back in front of himself and examined the second picture, all the while wagging his head back and forth in disbelief.

For a moment, Aaron sat quietly, deep in thought. She could tell he was processing everything she had shown them, making connections, filling in gaps, drawing unlikely conclusions. Then he spoke again, his voice jittery with excitement.

"So what this all means is that's no 'VR shack' out there in the woods. That thing is actually...."

Knowing what was coming, Ryan groaned. "Don't say it, man!"

Ellie ignored him, nodding excitedly as she completed Aaron's thought. "A time machine. Yeah."

17

Ellie backed up and briefly related the events of the day before, how the photos in her book had seemed different from what she remembered seeing earlier in the week. She explained how, even though the faces of people in the picture with the Teolis were mostly turned away—and despite the idea being completely ridiculous—she'd been sure she was looking at a photo of the four of them from over a hundred years ago. A Google search for similar images had done nothing to clarify the situation, so she had made a last-minute trip to the library in a fruitless search for books with similar photos from different angles. Failing everywhere else, she had finally pulled the older edition of the *Bread and Roses* book off the shelf in the hope that it would prove she was simply misremembering the photo. Instead, it only confirmed her original recollection.

Ellie said nothing when Sam, to whom all of this was old news, grew bored and wandered down the slope to the water's edge. She sat on the low stone wall that surrounded the pond, gathered up a handful of small pebbles, and began tossing them one at a time onto the water's smooth surface. Ellie suspected Sam was still listening, even as she pretended to be wholly engrossed in the patterns of rings that slowly expanded across the pond's surface.

Ellie kept her eyes on her sister, but directed most of her awareness toward Aaron, listening intently as he voiced his theory on the matter at hand. They had moved beyond arguing over the shack's true nature with a speed that surprised her. The Sherlock Holmesian device of eliminating the impossible and accepting whatever was left, however improbable, had gotten them most of the way there. The contradictory sets of photos remained a sticking point, but they agreed to set that incongruity aside for now and had moved on to discussing the broader implications of the device.

"Look. What if those bombs that were designed, like, right here," Aaron said, pointing at the ground between his feet, "literally this spot where we're now sitting, hadn't worked. World War Two would have ended in some completely different way. It might have lasted *years* longer, at least in the Pacific. From our perspective, history would seem, I don't know… *broken?* Its path would have veered off in some totally divergent direction from what we know. Or might not have happened at all, at least not for us. What I'm saying is, depending on how much things changed, we might never have been born. Maybe that's sort of what we did, except instead of breaking history, we only *bent* it a little. There's this minuscule new curve in the road, and only the four of us can tell because we're the ones who made it. Because we were outside of the, ah, 'time stream,' I guess, when it happened." He paused a moment, and a new thought clouded his expression. When he spoke again, his tone was more somber. "You know, we could have seriously messed things up!"

He sees it! Ellie's thought, experiencing a profound sense of gratitude. Thinking about their close call felt like a physical blow to her gut. They had innocently played hopscotch in a minefield and gotten away with it due to nothing more than dumb luck. She felt herself tearing up, relieved Aaron didn't consider her idea to be crazy, and even more relieved that he had so quickly recognized how extremely dangerous that innocent-looking shack in the woods truly was. For a moment, her view of Sam and her circles on the pond dissolved into a shapeless blur.

Ellie blinked to clear her vision and returned her attention to Ryan. It struck her as odd that, of the four of them, he remained the least convinced.

"Okay, let's agree that this thing is really what we're saying it is," Ryan said. "Maybe we changed something, maybe we didn't. Nothing either of you has said explains the different pictures, though." He jabbed a finger at the books that were once again on the bench beside Ellie's thigh. "If what we did in that device made any actual difference, why aren't both photos the same, huh?"

Back to that already. It was the one question to which no one had even a guess, much less an answer, and Aaron could do no more than bow his head and shake it from side to side, a silent acknowledgment of his cluelessness.

Ellie knew Ryan was right. Either they went back in time and changed history, or they didn't—it was as simple as that. As impossible as it seemed, one photo suggested that was precisely what had happened. But there was also the other one. *Or two, I guess, if we count the one that may or may not be of me in the tree.*

She caught motion at the corner of her eye and shifted her gaze back to the pond as another pebble arced from Sam's hand and splashed into the water. She watched as a new set of rings began spreading slowly outward. She gasped, struck by a sudden idea. *Could it be that simple?*

"Ripples," she breathed.

Aaron and Ryan paused in their argument and stared at her.

"*Ripples!*" she repeated, louder this time and with real excitement in her voice. *Yes, that's it!* She pointed to where Sam sat by the water's edge, and they twisted around in their seats to look at her. "Sam!" she called. "Sam, come here!"

Sam turned her head to see her sister frantically waving her back to the picnic table. She rose and started toward them, brushing dust off her rump as she walked. Ellie waited until she was seated before sharing her idea.

"I think our trip to Lawrence created ripples, just like Sam throwing rocks into the pond. Except these are *time* ripples. They've reached 2012, but not 1987. *That's* why the books aren't the same!"

Aaron stared at her, his face scrunched in an expression of intense concentration. Sam and Ryan were likewise mulling her idea over.

"So, if I get it," Sam said at last, "you're saying that it takes time, well, *time* to change."

"That makes sense, right?" Ellie framed the thought as a question even though she was convinced her hunch was correct.

Aaron nodded slowly. "I like your idea of ripples," he said. "But why would they move from now toward the past? Wouldn't they move outward from the point of change? From where the rock hit the water, in other words. In this case, from 1912 forward? That's the part I'm stuck on. It seems sorta backward." He looked from Sam to Ellie and then to Ryan, but no one had a ready answer.

"I have no idea," Ellie said, her exuberance fading.

"I got nothin'," Ryan said.

An even longer pause followed while everyone pondered the apparent contradiction. Finally, Sam spoke, her voice soft, hesitant, as if calling up a fragmented file from a dusty and long-idle hard drive.

"Maybe it's like that 'quantum collapse' thing?"

Ellie was surprised—shocked, in fact—at a suggestion like this coming from, of all people, "I'm-not-a-nerd" Sam. She saw Aaron's expression go dim as he ingested this tidbit and mentally chewed on it.

Ryan looked at Sam, waiting for her to elaborate. She didn't.

"What do you mean?" he finally prodded.

"I don't know. I mean, we were in physics class last month, or two months ago—whatever—and Mr. Boltzmann was going on about this cat in a box... there was something about poison...."

"That was all the way back in *November*," Ryan said.

"...and we had just put Mr. Pib to sleep...."

"That was *definitely* November," Ellie said.

Sam raised her voice to indicate that she was more than willing to talk over any further interruptions. "...so I wasn't really listening, but I remember him saying that when you looked in the box, something collapsed, and...."

"The wave function. Yes!" The light behind Aaron's eyes was back to full wattage.

Sam shrugged. "Whatever. Like I said... Mr. Pib—not listening." She turned to glare at Ellie and Ryan. "And I'd do better without all the running commentary, thank you!"

"I think she's right," Aaron said. "He was talking about the famous thought experiment with what's-his-name's cat."

"Schrödinger," Ellie said, thinking of her nightshirt.

"No, that was what's-his-name," he said, too focused on his new theory to notice how bonkers that sounded. "Anyway, the basic idea is that if something can be one way, or it can be some opposite way," he explained, avoiding any upsetting references to cats, radioactive decay, and poison, "that until an 'observer,'" he hooked air quotes around the word, "checks to see which way it is—*collapses the wave function*, as he would have put it—it's *both*."

"In other words," Ellie said, "we help determine reality merely by witnessing it."

"That's *nuts!*" Sam said. She seemed deeply offended by the suggestion that the world could work that way, and it was clear to Ellie that she had tuned out during more than that one day of class.

"That's quantum physics," Ryan said, smiling broadly.

"What, you mean you *buy* that?"

"Okay, so not about the cat thing, necessarily, but with atoms and smaller particles, sure," Ryan said. "Remember, it all has to do with how the world works at the tiniest scale."

"Maybe the cat is not the best, ah, 'conceptual metaphor,'" Aaron said. "Think of it this way—when you flip a coin, it always lands as either heads or tails, right? But when it's up in the air, spinning around, it's neither heads nor tails. Or you could say it's both heads *and* tails, right up until the instant you catch it and 'make' it be one or the other. That's kind of it, anyway."

Sam waggled her head in a noncommittal gesture that suggested she was more comfortable with this way of looking at the idea, but she was still unwilling to concede that the world was fundamentally that strange. Ellie enjoyed a conversational foray into theoretical physics as much as the next card-carrying nerd, but now was not the time. She tried to get the discussion back on track.

"So you're saying that in this case, we," she made a circle in the air with her finger, looping them all together as a group, "played the part of the 'observer.'" She mimicked his air quotes gesture. "And that it's our knowledge of what happened—here, in this time—that's causing the changes?" Aaron nodded. "So *we* started the ripples traveling back through time!" She laughed. "That *does* sound nuts! But at the same time, it makes sense."

"Very Heisenberg of you, Grasshopper," Ryan said.

Sam remained unconvinced. "No, it *doesn't* make sense!" She glared at them, her arms folded tightly across her chest.

"Look," Aaron said, his tone low and calm. "We have no way of truly knowing what's going on here, let alone being able even to begin explaining it. We're just making guesses based on a couple of photos in a book. As it happens, I believe they are very good guesses."

"Besides, it was your idea, Sam," Ryan said.

"Yeah, well, I didn't even know what I was talking about." Her reply was sullen, but she relaxed a little.

Ellie clamped her jaw shut and struggled to keep her eyeballs firmly centered in their sockets. She awarded herself both an A-plus *and* a gold star for being such an excellent younger sister in the face of such irresistible temptation.

"There's still that other photo, though," Ryan said. "What does our theory say about it?"

"Look, I think it's…. Wait, hold on a sec." Ellie closed her eyes and tried to work through the problem in her head. She pictured Sam's ripples on the pond. The edge of a ripple moved outward at a steady pace, but the area of the circle it made got larger at a much faster rate. If they were dealing with a similar phenomenon, then the effect on time might also be geometric, not linear. She scrunched her eyes even more tightly closed as she concentrated on the math.

Okay, it's Sunday afternoon. We were there on Friday, and I noticed the first picture on Saturday morning. Six years in less than a day… twenty-five more years… so maybe, just maybe… Unless I am nuts!

She opened her eyes and, without explanation, brought up the 2012 edition and placed it on the table. She positioned the book in front of the other three and opened it to the photo of her talking to Carmela. Her hands shook as she reached for the second book, and she clenched and unclenched them several times, trying to steady them before she picked it up. She was convinced she knew what they would see when she opened it, but that certainty only added to her anxiety.

The others watched in attentive silence as she placed the 1987 edition beside the other book and fumbled it open. When she reached the correct page, her anticipation fizzled. The picture showed only the three members of the Teoli family, exactly as it had before. She had been so sure!

Sam looked up at Ellie to ask what they were supposed to be seeing, so she missed the change when it happened. It wasn't a slow fade, a gradual transition from one image to another. Instead, it occurred with a quick, almost audible snap that startled Aaron and Ryan so much that they both reflexively jerked away from the book. Sam looked back down, her unasked question dying in her throat. That split second confirmed both Ellie's wildest speculations and her deepest fears. The two pictures were now identical.

They decided to put their discussion on hold and get lunch. A few minutes later, arriving there by way of some mutual yet unspoken agreement, they were seated at a window table in Diamond Dee's, across the street from the park. Everyone had ordered a bagel sandwich, a bag of chips, and a drink. Nobody was eating.

"Okay," Ellie said, picking up the conversational thread. She was feeling more confident since they had seen the photo change. "Forget about the pictures and whatever they might mean for a minute. Look at it this way—when we assumed we were dealing with a VR simulator, we kept running into all kinds of things that didn't make sense. But assume, just for the sake of argument, that it really is what we think it is. Do that, and all those contradictions disappear."

"Contradictions," Ryan repeated. "Such as?"

"One—why all the batteries if it has power running to it? Because it only has that power when it's here. It needs to take power for the return trip back with it, hence the batteries. Two—why can't you set the year earlier than 1903? Because the further back you go, the more power the device requires, and the batteries only hold so much. We had roughly four hours in 1912. It might have been closer to an hour or two in 1903. Three—the clothes. You guys were right. Having to change clothes doesn't make any sense in a simulator, but it does if you're actually going somewhere.

"I mean, there are all *kinds* of things! Why hasn't my camera ever turned up? That alone should have been a big, huge, glowing neon sign! We saw it go into the canal and what? Just accepted that it was lost? No, it should have been in Aaron's pocket at the end of the 'simulation.' Somewhere inside the shack, certainly."

She paused and chomped loudly on a chip.

"And here's another thing, something even more basic. If you were going to hide something in plain sight somewhere around here, what would you make it look like? An old wooden shack, maybe? And if you were making something that could blend in at any time from today back to, I don't know, say 1903, to pick a random year, what would *that* look like?"

Aaron answered, nodding slowly. "An old… wooden… shack."

"*Ding-ding-ding!* In fact, you could beam that thing back to 1803, or even 1703, and, in the right setting, nobody would give it a second glance."

"But if it's that obvious now," Sam said, "why didn't we see it before?"

Ellie recalled approaching the shack at the end of their visit to Lawrence, how she had seemed to feel a kind of vague malevolence radiating from it. She decided to keep that thought to herself and limit her response to the evidence they had all experienced. "I think we did. At least subconsciously. We kept asking all the right questions."

"It's human nature," Aaron said. "You know the saying about when you hear hoofbeats expect to see horses, not zebras?"

Sam nodded. "It means to look for common answers, not exotic ones."

"Right. And you notice how it doesn't say a word about unicorns?"

Sam rolled her eyes. "Yeah, but—*duh!*—unicorns don't exist! Everybody knows that."

"Yes, and that's exactly why we didn't automatically think *time machine*. We know they don't exist."

"Didn't use to, anyway," Ellie said.

"I've gotta sit down," Ryan muttered.

"You are sitting," Aaron said. "And drink some of that soda," he added, trying to be helpful. "You look like you're going to keel over."

He did look bad, Ellie thought. After she opened the 1987 book and they saw the picture change, it was as if they'd had the collective wind knocked out of them. But for Ryan, it had been worse. Realizing how close he had been to death hit him hard.

"I thought I had just fake-died, you know, like in a video game. But, man,

I *died*-died. Like, for *real*." He groaned and managed to look even greener. "I gotta sit down."

Ellie and Aaron shared an amused glance. The humor in their expressions did not escape his notice.

"Oh, yeah, it's real funny!" His sudden outburst was loud in the small dining area, and for a moment they held the attention of everyone around them. When he continued, he spoke so quietly Ellie could barely hear him.

"When that guy hit me with his bat... for a split second.... You know? You can feel it when your heart stops beating." His chin dropped to his chest and he clutched at his shirt where the bat had struck him, the place directly over his heart. He sniffed back tears and spoke quietly through a tight throat. "I can still feel it just thinking about it."

Sam put her arm around him and rested her head on his shoulder, comforting him with her touch. He did not acknowledge her gesture, but neither did he pull away.

He wouldn't have let himself be consoled in public like that before. Not the 'manly' way. And Sam being so supportive today? Have we all been changed by what happened? She glanced at Aaron, who looked abashed in the face of Ryan's distress. *How are we changing?*

"Sorry," Aaron said, contrite. "I didn't get it, okay? I figured you're still here, so you must be fine. How's this... next time, I'll be the one to die, then you can make fun of me all you want. I promise I won't say a word about it."

Ryan coughed out a short laugh and wiped his eyes on his sleeve before looking up again. His color was finally starting to improve. "I'm going to hold you to that, *Hedwig*."

With Ryan starting to act more like his usual self, Ellie felt some of the tension of the past day and a half begin draining from her body. She crunched idly on a few more chips as she thought. They had some answers —guesses, to be honest—that they all mostly agreed on, but there were still many more questions.

"One point of correction," Aaron said. "The batteries power it both ways. They'd have to. As soon as the process starts—the what? The 'transition?' The...."

"I've been thinking of it as a *flip*," Ellie said.

"That works. But whatever you call it, at that point the connection would be lost. I guess you could use massive capacitors for the first jump, but charging them up right before leaving would impose a huge, very noticeable drain on the power grid."

Ellie scowled, irked with herself for having missed something so basic. "So either the power needed is less than you'd expect, or those batteries provide a *lot* of juice."

Aaron nodded and held up two fingers to say it was the second part he agreed with.

"Hold on," Sam said. "I still don't understand the part about how long you can be someplace. I can see why you can only go back so far, but why can't you stay there as long as you want?"

Ellie looked at Aaron and raised her eyebrows, asking if he wanted to field that one. He took a moment to consider Sam's question, then nodded to himself when he had the answer.

"Okay, let's pretend that when you drive somewhere, you can't turn your car off again until you're back home. A typical gasoline car, right? Not your mom's Focus. You get to the store, leave the car running while you go inside, and then you drive home, turn the car off and fill the tank back up. Got it?"

"Uh-huh...."

"Good. So, when your car is idling out there, it's barely using any gasoline, but it is using some."

Ellie could see where he was going with his analogy. "This is good!" she said, encouraging him. She would have gone the pure math route, but for Sam, this way was better. He smiled at her, then went on.

"So if you drove from your house to White Rock, which is maybe ten miles each way, you could get out and do a little shopping, have a long lunch —you could spend a few hours there and even with the car running the whole time, you'd still have plenty of gasoline in the tank when you got back home. But if you drove all the way to someplace like Santa Rosa, you'd barely have enough spare fuel to allow you to run into a convenience store and buy a soda. At the edge of the maximum range, just a few extra minutes of idling could mean not making it home. In this case, though, it'd be a lot worse than getting stranded alongside the road with an empty tank."

"So it's the power the shack needs to make the trip there and back, plus whatever it uses while it's just sitting there, and that's what determines how long you can stay. I get it!" Sam said, sounding pleased with herself.

"Plus a presumably generous margin of error," he added.

"But why not simply turn it off? You know, until it's time to come back?"

Aaron considered her question, then grimaced as the answer occurred to him. "My best guess is that if the computer lost track of even a single millisecond of elapsed time, you wouldn't make it back. Not all in one piece, anyway."

"Okay, hang on a second," Ryan said. "So, that thing out there is an actual..." He caught himself and looked around the café before continuing in a quieter voice. "...an actual *time machine,* and we can use it to go anywhere at any time we want?" Only moments before, he had seemed on the verge of passing out, but now he was acting like a kid who'd just been handed the keys to the ice cream truck. "This is incredible! We could... I don't know... go back to 1960 and watch the Yankees lose the World Series!"

"Wait," Sam said, confused. "You *like* the Yankees."

"Yeah, but what a game! And to see what this place was like in 1944? Can you imagine shaking Oppenheimer's hand? No, wait—forget Oppenheimer. Feynman! *He* would be the guy to meet. Like we could even get in, but *still!*"

Ellie was horrified by Ryan's enthusiasm. "No! Absolutely not! Haven't you been listening?! We were very lucky. I mean, aside from you, you know, with the bat and all." She gave him a smile that she hoped conveyed sympathy. "But ever since I began to suspect what really happened on Friday, I start feeling half sick every time I think about it. Maybe Aaron is right and we only bent time a little, but we could just as easily have been breakers instead of benders. We go back in time and end up in a photograph or two we were never supposed to be in. Let's hope that's all of it!"

"Well, at least five people already know Han shot first," Aaron said.

"And there's that," she said, and couldn't help but laugh at the quip. Then she turned to face him. "But seriously, you lost your camera—*my* camera, actually—in that canal. What would've happened if you had dropped it along the road, instead, and someone picked it up? How much of an impact might something even that simple have had on the future? On our *now.* Nobody ever did find it, obviously, or we'd all have flying cars and cybernetic implants by now. But the fact that we didn't come back to find ourselves in some messed-up world like that was only because we were very, *very* lucky!" She paused for breath and continued more calmly. "What I'm saying is that everything could have turned out much worse."

Everyone nodded somberly, then Ellie asked the question that still bothered her most. "Putting all the bad sci-fi stuff aside, the real question is...."

"I know," Aaron cut in. "Who built the shack, and what are they using it for?"

"'Enquiring minds want to know,'" Ryan said. But this time, the humor seemed forced.

Sam and Ryan began exchanging ideas on this topic, but Ellie didn't bother listening. Instead, she turned her attention to Aaron. Deep in thought, he absently pushed chips around his plate with the tip of a pickle spear. Her focus settled on the pickle, and she wondered what percentage of those things went directly from jar to plate to trash. She always forgot to say, *No pickle, please,* and always wound up pitching it at the end of the meal. Sooner, if it started oozing juice all over her plate.

She had been thinking about the shack for more than a day and was convinced it had to be—hands down, no competition at all—the most dangerous invention of all time. Aaron had reached a similar opinion only minutes after learning what it truly was. She wondered if, in his silent contemplation, he was already coming to the next logical conclusion.

When he finally became aware of her eyes on him, he looked up and met her gaze. Her mouth twisted into a grimace of regret and resignation, and she raised her brows in a silent question, wondering if they were truly sharing the same thought. She held her focus on his eyes until finally his shoulders slumped. He nodded slowly and sadly. She silently mouthed the words, *I know.*

Returning her focus to Sam and Ryan's discussion, she heard him tossing out the usual "go back and kill a young Hitler" scenarios that any discussion of time travel inevitably inspired. She sighed and waited for a break in the conversation. When Ryan finally paused for air, she spoke.

"Guys, I think we, uh...." The others looked at her expectantly, but suddenly she couldn't bring herself to finish the thought. She glanced at Aaron, hoping for some help. He nodded again, more firmly this time, but said nothing. She swallowed hard and tried again.

"We need to blow it up."

18

Seconds ticked by as Sam and Ryan, stunned into silence, gaped at her. Then they both started speaking at once.

"You can't run around blowing things...." she said.

"Are you *kidding?!* Blow up a thing like...." he said.

They both stopped in mid-sentence and looked at each other. Ryan swept his arm in an arc in front of him, an *after you* gesture. Sam opened her mouth to continue, but Ellie jumped in first.

"Okay, so not literally 'blow it up,' maybe, but we have to get rid of it. We have to make it be... not *there* anymore."

Sam gaped at her. "And precisely how are *we* supposed to accomplish *that?!*" she demanded.

Ryan waved a hand in the air, wanting to preempt Ellie's answer with a question of his own.

"No, wait a second!" he said. "*Why?* If that shack really is a," his eyes darted around the room again, and he lowered his voice, "you know, a 'gadget,' how can you even *suggest* destroying it?" He sounded genuinely curious but also more than a little outraged.

"Because it might just be the most dangerous 'gadget' ever made, that's why!" Ellie shot back. That he wasn't seeing something so obvious for himself was getting her worked up, too.

"That's ridiculous! How could it possibly be dangerous?"

"*Seriously?!*" She didn't get it. *He's seen all the movies, and they never end well,* she thought. *How could he not understand this?* She opened her mouth to grill him on that point when Aaron spoke.

"She's right." His calm, neutral tone caught everyone's attention. That tone said *I've done the math—twice—and, sorry, but that's the way it is.* They stared at him, waiting for him to elaborate. Ellie, breathing hard and struggling to regain her composure, was happy to let him take the lead. The waiting stretched on.

"Go on," Ryan finally said.

"It has to do with what Ellie said before. About the camera. If I had lost it anywhere other than in that canal, it would have messed up the future so badly that there's almost no way the four of us would be sitting here together like this today. Even if we were still subsequently born, the new world we would have created wouldn't look remotely like this one. Even the smallest events create ripples. Then those new ripples create ones of their own, and so on. Tossing a twenty-first-century device into the waters of the early twentieth century would make a *huge* splash. I can't imagine what we would have returned to after making that great a change, but I doubt it would have been as benign as flying cars."

They considered that for a minute, then Sam spoke.

"But who's to say it wouldn't be a *better* world?"

Finally trusting herself to respond calmly, Ellie waded back into the conversation. She pointed at her sister. "You. Me." She spread her arms wide to encompass everyone in the sandwich shop, Los Alamos, the world. "Them... everyone! This is *our* reality, for better or worse. Like it or hate it, we made this world what it is, and it's our right to be able to expect it to still be here tomorrow."

Ryan, too, was calmer but remained skeptical. "But we don't know what whoever made the shack intends to use it for," he said. "Maybe all they want is to study history. Or maybe there's some big, important, lost secret they're trying to recover. *I* don't know. But I guess that's my point—we just... don't... *know!*"

Ellie's frustration surged again. "That has nothing to do with it, Ryan!"

For a moment he silently frowned at her, stung by her brusque rebuke. "I can see I might as well keep my opinions to myself."

Ryan's defensiveness only made Ellie even more snappish. "It's not like that!"

His expression darkened and she immediately regretted sounding so sharp. She took a slow, deep breath, using the few seconds to calm herself. Under any other circumstances, she would've been perfectly content letting Ryan go on being mad at her, but this discussion was too important to allow emotions to get in the way of coming to a decision they could all accept.

"I'm sorry, Ryan. I am. I always want your opinions. *Especially* when you disagree with me. What I meant was that their reasons for building that thing have no bearing on how much of a threat it poses. They're entirely separate issues. Can't you see?" She stretched her arms out on the table in front of her and leaned toward him. She was pleading now, desperate to make him see the point he was missing. "Their intentions—good or bad—don't matter. It's only the *possibilities* that do, all the things that *could* happen, not what's *supposed* to happen. Neither you nor Apple 'intended' for you to wear your watch into the pool, but…." She shrugged. "Look—I'm not pretending I know any more about that device than you do, but I have had a little more time to think about it. There are so many things that could possibly go wrong and screw everything up that absolutely nothing, no matter how important, could be worth the risk."

Everyone remained silent as that idea sank in, and Ellie exhaled a quiet sigh of relief. At least they were now taking the time to consider her side of the issue.

"Look, guys," Aaron said. "In the abstract, that shack may be the coolest invention ever, but this is not a purely abstract debate." His voice was still calm and reasonable. "We know it works and that it's sitting out there, this very second, ready to go. True, we don't know who made it or what they made it for, but, as Ellie correctly points out, that's not what matters. Here's what does—how well will you sleep from now on knowing someone could use that shack, go back in time, and, without even meaning to, change things just enough so that Sam would no longer be here?"

Ryan blinked at him. He considered that for a moment, but to his credit, it was a very brief moment. Sam barely had enough time to turn her gaze up to his face before he answered.

"So—what do we need to do?"

The discussion that followed was brief and anticlimactic compared to the emotionally charged exchange of moments before. Neither Ellie nor Aaron had an answer to that seemingly simple question. In the end, everyone agreed to think about the problem in the days ahead and throw out for discussion any ideas as they occurred to them. Only Sam had one right away.

"Why don't we tell someone what we found and let *them* deal with it?"

"The minor matter of prison jumpsuit colors aside," Ryan muttered, much to her annoyance.

"I'm serious! We didn't create the mess—why should we have to clean it up?" She folded her arms across her chest and waited for an answer.

Aaron shook his head slowly as he thought about how to respond. Ellie instantly came up with several reasons, but she knew better than to be the one to shoot down Sam's suggestion. While waiting for him to answer, she noticed Ryan was again rubbing absently at the middle of his chest. He seemed to be elsewhere, lost in thoughts unconnected to the ongoing debate. He caught her watching him and let his hand drop to the tabletop. She offered him a comforting smile.

"It might eventually come to that," Aaron said at last. "We would have to be extremely careful in deciding who that would be, and once whoever that someone was started asking questions, we might find out the shack had quietly disappeared." He shook his head again. "We know the thing is there, but no one knows we know. For now, I think keeping this strictly to ourselves is the best way to go."

"Okay, fine. Whatever," Sam said, but her expression said she felt otherwise.

"Listen," Ellie said. "School doesn't wrap up for a few weeks, anyway. Let's get through that, and maybe by then we'll have thought of something. I don't like putting it off, but it's not like we can set everything else aside, especially since we don't have anything remotely like a plan. Does that make sense?"

"Works for me," Ryan said.

Sam hesitated, still looking displeased. At last she nodded.

"You and I should work together on the research end of things," Aaron said, singling out Ellie. "If there's anything more we can learn about it, we should try to do that. But yeah, for now, that plan sounds good."

An hour later, Ellie was filling a water glass at the refrigerator when Sam returned home and joined her in the kitchen. Ellie spoke to her over her shoulder.

"Hey! So, how'd I do today?"

"He's fine, thanks for asking."

Sam's tone was breezy, but the note of false cheer it carried made Ellie wary—Sam was upset. She finished filling her glass and turned around.

"'He' who? Ryan?"

"Yes, *Ryan!*" Now she sounded exasperated. Ellie braced herself for an outburst, but Sam merely went on in an even calmer tone as she edged past her and placed the uneaten portion of her lunch from the diner in the refrigerator. "Finding out what he went through on Friday actually happened really messed him up."

She closed the refrigerator door and strode back out of the kitchen. Ellie remembered seeing him rub his chest, the distant expression on his face, and she felt guilty all over again. "I'm sorry," she said, trailing Sam down the hall to their bedroom. "I was so worried about how I was going to convince them, I guess I didn't stop to consider how that part of it would affect him."

"But you never do, though, do you? Think about people's feelings?" Sam shot back, her underlying anger boiling to the surface. "It's all just facts and figures with you. You jump in with both feet.... No, not with 'both feet.' With your *big, giant brain*—straight to the logical heart of things, without ever considering how other people will be affected."

Ellie didn't know where to go with that. She felt sure Sam had meant 'giant brain' as some kind of put-down, but she couldn't work out the angles necessary to make that work. Sam opened the bottom drawer of her dresser and rifled through its contents. She pulled a shirt out from the middle of the stack, tossed it onto her bed, and roughly shoved the drawer closed.

Ellie shook her head. "Hey, why am *I* the bad guy here? You heard what Aaron said. He was thinking the same thing I was!" She believed it was a valid point, even if not entirely sure how it was a defense.

Sam pulled her top off over her head, tossed it into the laundry bin, then slid into its replacement. Finished changing, she snatched a jacket from a hook on the closet door and stormed out of the room. "Yeah, well, you two *are* quite the pair, aren't you?"

Now Ellie was totally confused. She called out to Sam, who was already striding noisily down the hallway.

"What do you mean by...." The solid slam of the front door cut off her question, and she was left muttering to the empty house. "...'quite the pair?'"

Ellie tried working on her paper but found it hard to concentrate after the angry, confusing conversation with her sister. Eventually, she gave up in favor of tackling a reading assignment for Spanish class. She had long ago discovered it was much harder obsessing over problems while trying to think in a language she could barely speak.

It was a long time before Sam came back. The bedroom lights were out and Ellie was lying on her side, facing the wall, when she heard the bedroom door open and then softly close.

"Hey," she said, just to let Sam know she wasn't yet asleep.

Sam sighed. "Hey."

Ellie felt the side of the mattress droop as Sam sat on the edge of her bed. She remained quiet, afraid of saying something to upset her once again. Then she felt the warmth of Sam's palm on her shoulder, and she rolled onto her back to look up at her.

"You were right," Ellie said. "And I *am* sorry."

"Yeah, I was right," Sam agreed. "But so were you."

"Huh?"

"I mean, yes, it should have been obvious how he would react, but I also know that even someone with your...."

"*Giant brain?*" Ellie prompted.

Sam snorted. "I was going to say 'intelligence,' but yeah, even with your giant brain, you can only be aware of so many things at once. You told me first thing this morning, and *I* didn't put it all together, either. Obviously! Not until we were all sitting there at lunch and he was starting to lose it. And besides, Ryan isn't your concern, is he? Not like he is mine, anyway."

"I think... I still don't get it. About him, I mean."

"After we left town and walked back up to his place, he broke down again. Like he did at lunch, but a lot worse. He started sobbing. Hard. He couldn't say a word, and it scared me. Well, not 'scared' me, exactly. That's not it, but I didn't know what to do. Feeling so useless while he felt so bad... I guess that was the scary thing. All I could do was hold him. We were on that old, squeaky glider they have out behind the house, and we rocked slowly back and forth until he calmed down."

Ellie scooted back to sit upright against the wall. Sam paused to dab at her eyes with the corner of the sheet, and after a moment, she sniffed and went on.

"After what seemed like forever, we went inside. He lay down on his bed, and I sat with him until he finally drifted off. So that's what happened right before I came home earlier. That's why I was so angry, but I was mostly upset with myself for being so—I don't know... *inept*, I guess—while trying to help Ryan, but I dealt with it by blaming you. I'm sorry, El."

Ellie pictured them on the glider, Sam holding Ryan's head against her shoulder as he cried. Now she thought she understood the earlier change of wardrobe. "I get it. No problem."

"Anyway, I just came from his house again. He texted me an hour after I left here this afternoon, so I went back over. He seems to be much better now. Maybe all he needed was to get something out of his system, I don't know. But he said, and I quote, *I assume you let Ellie have it when you got home, so tell her from me, 'we're still good.'* So—message delivered." She smiled.

Ellie smiled back. "He's a good guy."

Sam's gaze drifted up to the ceiling and she sniffed again. "Yes, he really, really is."

"And you?" Ellie said. "How are you?"

"I'm okay." Sam returned her attention to Ellie's face. "Better now than earlier, certainly. But—and I'm being totally sincere here—thanks for asking."

Ellie leaned forward and wrapped Sam in a tight hug, smiling when she felt her sister's arms enclose her waist. "I'm glad."

After a moment, Sam released her and they sat up straight.

"And as to your other question, I think you were brilliant." Ellie's eyebrows went up, questioning. "You asked how I thought you did. You did great."

"Thanks," she said, but found she no longer cared about that.

"And, so… now what?"

Ellie knew it was a perfectly reasonable question, but it was not one for which she had an answer. "I wish I knew."

19

For the next two weeks, to the extent such a thing was possible, they focused on getting through the end of the school year, all the while pretending a potential doomsday machine wasn't sitting in the woods a few short miles away. The shack was too much of a technological marvel to be ignored entirely, and Ellie and Aaron sometimes discussed it and its implications on the short shared portion of their walk home in the afternoon. He was curious in a general way about the science and mechanics of the device, of course, but he seemed oddly obsessed with one puzzle in particular. If they weren't there to create an interface with a virtual world, then what was the role of all those nerve induction studs?

Ellie, on the other hand, needed someone with whom she could share her nagging fear that they were all living on borrowed time. Every attempt she made to talk about it with Sam was flatly rebuffed, and she quickly gave up trying. Forcing the device out of her mind and concentrating strictly on her upcoming finals and end-of-the-year projects was the only way she could sleep at night. Ultimately, that meant no longer discussing it with Aaron, either.

The swim team made it into the state-wide NMAA Championships in Albuquerque but washed out in the first round. Ryan personally performed very well under the extra pressure, and he seemed unbothered by his team's early disqualification. But Sam, who had been looking forward to spending more time in New Mexico's closest thing to a big city, had a more difficult time letting go of her disappointment, even days after returning home. While sitting at the table in the back yard one sunny Tuesday afternoon, she continued to rail against the injustice of it all.

"Two-hundredths of a second! I swear—if that Billy Peterson comes anywhere near me, he's gonna wind up needing a smaller Speedo!"

"You know," Ryan said, "maybe we could go back in time and…."

"Oh, shut up!" she said, and stormed off. He looked at Ellie, and they both shrugged—*What can you do?*

For Sam, the school year drew to a close without any other major letdowns. Of the four of them, she seemed to have the least trouble setting aside their recent experience and settling back into her usual routine. Suddenly determined to end her high school career on a high note, she spent an uncharacteristic amount of time isolated in their parents' small office or sitting cross-legged on her bed, surrounded by books. Occasionally, Ryan hung out in their room while Sam and Ellie studied.

"This school is seriously screwy," Sam observed one day. "On what planet does Newton's *Opticks* belong in an English Lit class?"

"In what other school do you have to be able to explain the physics of buoyancy before they'll let you join the swim team?" he pointed out. "But it is LA High, after all. I'm just glad I didn't try out for baseball! Don't get me wrong—I love the game, but have you ever seen a formula for the aerodynamics of an irregular spheroid?"

"*Out!*" she said. "Go! I need to finish this paper. Don't you have studying to do?!"

Ellie, trying hard to focus on her own studies, did her best to tune them out. She knew Ryan would have to receive some abysmally low marks for his year-end grades to have any impact on his GPA. He had already done well enough—both academically and on the swim team—to earn a partial scholarship to the university, and he wasn't feeling particularly motivated to spend time hunched over books. She looked up at him as he rose from the edge of Sam's bed. He smiled and gave her a wink as he headed out the door.

In the end, Sam did even better on her finals than she expected. Ellie wondered at her sister's new nose-to-the-grindstone attitude, but was privately pleased. *Maybe she's gained a new appreciation for the importance of knowledge.*

Aaron spent nearly every afternoon and evening alone at home, using that time to start from scratch on an entirely new Science Fair project. Unfortunately, the judges thought his presentation, *Practical Limits to Retrograde Time Travel*, was more science-fiction than legitimate science, and he didn't finish anywhere near the top three spots. Ellie was immensely relieved—she thought his project had carelessly risked drawing unwanted attention to their illicit adventure. Even so, she could not help but be amused by the fact that the judges had so perfunctorily dismissed a project that was not only entirely accurate, but one of just a few based on first-hand, real-world experience. It wasn't the first time she had questioned teachers as the ultimate source of wisdom, even teachers such as these.

"Sorry, buddy," Ryan said after the ribbons had been awarded. "I guess that was your last chance to be the first one to have his name on the plaque twice."

"Thanks. But the more I think about it, the more I think we dodged a bullet. That was kinda dumb."

Ellie couldn't have agreed more. "Being smart is one thing. Being wise? *Priceless!*"

The school year ended a week earlier for seniors than for underclassmen, and this arrangement gave Ellie a foretaste of the coming year when she would be making the daily walks to and from school alone. Unless Sam signed up for an early class or two, that is, which Ellie very much hoped she would. Since Sam had started spending more and more time with Ryan over the past few years, Ellie had grown to cherish the limited amount of "together time" the short walks afforded them.

Finally, all the studying and tests were over, and Ellie finished the year with her 4.0-grade point average intact. The pleasure this brought her went beyond an enormous sense of self-satisfaction. Thanks to a long-standing deal both she and Sam had with their parents, the accomplishment also relieved her of the obligation of finding a summer job just when having free time was more important than ever.

Her paper on the millworker strike earned her a grade of 100%, which, to her surprise, pleased her more than any other achievement of the year. Following their Lawrence excursion, she had worked into her paper as many of her impressions of the city and its people as she could. Having moved among the very people about whom she was writing, she discovered it was now very easy to express the emotional depth and sense of empathy her earlier draft had lacked.

The Power of One—Carmela Teoli's Impact on U.S. Labor Laws
L. E. Henderson

Every morning you wake before dawn, leave your pale yellow home, and trudge the same rutted path to the giant, red brick mill. You pass beneath towering oak and maple trees that shade the yards and houses of your fellow workers who join you along your daily route. The leaves are deep green in the summer, turn brilliant orange and red in the fall. But if the sky is a perfect, cloudless blue, or a shopkeeper's hat an especially jaunty shade of green, you do not notice. Your life is dominated by gray. It's the color of the faded, over-washed, over-mended clothes you wear. It's the color of your morning porridge, the color of your beans at night. It's the color of your mother's hair, a woman who is not quite forty. Coal-gray clouds pour from the mills' towering smokestacks to settle as soot on everything in town. You are only fourteen, but already it is the color of your hopes, your dreams, of any future you dare to imagine….

Her teacher had been impressed not only by her meticulous research into the facts of the strike, but also by her uncanny ability to evoke a sense of life at the time. The notes she penned on the essay's title page practically gushed—

I have been teaching for eighteen years, and I do not say this lightly—yours is one of the finest papers I have ever had the pleasure to read. Your descriptions of Lawrence, the mills, and the people who worked there are intensely intimate and evocative. I could almost taste the tart tang of coal smoke in the air and hear accented conversations all around me. When I finished your account of the final vote at Lawrence Common, I felt as if I had personally met Carmela and her family. It's hard to imagine how you, living in a small town on a high-desert mesa, could so deftly convey the gritty feel of an East Coast industrial city from another century—and with such abundant and realistic detail—but you did it splendidly! — Best wishes, Anna-Marie Comnena

The note brought a wry smile to Ellie's face. *I guess you just had to be there!*

After Ellie completed her last final, they all biked into town for celebratory gelatos at Danny's. They sat in the shade of a locust tree beside Trinity Drive, silently savoring their treats. Everyone had the same thought, and no one wanted to be the first to bring it up. At last, Ryan spoke, his sardonic tone capturing the mood perfectly.

"My, aren't we festive."

"Yeah, well...." Aaron said.

"I know," Ellie said. "We can't avoid it any longer. Time to come up with a plan."

"Seriously," Sam said. "Do we *have* to?"

Ellie looked at Ryan, letting him be the one to answer.

"Yeah, we do," he said, "I still think Ellie's right."

"And *I* still say we plop the whole thing in someone else's lap and let *them* deal with it!"

Believing at least that much had already been settled, Ellie was surprised by Sam's petulant attitude. She responded as patiently as she could. "We've been through this. Once people realized how much we know about that thing, we'd be hauled off somewhere—and probably our parents, too—while they hid it somewhere else, someplace we'd never find it again. And if we did go public, what are we going to say? 'Hey, everybody, we thought you should know there's a time machine hidden in the middle of the woods!' They'd call us wackos and, again, the shack would disappear. Whatever we do, we have to do it without letting anyone know we know about it. Got it?"

Sam still wasn't mollified, but she gave up resisting. "Yeah. Got it."

"As far as the 'whatever' is," Ryan said, "you'll have to start working on that without me. At least for a while."

"Oh? And why's that?" Aaron said.

"Because *Mister Collins* is going to be visiting the motherland for the next two weeks, that's why," Sam said.

Ellie raised her eyebrows at Ryan.

"She means my dad's taking us to Ireland. *Surprise!* We leave a few days after graduation."

This information cast her sister's foul mood in a different light. As she had for the past few years, Sam had taken a job at the aquatic center where Ryan continued to train over the summer while the high school pool was inaccessible. It meant that they could spend that much additional time near each other, even if they weren't technically "together." Now he was taking off for a few weeks of fun, and she was stuck at home working a job missing its primary perk.

"I thought your family was English," Ellie said.

"My grandfather came over from England in the fifties, yeah, did the whole 'Ellis Island' thing. But *his* grandfather was born and raised in County Wexford, Ireland, like all the Collinses before him. Family legend says that after he turned twenty, he woke up one day and said, 'I'm outta here!' He jumped on a boat to Bristol, got a job on the docks, and married the first Hore he met."

The climax of his story was met by three bewildered looks.

"That was his intended's last name. H-o-r-e? I guess it's funnier if you know that part up front." He flapped a hand dismissively. "Forget it."

"You said 'us'—are your sisters going, too?" Aaron said.

"They're going to fly out of JFK and meet us in Dublin."

"Ireland," Ellie said, bemused. "How did I not know this?"

"It's true. Speaking of, you know JFK's family was from Wexford. They have cows there. And sheep. And, from what I've heard, strawberries to die for." This short list of facts seemed to exhaust his knowledge of County Wexford. "I'm looking forward to it," he said, sounding the opposite of enthused. "Really."

"He's just pretending to hate the idea to make me feel better," Sam said.

"That and I promised to bring her back a leprechaun." Ryan gave Sam a wink.

"You said a pot of gold!" Sam's mood was finally beginning to perk up.

"Point is," Ryan said, "that you guys will have to do the first part of this on your own. I'll be too busy to give it much serious thought."

"What with the sheep and all," Aaron said.

Ryan snorted. "Good one!" He winked and fired a finger pistol at him.

Ellie wondered at Aaron's witty response. *That actually* was *a good one.* Suddenly Ryan was Irish. Now there's this wise-cracking Aaron. All at once, she felt like she didn't know her friends as well as she had always thought. What surprises was her sister keeping under wraps?

As if on cue, Sam sighed. "I don't know what help I could possibly be, but whatever you think I can do, let me know. I don't like any of this, but I'll do whatever I can."

Well, there's that!

20

W hile Ryan was away discovering his roots, Ellie and Aaron got together every few days to brainstorm about ways of getting rid of the device they continued to refer to simply as "the shack." The name stuck partly because a shack was precisely what it appeared to be, but mostly because everyone felt too ridiculous calling it the "time machine." Between sessions, they continued to work separately, attempting by whatever means they could devise to learn who was responsible for its creation.

Hacking into the computers at any of the research facilities was all but impossible, and getting onto one of the internal LAB networks specifically? That was like "nuclear rocket surgery," as Aaron put it. Merely trying was risky, and they made any such direct attempts at cyber-intrusion from the library, from public computers at cafés, or by sneaking into hotel business centers. Otherwise, most of their time online was spent at home poring over every published article, press release, or interview they could find from the past five years that might hold a clue to the shack's origin.

They concluded early on that destroying the shack would do nothing more than remove the threat it presented for only the exact amount of time it took to build a new one. They needed an altogether different approach, ideally one that ensured it never got made in the first place. She had no idea what such a plan might look like, and she spent many sleepless hours staring up at the shadows on her ceiling while pondering how, from a conceptual standpoint, they might set about accomplishing such a thing.

Aaron eventually thought to go back to the website of the company that made the shack's palm scanner. He hoped that if they could find a client list, they might discover a connection to one of the research facilities at the LAB, and narrowing down who might have built the thing would give them a better sense of where to look. Using his previous approach, he found the site map and linked from there to a lengthy list of companies and institutions to which the firm had sold products. It was merely an alphabetical list of names without context, nothing to indicate a time frame or what items had been purchased. This left them with no alternative but to Google each entry one by one to see if it had any presence in Los Alamos.

Following two days of tedious research that had yielded zero connections, Ellie was deeply irritated by their lack of progress. "So… what? You think they *stole* it?"

He shrugged. "Got ahold of it second-hand, repurposed it from another project somewhere else, bought it under a fake name or through a shell company…. There are lots of possibilities."

In her current mood, she refused to give them any benefit of the doubt. "I bet they stole it," she grumbled.

Their efforts continued to go unrewarded, and Ellie grew ever more frustrated. Although they worked hard, there simply weren't many avenues of investigation open to two high school students armed with nothing more than MacBooks and endless determination. *Well, one ex-high school student,* she amended. Ellie kept at it despite the steadily rising sense of futility, regularly checking in with Aaron to see if he was faring any better.

As they cleaned up after breakfast one morning, Sam suggested a trip to Santa Fe. Ellie, her brain numb from banging her head against a wall day after day, jumped at the offer. She texted Aaron to let him know she planned to be gone for the day.

Ellie—I'm going into town with Sam. That cool?

Aaron—Cool as 🔫 Got a family thing today

Ellie—Thx for not sending me an eggplant

Aaron—Cool as an eggplant? That doesn't make any sense

Ellie—😼 Later!

In less than an hour, Sam was trying to squeeze their mom's electric Focus into a tight parking spot along Alameda Street near its intersection with Palace. She was reluctant to get any closer to the plaza—too many lost, confused tourists clogging up the narrow streets and alleys. Plus, parking here meant they could finish their outing at The Teahouse and have a short final walk back to the car.

"Are you sure we don't have to charge it up before we head home?" Ellie said, opening her door. She stepped out onto a sidewalk that was tinted a muted pink.

"Yep. We should pull into the driveway with more than thirty miles to spare. Got your bag?"

Ellie raised the small, sling-style bag she clutched in her hand. "Got it." She slipped the strap over her shoulder. "So, where to first?"

Ellie heard the click of the locks, then Sam closed her door.

"If we want to eat at Pasqual's, we should get a reservation there before we do anything else. After that, I'm up for whatever. Mostly I just needed to get off the island for a while. And to spend time with my *favorite* sister, of course!"

It was an old joke and one that went both ways. Ellie blew a wet raspberry at her. "*Thppt! Funny, only* sister. Let's go."

As they walked toward Santa Fe's historic plaza, they were grateful for the cool shade cast by the enormous cottonwood trees that lined their route. Ellie glimpsed patches of the cloudless, early-summer sky through gaps in the dark green canopy, and all around them rose the smooth, organic shapes of terracotta-colored adobe houses. A light, floral scent permeated the air, but she failed to identify its source.

She thought about how bleak Lawrence Common had looked the day they were there. *Yes! Actually were there!* She felt a chill run down her spine. It was still hard to believe they had truly stood in the heart of Lawrence, Massachusetts, more than a hundred years ago. She thought she knew how

Neil Armstrong must have felt. Then again, he merely walked on the moon!

As if reading her mind, Sam asked, "Have you and Aaron had any luck coming up with ideas about the shack? I don't feel like I've been any help."

"There's nothing to help with, at least not yet. We're trying, but it's not like you type 'secret Los Alamos time machine project' into Google, and it all pops right up! Well, I have no idea about that, actually. We've been too worried about drawing attention to our snooping around to try anything that direct. We've been poking at every little reference we can find, but it's like looking at each individual part of a car," she flapped her hand at the line of vehicles parked along the curb, "and trying to imagine what the thing looks like all put together. The best lead we've come up with so far is one word—*Backspace*."

"Backspace? That somehow refers to the shack?"

"We found a TV interview online, and this guy—the Projects Director or something—was discussing projects at the LAB and how they get their names. Part of some PR puff piece from a few years ago. Anyway, he starts rattling a bunch of them off, but when he says 'Backspace,' he gets this look on his face like, 'I shouldn't have said that,' and then he recovers and says something along the lines of, 'yep, just like on your keyboard,' lists a few more names, then changes the subject."

"'Backspace?' *Hmm....*"

"Exactly. If that *is* the name of the shack project—and we're not totally sure that it is—that kind of worries us. Why do you use the backspace key? To go back and change something, maybe? Do a little of the old cut and paste?"

"I have an idea," Sam chirped. "Let's talk about—oh, I don't know —*anything* else for the rest of the afternoon."

"Agreed. That's mostly why I came along. To get away from it all for a while." Ellie was quiet for a moment. "Have you heard from Ryan?"

"Twice. I gather the Collins homestead is pretty far out in the sticks, so he can only get an internet connection when they go into town. He seems to be having a good time, though. Loves the strawberries, he says. He's said that several times, actually."

"And the sheep?"

Sam laughed. "He's mum on the sheep."

At Café Pasqual's, they were told they couldn't get a table until two o'clock, leaving them with several hours to kill.

"Want to check out the bookstore?" Ellie said. "It's close."

Sam shuddered. "*Ugh!* Too soon."

"They do have fiction there, you know. Even coloring books." Sam showed Ellie her tongue. "Okay, then," Ellie said, and gave Sam a mischievous smile. "How about the history museum? Wanna take a little step back in time?"

"How about *you*...."

But Ellie cut her off. "Wait, I know—*Maya!*"

Sam beamed at her. "And *that's* why you're my favorite sister."

Starting with Maya, a clothing and jewelry boutique only a block from Pasqual's, they spent the next three hours meandering from shop to gallery to boutique, gradually nibbling away at the time remaining before lunch. They wandered slowly past the jewelry stalls lined up under the colonnade that fronted the Palace of the Governors. Sam took the time to examine a few pieces, including a tooled leather cuff she thought Ryan might like, but she left empty-handed.

As they crossed the plaza for what felt like the tenth time, Ellie's stomach rumbled loudly. "I'm ready to give up on Pasqual's and try our luck at The Shed."

Sam glanced at her phone. "It's almost time. Let's go see if we can get in a little early."

Back at Pasqual's, they were told they'd have to wait fifteen more minutes. Ellie's stomach growled again as if making sure she had gotten the message.

Sam pointed across the street. "Let's go in there."

"I *love* Doodlet's! I wonder if they still have *The Cookie Sutra.*"

"I almost got you that for your birthday, you know. Thought you and Aaron might put it to good use."

Ellie snorted. "Yeah, right!"

Once inside the store, they quickly became engrossed in browsing through everything from its offering of retro toys to the Mac and Cheesus Divine Pasta Mix. They were stealing a peek at the book called *The Cookie*

Sutra when Sam noticed they were almost late for their reservation. Moments later, they stepped back out into the sunshine. Ellie dropped a small, gift-wrapped item into her sling bag as they started across the alley.

"I'm still trying to picture exactly how that one position would even work with actual, you know, non-gingerbread people," she said.

"Page fifty-six?"

"That one, too, now that you mention it."

Sam gave Ellie an impish smile. "You really wanna know?"

"Nope! Let's let that be a surprise." Ellie hastened to change the subject, if not by much. "Did you see they had cookie cutters, too?"

"What? You mean, like, in the *book?*"

"Yeah!" Ellie said.

"*That* would certainly perk up Santa's night!"

They were still laughing as they followed the host up a short flight of stairs to a small, round table at the edge of the raised section of the room. Their seats offered them an excellent view of the famous restaurant's decoratively tiled, art-filled dining area, but made Ellie feel a little on display herself. Even so, she felt more relaxed than she had at any time since school ended.

"Thanks for asking me to come along. I needed this like... *yeah!*"

"I've been watching you and Aaron ever since Ryan left. I figured this would be more helpful than anything else I could do. Besides, he had that family thing."

"Wait, you knew about that? How long have you been planning this 'spontaneous' trip?"

"Only since yesterday."

"Well, thank you," she said again. "I appreciate it. It's been very frustrating recently."

The waiter came, and they both ordered iced tea and a bowl of tortilla chips with salsa to share.

"Know what you want?" Ellie said.

"I want what I always want. The Green Chile BLT. *So* good!"

"I'm getting the enchiladas."

The waiter returned with their drinks, then left again with their order.

"Speaking entirely hypothetically here," Ellie said, "if you could go back to any time, any place, where would you go? Someplace glamorous, I assume?"

"Before Lawrence, I might have said something like that. Paris or Vienna in the 1860s, maybe. Or New York in the 1920s, check out the whole 'flapper' thing. If I went back to that period now, I would probably go to Tennessee to see the Nineteenth Amendment become law. Or go back to San Francisco in the late sixties."

"What, you mean, like, the Summer of Love? Flower power, 'turn on, tune in, drop out?'"

"Tens of thousands of people, not much older than us, came from all over to say, 'We're done doing things your way.' They were rejecting the rigidity of the past while being open to exploring *all* the possibilities of the future. And yeah, for some, drugs like LSD were part of that. But mostly, that was the beginning of the time when the younger generation began to matter, even dominate in some ways. Mostly in music back then, but in other ways, too, like the war protests. I think it'd be really cool to see that."

"Wow, that's...." Ellie shook her head, impressed by the seriousness of Sam's choices.

"Not that I wouldn't still be on the lookout for some cute shoes! How about you?"

"I've thought about it, but I don't know. There are so many possibilities. Florence during the Renaissance? I'd love to get a peek into Da Vinci's notebooks, or watch Michelangelo chip away everything that didn't look like David from a block of marble. Or maybe I would stand at Plymouth Rock in 1620 holding up a big sign that said, 'Pilgrims Go Home!'"

"Wouldn't that violate the 'Prime Directive' or something?"

"Yep, and that's exactly why we gotta do what we gotta do—it's *way* too tempting."

They were silent for a while, and when Ellie spoke again, she sounded more serious.

"I need to ask you something. Have you noticed anything unusual since our little adventure?"

"Like what?"

"Like...." She leaned across the table and whispered just loudly enough for Sam to hear. "My period should have started last week. It didn't."

Sam considered this. "Are you and Aaron... you know?"

"No." Ellie's tone was flat and matter-of-fact. Then, belatedly registering the question's implications, she repeated her answer more emphatically. "*No!*"

Sam raised her hands in a defensive gesture. "I was merely asking, not judging."

"What about you?"

"Me and Ryan?" She smiled enigmatically. "What do you think?"

Ellie once again felt a ghostly echo of Ryan's hands sliding down her hips, but this time she managed to suppress a shudder. "I think I don't want to think about it. Anyway, that's not what I meant."

"Oh. *Ha!* Well, I won't be able to tell you *that* until after this weekend. Are you worried?"

"No, not really. I mean, kinda, yeah, but not in *that* way. It just makes me wonder what that thing did to us when we were hooked up to it. Ryan should have had a massive bruise on his chest, but after we got back you could barely tell he'd even been hit. It didn't even hurt much. The flip itself must be incredibly stressful on the body. Maybe those chairs are made to monitor people and make some kinds of adjustments, look for infections, or even repair some types of injuries. Maybe we were vaccinated against certain diseases somewhere along the way." She paused and considered that last idea. *Vaccines take time to start working, though, don't they? How long does the process take?*

"Hold on," Sam said, her eyes widening with sudden realization. "My feet!"

"What about your feet?"

"In Lawrence, when we got back to the shack and were changing out of the old clothes, I pulled off the stockings and saw that my feet were all red and sore. I remember hoping that they wouldn't be covered in blisters later. I didn't say anything right then because it was nothing compared to Ryan's situation, and I was totally focused on helping him. But that night, when I was getting ready for bed, I noticed they looked fine. I figured that the redness I had seen earlier had been part of the simulation, but now.... Are you saying it somehow healed my feet?"

Ellie added this ability to mess with their bodies to her list of things she hated about the shack. She decided she didn't want to discuss that any longer and changed the subject.

"How's Ryan doing, by the way, regarding...." She trailed off, not sure how to finish the question.

Sam fixed Ellie with a hard stare. "What? You mean regarding having been *dead?*"

Ellie dropped her gaze to the table. "Regarding that, yeah," she mumbled.

"He says he's okay, but I also know he still has bad dreams about what happened. Sometimes I'll wake up and find he texted me at two or three. If I hear my phone buzz, I'll text him right back and we'll talk. He doesn't bring it up during the day, though. He says he just doesn't think about it, but I think he thinks really hard about not thinking about it. Know what I mean?"

"Yeah. It's okay if you want to leave your ringer on at night. I won't get mad if he wakes me up."

At that moment their lunches arrived, and they put their conversation on pause while the waiter set their plates before them. Then they waited some more for him to top off their glasses with more tea. They gave him appreciative *thank you* smiles, and he went away again.

Sam responded as she set to work carefully removing the long, wooden skewer that held the four sections of her sandwich together. "Thanks, but like I said, I haven't heard much from him since he got to Ireland. I don't know if he's still having the dreams or not. Guess I'll find out in another week."

"I was surprised when Aaron asked if his sisters were going on the trip. I always forget he even has sisters. He never mentions them."

"The younger of the two, Claire, is six years older than he is. She started college back east right before he and his dad moved out here. The other was already two years in. He was still in middle school. He says they seem more like aunts than sisters." Sam shrugged as if to ask *what more is there to say?*

"I dunno.... Seems strange to me. What about his mom—does he talk to her much?"

"I know they talk, but I don't know how often. He gets how she couldn't take yet another move after following his dad all over the place back when he was in the Corps—especially out here to the middle of nowhere—but there's some resentment there, too. That he's only gone back to visit twice since he's lived here says a lot about that." Sam shrugged again. "I dunno. He doesn't talk about that kind of thing much."

After that, they concentrated on their lunches. Sam, delighting in her BLT, occasionally let out a moan so borderline erotic that Ellie glanced around at the tables beside and below them, afraid they might be attracting attention. Reminded of one of Sam's favorite movies, she kept expecting someone to call the waiter over and tell him, "I'll have what she's having."

"Did you enjoy your sandwich?" Ellie asked, her tone dry.

"*So* good!" Sam mumbled around the last bite.

"I remember you saying that," she said, just as dryly.

Sam paid the bill, and afterward they stood outside the restaurant debating what to do next. "Mom gave me a list of things to pick up at Whole Foods. That's the only thing we definitely *have* to do. Otherwise, I'm open to anything."

"I like the usual plan," Ellie said. "Let's walk back on Canyon, peek inside a couple of galleries along the way, then get coffee at The Teahouse."

"And pastry!"

"Only if you promise not to have another foodgasm. Seriously—it's embarrassing!"

Sam bumped her shoulder against Ellie's as they started down the sidewalk toward Canyon Road. "Poor baby. Come on. I promise—no more embarrassing Little Sister. Besides, I bet you feel the exact same way when you see some… undifferentiated polynumerator or something," she teased.

Ellie laughed. "That's not even a thing! And, hey—I'm no more of a nerd than you are."

"Says the girl who can recite pi to twenty-five decimal places."

"Twenty-eight," Ellie corrected absently. "*You* alphabetize your side of the closet by label!"

"That's not nerdiness. That's just being organized."

"That's OCD is what that is."

"Which is still not nerdiness," Sam insisted. "*Nerd!*"

"*Food slut!*"

They both laughed. Ellie sighed and, still smiling, wrapped her arm around her sister's waist. "I love you."

Sam returned the gesture and tilted her head until it touched Ellie's. "I love you, too."

After dinner at home that evening, Ellie threw her sling bag over her shoulder and biked across town to the neighborhood behind the university where Aaron lived. He was already outside when she arrived, and she joined him where he sat on the curb in front of his house.

"How'd it go in Santa Fe?"

"I had a lot of fun! Don't tell her I said this, but I have a pretty great sister. How about you with your mysterious 'family thing?'"

"Not that mysterious. The parental units want to do a trip. All of us. We were deciding where to go. And when I say 'deciding,' I mean they were letting me know."

"And?"

"Montana," he said. "Glacier."

"Why there?"

"It's Dad's thing. He wants to collect the whole set."

"Of...?"

"National Parks. At least the major ones. I know—it's dorky. He could at least choose one in Hawaii while I'm still living at home."

"No, what you mean is at least he didn't pick Bandelier," she corrected. "That's what, twenty miles away?" She laughed.

"If you take the long way," he agreed. "That one's not what you'd call 'major,' though."

"I thought that your dad and the great outdoors don't really get along."

"You are not wrong," he said. "We're staying in the lodge by Lake McDonald, though, so it's remotely possible we'll all make it back in one piece."

"Oh, wait!" she said, suddenly remembering the item in her bag. She pulled the small, wrapped package from Doodlet's out and handed it to him.

"What's this?"

"You open it, and then you find out. That's how presents work."

"Yeah... no." He used his fingernail to slice through the tape, then began meticulously unfolding the paper from around the box. "I guess I meant, *why's* this?"

"No reason. Just thought you'd like it, that's all."

Aaron opened the box and slid the contents out onto his palm. He found he was holding five carved objects crudely rendered in some pale species of wood—a man in a hat, two animals, what might have been a giant water lily, and a boat. He looked at her and waited silently for an explanation.

"It's a logic puzzle. The little farmer guy there has to use his boat to get the sheep, the cabbage—that thing's a cabbage—and the wolf across a river, but he can only take one at a time. If he leaves the cabbage and the sheep behind and takes the wolf, the sheep will eat the cabbage while he's gone, and so on. You get it. You have to figure out how to get all of them across the river without anyone losing any bits."

"I see." He considered this. "And why, exactly, does a farmer have a wolf?"

She looked down at the little wooden game pieces cupped in his hand. "You know? I wondered the same thing."

Back at home, Ellie sat with Sam on the couch, preparing to watch a movie. With Ryan away, Sam was missing not only him but their usual routine, and she was delighted that Ellie had agreed to join her.

"You can choose," Sam said.

"Anything but *When Harry Met Sally* is okay by me."

Sam laughed. "Likewise *Looper, 12 Monkeys,* or any of the *Terminator* movies."

Knowing Sam was infinitely more familiar with their current options, Ellie left the choice up to her. "Tell you what—you pick something, and I'll go make us some popcorn."

"Deal!"

They spent the remainder of the evening laughing together as scenes from *The Princess Bride* flickered across the screen.

21

Ellie was already seated at the kitchen table behind a bowl of yogurt topped with sliced strawberries when Sam came down the hall to join her at breakfast. She watched her open a cabinet door and weigh her cereal options. "The new granola is pretty good, but stay away from that muesli—tastes like sawdust. And not in a good way."

Sam twisted to look over her shoulder and cocked an eyebrow. "I won't ask how you would know, but I'll take your word for it." She opted for the granola and took a bowl from a neighboring cabinet. Once she had filled her dish and thoroughly drowned its contents, she took a seat opposite Ellie.

Ellie almost asked *want some cereal to go with that bowl of milk?* but that one had gotten old, even to her. Instead, she asked the question that had been nagging at her since the previous evening. "You and Ryan have spent more time with him than I have—what's up with Aaron and his family?"

Sam swallowed. "What do you mean?"

"To put it in movie terms, it's like the casting director was drunk when he put that bunch together. Aaron is so fair, and his dad is so... whatever the opposite of fair is. If you ran into them along the street somewhere, you'd never guess they were related." After a moment's pause, she added, "Well, his mom and dad aren't, of course, but he doesn't look very much like either of them."

"Really? I think he looks a lot like his mom. You know, except for the hair. But I think maybe she darkens hers."

Ellie considered this. She closed her eyes and tried to picture their faces side by side. "The eyes, I guess, and his mouth a little. But line the two of us up beside Mom, and we look like triplets."

"Yeah, well, some parents have all the luck!" Sam chuckled at her quip. "Why all these questions about Aaron?"

"It was only *one!* Anyway, I was just curious. Last night, I went to his house to give him the puzzle from Doodlet's. We sat out front on the curb for a while, and when we got up, I saw his dad standing at the living room window like he'd been spying on us. He stood there staring at me for a second, then turned and walked off. Didn't smile, wave, or anything. Kind of gave me the creeps. I didn't say anything to Aaron, though."

"I haven't been around Jeremy more than a handful of times, but yeah, he does give off an edgy vibe," Sam agreed. "He always struck me as being very… what's the word… smug? *Condescending*—that's it."

"I've noticed you almost always call him 'Jeremy.' Any reason for that?"

"Like I said, he's just so smug all the time, so full of himself. Ryan and I refuse to call him 'Dr. Siskin.' Unless Aaron is around, that is."

"And getting back to him, you have to admit there's *no* resemblance *there.*"

"The DNA works in mysterious ways."

"You said his mom dyes her hair?"

"'Maybe,' I said. I don't see her very often, either, but the color does seem to vary from one time to the next. It's likely a generational thing."

"Meaning...."

"At one time, the only thing harder than being a woman in science was being a *blonde* woman in science."

"Ah." Ellie let that sink in a moment. "So, you think she's blonde like Aaron?"

"Please—*nobody* is blonde like Aaron."

Ellie decided she couldn't argue with that. Instead, she stood, crossed the kitchen, and found spots for her bowl and spoon in the dishwasher. She turned to look over her shoulder at Sam as she began filling the kettle with water. "Want some coffee? I was waiting for you."

Sam, caught with a full mouth, nodded enthusiastically.

"'As you wish,'" Ellie said with a nod, bringing a big smile to Sam's face.

"Not having coffee would be 'inconceivable,'" Sam said. "I *love* that movie!"

Later that day, Ellie and Aaron were back at work. They met at the library, where they could use public computers to scour the web for any references to a project codenamed *Backspace*. Working at monitors set back to back on their table, they crafted meticulously honed phrases and entered them into every search engine available, but failed to find anything remotely relevant. They also failed to get as much as a micrometer closer to finding their way onto any of the LAB's servers.

"I wonder if they changed the name," he said. "After that guy slipped up in the interview."

"Could have, I guess, but whatever they might have changed it to, we have no way of knowing."

"*Time Out? Flashback?*"

She shrugged. "How about *I'm an evil, maniacal wack-job bent on destroying the future of all mankind?*"

"I bet they don't allow project codes that long."

Three tedious hours later, they still had nothing to show for their efforts. Feeling defeated, Ellie leaned back in her chair and waited as Aaron tried one last time. While he typed, she idly fidgeted with a ballpoint pen someone had left on their table. Holding it at one end, she waggled the other back and forth in a blurred arc. It was supremely frustrating having to attack such an important job with such limited and feeble resources. The alternative, however, was to do nothing, and they had agreed that option was unthinkable. He stabbed the "ENTER" key and started scanning returns, disappointment plain on his face.

"That's it," he said, sounding thoroughly dejected. "I'm fried."

"Can I ask you a question?" she said.

"Evidently." His literal response earned him a kick in the shin under the table.

"*Ow!* I mean, yes, please do."

"Sam once said you told her and Ryan that it was your dad who pushed for you to start school early rather than wait until the next year. Do you ever wish he hadn't?" She saw his expression darken and feared her question had crossed some invisible line. She spoke quickly, trying to take it back. "I'm sorry—if that's too personal to...."

"No, it's not that. It was quite a change of subject, that's all." He sat in quiet thought long enough that she began to think he wasn't going to answer her, but at last he did.

"It's just.... I can't really know that, can I? It's like me asking you if you would have preferred to have grown up with a brother instead of a sister, or to have been born left-handed instead of right. Not having experienced that alternative, it's impossible to say. My mom never wanted it, though, and it's been a sore spot on and off with them for as long as I can remember. I definitely would rather not have had *that* to deal with."

"I'm sorry," she repeated. "I didn't mean to bring up a painful subject."

He flapped his hand to say it was no big deal. "I'm over it. And besides, now that I'm out of high school, it should be better from now on. Okay, my turn."

"To bring up a painful subject? *Ow!* Okay, I guess that was fair." She reached down to massage her own smarting shin.

"What if we can't figure out a way to do this?" he said.

Anticipating a question of a similarly personal nature, she was disappointed by the abrupt return to topic. "I don't know. I'd like to think we're a long way from failing."

"That may be true, but at this point we're also a long way from succeeding. Pretty much *all* the way. Exactly what do we know now that we didn't know from the beginning?"

This uncharacteristic show of pessimism surprised her. "Do you feel like we're wasting our time? That we can't do this?"

"Unless we get some kind of big, huge, major breakthrough, I don't see how. I'm not giving up," he added quickly, "but it's probably not too soon to start pondering alternatives."

It was her turn to sound dismayed. "Well, *that's* cheery!"

She tossed the pen onto the table. He watched it slide his way and slapped his palm on it to keep it from going over the edge and into his lap.

"Didn't mean to be depressing," he said, looking up from the tabletop.

"Eh, don't worry about it. Just means I'll be spending some quality time with my good friends Ben and Jerry later. Come on, let's get out of here."

They cleared their browser histories, turned off the monitors, then headed for the front door. Once on the sidewalk, they turned right and headed down the hill toward the aquatic center. Ellie was just realizing that she and Aaron had never before had such a personal conversation when he spoke again.

"You know, I was always much more upset he made me give up playing guitar."

"The *guitar?!*" The notion of him plunking out folk tunes around a campfire simply did not compute. The oboe she could picture. Or cello, perhaps. But the *guitar?*

"Is it that bizarre? My mom got me one when I was what, eleven? It was a while before we moved here, anyway. It was just a cheap, little, kid's guitar, but I took lessons and everything. You know, scales, chords—some super-easy classical stuff. Dad got all pissy about it, though. Never said why, at least not to me, but he made a real stink about it for months until one day it was suddenly gone from my room. When I asked my mom, she said it wasn't a discussion she was prepared to have with a ten-year-old. Oh, so I guess I was ten. I never brought it up again."

"Wow. That's horrible."

"My teacher said I had a knack for it, too. Said I was 'a natural.' Yeah, like I'm a distant descendant of Segovia or Sor! I figured that was something he told all his students. I did enjoy playing, though."

"Have you ever thought about getting yourself another one?"

He sighed. "No. No need to poke *that* hornet's nest again."

"We should get you one. You could keep it at our house!" She suddenly wanted to see him with a guitar in his lap, but mostly she felt sad for him.

"Really? Well... maybe. I'll think about it." She squinted at him, skeptical. "I mean it—I will," he assured her.

They stopped in front of the aquatic center.

"I'm going in to see Sam. Wanna come?"

"I should go pack. We're leaving tomorrow morning. The flight leaves

Albuquerque at eight something, so we're leaving here crack-of-dawn early," he said.

"Don't be so glum. At least you're not camping. There might not even be any bloodshed."

He laughed. "We'll see. You'd be surprised."

Without knowing she was going to do it, she stepped forward and wrapped him in a hug. His whole body stiffened at the unexpected gesture. "Have fun," she said, then she released him and stepped back. "I'll miss you."

"Um, thanks," he said, flustered. "I'll, uh… I'll try."

Ellie pushed through a double set of heavy glass doors into what always seemed like an alien atmosphere. The humidity, about five times higher than on the outside, made the air feel dense. Within seconds she could feel every square millimeter of exposed skin responding gratefully to the abundance of moisture. It was like a silent, whole-body sigh of relief. The scent of pool chemicals filled the air, and their acrid odor further amplified the impression of having entered an environment perhaps created for some chlorine-loving visitors from another world.

She made her way to the main pool area. Three people were making languid laps, fifty meters up, fifty meters back, but she knew instantly none was Ryan—his laps were anything but languid. She nodded a greeting at a figure she didn't recognize perched on the lifeguard's chair. Aside from those four, the cavernous room was empty.

She backtracked her way to the hallway and followed it until she came to the women's locker room. Entering, she immediately heard soft noises. She walked along the side aisle that ran the room's entire length, peering down each row as she passed. She had almost reached the far end when she found Sam.

"Hey!"

Sam was working her way through the muggy, tile-lined space collecting damp towels from the rows of long benches that ran between the facing sets of lockers. She added another to the large bundle of them she held in the crook of her left arm before turning around. "Hey yourself. Finished with Aaron?"

Ellie nodded. She snatched a balled-up towel from the bench in front of her and followed Sam into the next row, where they gathered a few more. Ellie lent a hand whenever she stopped by, and today it seemed that there were more towels than was typical for a mid-week afternoon.

"Did you have a team in or something?"

Sam shook her head. "No. Teams are usually pretty good about using the bins. This was a birthday party. A bunch of ten- and eleven-year-olds."

"Ooh, I bet *that* was fun!"

"Still beats flipping burgers. Still better than *your* job. Any luck today?"

Ellie picked up the lone towel from the last row, and they headed for the pair of large, mesh bins near the exit. "I found out Aaron used to play the guitar. Took lessons, anyway. Other than that, zippo!"

"The *guitar?!*" Sam sounded as startled as Ellie had been.

"Right? That's what *I* said. So, you didn't know either?"

"Not a clue." She dumped her pile of towels into the hamper. "How'd that come up?"

Ellie answered while she dropped her load into the neighboring hamper, trying to sound nonchalant. "We were just talking. You know, about him."

"Oh, *really?!*"

"It was no biggie. I asked him if he ever regretted starting school earlier instead of waiting. Not that it was his decision, obviously. He said there was no way he could know if waiting would have been better or not. He brought up the guitar thing on his own."

"Well, regardless of what he said, I think the school thing is—or at least was—a pretty big deal."

Ellie remembered how his expression had clouded when she'd brought the subject up. "Yeah, I got that. He said it was a sore spot between his mom and dad. Anyway, he's off to Montana tomorrow, so we quit early. He's gone home to pack."

On their way out of the locker room, Sam kicked up the stop attached to the bottom of the door. It swung closed behind them as they headed toward the entrance. Ellie noticed a Red Cross poster on the wall that listed dates for upcoming CPR classes. It brought to mind the comment Ryan had made while lying on the road in Methuen.

"Have you made out with Annie yet?"

Sam knew what she meant right away and laughed. "Yeah, right after I started. But I figure I passed that test back in May." She gave her a wry smile. "Good to know it actually works."

Ellie nodded in solemn agreement. "Speaking of Ryan—Oh! *Duh,* I forgot! Ireland! When I first got here, I looked in at the pool to see if he was working out."

Sam sighed. "One more day."

"We ought to do something tonight. Just you and me."

"Like what—go *clubbing*? Have a hot night out on *this* town?"

Ellie couldn't argue with Sam's underlying point—Los Alamos had never been famous for its nightlife. But she had something altogether different in mind.

"Actually, I was thinking about having some Ben and Jerry's later...."

This suggestion brought an enormous smile to Sam's face. "That might be one of your best ideas ever! Is there any at home?"

"Yeah, I think, but it's Cherry Garcia if there is. And there's probably not much of it."

"*Hmm....* You said you're walking?"

"Yeah."

"I have my bike. When I'm done here, I'll go to Smith's and get us a pint. Something rich, and gooey, and chocolatey with...."

Afraid Sam's eyes were about to roll back into their sockets, Ellie interrupted her. "Stop! I don't need you doing that *thing* again. Besides, you could get yourself fired."

Sam laughed. "Fine. Any suggestions then?"

"Believe me, when it comes to decisions like this, I trust your judgment completely!"

Later that night, they sat in chairs placed side by side on the lawn, sharing a third chair as a footrest. A short, thick chunk of log standing on end between the chairs served as a table. The waxing moon had already sunk behind the distant Jemez Mountains, and it was so dark they could barely make out where their yard ended and the canyon began. The middle ground, extending to the far side of the canyon where the lights of town started, was a pit of pure black. They had turned off the kitchen lights to see the stars better, but Ellie could still make out the two silvery spoon handles poking up from the open pint of ice cream sitting on the log.

"I've been thinking that somehow going to the past had changed us. That the experience itself, or maybe the way the machine works, had some kind of side-effects.... I don't know." She was frustrated by sounding so vague. "Ryan has been doing less of his annoying *hello, ladies!* thing, you're being less self-absorbed...."

"Gee, thanks." Sam rolled her eyes at what was at best a backhanded compliment, but the expression was wasted in the dark.

"I know, I know, but I mean it in a good way, sweetest sister. You've been so encouraging to me and Aaron, even though you don't a hundred percent agree with what we're doing. And the way Ryan let you hold him in the sandwich shop.... That he would even admit he had a problem is different. *Everything* feels different since that day." She shrugged. "And Aaron... Well, he's basically still just Aaron, but even he seems changed somehow."

"He's started to loosen up a little. Stopped acting so nervous around you."

"Why would I make him nervous? He and I have been.... Wait, do you mean...?"

Sam snorted out a short laugh. "He *likes* you, you goof! I'm pretty sure that's the only reason he would hang out with Ryan and me—to be around *you*."

Ellie shook her head. "That's hard to believe. I gave him a hug earlier today, and I thought he was going to have a seizure." She peered across the table at Sam, trying hard to read her face in the dim starlight. "Really? You're not just.... You're *sure*?"

Sam nodded. "Are you telling me that after what—*six years?*—you honestly had no idea?" She picked up the tub and spooned a large scoop into her mouth.

Ellie hung her head, embarrassed. "We've been friends forever, yeah, but no, I never thought he liked me. I mean, *liked* me liked me." She remembered Jordan telling her she should pay attention to what was going on around her, and it galled her to admit someone she considered a total ditz might have had a valid point. "Wow… talk about being self-absorbed!"

"I always assumed the feelings were mutual. No?" Sam took another big scoop, replaced the carton on the log, and began nibbling at the large glob on her spoon.

In this new context, some of the comments Sam had made over the last few months suddenly made sense. Ellie shook her head and reached for the ice cream. She dragged her spoon around the wall of the tub, gathering up the softest parts as she pondered her answer.

"No. I don't know. Maybe? I definitely like him. A lot! I just never thought about him like *that* before, is all. I never thought of *anyone* like that. Why didn't he ever say anything?"

She stuck the overloaded spoon into her mouth and tasted caramel, coffee, and something crunchy. She squinted at the label but couldn't read it in the dark. She gathered up another spoonful, this time from the center, and happily discovered this part was chocolatey and had a different texture. She jabbed her spoon into the ice cream and set it back on the table.

"Oh, he might have eventually," Sam said. "In another year or three."

Ellie shook her head, bewildered. *Must be a boy thing.* Realizing she had been side-tracked, she returned to her earlier point.

"Anyway, what I was trying to say is this—we *are* changing, but I was wrong about why. Every day we make, like, a thousand decisions, right? What am I going to wear? What will I pack for lunch? Or do I buy lunch today? Who do I sit beside in American Lit? Do I do my homework before or after *Big Bang*? But none of it's important. It's all stupid, little-kid stuff. But since we did the thing in Lawrence and figured out what that shack is, we've been dealing with issues that actually matter. 'Future of mankind' stuff. I know it sounds cheesy, but I think it's that we're…. Oh, I don't know…." It did sound cheesy, and she didn't want to say it.

"Growing up?"

"I guess." Ellie suddenly felt exhausted. Her mind had been churning hard all day, first working on the shack problem with Aaron, now talking "feelings" with Sam, and she felt intellectually wrung out and emotionally drained. She doubted she could get excited if her hair were ablaze.

"I think you're right," Sam said. "And you know what? I've been noticing some things about you, too, over the last couple of weeks."

Ellie was genuinely curious. "Like what?"

"Like that, for instance. Wanting my opinion, or Aaron's... even Ryan's! You've always wanted to figure everything out first and all on your own, but now I see you looking for input from the rest of us. But more than that, it's you who's brought us together on this, got us working as a team. My little sister—a natural-born leader! Who knew?"

"I'm not a leader of any kind. *And* I was a C-section, or have you never heard Mom complaining about that scar?"

Sam laughed at Ellie's joke, then her expression went serious. "I mean it, though, El. You're a leader of the best kind. You lead not by giving orders or by trying to force people to do what you want, but by getting them to believe in the importance of what you're trying to do. Then they sign right up. Even me."

Ellie scoffed. "I don't want to disappoint you, but this 'leader' doesn't know where she's going." It felt like a confession.

"Look, what I feel—what I *believe*—is that we're heading in the right direction and that the path will present itself when the time comes."

"Really?"

"Yes, really. Thing is, you have to be ready to recognize it when that happens."

It was Ellie's turn to roll her eyes. "*Great!*"

Sam stood up to go inside. She picked up the nearly empty ice cream carton and started toward the door. She paused as she passed behind her sister and laid a gentle hand on her shoulder.

"I trust you, Ellie. We all do. You should, too."

Ellie considered this as she stared up into the star-filled sky. She had never thought she was leading anyone. She had seen something she believed needed to be done, and she couldn't do it alone. That was all of it. She suddenly felt a sense of responsibility that hadn't been there only moments before. At last she sighed, reluctantly accepting her new role.

"You'd better leave the ice cream."

22

As soon as Ryan returned to town, he dropped by to see Sam. Ellie joined them on the shaded patio to hear about his recent experiences. She poured three glasses of iced tea from a pitcher and passed two of them across the table. Sam was already familiar with much of his story via the many texts he had sent upon arriving back in "civilization," by which he meant anywhere with reliable cell service. Ellie, however, had so far heard very few details about his trip.

"So, how was Ireland?"

"It was very nice, I must say. I can see why old great-great-granddaddy Patrick was so keen to leave, but for two weeks, it was... nice. Beautiful countryside, although after living here for so long, anyplace that green looks very strange." He took a sip of his tea. "Whew, *sweet!* But good," he added quickly.

"And the strawberries?" she said.

"Now *they* were worth the whole trip!" He leaned forward in his chair, excitement illuminating his face. "I've had what I thought were pretty good strawberries before. You know, those tiny guys that grow up in the mountains? But *these* things...."

While Ryan passionately rhapsodized the miracle of nature that was the Wexford strawberry, Sam leaned close to whisper a not-so-serious rebuke in

Ellie's ear. "Did you have to bring up the strawberries? You should see the texts on my phone!"

"Don't give me any grief," Ellie hissed back, "or I'll tell about you cheating on him with your BLT!" Sam gave her a wicked smile in return. Meanwhile, Ryan was still on topic.

"I mean *these* things… I can't describe them," he said, then he went on trying to do just that. "They're super intense, like they have the flavor of ten regular strawberries crammed into one. Until you've had one of those babies, you haven't really had a strawberry. I wanted to bring some back, but it seems customs has this thing about transporting produce. We even lied about visiting farms, or I probably would've had to burn my shoes. Very twitchy, those people."

"And the cows?" Ellie said.

"The cows were good. Large, brown, smelly…. You know—cows."

"I'm glad you had a good time. I'm even *more* glad you didn't come home sounding like Teague or Mr. Thomas!"

"I didn't get my pot of gold," Sam pointed out.

"And you know, I didn't see a single leprechaun the entire time," Ryan said. "Shy little folks, I guess." He shifted in his chair to address Ellie directly. "How'd you guys do coming up with ideas for the—you know?"

She held up her hand and waggled it. "*Eh.* We have some general ideas, but we haven't made it much past 'it has to go.' Aaron is gone, as I guess you know, but he'll be back the day after tomorrow. He and the fam went up to Glacier for a few days."

"That bunch *camping?!* I can't picture it. The great Dr. Jeremy Siskin— 'DSc,' as he *loves* to point out—might be a brilliant theoretical physicist, but I bet that man could literally kill himself trying to set up a tent. You know, put a stake through his foot and bleed out on the spot. Remember that time with the flat tire? On their way back from Fort Davis a few years back?" Ellie did remember. Aaron's parents had taken him to visit the observatory there. While on their way home, a chunk of metal kicked up by an oncoming truck had taken out the sidewall of one of their tires. "Five bolts, one tool, perfectly flat road, and he *still* ended up in the ER!"

They all laughed, recalling how embarrassed Aaron had been describing the ordeal the next day.

Sam spoke between fits of laughter. "You can still see the scar on his hand where the crowbar got him."

"You're right, though," Ellie said after they had regained control. "They're not camping. They're staying in a lodge by a big lake there. McDonald? I think that's it."

"Well, that's good," Ryan said. "As long as he doesn't try to adjust the window blinds in their room, or fold a map or something, they all oughta make it back alive."

They spent the rest of the evening talking and laughing, reliving memories of their worst family vacations and most embarrassing moments involving parents, forgetting for a while the difficult task ahead of them. Later, Ellie would remember that evening as the last carefree time of the summer.

23

For Ellie, the day Aaron was due back crept along at a pace that made glaciers seem positively zippy. Sam and Ryan were halfway through yet another movie, some teen drama tear-jerker Sam had chosen, when she finally received a message late in the evening.

Aaron—I'm back. Progress-finally! Can you get everyone together tomorrow morning?
Ellie—They're both here. Hold on a sec
Ellie—9:15 work for you? At the park again?
Aaron—That'll work
Ellie—What's up?
Aaron—Sorry. Gotta go. Dad's calling for me. I'll have to tell you tom
Ellie—😩 Srsly?!
Ellie—Ok. Glad you're back
Aaron—Oh, man… me too!!!

They met mid-morning beside the pond, not far from the picnic table where they had sat in May to hear Ellie's theory about the shack. This time, Aaron insisted they convene at the park's western side, where an artificial cascade returned recirculated water to the pond. The noise, he said, would make it harder for anyone to overhear them. And if they were completely exposed there, so was anyone watching them.

Sam thought this was ridiculously paranoid, but he refused to say anything until they were all seated close to where the water made a particularly long and noisy drop. Ellie was privately amused that, despite Sam initially scoffing at Aaron's precautions, it was she who kept casting anxious glances at anyone who wandered even remotely close.

"Listen, Sam," Aaron said. "It's not that I believe we're being followed or anything. Not at all, okay? It's just that Dad said a few things while we were flying back from Montana, and I think it has to do with what we did last month. It made me glad we had been as careful as we were, that's all."

"Your *dad? Really?!* What did he say?" Ellie, forced to wait all night to hear the news, couldn't help but leap straight to the heart of it.

"*Ellie!*" Sam chided. "Welcome back. How was vacation?" She was addressing Aaron but giving her sister a stern, disapproving look.

Nonplussed, Aaron launched into a brief summary of his time away. "Uh, it was okay, I guess. The old lodge where we stayed was on the edge of the lake, McDonald, which was beautiful. We rented a car in Kalispell, so we could drive all through the park. We did a couple of hikes—Avalanche Lake was one—and we walked around some at the top of the pass, but we didn't hike any of the trails up there. It's weird to go there and not see any actual glaciers. And it would have been cool to camp, but," he shrugged, "you know."

"Yeah," Ryan said. "Your dad and a Coleman stove—not a happy combination."

"Man, my hands start to sweat just thinking about it," he agreed, then actually wiped his palms on his thighs.

"*Aargh!*" Ellie erupted, no longer able to contain her impatience. "*So?!*"

"Oh, yeah. We're flying home yesterday on this dinky commuter plane with only two seats on each side of the aisle, and on this flight, I'm in the row in front of Mom and Dad. Normally I would've had my earphones in, but I forgot to charge my phone the night before. So I'm sitting there, flipping through a magazine from the seatback for about the fourth time, when I realize I can hear them talking about work. Mom's saying how busy she's going to be when we get back, getting ready for all the big presentations she has coming up in D.C. Then Dad starts talking about some security breach they had last month and how everything's come to a grinding halt while they grill all their lab techs to find out who's responsible."

"And you think he was referring to what we did?" Sam said.

"I couldn't tell for certain. For one thing, I couldn't hear every word, and then, when Mom started asking questions about what kind of a breach and what the project was, he started to get all *need-to-know,* and *I'd-tell-you-but-then-I'd-have-to-kill-you* on her. So she got kinda angry at him, said, 'Fine!' and that was it. Conversation over."

"*Wow!*" Sam was shocked. "He *said* that?"

"Well, no, not in those exact words, but his meaning was clear enough. It was not a happy drive back from ABQ. It doesn't seem like they have any theories regarding us specifically, but it doesn't hurt to play it safe. Hence the white noise background." He jabbed his thumb over his shoulder toward the water splashing loudly beside them. "But here's the important part. I got to thinking about that conversation on the plane. What it implied, you know? So after we got home, I told Dad I was starting to consider majoring in biotech in college, saying how I thought the field was going to get bigger and more important from here on out. He points his finger at me and says, 'Plastics!' and I have no clue what *that* means, but I'm like, 'Yeah!' So I suggested I should go out to the LAB with him for a day or two and see for myself what it's all about, which he thought was a great idea.

"For weeks, Ellie and I have been trying to find a back door into the labs there. Now I'm going to walk straight in through the front one. I'm almost certain that out of the dozens of projects going on out there, his is precisely the right one. We're in!"

"That is so cool!" Ellie exclaimed.

"It is," Ryan agreed. "I mean, your dad's a *Graduate* fan? Who'd've thought?"

"Wait a minute," Sam said. "When you say 'the right one,' do you mean you think your father is somehow involved with whoever built that thing?"

"Apparently," Aaron said. "The timing certainly works. If we really were his big security breach, then he must be. Anyway, I'm set to go in with him on two days. And not only to his lab—he's going to take me around to see some of the other projects, too. Tomorrow, I'll kinda get the lay of the land while pretending to be fascinated by the wonder that is Los Alamos Biotechnologies. He said he's got meetings or something on Thursday he can't reschedule, so I'll go back in on Friday. Which is good, actually. Dad says most people leave early on Fridays. He *never* does, so I'm hoping I'll be able to do some real poking around then." He shrugged. "I guess we'll see."

"But see what, exactly?" Ryan wanted to know. "If they are the ones who built the shack, then I can't figure out what he's going to show you. He obviously can't show you *that*."

Aaron shook his head. "No idea. I've been wondering the same thing. Just finding that out is worth going out there."

Ellie thought for a moment. "If you can get on a computer, can you make it so we'd have access to the network from out here?"

"I seriously doubt it. After all of our failed poking around, I can only assume that our problem is that they have all the good stuff on air-gapped computers. We can't get in because they lack any connection to the outside world. I have this, though."

He took a small item out of his tee-shirt pocket. It was a rectangular piece of metal attached to an irregularly shaped bit of green plastic shot through with tiny wires. Ellie held her hand out, and Aaron dropped it into her open palm. She peered intently at it, not understanding what she was seeing.

"Thumb drive," he said.

"Really?" It looked like it had taken an extended ride through a kitchen sink's garbage disposal. "What did you do to it?"

"It used to have a case. I broke that part off, and all that's left is the USB plug and the circuit board. If I tape that behind my belt buckle, it'll make it through security. Even if they wand me and it beeps, they'll assume it's just the buckle."

"That is so cool!" she said again, unaware she was repeating herself.

"They make tiny ones, but I couldn't get my hands on one by tomorrow, so... *crunch!*"

"'Siskin. Aaron Siskin,'" Ryan said in his best Connery voice, which, Ellie had to admit, was far better than his Roosevelt.

Sam looked deeply concerned. "Aaron, please be careful."

"Don't worry. I know we need to get rid of that thing, sure, but I won't do anything stupid. Something else did occur to me, though. It's a good thing Dad's interest in my school work doesn't extend beyond my grades—if he had seen my Science Fair project, he would have been onto us right then."

Ryan stood and offered a hand to Sam. She took it, allowed herself to be pulled up, and brushed the other hand across the seat of her shorts.

"On that cheerful note," Ryan said, "we need to split. She has to get to work, and I need to do some laps." He gave Aaron a big grin, backed it up with a sloppy, two-fingered salute. "Good job, dude!"

Aaron nodded and smiled back. "Thanks."

Ellie and Aaron remained where they sat while Sam and Ryan climbed the steps and disappeared beyond the top of the waterfall. Unaware of doing so, she held him locked in an intense, penetrating stare, looking at him the same way she might study a stray dog to determine how likely it was to bite. Soon, Aaron began fidgeting under her scrutiny.

"What?" he finally said.

"*Hmm...?*" she said, barely registering the question.

"I feel like I'm being dissected. It's creepy."

She snapped out of her daze and chuckled self-consciously. "What? Oh, sorry." She flapped a hand dismissively in the air. "I was just remembering something Sam and I talked about the other night."

He eyed her warily. "Did it involve cannibalism?"

She responded with a genuine laugh. "No, but now that you mention it, I am getting hungry. How would you like to get lunch?"

"What is it... ten o'clock?" he said.

"Oh. Yeah." She thought a moment. "Okay, how about we do the loop?"

"Big loop or little loop?"

She considered this. The little loop was a three-mile combination of side-walk and hiking trails that skirted the downtown's northern edge. The big loop was twice as long and led all the way around the airport east of town. One route would take less than an hour, the other almost three, since nearly half was unpaved and often quite rugged. Glancing down, she saw he was wearing trail shoes, low-cut but with a suitably aggressive tread.

"You up for the big loop? Do you have time?"

He nodded once. "Sure."

"How's this sound? We'll take Rim out to the co-op, get something for lunch, and stop along Canyon Trail to eat. You know where it dips below the edge a little bit? Behind the airport?"

"You mean where Zipline drops down."

She nodded. "That's the spot."

"Sounds good." They started walking toward the eastern end of town but had barely gone a block when he changed his mind.

"You know… actually, I'm kind of hiked out."

She was disappointed, but he went on before she could respond.

"What if we went to the Starbuck's at Smith's instead? We can take our drinks outside and sit on the patio. I love the view there."

"Works for me," she said, instantly cheerful once more.

A second later, Aaron came to a sudden stop and knocked the heel of his hand against his forehead. "No, wait—I don't… I mean…." He looked embarrassed.

Ellie was pretty sure she knew what the problem was. She laughed and brushed away his concerns with a sweep of her hand. "Don't worry about it. I've been saving up my house chores money." She patted her hip pocket.

Now he looked even more embarrassed. "But…."

"Stop that," she said. "It's coffee and a munchie. It's not like I'm buying you a car!"

At last, he relented. "Okay. But next time, it's on me. I promise."

Ellie got the impression he was disappointed with himself, but she had no idea why. "Deal," she agreed, and they resumed walking.

They turned right at the end of the building and cut a zig-zag path diagonally across the next block. At the opposite corner, they crossed the four-lane road that skirted the southern edge of town to get to the enormous Smith's grocery store that housed one of the town's two Starbuck's. They walked in the shade of the massive storefront until they reached its far end, where they entered and got in line at the ordering counter.

"Whatcha want?" she said.

"Medium coffee. Black."

She fixed him with an exasperated stare, and he caved in less than five seconds.

"Fine! I'll have a double tall latte."

She smiled. "Was that so hard?" She turned to the young girl at the register and, truly focusing on her for the first time, was startled to find she knew her. "Oh! Hi, Hana! I almost didn't recognize you with that thing on your head. Been working here long?"

Hana suffered from perpetually looking like she had skipped a few grades, a trait that made her easy to underestimate. She fought just as fiercely as Ellie for their class' top spot, though, and out of all Ellie's class-mates, Hana was her only real competition for Valedictorian come the following June. She was also one of only a handful of fellow students Ellie regarded as friends.

"Hey. Just since the beginning of the month." She patted her white hair net. "I know—it's *so* attractive, right? Hi, Aaron. What can I get for you guys?"

"One double tall latte and one short mocha, no whip, please. And how about one of those." Ellie pointed through the glass front of the pastry case at a wooden tray piled with chocolate chunk-espresso brownies.

"That all?" Hana said.

Ellie looked at Aaron. He nodded. "That's it," she said.

Hana slipped the brownie into a paper bag with the company's ubiqui-tous logo printed on both sides and passed it over the counter. As Ellie reached for the bag, she again noted what she thought to be the world's oddest choice for a corporate design. And why "Starbuck's" to begin with? She had never been able to draw any connection between *Moby Dick* and coffee, and it's not like the character lived to retire from whaling and start a gourmet roastery. Moreover, she could never figure out how or why the company had come to decide that a depiction of a sperm whale and a pair of crossed harpoons was the perfect image for the marketing of said product. No closer to an answer now than before, Ellie passed the bag to Aaron, paid, then they waited together near the pick-up counter while the barista, someone they didn't know, made their drinks.

"Do you think this is the super, major breakthrough we've been hoping for?" she said.

"It better be. It feels like it is, you know? Like when I figured out the shack's entry code. Anyway, we'll definitely know by the end of Friday."

After a short wait, the barista placed their drinks in front of them. Ellie waved at Hana, who was busy ringing up another customer, and got a smile in response. Outside, they picked a table near the patio's edge and sat side by side, looking east by southeast across the dry, deeply etched landscape. The canyon below them dropped away to their left until it merged with another, which eventually opened up onto the wide Rio Grande Valley east of the plateau. Somewhere in the distance, its precise location easier to pinpoint by the glow of its lights at night, was Santa Fe.

"Not too many views like this in New York City," Aaron said.

"I would guess not." She had always known he lived in New York before moving to Los Alamos, but he almost never mentioned his life there.

"What do you remember about back then?" she said. Waiting for his answer, she removed the brownie from its bag, broke off a small bite, and set the remainder on top of the bag near her elbow. She popped the morsel into her mouth, chewed a few times, and mentally shrugged, unimpressed by its dry texture and surprisingly bland flavor.

"Well, first of all, it was as opposite as you can get to living here. The city went on for miles, and every so often there was a park. Central Park is pretty big, but most of them were kinda dinky. At least, that's my memory of it. But here, it's like the whole world is a park, and we're in this tiny town in the middle of it. It's much quieter here. And *dark* at night, which I especially like. And it smells tons better."

"Did you like anything about it there?"

"I guess. There's an energy, and I don't mean some lame, 'Taos vortex' sort of thing. It's the pace of the people—*go, go, go!*—all the time. You get caught up in it. I was what, twelve when we left? Even as a kid, I was aware of it."

"Do you ever wish you'd stayed instead of moving here?" She broke off another small chunk of the brownie and began nibbling at it without enthusiasm. *Maybe it's old.*

"I don't know. I didn't hate it. The thing I liked most about moving out here was the move itself. Until I met you guys, of course. First, the furniture went, then Dad, and then Mom and I drove out. We spent four days together in that old Volvo. It was sort of like a mini vacation. We stopped at a few cool places along the way, like the arch in St. Louis, but mostly it was just listening to music and watching the world go by. The whole drive was so… peaceful."

There was a wistfulness in his voice that made her heart ache. She tried picturing him on that ride, smiling, looking out the window… just a happy little kid on a big adventure. She could certainly picture his mom's car, a twelve-year-old white Volvo wagon, its rear end plastered with bumper stickers. She had always liked the one that said, "Well-behaved women rarely make history." And the "WARNING: Environmental Scientist with an Attitude" one. Recalling the slogans reminded her of something else.

"It was your mom who gave you that 'I Grok Spock' pin, wasn't it?"

"Yeah. Some guy gave her that when she was in college. She gave that to me a *long* time ago."

"Sorry. I didn't mean to sidetrack you."

"I was saying it was a nice time, that's all."

He was quiet for a moment as he relived a part of that drive in his mind. When he finally spoke again, it was about the present. "Things have been better between the parental units since we moved here—I do know that."

"They used to fight?"

"Not 'fight,' exactly. It was just so… *tense,* I guess is the word. Mom's projects always seemed to go better than Dad's, to get more recognition. Which makes total sense. His research is so much more theoretical, more abstract than hers. But still, he had a hard time dealing with that. It got a little better after he got his own project going out at the LAB. Of course, I spend most of my time with you guys now, so I'm not hanging around at home as much." He paused to consider that point. "Who knows—maybe it only *seems* better."

Ellie didn't know how to respond to that, so she pinched off another nibble of the brownie. Her parents each had their own separate lives when it came to their jobs, but they always supported each other. She'd never sensed the slightest hint of competition. That Aaron's father felt jealous of his mom seemed wrong at some very basic level. Remembering that Aaron's parents were potentially a sore subject, she chose to steer the conversation in a new direction.

"I was surprised when you said you were going to school here. I always assumed you'd be off to California or Massachusetts or somewhere."

"Yeah, well, that is part of 'the plan.' Two years here, then transfer to a big school on one of the coasts."

What?! No!! She had long known this, of course, but today imagining him being gone shook her badly. Trying to conceal her upset, she continued in a mild tone.

"Really? Like where?"

"MIT, Stanford, UC Berkeley—it hasn't been decided yet."

"What do you mean 'hasn't been decided?' Don't *you* get any say?"

"I'd just as soon stay here like Ryan and Sam. I know she doesn't like how small it is here, but it's hard to picture being back in a big city again. Mom's research isn't going to last forever, though, and once she's got everything figured out, they'll be off to someplace else—to wherever it is that wants her most, I guess. That'll probably be in right around two years, anyway. And you have to admit, UNM-LA is not known for its engineering program."

"It's not really Sam's choice. Mom and Dad can't afford for her to go somewhere else, as much as she might want to. But Ryan has his scholarship here, so at least they get to stay together."

"Yeah, they'll like that. Of course, as far as Dad's concerned, it's mostly about getting into the top-tier post-grad programs."

"*Hmm...* Aaron Siskin, PhD. Has a nice ring to it." She flashed him a bright smile. "I hope you do stay! I've been thinking I would take advantage of the dual-credit classes at UNM next year, maybe take a few extra classes over the following summers to catch up. I thought it'd be fun for us all to graduate together."

He pointed at the brownie. "Is that any good?"

She let the blatant change of subject slide and merely shrugged in reply. In truth, it had looked better in the case than it ended up tasting. "Sorry, I didn't mean to hog it." She slid the bag bearing its dark brown lump across the table toward him. "It's okay. There's chocolate, and then there's chocolate."

"And this is?"

"Definitely the former."

He pulled off a chunk and popped it into his mouth. "Not bad," he said, then washed it down with a swig of his latte.

"It's okay," she said again.

She let him have the rest of the brownie. When it was gone, they tossed the bag and carried their cups to the fence at the edge of the patio. They rested their elbows on the top rail and gazed south across the canyon in the general direction of the object of so much of their recent focus.

"It's like that's the Lonely Mesa, and the shack is our Smaug," he said.

"Would that make you an elf, a human, a dwarf, or a hobbit? Or a goblin —you can be a goblin if you want, I guess."

"Since it looks like we might need magic to take care of it, it'd be nice if at least one of us were a wizard. Might as well be me!"

She looked at his fair hair, noticing for the first time that he was allowing it to grow out. It wasn't long, not by any definition, but it wasn't spiky anymore, either. Maybe he thought it made him look less owl-like.

"'Aaron the White!' Because obviously. I think you'd make an *enchanting* wizard."

He smiled at the pun. "Thank you! There's no reason you couldn't be one, too, you know."

"I hope we don't need two, but it would be fun to be able to do some magic."

"I *can* say you are not entirely without your charms."

She looked at him wide-eyed, surprised by what she thought had to be the corniest—certainly the flirtiest—thing she had ever heard him say. She thought she detected a smile hiding in his expression.

"You started it," he said, and a second later, they were both laughing like happy little kids.

While Sam got ready for bed that evening, Ellie told her about her afternoon with Aaron. In particular, she described how it almost didn't happen at all.

"When he realized he didn't have any money with him, he got all weird and tried to back out of it. I was like, 'it's coffee, not a car,' and he finally said okay."

"No biggie," Sam said. "He probably imagined your first date a little differently, that's all."

Ellie was startled by the suggestion. "First *date?!* I don't *do* dates!"

"I could be wrong, but isn't that the first, you know, social thing you two have done together, just the two of you? I bet he's been picturing dinner at the Old Adobe Café or something."

"Wait, I've been on a *date?* Does having coffee even count?" She was still trying to process this news. Much to her amazement, she found herself quickly warming to the idea.

"And I bet he expected to pay, too, but yes, I'm sure that's how he saw it."

"I've been on a *date!*"

Sam rolled her eyes. "Should we call the papers? Alert CNN?"

"*Thppt!* I always assumed that if I went on a date, I'd be aware of it at the time, that's all." She shook her head, bemused. "*Huh!*"

Forty-five minutes later, the lights off and Sam presumably asleep, Ellie was still rehashing the event her sister had called a date. A week ago, she would have denied it had been anything remotely like a date and been telling the absolute truth. However, on the heels of her conversation with Sam concerning Aaron's feelings for her, and considering how much she had enjoyed hearing him talk of New York and joke about being a wizard, she had to admit that it had felt sort of date-ish. So there it was. She'd been on a date, and not only had the world not ended, but she had enjoyed it!

"*Huh!*"

24

Ellie felt anxious and aimless all of the following day. She spent half her time obsessing over what Aaron was doing, imagining what he was finding out. The other half was occupied by a looping replay of the time they had spent at Starbuck's the day before. She would suddenly realize she had come to a dead stop in the middle of some task like an android running low on juice, her brain fixated on some small, random detail from the previous afternoon. It happened once while she was in the kitchen rinsing some dishes, and she was suddenly confronted by a goofy-looking grin reflected in the window over the sink. Annoyed, she threw the sponge at it, splattering suds everywhere.

She finally got a text from him late that afternoon, a quick note letting her know all was fine but that they were running late and that he wouldn't be able to get together that evening.

Aaron—Looks like I'll be here another couple of hours

Ellie thought about how to ask if he was learning anything useful that wouldn't raise concerns if someone happened to be looking over his shoulder.

Ellie—Enjoying the tour?
Aaron—Very educational. Tell r & s we're looking good for Friday
Ellie—Ok ttyt
Aaron—Bye

Ellie was sitting on her bed, staring absently at her hands and making small, clicking sounds with her thumbnails, when Sam returned following her shift at the pool.

"Hey," Sam said. "Why are you hiding in here?"

"Just sittin'," she answered quietly. "Sittin' and thinkin'."

"Sounds like somebody needs a hobby." She began peeling off the red shorts and white, red-trimmed tee shirt that marked her as an aquatic center employee. She almost always wore her uniform home, having realized long ago it made no sense to shower there and then put on clothes that would themselves be reeking of pool chemicals by the end of her shift. "Hear from Aaron today?"

"He said to tell you and Ryan that Friday looks good. I assume that means he's got something to tell us." She watched as Sam selected fresh clothes from various drawers and their small, shared closet. She opened her mouth to say something more when Sam, outfit in hand, headed for the door.

"Hold that thought—I'll be right back," she said. Then she was gone, closing the door behind her.

Ellie turned on her bed and leaned back against the side wall, letting her feet dangle over the edge of the mattress. Spending the day mostly on her own had given her plenty of time to reexamine yesterday's—*go ahead and say it*—yesterday's *date* with Aaron. She had enjoyed being with him, but that was her only conclusion so far. Her feelings for him remained as undefined as ever. Maybe when you've known someone for six years, had more or less grown up together, it's different. It's not like "love at two-thousandth sight" was a thing. Sam and Ryan didn't seem to have any problem figuring out how they felt, though, and they'd known each other for only six days longer than she had known Aaron.

Maybe it's just me.

She heard the sound of the hairdryer whirring from across the hall. She thought about how Sam and Ryan seemed so happy, even though she knew his perpetual wisecracking sometimes got on her sister's nerves. She also assumed, based on her own reactions, that Ryan could get as irritated by Sam's quirks as she sometimes did. And yet....

The dryer went silent, and Ellie knew Sam would be back any second. Her mind raced, but try as she might, she couldn't see any way to avoid the impending discussion. She would have to do the unthinkable—there simply was no other choice. She was going to have to ask her sister for advice about boys!

"That's just *great,*" she muttered.

As if hearing her thoughts, Sam reappeared. Ellie noticed she was wearing the slightest hint of make-up and a dress she hadn't seen before. It was a simple design, deep olive in color, and looked like it was made from tee shirt material. It was long enough that she guessed Sam would call it a "midi." Once again, she had to admit it looked good on her.

"Nice dress," she said.

"Lulus. Like it?"

Sam twirled in a quick pirouette, and the bottom of the dress flared out from her legs. The fit was tighter from her hips up, cut to accentuate every curve, but the dress didn't seem to bind anywhere. The rear was open in a deep 'V' that ran from the shoulder straps down to a point very low on her otherwise bare back.

"I do," she said, and meant it. "Hot date?"

"Funny you should put it that way. We're going to see a movie at the theater—it's always *freezing* in there! And after, we're getting sushi at the Paper Crane. So 'hot' isn't exactly the word. Which reminds me...." She retrieved a light sweater from the closet and tossed it onto the foot of Ellie's bed.

Ellie felt a twinge of envy. Now that she was adjusting to the concept of dating, she wondered if Aaron knew how to use chopsticks. She tried to smile, but the expression evidently didn't come out as intended, and Sam's eyebrows drew together in concern.

"Hey. What's up?"

Ellie responded with a one-shoulder shrug and began picking distractedly at a spot on the bedspread between her legs. "Nothing, really. I wanted to ask you something. I don't want to hold you up, though."

"Don't be silly." Sam sat on the foot of Ellie's bed, smoothing her dress beneath her as she scooted back on the mattress. "Ryan won't be here for at least twenty minutes. And if we're not done when he gets here, then he can just wait!" She leaned against the wall and folded her hands in her lap.

Ellie opened her mouth, but no words came to mind. She tried again a few moments later. "When did you know you liked him? Ryan, I mean. And *how* did you know? And I don't mean 'liked,' but, you know, '*liked*.' Was it all of a sudden, or was it more of a gradual thing?" She sensed she was on the verge of lapsing into full-on babble mode and forced herself to stop talking.

Sam's smile was warm and understanding. She laid a hand on Ellie's thigh. "This obviously had to do with you and Aaron, so the first thing I'll say is this—Ryan and I are *not* you and Aaron. Every two people have their own situation going on, and sometimes even *they* don't understand it completely. Get it?"

Ellie nodded.

"But to answer your question...." Sam was quiet for a long half-minute. When she continued, her expression was solemn. "Do you remember Kyle Jeffries?"

"I knew who he was. I didn't *know* him."

Kyle Jeffries graduated two years ago. All Ellie knew about him was that he had been the school's quarterback for both his junior and senior years, which she gathered was some kind of a big deal, and that he had a reputation for partying pretty hard whenever his mom had to travel for work.

"Consider yourself lucky. Two years ago, back in that fall, the football team was doing unusually well. They were five and one or something, but then they lost a game everybody expected them to win easily. I didn't know this until later, but it turns out it was because Kyle and half the offensive line were drunk on the field. They started out okay, but at half-time, he passed around a bottle of Jim Beam... or was it Jack Daniels? One of those guys, anyway. He had snuck it into the locker room and split it with three or four other players, I guess. After that, the game went the other way.

"So, the following Monday, I'm walking down the hall after gym, late for class, and he and some of his friends came out of the guys' locker room. I said something like, 'Too bad about Friday's game. I'm sure you'll win the next one.' Totally innocent, just trying to be friendly, but then the next second, one of his hands is around my neck, his other arm is across my chest, and I'm crushed up against the wall, barely able to breathe. Only the tips of my toes are on the ground. He's got his big, bright-red face shoved right up into mine and he's, like, *snarling* the most disgusting things at me. Like, 'Think that's cute, you stupid, ugly bitch?' I remember that one pretty clearly. And he said some other, much nastier things I've tried hard to *un*-remember."

Ellie stared at Sam in shocked disbelief. She'd never had so much as a clue this had happened.

"His friends—there were three of them—were crowding around me the whole time like they were watching a show, you know? I kept wondering, 'Where *is* everyone?' All I could move were my eyes, and I kept looking from one of their smirking faces to the next, hoping one of them would pull him off me. Then I got a glimpse of movement, someone coming up fast behind them. There's a shout and Kyle's suddenly gone, and I'm sliding down the wall to the floor.

"I was sitting there, rubbing my throat and just trying to breathe again, so I didn't see everything that happened. But I heard it all—Ryan shouting at Kyle and the other guys to get away from me, him telling Kyle exactly what kind of a total shit he was for attacking little girls. And trust me, I felt like a little girl while Kyle had me shoved against the wall. The guy was huge, especially for a quarterback.

"The next thing I knew, they were gone, and Ryan was helping me stand up, picking my stuff up off the floor for me. He told me to wait while he disappeared into the locker room. He came back a few seconds later with some ice wrapped in a towel, told me to hold it against my neck to help keep it from bruising. He was so sweet!

"Another thing I learned later was that Kyle and his buddies had just found out that, in addition to getting suspended, they had been benched for four weeks—the rest of the season, in other words—and they were looking for someone to take their anger out on. So I come along all, 'So sad, better luck next time,' and *bang!* I'm pinned against the wall. I don't know what would have happened if Ryan hadn't shown up when he did, but I bet there would have been a lot more bruising."

For a moment, Ellie remained too dumbstruck by Sam's story to say a word. She'd had no idea about any of it. It certainly seemed to explained Sam's feelings for Ryan though. "So that's when you knew," she finally said.

Sam shook her head. "No. I was pretty much in shock at that point. It was because of something that happened the next day. We had just gotten to school, you and me, and you had already headed off to homeroom. I was at my locker changing out of my trail shoes when Ryan found me and asked me how I was doing. I said I was okay and thanked him for rushing in like that to save me. He said—and here's the thing—he said he didn't even realize it *was* me until he was helping me get onto my feet, that he hadn't been able to see who it was behind that wall of big guys. See, he didn't do it because it was *me*, his bosom buddy and bestest friend for four years, but simply because he had seen that someone needed help and because it was the right thing to do."

Ellie tried to picture the scene in the hall. Sophomore Ryan, all of five feet nine and a hundred and fifty pounds, going up against four pumped-up and pissed-off football players. Understanding why they hadn't needed to scrape him off the floor with a spatula was totally beyond her.

"Of course, then he went on to say some very sweet and flattering things, pretty much the opposite of everything Kyle had said, and that didn't hurt, either. After that, things were different between us. It wasn't because I was grateful—I was, of course—but because I had seen something good and true in him. The 'inner Ryan,' I guess you could say. At that point, I just *knew*— this is the guy!"

After hearing Sam's story, Ellie saw the incident in Methuen in a totally new light. Ryan stepping in to protect her, how Sam had fought to get him breathing again and her subsequent anger. Saying he was a "good guy" didn't even start to cover it.

"Thank you," she murmured. She wiped away tears with the side of her hand. "I never knew any of that."

"Part of a big sister's job is to make sure you don't have to deal with stuff like that. Anyway, it all happened so fast that I was too stunned to be trau-matized, I guess. What I remember most clearly from that day is not the sneer on Kyle's face while he was holding me against the wall, but the concern on Ryan's as he helped me up. Now do you see what I meant about how you and Aaron's story is different from ours?"

"Yeah. I'm still glad you told me, though." She had hoped learning about Sam and Ryan would help her untangle her jumbled feelings toward Aaron, but she wasn't prepared to get roughed up merely for the sake of achieving a little emotional clarity.

"Don't sound so depressed. I'm not done. My point is you need to think about your situation in a way that works for you."

"Meaning?"

"Well, if *I* wanted to know what something was, how something worked, I'd probably jump right in and start fiddling with it until either I figured it out or broke it. *You*, on the other hand, would take all kinds of measurements, formulate a hypothesis, figure out a way to test it.... See where I'm going?"

"*Umm...* not really."

"You enjoyed having coffee with Aaron, right? But you're still not sure how you feel about him—boyfriend or just friend—is that it?" Ellie nodded, still not sure where Sam was headed. "Okay. So say you're working in a lab, doing some experiment or whatever, and you get a result you aren't sure of. Or maybe one that's *exactly* what you were expecting. Either way, what's your next step?"

Ellie rolled her eyes. *Basic scientific method—ask me a hard one next time!* "That's easy! Repeat the experiment and see if I get the same result." Her eyes went wide as she finally realized what Sam was driving at.

"Need I go on?" Sam said. "This isn't something you can reason out. If you really want to know, you're going to have to 'run some field tests,' I guess you would say."

Ellie nodded, grinning. "'Clever girl!'"

"Ha! *Jurassic Park!* Ryan would appreciate that one."

They heard the front door open, then Ryan called, "Sam?"

"Speaking of...." Sam slid off the bed, scooped up her sweater, and headed for the door. "See ya!"

"Hey... about Ryan?"

Sam stopped in the doorway and turned around. "Yes?"

"Give him a big, sloppy kiss for me?"

Sam grinned devilishly. "That will be my pleasure!"

The idea of running a repeat experiment occupied Ellie's thoughts for the rest of the evening. She would not have been capable—even under threat of torture—of repeating a single thing her mom or dad said during dinner. She had smiled and nodded whenever it seemed appropriate, adding the occasional *mm-hmm* at random intervals. When the meal ended, she cleared the table and loaded the dishwasher in such a brain-dead, zombielike fashion that she had to return to the kitchen an hour later to assure herself she had actually done it.

Leaving the kitchen this second time, she glanced into the living room and saw her dad in his recliner, his peculiar, little half-moon reading glasses riding low on his nose, which was buried in a book. Her mom scrolled through the Netflix menu, searching for something worth watching. It had never been a mystery which of their parents she and Sam each took after. Her mom looked over in mid-scroll.

"Hey, El. Up for some *Stranger Things* tonight?"

Ellie couldn't help but laugh. "Thanks, but you know, things are strange enough already."

Her dad responded without lowering his book. "Too true. Too true."

"I'm just going to get into bed and read."

"That's my girl," he said.

Her mom looked up from the screen to lob an Alcott quote at her dad. "'She is too fond of books, and it has turned her brain.'"

He fired back with a favorite line of his own from Annie Dillard. "'She read books as one would breathe air, to fill up and live.'"

Ellie rolled her eyes. "Goodnight, you two."

As she headed down the hallway, she wondered, and not for the first time, how that pair had managed to produce two such normal, well-adjusted daughters.

25

Awake but still groggy, Ellie sat up, positioned her pillow against the wall, and leaned back on it. Glancing across the room, she saw Sam's bed was made and assumed she was already out somewhere with Ryan. She also noticed that Sam had left a mug blocking her view of the clock.

How late is it?

She picked up her phone from the desk, hit the home button, and checked the date and time. She had been wrong both about it being late and regarding Sam's whereabouts. It was Thursday, Sam's morning to go into the pool early and help with cleaning before it opened for the day, and it was not quite eight.

She unlocked her phone and sent a message to Aaron.

Ellie—You up and about?

While she waited for his reply, she checked the forecast. The app predicted yet another in a long string of sunny days with a high of seventy-nine degrees. *Who'd have guessed?*

The phone buzzed in her hand.

Aaron—Up. Not about. You?

Ellie—Same. Sam's at the pool early today. Meet here in an hour?

Aaron—That works.

Ellie—Coffee?

Aaron— ☕ ☕ ☕!

"Okay, then… coffee it is!"

She lowered the phone into her lap and closed her eyes. Ever since Sam had made her aware of Aaron's feelings for her, she felt like she was seeing him through different eyes. Or maybe it was more like she was suffering from a form of double-vision. She saw the boy she had long known as a friend, but also this other Aaron, who she now knew viewed her as something more. Either way, it was disorienting.

She had never given more than a passing thought to what love—romantic love—meant. She loved her parents and she loved Sam, and she knew that for an absolute fact. She also knew that was a different type of love, what the ancient Greeks had called *agape*. This according to Mrs. Foucault, the instructor who taught mythology, sociology, and psychology to sophomores. She said it was distinct from *eros*, the romantic emotion shared by people *in* love.

Eros and Aaron? Did those two ideas go together? When he had reminded her he would be leaving in two years, she'd felt an actual, physical pain in her chest. But is that all love was, the fear of losing someone? That couldn't be right. But what did she expect, fireworks? No, she wasn't *that* naïve. Where was the middle ground? Maybe feeling love was like seeing puce. She'd probably been surrounded by the color all her life, but couldn't say whether it was closer to red, blue, or some shade of green. Perhaps she was feeling some kind of love for him but simply didn't recognize the emotion for what it was.

On top of that, she was still disturbed by Sam's story from the day before. She couldn't decide which aspect of the telling of it she found most upsetting, the details of the attack itself or Sam's calm, matter-of-fact delivery. She was amazed all over again that something so significant had happened to the person in the world she cared most about, and she'd had not the slightest hint. On one hand, learning Sam had been keeping that secret made her sister feel a little bit like a stranger, and she didn't like it. But on the other, now she *did* know, and that made her feel closer to her than ever.

"*Aargh!* Does *everything* have to be so *confusing?!*"

Her mind was content to remain in bed as long as she wanted, but her bladder was working according to its own, more urgent agenda. She slid off the bed, tidied up the covers, then crossed the hall to the bathroom.

Ten minutes later she returned to her room, hair towel-dried into a tousled mess, her nightshirt draped over one arm. As she entered, she elbowed the door closed. She folded her nightshirt neatly and smiled when she placed it on the foot of her bed, message up. The design on this one mimicked an entry on the periodic table and read:

She opened one of the top drawers of the dresser built into the base of her bed, withdrew a bra and panties at random, and tossed them onto the bed next to her nightshirt. She squatted, opened a lower drawer, and pulled out a folded pair of shorts and a rolled-up tee. These she shook out and laid flat on the bed next to the underwear. She regarded her chosen outfit as she stepped into the underwear, and by the time she was sliding the bra straps over her shoulders she had decided she could do better with the shirt. She re-rolled her first pick and rooted through the drawer until she found a nicer one to swap it for. After spreading her second choice out, she realized that now the shorts no longer worked. She started to reach for them, but stopped her hand before it made it all the way. This was *not* normal behavior. Certainly not for *her*.

What am I doing? *Oh, my God—I've turned into Sam! One freakin' date and my brain's been reduced to mush.*

She laughed at herself, shaking her head. As ridiculous as she felt, an inner voice—speaking from that mushy part of her brain, perhaps—urged her to lighten up and go with it. She refolded the shorts, picked out a pair that matched the second shirt better, and in less than another minute she was fully dressed. When she turned to check her outfit in the mirror, she realized both the top and the shorts were hand-me-downs, items Sam had given her when she'd grown bored with them after a year or two. She rolled her eyes at her reflection and laughed again. *I really* have *turned into Sam!* She teetered on the brink of changing again, just on principle, but decided against it.

She ran a brush through her hair, pocketed her phone, and headed for the kitchen. Out of habit, the first thing she did was begin filling the kettle. When she had added enough water to brew herself a cup, she turned to set it down, remembering only then she was making coffee for two, and not for at least another half an hour. She added more water to the kettle and replaced it on its base, but did not turn it on. Still in coffee-making mode, she ground some beans and prepared the pour-over filter. As she herded a few errant grounds from the countertop into the sink, she scanned the back yard for Sunshine, but the furry little vagabond was not in any of her favorite spots.

Opting for yogurt with granola this morning, she handed the task of preparing it over to her mental autopilot and returned her thoughts to an earlier topic. *What is it I feel for Aaron?*

She thought back to Tuesday morning at Starbuck's. Aside from that occasion, she could remember only one other time when they had talked in such a personal way, and that had been right before he left for Montana. During all the rest of the time they had spent together, she had been too concerned with making sure that he took her seriously, that he didn't think of her merely as "Sam's little sister," to waste much time on small talk.

When she looked down, she saw that her autopilot had filled the bowl nearly to the top with cereal, leaving little room for anything else. She tipped most of it back into the box, then took a large tub of 2% yogurt and a dish of sliced strawberries out of the fridge.

Have I spent all these years trying to impress him without even realizing it? She had to admit it did seem that way. That certainly implied... well, something. She wasn't sure what.

As she spooned the yogurt and strawberries into her bowl, her thoughts returned to the previous day's discussion. Re-run the experiment. She understood Sam hadn't meant it literally, but why not? The coffee part was good to go. All she lacked was one mediocre store-bought brownie, and she was sure she could come up with something.

After finishing breakfast, she took out a large wooden cutting board and the bread knife and set them on the counter. She slid up the roll-top front of the breadbox, expecting to find a partial loaf of hearth bread from the co-op. She did, but there was also a day-old lemon-poppyseed muffin.

"Score!"

She placed both the bread and the muffin on the cutting board, sawed four thick slices from the loaf, and quartered the muffin. Two of the bread slices went into the toaster. She took butter and several varieties of preserves out of the fridge and added them to the cutting board. Finally, she weighted the two halves of a torn paper towel with a pair of small butter knives and, declaring that project finished, switched on the kettle.

She was down to the final few ounces of water when she heard a rap on the front door. It surprised her when the sound caused a literal flutter in her chest. She yelled to be sure Aaron heard her.

"Come on in!" She heard the knob turn and the door rattle, then remembered she had never unlocked it, so she yelled again. "Be there in a second!"

She poured the last of the water in as quickly as she could, filling the filter cone to its brim, depressed the toaster's handle, then dashed through the living room to the front of the house. She twisted the thumb latch on the deadbolt and pulled the door open. "Sorry—forgot it was still locked."

Aaron stepped in, and she closed the door behind him. Her brain belatedly registered something she had glimpsed beyond him as he stood on the stoop, and she opened it again. Leaning out, she saw Sunshine basking in a pool of sunlight along the side of the garage. The cat looked up and greeted her by way of a voiceless *meow*.

"Come around back if you want fed," she said, then closed the door a second time. "That goes for you, too."

"Actually, I...."

"Just some munchies," she added. "Come on. Coffee is also waiting."

Back in the kitchen, she saw the water had finished filtering through the grounds. As she reached out to the toaster, it popped up a pair of perfectly browed slices. She laid them on the cutting board and handed it to Aaron, then pointed unnecessarily through the window above the sink.

"Will you take this outside to the table?"

He took the board and carefully backed out through the screen door, an odd, contemplative look on his face. She followed with two mugs in one hand and the carafe in the other. After he placed the food on the table, he stood there, regarding her closely as she set their mugs down and began filling them. She was acutely aware of him watching her, and for the first time in her life, she felt self-conscious in his presence. Her heart was thumping so hard she was sure he could hear it through the wall of her chest, and her hands shook as if the outside temperature were ten degrees rather than nearly seventy.

This is getting ridiculous!

When she straightened and turned to hand Aaron his mug, she saw he was still eying her intensely.

"You look...." he began.

Don't you dare say 'like Sam!'

"...great."

"Thanks!" She quickly turned away to pick up her own mug, using the motion to hide what she was sure was an encore appearance of the big, goofy grin from the day before. Turning back around to face him, she tried toning the intensity of her smile back from eleven to somewhere closer to six.

"Cheers," she said, and clunked her mug against his. Too hard! Coffee slopped from their mugs and spilled through the wire mesh and onto the patio. By luck, it missed the tray of snacks.

"Whoops!" she said, embarrassed by her clumsiness. "I almost slopped our toast onto the toast!"

"Uh, cheers," he echoed. He took a sip, then used his mug to indicate the cutting board. "What is all this?"

"Didn't know if you'd have had time for breakfast, so I threw this together." She shrugged. "If you don't want any of it, that's okay."

"No, it looks great."

They took seats on opposite sides of the table. Aaron nibbled at a piece of muffin. Ellie chose a slice of the toast and, using her half of the paper towel as a plate, spread on some butter and slathered it with raspberry preserves. The patio was splashed with sunlight filtering through a neighbor's tree, enough to make it comfortably warm. The light was shining in her eyes, though, and she had to bob her head around to find a position that allowed her to see him as something other than a silhouette. He looked at ease, leaning back in his chair, a piece of muffin in one hand and his mug in the other. When he caught her studying him, he gave her a relaxed smile. She smiled back, thinking she didn't often see that expression on his face.

"This is great," he said.

She noticed he seemed to be stuck on that word. Maybe he wasn't as relaxed as he appeared. "Yes. It's very pretty back here," she said, then tried hard not to let the cringe she felt show on her face. *He wasn't talking about the landscaping, you idiot!* "I'm so very happy you could come over this morning." *Okay, so that sounded* totally *natural!* She had to fight a sudden urge to bury her face in her palms.

Her memory offered up a scene from several weeks before. In it, her parents were the ones sitting here on the patio, enjoying toast and coffee and reading the paper. The remembered image changed the morning's mood, casting it in an unintentionally domestic light. Once again, an inner voice urged her to go with it, but she had decided that voice was not entirely to be trusted.

The experiment was not going to plan. Ellie put her mug on the table and sat upright in her chair. "Listen—I know you want to tell me what you found at your dad's lab so far, and I want to hear everything, of course. But before we get into that, hear me out."

"What's up?"

She took a deep breath and pressed on before she lost her nerve. "What I would *really* like to do is get out of here, go do something fun for a change and stop obsessing over this whole 'shack' mess, even if it's only for a couple of hours."

"Fun?" He sounded dubious. Or confused.

She laughed. "Okay, I am not going to define *fun* for you."

"No, I meant, like, what did you have in mind?"

She was winging it, the idea of taking the morning off having just occurred to her, but it took her no more than a second to come up with an idea.

"I'm sure one of the cars is here. When's the last time you were at the top of Pajarito? I'll check with Mom to see about driving up to the ski area. Then we can hike to the peak." To her surprise, she found she was warming to the idea. "We could have a picnic!"

"I guess that could be 'fun,'" he said, and even without the air quotes he couldn't have seemed less enthusiastic. She felt like a balloon that'd been stuck with a pin. When her gaze dropped to the ground, a dejected frown on her face, he leaned toward her and placed his hand on the arm of her chair.

"No, Ellie, that was…. I'm sorry—that didn't come out as funny as it sounded in my head. I'd *like* that!"

She peered up at him from under her brows. Was that all it was—a failed wisecrack? Had he merely been channeling—and poorly—*his* "inner Ryan?" This morning was *not* going as she had imagined.

"Really?" she asked, doubtful.

"*Really* really."

She raised her head and looked into his eyes. Seeing only sincerity there, she relaxed and sighed. It finally occurred to her that this whole situation must be feeling as awkward to him as it was to her.

"Really," he said again.

"Okay," she said, at last convinced. "Let's go inside. You see what's in the fridge for making sandwiches, and I'll text Mom."

They cleared the table and carried everything inside.

"That bread should be okay to use if it didn't get too dry." She gestured toward the remaining slices on the cutting board. "If we need it, there's more in there," she added, pointing to the bread box.

Aaron examined the three slices of bread. He picked up the remaining browned one by a corner and held it out for her to see. "The other two pieces are fine, but this one's toast," he said, perfectly straight-faced.

"Har, har." It was a corny joke, but that didn't stop her from grinning.

She pulled the phone from her pocket and tapped out a short message, hoping her mom wasn't in a meeting.

Ellie—Hi, Mom. Okay to take the car up to Pajarito? 🧦 with Aaron.

She placed the phone on the counter and checked on Aaron's progress with lunch.

"What've we got?"

"Roast chicken from the deli or PB and J," he said. "Or there's a can of tuna up there." He pointed at the cabinet next to the refrigerator.

Her nose wrinkled at the prospect of future tuna breath. The same went for the peanut butter. She glanced around the kitchen while she considered the options. "Okay, let's go with the chicken. There's a tomato and an avocado in that basket by the sink. Add a little mayo, maybe some salt and pepper.... Sound good?" Her phone rattled on the granite, and she reached for it.

"Sounds grr... um, yummy," he said.

Mom—That's fine. Careful on West … road work. Don't forget water.
Ellie—Thanks, Mom. YTB!
Mom—This is true. ;-) Have fun!

"Look at you, Mom, rockin' those emoticons!"

26

They made lunch quickly. Aaron assembled the sandwiches while Ellie gathered additional munchies. She loaded one small plastic container with apple slices, another with mini-pretzels, and snapped on their lids. She filled two large water bottles, and everything, minus the bottle Aaron wanted to carry with him, went into her small daypack. She pulled on a lightweight, long-sleeve shirt over her tee, and then they were out the door.

On their way through town, they stopped at Aaron's house, where he swapped his sneakers for the sturdier trail shoes he had worn on Tuesday. He also picked up a light, wind-proof jacket, which he tossed onto the back seat.

Whatever road work had been going on earlier in the morning had been completed, and the West Road bypass of the LAB security checkpoint was clear. Ellie realized that although she had been up to the ski area many times, this was the first time she had driven the narrow, winding road herself. Los Alamos was so small that she had little need to drive at any time. Plus, a trip to Pajarito was typically a group outing, so someone else— Mom, Dad, Sam, or Ryan—was always at the wheel.

Fifteen minutes later, she guided the car into one of the many empty parking spots at the bottom of a valley between a forested slope to the north and the ski park to the south. Stepping out onto the gravel, she drew in a slow, deep lungful of fragrant air. The day was clear, and the warm air was richly scented by spruce and fir trees, a spicy aroma that always sparked thoughts of Christmas.

Ellie opened the rear door to retrieve her pack. She rolled up Aaron's jacket and threaded it through the elastic bungee cords that crisscrossed the pack's back. He waited mutely on the far side of the car, and as she slid her arms through the straps and positioned them on her shoulders, she mentally awarded him points for not offering to carry it for her.

"Got your water?" He nodded and held the bottle up. "Okay, then." She slammed the door and pushed a button on the remote fob. The door locks clicked, and the horn gave a feeble *toot*. "Off we go!"

They picked up the lower end of the route and started to climb. The trail they needed started as a jeep track behind the modest ski lodge and angled up the slope in a northwesterly direction. After nearly a mile, the trail turned sharply to the left and continued to climb, eventually curving around so much that they would wind up heading southeast, opposite the direction in which they were now walking. Beyond the switchback, a smaller hiking trail broke off from the jeep road and angled more directly toward the top, ending at the peak. It was the easiest, if not the most direct, route to the summit, and they knew it well enough that they didn't need to pay it much attention.

At first, they talked very little, content to enjoy the scenery and the sun's radiant, invigorating heat. High atop a tree somewhere to their left, a raven uttered an occasional, guttural croak. They passed through successive clusters of trees separated by the nearly parallel ski runs cut from the crest of the ridge down to the lodge. Stepping out into the second of these wide runs, Ellie recalled a thought she'd had the day before.

"This summer makes it six years here for all of us, doesn't it? You, Ryan, me and Sam?"

"Six years in August for me. I guess we all got here sometime that summer."

"Middle school—that seems like ages ago."

"Go Hawks!" he said.

"I remember when you three started high school, and I was still stuck there. I hated that year!"

"Me, too. It was so strange having only those two around. I think it was almost a month before I stopped expecting you to show up at our lunch table."

"Really? You missed me even way back then?" The notion genuinely surprised her. Aaron—and she gave him points for this, too—did not try to play dumb. He smiled at her, but it was a bittersweet expression.

"Oh, *yeah!*"

Not knowing whether to laugh or cry, she opted for a wan smile. "I had no idea," she said.

"Until?" he prompted.

"Until Sam said something a week or so ago. Honestly, I didn't have a clue. But that's entirely because of me, not you," she hastened to assure him. "I just never thought about it before. Being *with* somebody, I mean."

"Because?"

"I dunno. It's not that I chose not to. Not consciously, anyway. But I never wanted to be one of those ditzy, flirty, girly-girls at school, always messing with my hair or worrying about my make-up, obsessing over every zit or something, all to impress some boy. I *hate* all that crap! All I ever wanted was to learn stuff."

"All the same, I was impressed."

She remembered having a similar thought earlier that very morning. If trying to impress him had been a subconscious goal on her part, at least she had been successful. She decided it was time to turn the conversation around. "But what about you? Why didn't you ever say anything?"

"I was happy being around you, even if it meant having Sam and Ryan around, too. I liked spending time with you, watching the way your mind works, and how you always try to be one step ahead. You seemed to have a good time, too, but you clearly weren't interested in having a boyfriend. I was afraid if I spoke up, it might mess everything up, make it all weird."

"Weird like this morning, you mean." She shook her head, still not entirely over the recent awkwardness.

He laughed. "Yeah—*exactly* like that!"

The climb became steeper, their breathing heavier, and for a while they hiked in silence. When they crossed the last ski run and reached the western end of the basin, they turned left and started the final leg of the climb. The trail was narrower here, and their shoulders occasionally bumped as they walked. Once she had adjusted to the increased level of exertion, Ellie resumed the conversation.

"That's not true, actually."

"What's not?" he said.

"That I never thought about it. I just *thought* I never thought about it." He turned to look at her, but she continued before he could point out she hadn't clarified matters. "I've been rethinking things since I talked with Sam. Things having to do with you, I mean. I remember there were many times I would wonder what you were up to. You know, randomly, in the middle of the day or after school. Or I'd feel disappointed if you weren't waiting for us—for *me*, I guess—after class."

She paused and looked at him to be sure he was following her. He gave her a nod and waited for her to continue.

"What I'm trying to say...." she sighed in frustration. "I don't know what I'm trying to say."

"That you were falling under my manly spell without even knowing it?"

Her eyes jerked up to his face, and once again, she could tell he was trying hard not to smile. Then they both laughed at the ridiculous line.

"That is *totally* it!" she said.

The brush of Aaron's knuckles on the back of her hand caused her to look down. Acting on impulse, she wrapped her fingers around his and held her breath, hoping he wouldn't pull away. She kept her eyes glued to the ground while waiting for his response. She didn't want to see his expression if it turned out she had just made an enormous mistake.

On a field trip to the Explora museum in Albuquerque a few years ago, she had placed her hand on the silvery sphere of a Van De Graaff generator. The 300,000-volt static charge that made her entire body tingle and every hair stand on end that day was nothing compared to the thrill she felt when Aaron gently squeezed her hand in return.

She released the withheld breath and looked up into his smiling face. "Seriously... I never had a clue."

They found an open area slightly below the peak that offered them a view west and south, then began searching for a spot to sit. There were many fallen trees from which to choose, and it didn't take long to find one that offered a seat at a comfortable height. Ellie set her pack on the ground against the trunk, then walked to where Aaron stood admiring the view. Directly below them, stretching from the base of Pajarito Mountain to the west, was the Valles Caldera, the collapsed remains of an ancient volcano situated in the heart of the Jemez Mountains. Redondo Peak, its softly curved summit almost a thousand feet higher than where they sat, marked the far end of the bowl-shaped valley. When they looked left, they could make out the near end of the Sandia Mountain Range far to the south.

She made a broad, sweeping gesture that encompassed the entire scene. "Will this do?"

"This is beautiful. I can't remember the last time I was up here. You know—without snow."

Still comfortable in only his tee-shirt, Aaron untangled his jacket from the pack's bungees, folded it lengthwise, and laid it over their chosen log. It was barely large enough to accommodate them both if they sat close. Recalling Ryan's taunt from a few weeks back, she smiled to herself. *'You old smoothie!'*

She sat at one end of the makeshift cushion and set the pack between her feet. She placed her water bottle on the ground and rummaged around for their lunch as Aaron settled beside her. She passed him the sandwich she thought felt heavier, then took out the pretzels and the apple slices. After zipping the pack shut, she placed the opened containers of treats on top.

Lunch now served, she lifted her gaze to the horizon and swept her eyes slowly across the seemingly endless view. "It really is beautiful up here. Too often we take the treasures around us for granted and forget to stop and truly appreciate them."

She had been referring to the scenery, but she instantly recognized an unintended, more personal meaning, and the truth of it made her feel self-conscious. She tried to disguise her discomfort with the suddenly complex and all-consuming task of removing her sandwich from its wax paper bag.

"I just meant we should come up here more often, that's all."

"*Umm…* yeah," he said.

With the weight of that accidental *double entendre* hanging in the air between them, they began to eat. Ellie had never liked making small talk during a meal, and Aaron was never one for small talk at any time. Focused solely on eating, they finished their sandwiches quickly. She took a long draw from her water bottle to wash down the last bite.

Aaron's thin windbreaker might help keep the seats of their pants clean, but it provided nothing in the way of padding. It hadn't been even fifteen minutes since they'd sat, but Ellie's rump was already beginning to protest.

"Would you mind if we move down to the ground?"

"Oh, *please!*" He sounded relieved she had finally made the suggestion. "My butt's killing me!"

She didn't know why—maybe it was a reaction to the tension her earlier comment had created, or perhaps it was simply hearing the usually far more decorous Aaron say *butt*—but she found this innocent statement hilarious, and she began to laugh.

They stood, and he spread his jacket on the grass where their feet had been. She was still laughing as they took their new seats and leaned back against the log.

"What is so funny?!"

"*Butt!*" Her voice was loud enough to startle a nearby pair of crows into flight.

Aaron studied her closely, as if afraid he might have somehow accidentally drugged her sandwich. The concern in his expression made her laugh even harder, and it was nearly a minute until she got herself back under control. Her giggles eventually tapered off to mere aftershocks of occasional chuckles.

Okay, that *was odd!* "I'm sorry. I don't know what that was about." She smiled at him. "I guess I'm just happy to be up here with you."

"Uh-huh," he replied dubiously. He picked up an apple slice and bit it in half.

"Wanna know what's weird?" she said. He paused mid-chew and raised his eyebrows. "What's weird is that I really, *really* am. Happy, I mean. I'm glad we did this." She leaned toward him, laid her head on his shoulder, and closed her eyes. She felt him shift position and was startled a second later by the brief press of his lips to the top of her head.

"Thanks," he said, and breathed out a long, contented sigh.

She sat like that for a long while, not wanting to disturb the perfect tranquility of the moment. As she drifted in a feeling of quiet contentment, random bits of their earlier conversation drifted through her mind. In particular, she remembered a comment he had made near the beginning of their hike, and she sat upright to look at him.

"You said something before about 'the way my mind works.' What did you mean?"

He considered his answer for a moment. "Okay. Remember the day in the park when we were trying to figure out why the books changed in the order they did? You gave one answer, the one about the ripples, then Sam came up with another—the wave function collapse. Both of those were pretty big intuitive leaps. My mind doesn't work that way. I do better starting at point A and incrementally working to B, then moving on to C, D, E, and so on. You can do both. I've seen you grind away at a problem with brute force, chipping away at it bit by bit until you get the solution. But more often, it's like you see the overall pattern and jump straight to the answer. An even better example would be how you just *knew* where the door on the shack would be."

"And how's that different from Sam?"

"My guess is that Sam can sometimes sense a connection between ideas but that the nature of the connection usually remains hidden from her. She couldn't recall what the wave function was, nor explain how it was related to our problem. She felt that the two things were tied together, but only at a subconscious level. I don't think she ever—or rarely, anyway—sees that underlying pattern. But you? Once you see the answer, you also know *why* it's the answer."

"That's why she's so good with people? Because she 'gets' them without having to think about it?"

"Could be. Probably. You saw how she handled Mr. What's-His-Name in the mill—there's no denying she's good at it. She could go to the top of her field if she went into politics, public relations, marketing."

Ellie nodded in agreement. "And what would I be good at?"

He answered without hesitation. "R and D, for one. The research part of it can take you only so far, and sometimes that's right up against a wall. It takes a special type of person to see what lies beyond that wall. Or better yet, to see a new way to get where you want to go that avoids the wall altogether.

"Leibniz said *natura non saltum facit*, but in reality, leaps, are a basic fact of nature, starting with the tiniest of all, the quantum leap.Leaps happen in evolution. Name one important advance humans have made that wasn't a jump from one conceptual paradigm to a whole new way of seeing the world."

"What, off the top of my *head?!*"

"Point is, I don't think there is one. Time after time, we—humans in general, that is—make it to a certain point and then stop. We come to a wall. It takes somebody like Copernicus, or Galileo—or Newton, or Darwin, or Bohr—to show us how to leap beyond that wall. They were all people who could problem-solve in a linear way, like I do, but who could also see those larger patterns and therefore were able to make connections unimaginable to the rest of us. Their brains worked more like yours."

"Newton, Hawking, *Henderson?*" She shook her head in a silent rebuttal, not seeing it. "I don't think so."

He conceded the point with a conciliatory smile. "Yeah, well, probably not. Not to burst your bubble. But on the other hand, when the rest of us were still seeing a VR device, you made a leap and saw the impossible—a time machine."

She considered this a moment, then a wide grin spread across her face. "Wait—you know what you're saying, don't you?"

"Um, I'm thinking... not?"

"That I can see *unicorns!*"

It took him several seconds to recall Diamond Dee's and the conversation about hoofbeats they'd had back in May. When he made the connection, he joined her in laughter.

"*I* get what you mean," he said, "but I wouldn't run around telling everyone that!"

She held her right hand up as if she were preparing to testify. "I swear I will use my powers only for good."

"I'm sure you will." He took her hand and gave it a firm squeeze.

"This is cool! I've never thought about my own brain like this before. I'm not sure I want to spend my life doing research and development, though."

"You don't have to. I thought of that first because it's so obvious, but perhaps you'll have your own high-tech start-up. Or there could be a social policy think tank in your future. After all, that's essentially what we've been doing since the end of May. But who knows? What's important is that you find something to do that allows you to use both of your strengths, the analytical side *and* the intuitive. But I don't doubt that you will, and I'm sure you'll be great at it."

"How can you be so sure?"

"Call it a leap of faith."

They sat in silence for a while then, their hands joined, her head again resting comfortably on his shoulder. Somewhere in the middle of the conversation, she noticed that the usual halting quality was absent from his speech. Then she realized it had been all day. It seemed Sam had been right about him starting to loosen up. He sounded more self-confident, more comfortable with himself, almost like a different person. *Except when we were playing "House," anyway.*

With no direction on her part, her thoughts abruptly refocused on the challenge that still lay before them. Maybe Sam was right about that, too. How tempting it was to let someone else deal with it. She let out another long sigh, this one sounding unmistakably sad.

He registered her change in mood. "Ready to go back to the real world?"

"Never. But I guess we have to."

Ellie made sure anything that remained of their food and any trash they had made was back in her pack. She adjusted her trail shoes, tightening the laces for the steep descent, then stood and handed Aaron his jacket. The wind had picked up, so he shrugged into it but left it unzipped. They stood side by side to admire the vast panorama a final time before leaving. He slid his left arm around her waist and leaned against her. Tilting her head to look up at his face, she was struck by how young he looked. His gaze remained fixed on the view below as though he were trying to etch every detail into his mind. Then she felt him withdraw his arm and step away from her.

"It's time to go," he said.

"Yes, but that doesn't mean we can't take the long way down."

This brought a smile back to his face. "As I said—I like the way you think!"

The path they followed back to the lodge was only slightly longer than the hike up, and, being all downhill, they covered the ground more quickly. They stayed off the major trails as much as possible to avoid mountain bikers. They had yet to see any, but they heard occasional, exhilarated cries cutting through the trees.

At first, they spoke very little as they walked, both trying to avoid topics that would force them back into the real world. After a while, they were altogether silent. She cast repeated glances at him along the way, at his wrinkled brow, at the eyes that seemed focused more inward than on the beauty of their surroundings. It wasn't until they were nearing the lodge that he spoke.

"This was fun. Thanks for suggesting it."

Again there was that sad, wistful tone in his voice, the one she had noticed when he had described the drive west with his mom. Unable to interpret the tone, she responded solely to his words.

"I'm glad you had a good time," she said. "This was the best idea I could come up with on short notice. The old *cranium non saltum facit* on demand, apparently."

He rewarded her halting attempt at Latin with a delighted grin. "That's very good!"

"See that? It's not just my *brain*—I also have a very talented *tongue!*" She realized a split second too late how suggestive the assertion sounded. She inwardly groaned and felt her face burning with embarrassment. *Oh, jeez— tell me we're not back to that again!* To her relief, Aaron mostly let the comment pass.

"I've always thought developing multiple talents is admirable," was all he said. He did have an odd smile on his face, however, and she was glad they reached the car at that point.

"A lot more people here now," she said, desperate to change the subject. There were at least twice as many cars in the parking area than when they had arrived, and most of them sported empty bike racks.

She beeped the car open, put her pack on the floor behind the driver's seat, then slid in behind the wheel. After Aaron was buckled in, she backed the car out of its slot and aimed it toward town.

The silence of their hike down the mountain resumed once they were in the car. Aaron seemed content to stare out his window and watch the land-scape slide by. It wasn't until they were nearing the lower end of the road that either spoke.

"This is my favorite part of the drive," he said, suddenly coming back to life. "Especially at night."

She didn't have a favorite stretch of road, but she thought she could see his point. For more than a hundred yards, the road offered them an unob-structed, bird's-eye view across the research complex to the town beyond. The jagged profile of the Sangre de Cristo Mountains stretched across the distant horizon, providing the scene below them a dramatic background. On a clear evening, the city's lights would make the whole mesa sparkle. Then the road curved sharply to the right, and the view was lost behind them.

Two miles closer to home, they stopped at a light and waited to make the left turn from West Road onto Diamond.

"Want me to drop you at your house?" Ellie said.

"I'd rather go back to your place, if that's okay. I'll walk home later."

"That's more than okay, but if we're going to hang out, there's one stop I want to make along the way."

27

F ive minutes later, they pushed through the front doors of BB Wolf, Los Alamos' only department store. When they first moved to town, her dad had told her and Sam that the "BB" stood for "Big Bad," and that was still how they sometimes referred to the place. Big Bad's clothing selection was supplied mainly by athletic and outdoor apparel manufacturers. Although not inexpensive, the store was the source of much of Sam's wardrobe, strategically procured off-season.

They stopped a few feet inside the main entrance and peered into an enormous glass and faux-wood display case filled with chocolates, fruit jellies, and many other varieties of sugary confections. At the case's opposite end, the salesperson chatted with another customer.

Ellie crouched and gazed at the truffles, inhaling deeply. Unlike Sam, who could be transported to gastronomic euphoria by something as unlikely as an especially zesty jalapeño popper, her food triggers were few and far more specific. Topping that very short list was chocolate. "This is as close to a religious experience as I get, you know."

"It *is* the food of the gods, after all," he said.

"*Hmm?*" she said, distracted by the mounds of chocolate so tantalizingly close. She was more focused on deciding between the raspberry buttercream and a cappuccino truffle than on what he was saying.

"*Theobroma cacao* is the tree they get cocoa from. *Theobroma* translates literally to 'food of the gods.'"

She stood and turned to face him, an enormous smile lighting her face. "I love that you know that! You have to be one of the other four." He stared back at her blankly. "On Sam's list. She said I'm one of the top five smartest people she knows. You *definitely* are one of the others."

"You're telling me you didn't make her tell you the rest of the names?" His voice was heavy with incredulity.

"*Puh-leeze!* I can handle a little competition."

He raised an eyebrow at her, obviously prepared to challenge that assertion, but at that moment, the sales clerk's head appeared over the top of the case.

"Can I help you?" she said with a polite smile.

"Yes!" Ellie chirped. "We'd like some 'god food,' please,"

At home, Ellie carefully backed the car into the garage. She retrieved her pack from behind her seat, then plugged the car's charging cable into the port located forward of the driver's door. When three of the charger handle's four indicator lights came on, she was sure she had attached it properly.

"The first time I plugged it in, I didn't push it on far enough. It sat there all night long, quietly not recharging. Mom was not amused."

"That's better than spilling gasoline all over your shoes at the station," he said. "I did that in Santa Fe once. I pulled the nozzle out of the tank too soon, and the last bit dribbled onto my feet. Had to drive the whole way back with the windows wide open and the fan at full blast so I didn't asphyxiate. At least it was in June and not January."

As they stepped into the house, Ellie pushed the button to close the garage door. Aaron, bag of chocolates in hand, looked around like he was getting his bearings.

"I don't remember ever coming in that way before."

"Wanna go out back?" she said.

"Sure. If there's more water to be had."

"I think I can manage water." She pointed at the bag. "Take those out with you."

She filled two large glasses from the fridge dispenser. Passing the window above the sink, she saw that he was already seated at the table, and she stopped to study him for a moment. He was in the same chair he had used earlier, slouched down, his feet propped up on a second chair he had pulled around to face him. His head was tilted back, and his eyes were closed as if he were catching a quick nap. He looked as relaxed and at ease as she could ever remember seeing him. Sighing softly, she elbowed her way through the screen door.

He opened his eyes as she stepped onto the patio, and watched as she placed his water on the table beside their treats. "Thanks."

She grasped a third chair by its arm and dragged it next to his, and they sat side by side, sharing the makeshift footstool. Looking out across the back yard at the wall of trees that lined the edge of the canyon, she wished, as she often did after being someplace like the top of Pajarito, that they lived up on Arizona Avenue, where Ryan and his dad did. It was only a few hundred feet higher, but the difference in the view was dramatic.

"Here we are again," he said.

"Again we are here."

She leaned toward the table and, stretched out as far as she could without tipping the chair, barely managed to get her fingertips on the bag. Little by little, she carefully inched it nearer until she could get a full grip. Once she had it in her lap, she spread the top with her fingers, raised the opening to her face, closed her eyes, and inhaled a long sniff. She let it out slowly with a deep sigh that, although she didn't realize it—would have vigorously denied it—sounded every bit as erotic as Sam's moans had at Café Pasqual's.

"Oh, yeah... that's *amazing!*"

Aaron squirmed uncomfortably in his chair. "Do you want me to leave you guys alone?"

"*Ha!* Not on your life." She peered into the bag and spotted the piece she wanted. She reached in, pinched it gently between forefinger and thumb, and held it up between them.

"This is one of my favorites. It has a raspberry center with a dark chocolate shell to balance the sweetness of the fruit. This maker uses actual fruit in its fillings, not just extracts, so you might even get a seed or two. Here...."

She extended her arm, offering him a bite. He opened his jaws wide as if expecting her to drop in the entire piece. Instead, she jerked the chocolate away from his gaping mouth. "Hey! You only get half." He eyed her uncertainly. "It's fine. Just take a bite."

She moved the chocolate toward his mouth again. This time, he leaned forward and carefully nipped off a portion.

"Now, don't chew right away. Let it melt a little so you get the full effect." She mushed her half against the roof of her mouth with her tongue. Once it had warmed almost to body temperature, she began chewing.

Aaron went bug-eyed as the intense flavor hit his senses. "Oh, man—that was *good!*"

"Okay, next one. Have a little of your water first."

She peered into the bag and selected a second piece. She held it up in front of him as he placed his glass back on the table. "This is a truffle," she said, displaying a cone-shaped, cocoa-dusted morsel before his eyes.

"What do you mean?"

"Don't try to tell me you've never had chocolate before."

"If *this* is chocolate, then no. Whitman's, I guess…. But what I meant was I thought that last thingy was a truffle, too."

"So, Chocolate 101. Even though most people call them all truffles, technically? That was a buttercream. Did you notice it was pinkish inside instead of brown?" He nodded. "A truffle is chocolate mixed with heated cream, often infused with an added flavor like mint, for instance, to make what's called *ganache*. After it cools, the ganache gets rolled into balls. Used to be that then the balls were rolled in cocoa powder, and when they're made that way, they look like the mushroom truffle, get it? These days they're often coated with a hard chocolate shell. Prettier. Less messy. This one has a shell, but it's also been dusted on top with a little cocoa. Here."

She held it out for him to take a bite, then let him see the chocolatey brown center. She watched as he closed his mouth and began savoring it.

"*Mmm!*" he said through sealed lips.

"I know, right?" She put her half in her mouth and let it start to melt. "What do you taste?" she mumbled.

His eyes went out of focus as he concentrated. "Well, chocolate, obviously, and… more chocolate?"

"*Ding-ding-ding!* It was a trick question—good chocolate does not need additional flavor."

He swallowed. "And I thought the *last* one was good!"

"There's a reason that one is called 'Decadence.' I'm glad you liked them. You can take the last one home with you. Tell me tomorrow what you think."

Suddenly he looked glum. "Yeah, tomorrow...."

"Not looking forward to it?"

His mouth tightened into a grim line as he considered this. "I already know for certain that we're looking in the right place. There were some things at Dad's place that were definitely related to the shack, and there was absolutely no connection with anything I saw in the other labs I went to. I'm starting to get some ideas about what we might have to do, but I'm hoping I'm wrong. I won't know for sure until I can look at some actual facts, and until then, I'd rather not say anything."

She looked at him curiously. It wasn't like him to keep his ideas—even his half-formed ones—to himself this way. She decided not to spoil the good feelings the day had created by pursuing the matter. "Okay," she said at last.

They sat and watched as the sun dipped ever nearer to the mountains. At last, Aaron rose and said he needed to go, and they walked together to the edge of the back yard. For a moment, they stood silently facing one another. She studied his expression while trying unsuccessfully to turn her jumble of feelings into a coherent thought. Finally, she started talking and hoped that whatever came out would not sound too nutty.

"I had a *really* good time today. I know I probably seemed kinda wacko, but...." She sighed and started over. "Look at it this way—I bet you've never given much thought to chocolate before today, have you? Like, beyond genus and species." She smiled at him, and he nodded. "But now that you've had a taste of the good stuff? You see it differently, right? For me, it's something like that, except about you."

He nodded slowly, evidently finding some sense there. "I get it. I had a good time today, too, you know. It was, uh, 'great,'" he said, and they both laughed at the reminder of the morning's awkwardness.

Before he could turn away from her, she stepped forward and hugged him. This time he did not tense up. He returned the gesture uncertainly, but she could feel real emotion behind it. When he stepped back, she saw in his eyes the same warmth she had observed that morning. She saw something else there, too, a darker thought lurking like a shapeless, sinister figure in the shadows. Then he turned and started walking away along the trail. She stood there until he disappeared into the canyon, all the while wondering what he was so reluctant to share.

Ellie was in bed by nine. She was thoroughly worn out, although more by the emotional energy she had expended rather than from the effort of hiking up the mountain, yet she remained too keyed up to go to sleep. She tried to distract herself with a book but gave up after repeatedly reaching the bottom of the same page without being able to remember a single word of what she had just read. Eventually, she put the book aside and let her mind wander randomly through the day's events.

Remembering sitting on the mountain with her head on Aaron's shoulder gave her a warm, fizzy feeling in her stomach. She smiled when she recalled how much he had enjoyed the chocolate. As experiments went, today's had been even more enjoyable than breeding mutant fruit flies.

Shortly after ten, Ellie heard the TV go quiet, followed by Sam saying goodnight to Ryan. She was sitting cross-legged in the middle of her bed when Sam opened the door.

"It's all your fault!" she said, even before Sam was completely inside the room.

Sam was unfazed by the accusation. "Exactly what, may I ask, is supposedly my fault?"

"All of it! Everything!" Ellie pressed the pillow into her face and collapsed backward onto the mattress. "*Aargh!*" Her cry came out muffled through the pillow.

"Well! If I didn't know better, I would say *somebody* was having boy troubles!" Sam sounded delighted by this development.

Ellie sat up again and let the pillow drop into her lap. "Yes! I was with Aaron all day. You know, 'experimenting,' like you said. I spent the whole time feeling like I was about to take a final exam, but I didn't know in which subject!"

"*Ha!* That's... actually... very good!"

Ellie was bothered that Sam considered her summary of her day with Aaron to be in any way an apt one. She sighed.

"It wasn't actually *that* bad. He came over for coffee this morning. I made up a tray of toast and jam and a muffin, and we sat out back with it. That part was totally cringey. I felt like we were Mom and Dad out there, and I kept saying stupid things, spilling the coffee.... Finally, we decided to hike to the top of the ski park, and that was a lot better. Well, except for the one giggle-fit I had. And then there was that 'tongue' thing." This she muttered as an afterthought, but even that memory made her smile.

Sam's eyebrows arched with surprise, but she said nothing. Instead, she nodded toward the laundry basket where the clothes Ellie had worn that day —the hand-me-down outfit—sat on top of the pile. "At least you looked good," she teased. "Can't overestimate the importance of that, you know, stuck out here in the boonies."

"*Thppt!*" It was the only response Ellie could muster. She couldn't help but grin, though, remembering that long-ago conversation. She placed her pillow against the wall and leaned back against it.

"After the hike, we came back here and had chocolates from Wolf's. You should have seen his face. Eighteen years of M&Ms and Snickers Bars, then *boom*, Le Grand truffles! He was so cute!"

"So, you had a good time, then." It was more a statement than a question.

Staring up at the ceiling, Ellie laughed and shook her head as if she couldn't believe it herself. "Yeah, I did. I actually did." She sighed again, this time happily.

"*Ellie's got a boyfriend!*" Sam gave her words the bouncing lilt of a playground taunt, but Ellie ignored her.

Sam continued to get ready for bed, and Ellie, eyes closed and lying perfectly still, found she could easily identify most of the noises coming from the far end of the room. The sound of a drawer opening and sliding shut again meant Sam had taken out a pair of shorts and a tank top to sleep in. Then there was the soft clap of her jewelry box lid closing—she had removed her earrings and put them away. A minute later, she heard the swish of Sam's dirty clothes, wadded into a tight ball, arcing through the air and landing in the laundry basket with a soft *whump*. The quiet rustle of cloth against skin was Sam getting dressed for bed, and that was followed by the whisper of her brush sliding through her hair. These were the familiar sounds of their nightly routine, and she generally found them comforting. Tonight, however, she could swear there was a different sound in the room, and this one she found ever so slightly irritating.

"Stop that!"

"Stop what?" Sam said, all innocence.

"I can hear you grinning!"

28

It wasn't until seven-thirty the following evening that everyone could get together to hear Aaron's news. Sam rarely worked at the aquatic center until close, and Friday was one of her three usual days off, but on this particular Friday, she had volunteered to fill in for someone away on vacation. Ellie caught a whiff of the acrid odors wafting from her sister's clothes, and she hoped her imaginary visitors from the chlorine planet were enjoying their time on Earth.

They met at a spot chosen for its convenience, a small, unadorned courtyard nestled among the buildings on the university campus. It was close to Aaron's house and on the way home for Sam and Ryan. Ellie hiked the same trail she used to get to the high school and then crossed Diamond to reach the university. They sat together on a low, concrete wall encircling a large, raised planter.

"How did the big undercover op go?" Ryan said. "Were you able to sneak your thumb drive in?"

"Yeah, right!" Aaron rolled his eyes. "I could have gone in and out of there with a ten-terabyte hard drive tucked under my arm, and they wouldn't have cared. Technically, there is security, but they've gotten pretty lax. Granted, I couldn't have gotten in on my own, but I bet if I went back out on Monday, waved, and said, 'Hey, Frank. I left my pencil on my dad's desk,' or something equally stupid, he'd probably let me waltz right back in."

"Could you?" Ryan said. "Waltz? I'm trying to picture that. Personally, I'd rather see you jitterbug in. Or limbo."

"Or *twerk!*" Ellie added. "Now, *that* would be something."

Sam laughed. "I was going to say 'mambo,' but I prefer Ellie's twerking idea."

"All right, all right...." Aaron's ears had become an alarmingly brilliant shade of pink. "Point is, once I was there, nobody paid that much attention to me. On Wednesday, I taped the thumb drive to the bottom of one of the chairs and left it there. Today I retrieved it and loaded it up."

"And?" Ellie said. "Did you find out anything new at all?"

He shook his head. "I haven't had time to go through any of the files yet. I did find this out, though—the new project code? *Backstep.*"

"Wow," Ryan said, unimpressed. "That bunch seriously needs to hire a marketing guy."

"Agreed. And to answer your question, Dad's lab is staged so that anyone coming in sees research on a concept to create a remote neural interface with things like drones, for instance. Or bomb disposal robots. Submersibles. He said the idea is to remove the intervening layer of technology—screens, buttons, joysticks—from between the operator and the device. So they have a few of the studded chairs there, presumably to demonstrate how the connections work, and they were virtually identical to what we saw in the shack."

"Are they really working on the remote control idea?" Ryan said.

"If not, they should be. It's a great one. I never saw anyone so much as glance at any of it, though. But I didn't spend a lot of time there on Wednesday. That morning there were about fifteen people sitting at computers in a separate room. It looked like they were doing research, taking notes. I was looking through a glass wall, too far away to read their monitors, but I could tell it was all text. No CAD, no formulas, and they didn't look like techs."

"Researchers... like maybe historians?" Sam suggested.

He shrugged. "That was my guess. It would make sense."

"The few people who clearly were technicians were in a different area. From what I could overhear, I gathered they were still trying to wrap up their investigation of what happened back in May, not on some bogus 'neural interface' project.

"After only twenty minutes at his place, Dad had one of the junior techs —Ishanvi, I think her name was—take me around to a couple of other labs out there. Some of the projects I saw were pretty interesting, but none of them had anything to do with the shack. One group was working on test modules to be installed on rovers looking for life on other planets. I could have stayed there the whole time, but as it was, we didn't get back until almost the end of the day. Then I had to wait around while Dad was in a meeting for two hours, and that wasn't even in his lab but over at the Admin building."

"And today...?" Ryan said.

"Mostly, it was pretty boring. Like Dad said, Fridays are usually slow, but that did give me that chance to look around. There are a couple of real labs, cleanroom types of places, but nothing was happening in either of them. The first one was where they developed the nerve induction components. I saw a shelf full of things that looked like early versions of the helmet devices. Some of them had spikes instead of rounded studs."

Sam winced. "*Yowch!*"

"That's what I said. The other room had more to do with straight-up electronics rather than biotech. They had a few panel prototypes leaning against a wall, not hooked up to anything. There was also a stack of those big, GraphMax batteries in one corner. And maybe they did the programming for the computer control system there, too, but today everything just seemed to be collecting dust.

"I never got to see inside the third area. That was a separate building a hundred yards away from the main one. Like a small, concrete bunker, almost out at the tree line. When I asked, Dad said they conduct 'sensitive tests' out there and wouldn't say any more about it."

"Do you think that's where they tested the time-travel part of the device?" Ryan said.

"Again, it makes sense, but I can't be sure. I suppose they could control everything remotely, rig it up with a camera and an auto-return routine. Send the device back, have it grab a couple of photos so you know it's working. Presumably, even if you were standing beside it, you wouldn't notice anything happening while it's doing its thing. One second it would be there, and the next it would still be there, having gone and come back in the same micro-instant. At most, you might hear a faint *pop* or something if the timing wasn't perfect. Air displacement, like a tiny thunderclap."

"That is still so hard to grasp," Sam said. She raised her hand and rubbed her left temple as though trying to massage away a headache.

"Something I realized, looking out at that tiny, remote lab? Dad's building is at the edge of the complex out there. Which sorta figures, since it's one of the newest. But it struck me how easy it would have been for someone to dig that utility trench without anyone noticing. Of course, they'd have to tie it directly into the main trunk somewhere—running it straight back to Dad's lab would defeat the whole purpose of hiding it in the first place.

"And one other thing." He looked at Ryan. "They have their own, separate security there. There's a fence around the place, and your dad's guys take care of everything up to it, but I don't think even *they* could get past the gate."

They all considered this for a long, silent moment. It was interesting, Ellie thought, but it didn't bear directly on their problem. "Given everything you've said, especially about the researchers, it sounds like the engineering phase is done and they're getting ready to put it to use."

Aaron nodded. "That's what I thought, too. We need to come up with a plan fast."

"But you did get some files out of there?" Ryan said.

"Yeah. Toward the end of the day, Dad got called out of the lab for a while. That was my chance to get on his computer, only I didn't know how long he'd be gone, so I couldn't be very selective about what I grabbed. I started copying whole directories that were named anything that looked relevant and kept going until the drive was full. I had just finished hiding it behind my belt buckle when he got back. I have no idea what I got, but there's a lot of it. I'll know more by the end of tomorrow, but my guess is it'll be Monday—Tuesday, maybe—before I have a good handle on it."

"So that's it for now?" Ryan said.

Aaron hesitated. "There is one other thing. I don't know what it means, or even if it means anything at all." He glanced briefly at each of them before continuing. "When I was in that first cleanroom, the one with the spiked helmets, I saw things that reminded me of thin wetsuits hanging in a cabinet."

"Wetsuits?" Sam said.

"Or adult-sized, onesie pajamas, if you like that image better."

"I'm squarely in the anti-pajama camp," Ryan said.

"What do you think they were?" Ellie said.

"The cabinet was locked, so I couldn't check them out. They might have been merely a uniform, some lame *esprit de corps* sort of thing, but I doubt it. I could see things running under the surface. Wires, maybe. Or tiny tubes. Remember that little hole or socket between the two pairs of wrist studs?" She nodded. "I've been wondering if the suits actually do something, like if they plugged into the chairs there."

"Maybe they keep you from feeling so sick," Sam suggested.

"I'd like to believe that isn't supposed to happen, so that could be at least part of it. Anyway, I thought you should know we might be missing something important, maybe some form of protection, by not having the suits. But again, I'm only speculating here."

Sam looked at Ellie and raised her brows in an unspoken question. Ellie frowned and responded with a subtle shake of her head. She thought the idea of suits might answer one minor question, though. "If we were supposed to be wearing them, that would explain why the clothing bins opened after we got to Lawrence rather than before we left. I've been wondering about that."

"Yeah," Aaron said. "That makes sense."

"Anything else?" Ryan said.

"That's all I have so far."

Ryan stood and offered a hand to Sam. She took hold, and he pulled her to her feet. "All right, then—good job. Keep us posted," he said, then they turned and walked hand in hand out of the courtyard.

Ellie waited until they were gone. "Do you want me to help?"

"No. I mean, yes, I'd like that, but no, I can't let you. I'd prefer none of you even knew I have that stuff. Ryan makes it seem all cool and James Bondy, but stealing those files is serious. I don't want you guys involved any more than you already are."

She was disappointed, but she nodded. "I get it. So... Monday?"

"I hope. As soon as possible." That was all he would promise.

"Anything more about what you were thinking yesterday?"

"No. Except I still *really* hope I'm wrong."

"And you won't...?"

He shook his head. "No. Not yet."

They had worked closely together for so many hours since the end of school, and suddenly she felt excluded, unnecessary. Understanding his reasons didn't make it sting any less. She tried to keep the disappointment out of her voice. "Okay. It just seems like an awful lot to sift through, that's all."

"I'll get rid of the garbage first. There shouldn't be much to deal with after that. Figuring out how we can use whatever's left... that will be the *real* challenge. That's where I'll need you the most."

They stood and regarded each other from a few feet apart. Again she got the impression that he was going through some internal struggle. Whether it involved their efforts with the shack or had something to do with her—with *them*—she couldn't tell.

"Are you okay?"

"Yeah, yeah, I'm fine," he said. "Very tired, a little stressed, but... I'm okay."

His smile, meant to be reassuring, left her unconvinced. She thought "exhausted and totally frazzled" might have been closer to the truth, but she let it go.

"If you need to... I mean, I'm...." She stammered, not knowing what to say. Or do. They had felt so close only the day before, and now she could only stand there, thumbs hooked into the pockets of her shorts, feeling awkward all over again.

"I know. Thanks. We'll go over everything in a few days."

"Okay. Well... goodnight." She remained where she stood. This didn't feel like a "huggable moment."

"Goodnight," he said. He gave her a slight wave, then turned around and headed toward his house.

She walked home slowly, returning via the same route by which she had come. By the time she reached the trail along the canyon's rim, the one that led to her back yard, the lack of daylight would have been an issue had she not known the way well enough to travel it safely both backward and blindfolded. She was crossing the middle of the lawn when she felt her phone vibrate in her pocket.

Aaron—Sorry that was weird. Thanks for understanding. As soon as I find something out I'll let you know. Promise.
Ellie—Thanks. Don't stress over it too much. Good luck!

She hesitated on the verge of deleting the heart, but that little "go with it" voice was back and sounding pretty sure of itself. She took a deep breath, held it in, and pressed the "Send" arrow. The "Delivered" notification appeared below her message a second later, and she stopped at the edge of the patio to wait for his reply. Five seconds ticked by. Ten. And then—

Aaron—❤️!!!

Equal parts excited and relieved, she let her breath out with a loud *whoosh!* Her grin was bigger and goofier than ever, but as she pulled the screen door open and stepped into the kitchen, she realized she didn't care who saw it.

She repeatedly checked for another message over the course of the evening, but he had gone dark. That little red heart was the last she heard from him until Monday, save for a single message he sent during the waning hours of Saturday night.

Aaron—

29

Over the weekend, Ellie worked hard at keeping herself distracted. She and her mom left early Saturday morning on a shopping trip to Albuquerque. With vacation just days away, her mom wanted to pick up a few new outfits and had asked Ellie to accompany her, mainly to provide a second opinion she could trust. It was not the first time Ellie had helped out in this way, and it was a perennial mystery why she, rather than the more fashion-conscious daughter, was usually chosen for this decidedly dubious honor. Or rather, it had been a mystery until one day Sam confided that the one time she had gone along, she had talked their mother into making several buying decisions the price of which had nearly sent their father into an apoplectic fit. His objections had vanished, however, once he saw her wearing the new ensembles. Sam chalked it up as a win for good fashion sense, but she had never been asked to go along again.

"And I call that a win-win scenario if there ever was one," she said.

Driving non-stop to Albuquerque pushed the limits of the Focus' range, and although it had always made it, wondering if this were the time it wouldn't made each trip a little nerve-wracking. The return drive was a different matter since, along with the distance, it also required gaining two thousand feet in elevation. The climb, plus the need to use the air conditioner in the often scorching afternoon heat, meant attempting a non-stop return was almost guaranteed to fail. The obvious solution was to stop in Santa Fe to at least partially recharge before driving the final leg. Why her mom insisted on taking her own car rather than the gasoline-powered Subaru was yet another long-standing mystery. Ellie decided it was her way of living on the edge.

Whatever the reason, the promise of a Santa Fe layover made the entire outing worth it. She knew her mom would indulge her desire to visit her favorite bookstore and that afterward, they would likely have an early dinner somewhere near the plaza. Even if she didn't appreciate food with the same euphoric intensity as Sam, she believed that any day that ended with dinner in Santa Fe was a good one.

They arrived at the ABQ Uptown shopping center with "whole miles," as her mom put it, left on the battery. They found an open spot at a charging station in a nearby parking lot, and Ellie plugged the car in. She spent the following several hours tagging along from store to store, her role frequently alternating between that of fashion consultant and pack mule. For reasons she wouldn't have been willing to explain, she welcomed the distraction the day's excursion offered, and happily performed either task as required. Moreover, she found herself actually enjoying helping her mom pick out clothes, and even contributed one selection of her own to the new vacation wardrobe. And from the sale rack!

In Santa Fe, Ellie scoured the shelves at the Collected Works Bookstore. Her goal was to find something engaging enough to keep her mind from fixating on Aaron until he was ready to share what he had learned. After twenty minutes of intense browsing, she ultimately chose a book she had noticed on the New Fiction display when they had first entered. *The Boy on the Bridge* was a prequel to a story she had enjoyed a few years before. She figured if it were only half as good, it would more than do the trick. As a bonus, her mom insisted on paying, which Ellie thought was the best of all possible win-win situations.

It was still too close to lunch for either of them to have much of an appetite, so they opted for something light. They lucked into a railing-side table at a taproom that offered a second-story view of the plaza to go along with the local beers and gourmet pizza they served. A waiter appeared as soon as they had seated themselves under a dark blue umbrella, jotted down their order for two sodas and a Santa Fe Chicken pizza, then walked away to check on his other tables.

A second later, a bright flash caught Ellie's attention. When she glanced in that direction, she saw it was merely sunlight bouncing off the glass door as a different waiter pushed through it with a tray laden with beers for a nearby table. The flash struck her again as the door swung the other way. When it closed, she found she was staring at the unremarkable reflection of a young girl preparing to share a mid-afternoon meal with her mother.

That it was her own image in the glass brought home the absurdity of her situation. Sitting across the table from her mom, a new science fiction book in a bag at her feet, she couldn't help but see herself as she knew the rest of the world viewed her—as little more than a child. The weight of the secret burden she shared with Sam, Aaron, and Ryan was one she believed few adults had ever shouldered, but that didn't change the fundamental fact that they really were just a bunch of kids.

She was instantly overcome by a frigid wave of self-doubt, an icy sensation that spread outward from her stomach into every part of her body and left her chilled, despite the day's heat. In addition to *agape* and *eros*, Mrs. Foucault had taught about another Greek concept, *hubris*. Was her insistence that they deal with the shack on their own nothing more than an expression of misguided and ill-concealed arrogance? Did it all come down to ego? It was arrogance that had gotten them into this situation to start with. Was she making the same mistake all over again?

She reconsidered Sam's preference for dropping the entire problem in someone else's lap. Would it hurt to talk it over with her mom, if only in hypothetical terms? It wasn't until she looked away from her reflection that she realized her mom was saying something.

" ...and then there he was—*your father*—sprinting across the middle of the quad without a stitch on!"

"*Huh?!*" Ellie gaped in confusion. She could not imagine a story her mom could tell that would end that way, but she was certain she didn't want to hear it.

"Welcome back." Her mom smiled, amused by Ellie's bewildered reaction to the risqué ploy she'd used to pull her focus out of her head and back into the real world. "As I was saying, the other night you said something like, 'things are strange enough already.' That made me wonder if everything's okay."

Ellie thought fast, trying to conjure up a suitable response, preferably one that didn't involve trespassing on restricted federal lands, conspiracy to destroy government property, and, most especially, time machines. "Yeah, I guess. It's just…. I've been picturing how different everything's going to be next year when I'm still stuck in high school and Sam and the rest of them are across the street. It'll be weird. For a while, anyway."

"It's only one year, and then you'll be there, too. You survived the last time, when...."

Her mom was interrupted by the arrival of their drinks. The waiter placed small, square napkins on the table, then set their glasses on top.

"Thanks," Ellie said.

"Your pizza will be out in a minute," he said, then left.

"…when they started going to high school," her mom finished.

"I know," Ellie said. "It's not a big, huge deal or anything. Just something I've been thinking about, that's all."

"It's possible to do too much of that, you know. Thinking, that is." After subjecting Ellie to a brief, pensive appraisal, her mom smiled. "Okay, then. But remember—big deal or not, you can always come to me if you need to talk. Got it?"

Ellie nodded. "Got it."

She felt it again, the seductive tug of the idea of dumping their problem onto someone else. Should she? Would that be better, or simply easier?

She mentally reviewed the various arguments for dealing with the shack themselves, alert to signs of rationalization. Not ego, she decided. And not arrogance. All their reasons were valid ones. She was sure they were handling the situation exactly right, and was equally sure Aaron would find the answers they'd been after. Okay, so she might be guilty of over-confidence, she allowed.

Her mind was made up. She wasn't going to discuss it in any way, hypothetical or otherwise, with her mom. Instead, she smiled across the table at her.

"So, what's this about Dad streaking?"

After eating, they walked slowly through town, staying within a block or two of the plaza. They'd already been to the one place she'd had on her list, but she could never pass on the opportunity to enjoy the beauty of Santa Fe's old, historic center. As they strolled by the front of Saint Francis' Cathedral, During the day, it was a muted yellow, but the color intensified as the sun sank lower toward the western horizon, and she had seen the building glow brilliantly near sunset. Even at this early hour, with the sun still high over-head, it was a striking scene.

Ellie exhaled a long, contented sigh. "Okay. I'm good."

Back at the Convention Center charging station, she urged her mom to let her drive home. Despite having her provisional license for nearly a year, she had rarely driven outside the undemanding confines of Los Alamos and nearby White Rock. She wanted to see if she was up to the challenge of navi-gating the narrow, busy streets of downtown Santa Fe on a Saturday after-noon. Her mom, obviously reluctant but unable to argue with its reasonableness, acceded to the request. Ellie thought she did well, even if her mom did stomp on an imaginary passenger-side brake pedal more than once, and despite hearing her heave a theatrically loud sigh of relief once she had merged the car onto the broad, six-lane highway that ran north toward home.

She helped her mom carry in the bags of new clothes, said a brief hello to her dad, then curled up with her new book for the rest of the evening. By the time she turned in for the night, she was grateful they had only an inani-mate time machine to deal with and not a world full of fungus-addled "hungries."

Aaron's short, pictographic message gave her flagging optimism a much-needed boost, and she began Sunday feeling better than she had the day before. Still, she would have given nearly anything for some actual details. She sat in bed, thumbs poised over her phone's screen, debating whether or not she should try to pry some out of him. Eventually, she decided to trust he'd let her know what was going on as soon as he was ready, and she set the phone back on her desk.

She started attacking her chores list by first emptying half of the contents of the laundry hamper into the washing machine. The month she had agreed to was up, but she still felt so bad about the beating Ryan had suffered in Lawrence that she continued to do every load. It was almost literally "the least she could do," she acknowledged, but it helped assuage her lingering feelings of guilt.

In the kitchen, she went through the refrigerator shelf by shelf, then inspected the two crisper drawers for anything past the point of edibility. They appeared to be doing better at using stuff up because the only things she found to toss were a container of homemade salsa that was getting green and fuzzy around the edges, and a bag of cilantro, mostly stems, that had turned dark, slimy, and unbelievably foul-smelling. Three of their oranges were beginning to look withered, but she promised herself she would make juice out of them before it was too late. She gave each shelf a quick wipe, then moved on to the next task.

Her father had already hauled the old-fashioned push mower around to the rear of the house when she joined him in the back yard. While he made nearly silent passes back and forth over the sparse grass, she used her gloved hands and a flat-bladed screwdriver to pull out any weeds growing between the patio's bricks. Above the rapid *snick-snick-snick* of the mower, she could hear her father whistling a vaguely familiar melody as he made his laps, something peppy she recognized but couldn't quite identify. Her dad was not usually a whistler, so she guessed he was trying to make some subtle point. He often tossed out random brain teasers for her and Sam to solve.

She let the back of her mind pick away at the puzzle while she worked. In time she decided the melody came from an old album they had acquired, along with a pile of others and the turntable needed to play them, after her grandfather died. They had spent a winter night a few years ago listening to several of the albums as a sort of tribute. Everyone agreed that the record she thought this tune was from, a collection of jazzy trumpet pieces, was one of the best. She recalled the track had an odd, repetitive-sounding name but was having trouble dredging it up to the surface.

When the title of the piece finally came to her ten minutes later, she had to laugh. *More and More Amour!* Although in this case, it was undoubtedly supposed to be something like—

"More and More I Mow 'er! Good one, Dad!" she called across the yard. She had to give it to him—his 'dad jokes' were the best.

He acknowledged her praise with a wave and a gratified smile. "I'm glad you finally got it. I about wore out my whistler!" Then, mere seconds later, he went right back to whistling.

With the weeding done, she stripped off her gloves and went inside to move the clean laundry over to the dryer, then started the second load. While in the garage, she lifted the long-handled squeegee from its hook on the wall and carried it through the house to the back yard. Moving from window to window, she gave each a thorough spray from the garden hose, then used the squeegee to wipe it dry. When she finished the back side of the house, she coiled the hose over her arm and walked to the front yard, where she repeated the process until all the windows sparkled.

After putting away the squeegee and hose, she extricated the vacuum cleaner from among the many jackets filling the entry closet and zoomed it around the living room and hallway. Sweeping completed, she stepped on the button to retract the cord and placed the heavy machine back in the closet. Lastly, she wiped a cloth over all the room's horizontal surfaces and declared her work done for the day.

Whoops! Except for the laundry, she remembered. She emptied the dryer, transferred the wet second batch over from the washer, and took the first load to her bedroom for folding. She was sliding the final few items into her drawer when Sam came in, her half-day Sunday shift over.

"Aww, thanks, El!" she said when she spotted the empty hamper.

"No problem. If you're missing something, the other load should be done in twenty-five minutes or so."

"I'm good. Any word from Aaron today?" Drawers slid open and closed again as Sam began piecing together a new outfit.

"Nope. Not a peep. Well, one peep, I guess. He seems to be on to something, but all I got was a 'thumbs-up' in the middle of the night. Kinda worries me. I think he'd let me know if he's getting somewhere."

"I bet those files he took had all kinds of charts and schematics, lots of long, complicated formulas—maybe he's just having too much fun to remember to text you!"

Ellie laughed. "You're probably right. He's finally achieved nerdvana and can't be bothered with us poor, unenlightened souls!" Remembering how he had not long ago abruptly left her standing alone in front of the school so he could rush home and check on his bacteria cultures, she decided that Sam's guess might not be far off the mark. If that were the reason for his silence, she guessed she was okay with it.

She watched curiously as Sam slipped out of her pool uniform and changed straightaway into a similar outfit. She pulled on a thin, white tank top over a vivid blue sports bra and stepped into a pair of black spandex shorts. She completed her *ensemble* with a pair of ankle socks. It was not a typical Sam outfit.

"Off to see Mr. Collins, I assume?" Ellie said.

"Mm-hmm. He hasn't run much since track season ended. He wants to get back into it over the summer. I'm going to try to keep up."

"Ah." This explained both Sam's choice not to take a shower and her atypical selection of athletic wear.

"What about you?" Sam took an elastic hairband from a small basket on her dresser and used it to draw her hair into a ponytail.

"*Hmm…?*"

"What are you doing this afternoon? Want to come? He'll take it easy on us—I promise."

Ellie considered the offer. Running, outside the white outlines of a soccer field, was not normally an activity she enjoyed, but some mind-clearing physical exertion was perhaps exactly what she needed right now.

"Sure, why not? Thanks." She looked down at the clothes she'd worn for doing her housework and figured the old cotton shorts and tattered tee were equally suitable for a short run. She saw only a few dirt smudges left from weeding the patio, and she was mostly dry again after washing the windows. She chose a pair of socks from her drawer and turned to face Sam. "Okay, I'm ready."

Sam eyed her shabby outfit skeptically but made no comment. Instead, she turned and led the way out of their bedroom. "Alrighty then, let's go. This'll be fun!"

"You're starting to oversell it."

"It. Will. Be. Fun."

Hearing the firm emphasis on each word, Ellie realized it was not her Sam was attempting to psych up. She tried to sound encouraging. "Ah, I see now. Yes, I'm sure it will be!"

They finished their run at the top of the long, steady climb Diamond made after it passed the two school campuses and entered the residential north side of town. Ellie leaned forward, hands on knees, trying to catch her breath. Sam, face blotchy from the heat and exertion, also panted heavily. In contrast, Ryan's stance was relaxed, and his breaths came at slow, even intervals. He was sweating, but he otherwise looked like he might have just risen from taking a nap.

I guess he was taking it easy on us. Ellie forced herself to stand upright and concentrated on slowing her breathing, counting to three on the inhale, four on the exhale. She would not have called it "fun," but the hilly, three-mile circuit had the desired effect on her mood. Her thinking felt less fuzzy than it had in days. *Gotta love those endorphins!*

Watching from the corner of her eye, she saw Ryan lean close to Sam, lay his hand on her arm, and speak softly into her ear. Not softly enough, though, because she caught the words *to my house* and something that sounded like *already sweaty*. He stood up straight and grinned at her, left eyebrow raised expectantly.

"*Ryan!*" Sam exclaimed and gave him a playful shove on his chest. She sounded more amused than scandalized, but she blushed as she cast a self-conscious glance at Ellie.

Ellie, already choosing to assume he had suggested something as innocent as cleaning the garage, managed to keep both her expression and her tone neutral. "Want me to tell Mom you won't be home for dinner?"

Sam turned to look at Ryan while she answered, speaking mainly for his benefit. "No. I'll be there." Then she spun around and began striding purposefully up the sidewalk toward his house. Ryan remained rooted in place, held in thrall by the sinuous sway of her body as she walked away, a look of total adoration on his face.

"C'mon, you!" she called over her shoulder. He came to then and, still smiling, jogged off after her.

Ellie covered the final few blocks to her house at a slow trot, grateful it was all downhill. By the time she reached her front door, she had cooled off and could breathe normally again.

She filled a tall glass with water from the fridge's dispenser and stood by the kitchen sink while she downed it in small swigs. Her dad was at the far end of the back yard where he seemed to be doing some maintenance work on the fence. Her mom was resting on one of the lounge chairs, its back raised to nearly vertical, reading a magazine.

She wondered if her mom had likewise struggled to define her feelings for her dad back when they had first dated. Or had it been more like Sam with Ryan, their relationship coalescing in a single 'aha' moment? She tried to imagine some remote point in the future when she and her as-yet-unknown husband would while away Sunday afternoons together. She couldn't picture it.

She drank the last of the water and set the glass on the counter beside the sink, still studying her parents.

What I wouldn't give for a time machine that went the other way.

Ellie was sitting upright on her bed, absorbed in the final chapters of her new book, when Sam returned a few hours later. She still wore the workout clothes but appeared to have showered at some point during the afternoon. This guess was confirmed when she began changing directly into fresh clothes for dinner.

"Have fun cleaning the garage?" Ellie said, not looking up from her book.

"*Cleaning the garage?*" Sam echoed, confused. "No, he wanted help moving some boxes around in the attic. His dad asked him to find some paperwork from back when they lived in Jersey." Her face reddened as she realized Ellie must have overheard Ryan's suggestive invitation, and she began to stammer. "Wait... why did you think we... I mean...."

Ellie did not respond. Delighted at suddenly appearing omniscient, she merely gave Sam a smug, knowing smile.

"All right, fine!" Sam said. "So yeah, he said, 'If you want a different kind of workout, come on back to my house. After all, you're already sweaty.' Of course, what I *thought* he meant... never mind. So anyway, we get there and then spend the next forty-five minutes digging through dusty, old U-Haul boxes until he finally finds the stuff his dad wanted. It must have been a hundred and ten degrees up there! I was *sooo*...."

"Disappointed?" Ellie suggested impishly. *"Frustrated?"*

Sam flashed her an equally impish grin. "Yeah, well... only for the first forty-five minutes!"

Hours later, Ellie lay in the dark staring at the phone on her desk, willing the screen to light up with a message from Aaron. If the information she was waiting for weren't so important, she would have felt foolish, even more mush-brained than she had while getting dressed for the hike up Pajarito. She had certainly gone a lot longer than forty-eight hours without hearing from him before, but tonight each passing minute felt like an hour. And besides, she felt more like a spy waiting to hear from a fellow agent than a love-struck schoolgirl.

She fought to stay awake until she got word from him, even just another "thumbs up" emoji, but as the minutes literally did become hours, drowsiness began to get the upper hand. Her mind would wander off in pursuit of some interesting thought, then she would jerk back into consciousness and realize she had been dreaming. Despite her best efforts, sometime after eleven the dreams won for good.

30

E llie woke up early and immediately checked her phone, squinting at the bright screen through one partially opened eye. Nothing. At the same time, she noticed Sam was already up and out of the room, her bed neatly made. She sat up and rubbed her face with both palms, giving the last tendrils of sleep time to withdraw themselves from her brain. She took a deep breath, closed her eyes, and leaned back against the wall.

She felt uneasy. It was a vague anxiety with no specific cause she could point to, but the sense of foreboding gave her a tight knot in the pit of her stomach. She kneaded the ache absently with the heel of her right hand. Maybe the feeling had to do with the odd way Aaron had been acting recently, she thought, and the sense she'd had that he was keeping something from her.

"Anything yet?"

She opened her eyes to see Sam leaning in through the half-open door. She shook her head. "No, not yet."

"Then I'm outta here. Let me know if anything big comes up?"

Ellie nodded. Sam closed the door, and she was alone again.

After showering and dressing, she poured herself a bowl of granola, but found after a few bites that she didn't have much of an appetite. She forced herself to eat as much as she could before emptying her bowl into the garbage disposal and *whirring* the remains down the drain. She picked up the electric kettle from its base and turned toward the fridge, but hesitated. No coffee today, she decided—she felt jittery enough already. She had just replaced the kettle when her phone finally buzzed.

Aaron—Hi. In front of the library in half an hour? Just you
Ellie—Hey. I'll be there

She left as soon as she put her shoes on, knowing she'd be early but feeling too anxious to sit idly around the house for even another minute. That he had asked to see her alone made her more uneasy than ever. She exited through the back door and crossed the lawn to where the trail started. She ate up some of the extra time by taking a few detours along the way. The distractions of the canyon—the trees, the rock formations, the occasional streak of blue or black slashing through the air ahead of her, plus the need to focus a significant portion of her attention on where she was putting her feet—began to have their usual soothing effect.

She re-emerged into town after many twists and turns, feeling better than she had all morning. A few minutes later, she entered the small playground in front of the library, sat on the ground under one of the towering ponderosas, and rested against its rough, substantial trunk. Early, as anticipated, she tilted her head back against the tree, closed her eyes, and waited patiently. She let her thoughts drift and felt almost like her usual self when Aaron arrived and pulled her out of her reverie.

"You're going to get pine pitch on your shirt."

She opened her eyes to see him peering down at her. She didn't bother to check her phone, knowing he was on time, probably to within a few milliseconds.

"I've got gas," she said, sitting up straighter.

He blinked at this bizarre non sequitur, and she laughed when she realized how crude her announcement had sounded.

"*White* gas—like for a camp stove? Takes the pitch right out."

Now they were both laughing.

"All the same, I'm going to sit over here. You know, up-wind, just to be safe." He plopped himself onto the ground at the base of the nearest neigh-boring tree, facing her.

She was about to blurt out, *So, whatcha got?* but caught herself. *This social etiquette crap is such a pain!* "How'd it go over the weekend?" she said instead.

He yawned and rubbed his eyes. "It went okay, I guess. I started by sorting through all the stuff I got on Friday. Like I figured, most of it was useless, but there were a few files that helped a lot. I learned enough to know what we need to do. My first guesses were right, it turns out. I went over it all again last night, but...." He yawned again, then gave his head a quick shake. "Sorry. I'm totally wiped."

He looks more than 'wiped,' she thought, but didn't say so. "Do we need to go inside to use a computer?" she said instead, fighting a sudden urge to yawn.

"I thought we might. That's why I suggested meeting here. But I decided on the way over we don't have to. It's easier if I just tell you. If you want to look at anything afterward, we can go in. The solution isn't in the files, though."

Haggard—that's the word. This bothered her deeply, although she couldn't have expressed why. She sensed that earlier anxiety stirring in the back of her mind, a dozing cat perking up its ears because it's heard potential prey scuttle into range. *Stay!* she told it.

"Okay, sure. Whatever's best."

He sat quietly for almost a minute before speaking. "Remember Ryan saying his grandfather came to the U.S. in the fifties? That got me thinking. My grandfather, Dad's father that is, came to New York, too, but a little earlier. In the thirties. He got out of Germany right before everything started to go seriously downhill, and by the time the U.S. got into the war, he was too old to get drafted. Actually, he went to London first, in 1932, and stayed there for a few years. Then he got on a steamer for New York in '36.

"Once here, he got a job as a tailor and later owned his own men's suit shop, which is where he worked almost until the day he died. You know, I should have thought of this earlier. Some of the cloth he used probably came from those mills in Lawrence. He died in 1984, so I never met him. I always wished I had, though. From the family stories, he sounds like a pretty inter-esting guy."

Try as she might, Ellie couldn't see how this had anything to do with their problem. She knew Aaron well enough to assume he must have a good reason for laying it all out for her, so she decided against trying to prod him into moving the story along any faster than he wanted. And besides, Aaron so seldom discussed his family, even his mom or dad, that she was genuinely interested in what he was saying.

"I'm sorry. I never knew that."

He shrugged. "Ancient history. But still very important to us." He shifted his position so he could lean back against the pine tree.

"Important? How so?"

"See, there's a story in my family about how my grandparents met. He's been in the U.S. for just a few years, and at this point he's still working at a tailor shop in Brooklyn a couple of blocks from his apartment. He's walking to the shop one morning, and he stops at one of those sidewalk newspaper stands because a headline has caught his eye. He's standing there, absorbed in the article, when the guy running the stand says something like, 'Buy it or beat it, Bub!' Startled, my granddad kinda snaps to and backs up a step. He hasn't seen her coming along the sidewalk because he's so focused on the paper, so when he steps back, he crashes into a woman who right that second is passing behind him. He almost knocks her down, but he grabs her arm and manages to keep her from falling. He's so embarrassed that he offers to take her out for dinner or something as a way to apologize. Also, so the story goes, she's quite beautiful. She agrees to meet him for lunch later that same day, and they hit it off. Long story short—*ta-da!*" He spread his arms wide as if to say *here I am!*

"Did you ever get to meet *her*?" Despite the sense of dread she still couldn't shake, she'd become engrossed in the story.

"You'd think. She was quite a bit younger than he was, ten or eleven years, I guess, but no, I never did. They had problems having kids, and they were both pretty surprised when she finally got pregnant with Dad. She was almost fifty—*was* fifty when Dad was born—and there were complications. She died shortly after giving birth."

Ellie nodded, not knowing what to say to that.

"It's always felt strange that our family is so small. I have a few aunts and cousins on my mom's side, but we almost never see them. And on my dad's side, it's just him. If any of Granddad's relatives made it through the war, they never managed to reconnect."

They both pondered that for a respectful moment, but Ellie's anxiety was returning, and she wanted to get to the end of this family history and on to the plan. "So, how does all of this…?"

Aaron raised a hand to quiet her. "Please, I need to…. Trust me, we'll get there."

Once again, she noted the fatigue in his expression. "Sorry. No, take your time." She continued to study his face while he stared at a spot on the ground between them. He seemed to be gathering his thoughts, organizing the next part of his story. After nearly a full minute, he went on.

"It's funny, you know? It was because of Mom that we moved out here, because of the new ways she found for getting energy out of microbes. People at the LAB thought it might lead to a way to satisfy both the electricity and oxygen needs for the proposed Mars colonies, if we ever get there, with only one operation. Solar and batteries work, of course, but batteries, especially, are heavy… expensive to transport. With microbes, though, you carry a small vial of them up, and, after a brief flurry of reproduction—*presto!*—instant power plant. And breathable air, too. And the brilliant part is this—if you can get the microbes to thrive on the, um, 'waste' of the colonists, that means they eat for free. That problem is where the hang-up is for Mom right now."

Ellie already knew all of this and wondered why he was being so uncharacteristically circumspect with this rambling effort to avoid the real topic.

"So, like I said, Mom got hired at the LAB doing her thing, and Dad and me just kind of tagged along. We lived here for almost eighteen months before he started working out there. From what I learned over the past few days, I guess he must have spent all that time 'checking his math' or something. Who knows? Anyway, when he goes to work out there, it's at a whole new facility created solely for his project. He gets his own brand-new, tailor-made lab on the edge of the campus, and gets to hand-pick his entire staff. And the computers—you should see the computers they have! Anything he wanted, *anyone* he wanted, he got it. It seems like money was no object."

"So, whatever he started on was big," she said. "When did he move from that project to this?"

"That's just it. This *is* that project. Or really, I should say *he* is this project because, as far as I can tell, all of it is based on theories he came up with entirely on his own. He's been working on this for the past four and a half years. I read emails, proposals, saw pages and pages of calculations I could barely even begin to follow, all about how to design, then build our little problem-child in the woods out there." He laughed, but there was no humor in the sound.

"I even found emails where he and the head of the LAB discussed how they could camouflage the massive amount of power the device would eventually need. Dad solved the problem by having one of his techs write some malware that they turned loose on the LAB's intranet. It makes random increases to other departments' power usage reports, anywhere from six to nine percent. It's not much on an individual basis, but there are a lot of projects out there. Dad's lab reports a large but not unreasonable amount of consumption, and all the electricity going out through that new trench gets hidden in among all the other projects."

"It's kinda like signing up for basic cable, then stealing HBO, Cinemax, and Showtime, each from a different neighbor," she said.

"Yeah, that works. So, a little over four years ago, he gets his own lab and sets to work engineering—and I still can't believe I'm saying this—a time machine. I have no idea what anyone plans to use it for. I think that to Dad it's nothing more than a theoretical puzzle to solve, but he got the Head of Projects to sign off on it—you know, the guy from that 'Backspace' video—so maybe *he's* the one with the plans. Or somebody in the government. Or the military. I can imagine any number of very nasty things that could be accomplished with a little nip here and a little tuck there at carefully chosen places in the fabric of history. And this is just version 1.0. We could set it back to only what… 1903, was it?" She nodded. "Imagine being able to go back as far as you want. You could change the outcome of any election, any war. You could erase whole cultures, even entire races if you went back far enough. I can't conceive of anything more dangerous."

In the pause, Ellie considered what she had heard so far. "I'm trying to decide whether or not I should take back that 'evil wack-job' comment, seeing as he's your father."

He barked out another humorless laugh. "I've been going over this for three days now, and even I'm not sure yet.

"We were right about the monitoring, you know. They have nothing on the shack itself. No cameras, no infrared tripwires or motion detectors... nothing! And it's made specifically not to keep records of what it does. Their security—aside from that palm scanner I got us past in under five minutes, that is—mostly seems aimed at maintaining deniability. That's why they've had so much trouble with their 'security breach.' All they know for sure is that there was a huge power drain. Their first assumption was that the shack had been used, but all the rest has been guesswork. Who did it, to where and when it went, if it went anywhere—they don't have a clue, although they clearly suspect someone inside the project. But that specific approach to security may also explain why we're still walking around free."

She was shocked. "What do you mean?!"

"You, me, Ryan... we each added our palm prints to the shack's database, but there's nothing about checking on that in any of the files I got. My guess? That information gets encrypted in a way that allows the shack to use it while preventing anyone from seeing it directly. Converts the print's pattern into something like a QR code, maybe. Like I said, they mostly seem concerned with deniability. If you dissected the thing all the way down to its molecules, went through its programming line by line, I bet you wouldn't find a single clue as to where it came from."

She could feel cool sweat on her forehead and palms, and that earlier queasy feeling was back now, too. She had utterly forgotten about adding the new entry codes before they exited the shack in Lawrence. She was glad she had—she was sure it was impossible to survive going more than five weeks without sleep!

"What about actual prints, like from the glass itself?"

He shook his head. "The scanner had an anti-fingerprint nano-coating. I saw that at the time, but it wasn't noteworthy then. It's just the way those things are made. And besides, without a pool of suspects to check prints against...." He let the thought go unfinished.

Realizing that made sense, she merely nodded and remained quiet until he went on.

"When I was there on Wednesday, they were looking mainly at the power systems. My prediction is that they're going to conclude that the shack didn't actually go anywhere, but that the batteries spontaneously discharged, causing the whole thing to have to charge up again. I think they *want* to conclude that. They were busy looking for some reason they could pin the drainage on, like a glitch in a control circuit or something."

She was surprised that they'd even dare mention the shack where he could overhear them. "And they were discussing it? Out in the open?"

He shook his head. "No, not exactly. It was like they were talking in code, sort of talking *around* the device rather than *about* it, if that makes any sense. But since I already knew what they meant, it was pretty easy to follow along.

"We bought ourselves a lot of time there, you know. An unexplained power drain is just the type of problem that would keep them from using it. If they hadn't spent the last month trying to figure out what happened, who knows what they'd be doing with that thing by now?"

She nodded again, indicating that she understood.

"Another thing I found out is that they finished that thing very recently. Seven weeks ago, or about a week before we found it. That's probably the reason we could still see signs of the trench. That must have been dug within the past six or eight months. Our little adventure might even have been its first manned test!"

"Okay, so *that's* scary!" Being reminded yet again of how her arrogance—there was no other word for it, she had to admit—had put them all in danger and had gotten Ryan killed, however temporarily, made her stomach feel more unsettled than ever.

"Ha! You want to hear something *really* scary?"

"I don't know—do I?" She was pretty sure she didn't.

"Okay, remember how when we got back to the shack there were only eight and a half minutes left on the clock? I've given that a lot of thought. This is just another guess, but I have to assume that the thing is programmed to come back automatically at the last possible second, even if it's empty. Wouldn't be good to leave it back where it could totally screw up the timeline. And you should see your face right now."

Without warning, the dozing anxiety cat opened its eyes and pounced. The world grew dark and distant and seemed to spin around her. It was the

shack all over again, minus the possibility of adventure. The sense of spinning intensified until it filled her entire awareness, save for one clear
thought—*don't throw up in front of Aaron!*

The next thing she knew, he was kneeling in front of her. She felt a cool
hand on the back of her neck and heard his voice as though it were far away
but drawing nearer.

"You okay? Ellie?"

Realizing she was still breathing much too fast, she leaned forward as far
as she could, dropped her head between her knees, and focused on taking
long, deep breaths until the nausea began to fade. After a minute, she felt
recovered enough to sit upright.

"That was… *wow!* Did I pass out?" She had never come even close to
fainting before, but as reasons go, the idea that they had missed getting
forever trapped a hundred years in the past by a handful of seconds seemed
a good one. She thought of Ryan and believed she finally understood his
reaction to learning his near-death experience in Methuen had been real.

Seeing that she was now okay, he let go of her and leaned back against
his tree. "I don't think so, but you did turn pretty green. And it sounded like
you kept saying, 'don't throw up.'"

She cringed, embarrassed. *Jeez! How vain can you get?* "Yeah, never fun.
Aaron, I am *so* sorry. I really thought…."

"Hey, it was my screw-up, too. I was totally on board with the idea it was
just some ultrahigh-tech VR chamber."

They sat silently for a few minutes, absorbed in their own thoughts. She
still felt weak and shaky, and her hands remained ice-cold, but her head was
clearing.

"But that makes our whole point, though, doesn't it?" she said. "The
'auto-return' idea, I mean. We got hung up on our way back to the shack
because of the run-in with Angelo's guys. Something like that could happen
to anyone who uses it. They could be in an accident. Or get lost—*anything*
could happen! And there's no way that somebody who got trapped back
there wouldn't eventually cause some major kinks in the timeline. Even if he
or she knew better. It's not a question of what they plan to do with it. It only
matters what might go wrong.

"Think about it. If we had made it back to the woods and the shack was gone, we would have found some way to blend in—get jobs, get into colleges somewhere—whatever. At first, it might even seem like an adventure. No TV? No iPhones? How can we possibly survive?! But also no antibiotics, no regard for the environment, no civil rights. Knowing what we know, how long would it take before one of us could no longer resist the urge to speed things up, help things along? I don't know how to make an antibiotic, but I know penicillin was discovered in mold. How many millions of lives would be saved if one of us could somehow 'discover' it decades earlier? How could we be aware of the suffering going on all around us and not try to do something? Which decision is actually the 'evil' one?"

She paused and gazed down at her hands, clutched tightly in her lap. She took a moment to review everything they knew, then looked up at him. "No, it definitely has to go. Whatever it takes."

The look he leveled on her was penetrating, but his expression was unreadable. "Yes. I agree."

"No, really!" She went on laying out her case as if he had contradicted her. "They must know how potentially dangerous that thing is. Even if their only intent was to go back and erase Barney the Dinosaur—which I would wholly support, by the way—still, they never should have built it."

"I'm sure the same arguments were made against making Fat Man and Little Boy," he quickly held a hand up, "and no, I'm not equating the two. I'm saying that a lot of people felt the same way about developing nuclear weapons—even people who worked here—yet they got built anyway. People can argue over whether it did more good than harm, but it's still a terrible, terrifying technology. My point is that there's always someone willing to do the unthinkable. And before I forget, can we add the Teletubbies to the list along with Barney? They're back, you know."

"Are you kidding? Who thought *that* was a good idea?! Consider it done! But seriously, what about all those researchers? They, of all people, would have to see what a bad idea that thing is. I bet they were told they *are* making some kind of historical VR device." She laughed coldly. "I mean, can you imagine working day after day on a project that might ultimately result in your own...."

She stopped mid-sentence, drew in a sharp breath, and stared wide-eyed into the distance while the intuitive part of her mind leaped ahead. The unfinished question acted like a key unlocking a door in her brain, and she could sense bits of Aaron's story realigning themselves, settling into new, meaningful relationships. She suddenly understood the cause of his upset as the nature of his plan assumed a vague shape in her mind. She lacked enough data to lay out every detail, but its general outline and ultimate, horrifying consequences were plain enough. When she brought her gaze back to his face, she could tell he knew exactly where her thoughts had gone.

"No!" Her tone was at once defiant and pleading.

"Yeah. I'm afraid so."

Unable to focus on him through sudden tears, she dropped her gaze to her lap. A second later, a dark spot appeared on the front of her shorts. Then another. She hated being wrong more than almost anything else in the world, but she desperately hoped she was wrong now.

"Okay," she said, her voice husky. "Tell me."

"You know the classic time travel paradox where you go back in history and somehow kill your own grandfather, thereby making it so you could never be born?"

"But if you are never born, how do you go back and kill your grandfather? That one?" She sat up straight again and stared hard at him. "So, your plan is we go back and *murder your grandfather?!*"

"No, of course not!" he said, and she relaxed.

She saw him bow his head and shake it, and she thought he might have been trying to blink away tears. But when he raised his head and looked at her, his eyes were dry.

"My father, actually."

31

Although Ellie had already guessed that Aaron's story was leading to this or some similar conclusion, hearing him express the idea aloud wiped the distress from her mind and triggered a powerful reaction she could not control. She surged to her feet and stormed five paces away before she could stop herself. She stomped back to where he had remained seated on the ground and stared down at him, her hands clenched into tight balls.

"If you think for one sec.... How can you even.... *Are you out of your...?!*" She was too upset to form a coherent response. Only after forcing herself to take a series of slow, deep breaths was she able to form a complete sentence. She glared fiercely into his upturned face, finding his expression as inscrutable as before. "We cannot go to them with this! I am *not*...."

He raised a hand to cut her off. "It's not like that. Just sit back down and let me explain." He spoke calmingly and patted the ground beside him. He turned his head fractionally, and the glare disappeared from his lenses. The anguish she saw in his eyes made her realize that however difficult his plan was for her to accept, the situation was infinitely worse for him. "Please? Sit?" He patted the ground again.

For a moment she stared down at him, still too shocked to think clearly. What did he mean by *it's not like that?* Killing somebody was just that—

killing! He couldn't really mean that, could he? No, she decided. The idea that he would suggest they murder someone was ludicrous, of course. She returned to her seat on the ground, tucked her legs under her, and folded her arms tightly across her chest. She took another deep breath, let it out slowly.

"All right. I'm listening."

"There's a little more to the first part of the story, and our answer is in the details. It turns out that my grandmother—her name was Judith—didn't live in Brooklyn. Her family had been in the U.S. a lot longer, and they had settled in Manhattan. She was across the river running an errand for her father that morning when she basically got body-checked by my grandfather, Daniel. More than that, she later told him that she couldn't remember even being in Brooklyn before that day and was, in fact, near *that* newsstand on *that* morning only because she had gotten lost on the way to wherever she was supposed to be, turned right when she should have turned left, or whatever. The place she was trying to find was half a mile on the other side of the tailor shop." He paused as if waiting for a question or comment.

She said nothing. Her initial revulsion at the thought of killing someone had temporarily masked her pain and grief of moments before. Now those feelings were back. At first, she had been curious about Aaron's story welcoming the chance to learn more about his family. Now that she understood where all the talk about his grandparents was leading, she no longer wanted to hear it, even though she knew she must. However, she wasn't going to prolong his explanation with unnecessary discussion. She remained silent, and soon he went on.

"The important thing to understand is that the chances of my grandparents meeting on any other day, at any other time, are incredibly small. *Vanishingly* small, as Mr. Hardy would say. It's pretty much that day or never. Get it now? If they don't—quite literally—bump into each other at that one precise moment, they never do. If they never meet, Dad never gets born. No Dad, no device. All we need to do is prevent that meeting from happening. That's not so bad, right? They'll go on with their lives, marry other people... See what I mean? It's not like we're *killing* anybody. Dad just never *is*."

She found she couldn't argue with him on that specific point. He was right. Merely preventing two people from marrying was not the same as murdering their future son. The irony that this kind of messing around with people's lives was the very thing they were trying to prevent was not lost on her, but she forced herself to stay focused on the main issue.

"Okay... sure.... I suppose I can go along with that. But, still, nothing in that story says exactly when that happened. It could have been any day of the year."

"No, it couldn't. *In the details*, I said. See, the headline that caught his eye that morning was a pretty big deal. It went something like, 'Japan Wars on U.S. and Britain; Makes Sudden Attack on Hawaii... ' It was the New York Times headline on the day after the attack on Pearl Harbor. It was *exactly* the morning of Monday, December 8, 1941."

She sat silently for a long time, staring at the ground and trying to process the implications of the scenario he had just laid out. She instantly saw that he was correct, at least regarding the effect his plan would have on subsequent events. Each piece of it clicked smoothly into its place, adding detail to the skeletal framework in her mind.

She tried to work out the logistics of carrying out the plan. She imagined Brooklyn in December. *Why couldn't it be June?* Then she wondered where you could stick a beaten-up old shack anywhere in Brooklyn and not have it look totally out of place. *Maybe that particular camouflage isn't so good after all.*

She struggled to find a flaw—any flaw would do—in this horrendous idea. His logic was as impeccable as always, however, progressing smoothly from A to B to C. *No meeting* ergo *no marriage* ergo *no Aaron's dad. No Dad, no device. But also no Aaron!* This was the final consequence of the plan that her flash of intuition had shown her.

She looked up and saw him watching her patiently, his face still devoid of expression. When she tried to imagine him suddenly gone, she felt a vast emptiness open inside her heart. The feeling terrified her, and she shook her head to clear it of the thought. She was breathing faster again, and her whole body felt cool and clammy. That coldly calculating part of her brain she thought of as her logic module refused her urging to come forward and take over, forcing her to deal with Aaron's plan on an uncomfortably emotional level. She sensed the cat crouching in the back of her mind, preparing to pounce again, only harder this time. Rather than remain its helpless target, she abruptly rose to her feet.

"Let's walk. I can't sit here anymore." She turned away and began striding across the adjacent parking lot, still clasping her arms tightly in front of her. Caught off guard, Aaron got to his feet late and trailed a few steps behind. Her pace became progressively slower until she stopped altogether. Standing at the far edge of the blacktop, she bowed her head and began to cry, each sob a convulsion that shook her entire body. Aaron closed the distance between them and gently turned her so that she was facing him, then wrapped his arms around her and pulled her close.

"*No!*" That single syllable was all she could manage, and she muttered it over and over as she clung to him.

He could feel her shuddering spasms as she silently wept, and he continued to hold her against him until her body finally relaxed and her breathing eased into a steady rhythm. He stroked his hand along her back, giving her whatever time she needed to regain her emotional control. "I know," he said into her hair, "physics can't explain it, but this situation somehow both sucks and blows at the same time."

The joke was not an especially original one, but it had its desired effect. Her laugh was a harsh, bitter snort. "Yeah! It really, *really* does."

"You okay to walk a bit? Let's go over by the lodge," he said. She detached herself from his embrace, and they walked side by side under the trees along the edge of the library grounds. When she felt his hand brush against hers, she took hold of it, laced her fingers through his, and gripped it tightly.

They crossed the street and entered another small parking lot in front of Fuller Lodge. The huge, extremely old log building had been a dining hall in the long-ago days before the city, even before the World War II research lab, back when the only reason to visit the plateau was to attend the rustic Los Alamos Ranch School. They passed between the massive structure and a tiny museum and entered a wide, grassy area. They found a park bench at the base of an enormous cottonwood tree, and there they sat, still holding hands.

"Oh, yeah." He tilted slightly to one side, reached back with his free hand, and pulled a folded square of white cloth from his hip pocket. He handed it to her. "I almost forgot."

It took her a second to understand what she was holding. Despite everything she was feeling, she nearly laughed. "What's…? A *hanky?!*"

He shrugged. "I figured at least one of us was going to end up needing it."

"Thanks," she muttered. She stared at the ground and dabbed at her eyes until she felt she could trust herself to talk without bursting into tears.

"How can you possibly be so calm about all this? We're talking about your own father. And *you!*"

"It's like that logic puzzle you gave me. You know, the little wooden toy thingy." She nodded, but she couldn't see the relevance. "Figuring out how to get everything across the river? It's not an emotional exercise. Once you figure it out, it's like, 'Oh, okay. So that's the answer.' It feels good, that sense of clarity replacing the uncertainty and knowing it can't be any other way. But the solution itself? It is what it is.

"Coming up with this plan was like that. I've tried to think of an alternative, but trust me—I honestly don't believe there is one. So I moved on from *what* to *how*. I guess the short answer is I just accepted it. What else can I do?" He considered her question further. "And I'm not calm. Not on the inside. It's just that I did all my major freaking out over the weekend, I guess."

"Well, I *can't* accept it. I *hate* it!" More sobs shook her body. "*I don't want you to go away!*"

"'Whatever it takes,' is what you said, and you were right."

"*Whatever* wasn't supposed to include *this!*" She hung her head in despair, burying her face in the damp handkerchief.

"You know we are running out of time. It may already be too late. We'll give it one more day, but if we can't think of something else, we go with this. Deal?"

Her throat was too tight to speak, so she merely nodded. Then she sat up and noisily blew her nose into the cloth. He watched as she folded the damp portion into the handkerchief's center.

"You can, um, keep that, if you want."

· · ·

Ellie was determined to find a plan that didn't end with losing Aaron. She found that as long as she could keep focused on finding an alternative to his mad scheme, she could keep her emotions mostly in check. For their first step, she insisted on seeing the files he had brought. They retraced their path through the parking lot and passed under the library's massive *porte cochère* toward the front door.

"Listen," Ellie said. "When it comes to something like this, I trust you as much as I trust Sam. It's just that if I'm going to sentence someone to—what do we call it, *deletion?*—I want to see the evidence for myself."

Once inside, they found a computer station that faced a blank section of wall. Ellie sat in front of the monitor and mouse-wiggled the CPU awake. Aaron glanced around the room and, seeing no one, crouched under the table and deftly unplugged the network cable from the rear of its housing.

"Make sure the wi-fi is off," he said.

"Off," she confirmed.

He handed her a thumb drive, this one bright red and intact. She looked at it, then at him, then plugged it into a slot on the end of the keyboard.

"I was afraid the other one was going to fall apart," he said. "I transferred everything that's relevant to this one."

The window that opened on the monitor listed twenty-two files. About half were PDFs. The remaining files were a mix of various formats, a few of which she was pretty sure couldn't be opened by any of the programs on the library's computer. He pointed to a file named *proposal.pdf.*

"Start with that one. Then read the one right below it. After that, you can go in whatever order you want." He yawned. "I'm going to go collapse over there, but come get me if you need anything."

She watched him settle onto a nubby, turquoise loveseat, tilt his head back, and close his eyes. She couldn't remember ever feeling as tired as he looked. After making sure they were still alone, she clicked on *proposal.pdf* and began to read.

Twenty-five minutes later, she removed the thumb drive, cleared the "Open Recent" menus from the programs she had used, shut off the monitor, and walked over to join Aaron on the tiny sofa. The slight jostling of the cushion was enough to wake him. He opened his eyes to find her looking straight ahead, offering him the thumb drive in a backhanded gesture.

"Oh, hey. How long was I out?" He still sounded groggy. He took the drive from her hand and pocketed it.

"Not long. I didn't read everything, but I read enough. I'm sorry, but I agree with you." She finally turned to face him, regarding him with eyes that were red but dry. "What are we going to do?"

They left the library. As soon as they reached the sidewalk, Aaron took the thumb drive from his pocket, dropped it on the ground, and crushed it under his heel. Once the case had broken away, he flexed the inner circuit board until the memory chip popped free. It was tiny, but by pinching it carefully between the nails of the thumbs and index fingers of both hands, he was able to bend it back and forth until it snapped in two. He dropped half of the memory chip and pieces of plastic shell into the first trash can they passed. He pocketed the other half of the chip until they found a different can to throw it in. Ellie suspected that, at least at some level, he enjoyed the "James Bondy" aspects of their mission.

"Can I assume you gave the other one a similar sort of funeral?"

He managed a faint smile. "That one involved a hammer!"

They walked as they talked, making large, random circuits through the edge of town, returning at some point during each lap to the bench beneath the giant cottonwood. For a while, they explored the possibility of merely disrupting his father's research, interfering somehow with the process by which he had come to develop the concepts crucial to the shack's creation. That idea quickly fizzled after he realized there was no way to work out how or when that had happened. Furthermore, complications could arise from going back to a point in time already populated by their younger selves.

"It's not just about avoiding running into ourselves," he said, "but if we're supposed to be in school and someone saw us sneaking around my house? Or if your mom drove by you and Sam walking down the street, then found you at home when she got there? Too risky. Not to mention the fact that we'd be years too old."

"I don't think any of that matters. When I was trying to figure out the control panel settings, I noticed the most recent year I could pick was 2006. Was he even working on this that far back?"

He thought for a moment, then shook his head. "Twelve years ago? Probably not. If he had been, he would have gone to work on it as soon as we got here, not more than a year and a half later."

"Maybe. How long would it take *you* to convince somebody to give you money to build a time machine? If you really could build one, I mean."

"Good point," he conceded. "But I still say no."

"Well, then... let's keep moving on."

They spent the rest of the day bouncing ideas off each other, but, much to their frustration, having a viable plan in hand—even a mad one—only served to make coming up with new ideas even harder. All other possibilities lacked the laser-like precision of Aaron's original plan, and when the end of the day arrived, they had found no place to move on to. Nothing she thought of hadn't already occurred to and been dismissed by Aaron over the preceding days. She gradually realized that all the brainstorming they were doing was solely for her benefit. He was patiently giving her the time to come on her own to the same conclusion he had already reached—they would never come up with a plan B.

They stopped on their way home to sit side by side on a low wall near the entrance to the high school auditorium, oblivious to the traffic that sped by on Diamond. She reviewed the plan for what seemed like the hundredth time and once again failed to find any flaw. She was finally forced to concede that his idea wasn't a 'mad scheme' at all. It was quite brilliant, in fact, even elegant in its minimalist simplicity.

"Just the teensiest bit suicidal, that's all," she muttered.

"What's that?"

"There has to be another way," she said, this time loudly enough for him to hear her clearly.

"I am wide open to alternatives, believe me. I did not want to have to tell you this. I thought about giving you a heads-up on Thursday, but I wasn't a hundred percent sure yet, and I didn't want to put any of this on you until I was. Then, when I got to your house and saw what you were up to, I just couldn't. That was wonderful, by the way." He smiled at her, but his eyes were sad. He cleared his throat and went on.

"Anyway, we've already been going at this hard for almost a month, and so far this is the only idea we've come up with. Like I said before, I went through it all again last night, forward, backward, every other way possible. I was up until four. And it's not simply that this plan will work, but it's something we can actually *do*." He paused. "Unless I've missed something."

She hung her head and sighed. "No. I don't think you have."

"Me neither. It's just that he's the guy. Every important part of that thing is based on his ideas. If it doesn't get built now, it could be decades before someone else comes up with the same theories. Who knows—maybe by then people will be smart enough not to build it at all."

"*Pfft!*" she scoffed. "I guess we can dream!"

They walked together to the base of the pedestrian overpass, then went their separate ways. In no mood for company or conversation, Ellie was relieved to arrive home to an empty house. Sam, she assumed, was where she always was when not at home or working—out somewhere with Ryan. Where her parents were was more of a mystery until she remembered they were having dinner with the couple joining them on their upcoming golf trip. Was that already the day after tomorrow? She was amazed by how quickly the month was going by. Aaron was right—they needed to act soon.

Since she was in the kitchen anyway, she opened the fridge, peered inside, and discovered the contents had not changed much since she cleaned it over the weekend. Nothing she saw was remotely appealing, despite not having eaten since leaving the house nearly eight hours ago. She considered checking the freezer, too, but knew not even the considerable magical power of Ben and Jerry's would be enough to lift her spirits. She knew she should eat something, however, and in the end she opted for that simplest of all meals and poured herself another bowl of cereal. She ate in a mechanical fashion—raise spoon to mouth, chew, swallow, repeat—until the bowl was empty.

Empty. That was how she felt, she realized. *Hollow.* She guessed she should be feeling all kinds of things—sadness, anger, bitterness. She should be outraged by the fundamental unfairness of it all. She had felt all of those emotions burn hot inside her earlier, right after she had first grasped the full implications of Aaron's plan, but at that moment she had lacked the time to deal with them. Instead, she had forced them into a box and shoved the whole flaming mess to the back of her mind. Opening the box now, instead of a raging fire, she found only ashes. By suppressing her emotions all day, had she somehow robbed herself of the opportunity to feel them? Or was this emptiness itself an emotion, the one feeling that remained after pushing beyond all the others?

As Ellie returned her dried bowl to the cabinet, she wondered how to deal with her sister when she got home. Still hoping against hope to find an alternative, she wasn't ready to share the plan with her yet. The problem was that even though Sam might not know how to handle an "undifferentiated polynumerator," her knack for reading people guaranteed that she would know something was wrong as soon as she saw her. Deception seemed the likeliest way to avoid an unpleasant conversation, but that relied on Sam returning suitably late in the evening.

Assuming she had at least a few hours before anyone got home, she decided to indulge herself with a long, hot shower in the hope it would ease the tension her body had accumulated over the course of the difficult day. She stood directly under the spray, closed her eyes, and allowed the water to cascade down the entire length of her, from scalp to toes. She rotated slowly to present every inch of her body to the spray's soothing warmth. Growing up in the southwest had made her acutely water-conscious, but on this occasion, she stayed under the flow until even with the cold valve completely closed, the temperature had become too cool for comfort.

Back in her room and wearing a fresh nightshirt, she pulled the covers back and sat upright on her bed. She dragged her MacBook from her desk to her lap and passed part of the first hour idly clicking from one BuzzFeed list to another. The rest of the hour she spent trying in vain to find a YouTube video humorous enough to make her smile. Unimpressed by anything the Internet had to offer, she returned the computer to her desk and retrieved *The Water Knife* from her bookcase. As she flipped past the cover to the story's opening page, she wondered if her long shower had subconsciously influenced her choice of books. She switched her desk lamp to its lowest setting and slid it close to the edge of the desk, hoping the dim glow would not be noticeable through the closed window blinds.

She was nearly a third of the way through when she heard the front door deadbolt clicking open. Since nine o'clock, she'd been wondering who would get home first, her parents or her sister. Sounds from the front door, rather than from the garage, meant it was Sam returning. She turned off her bedside lamp, quietly laid the book on her desk, and slid beneath her covers to face the wall.

The ritual of two smitten teenagers bidding each other goodnight being what it was, it was several minutes before Sam made her way to their room. Ellie used that time to slow her breathing to a deep, steady rhythm, realizing for the first time she had no idea how she actually breathed in her sleep. More minutes passed while Sam moved about the room, quietly opening and shutting drawers. There was a prolonged silence during which Ellie was certain Sam was standing there, staring at her. Finally, Ellie heard Sam leave and the bedroom door close. She puffed out a sigh of relief. Who knew pretending to relax could be so stressful? She shifted to a more comfortable position and continued taking slow, calming breaths until she truly fell asleep.

32

That night Ellie did dream. It was early morning, and she stood on the porch of a small house in the country. Its unfinished boards felt rough on the bare soles of her feet, and they creaked softly with every subtle shift of her weight. She faced the brightest spot on the horizon, waiting calmly for a sunrise only minutes away. Although the still air was cool and damp with dew, she felt warm with Aaron standing close by her side. She didn't know where the house was, but the expansive front yard dropped away eastward before rising again to merge into a broader landscape of green, softly rolling hills. The scene was silent except for the sound of birds chirping from the depths of nearby trees she thought might be sugar maples. They weren't in New Mexico anymore, that was for sure. Kansas? Kentucky? She hadn't a clue.

Most of the front yard was taken up by a strange-looking garden unlike any she had ever seen. It was divided into an array of individual, nearly square plots, seven across and five down. Most of these were planted at random with a mix of either vegetables, herbs, or flowers. The two upper left plots were empty, as were the last three, those in the lower right corner. For some reason, she found that particular configuration comforting, and in the dream, she smiled.

It's not time yet.

She felt Aaron wrap his arm around her waist. She returned the gesture and leaned her head against his shoulder, enjoying the simple happiness of this perfect moment. She tilted her head back to look up at his face and was shocked by the age she saw there.

No! We're young! her mind protested.

"We're not kids anymore," he said, keeping his gaze directed outward across the brightening landscape. "But you're right—we still have a little time. Let's make the most of it." He pulled her closer.

She thought he sounded sad and wanted to reassure him, to say *of course they would*, but at that instant, she became aware of a new sound in their surroundings. It came from no specific direction, a slow, rhythmic ticking that reminded her of the metronome from her days of piano lessons years ago. It gradually got louder and louder, although the tempo remained the same.

Not a ticking, she realized. *A tapping*.

It was bright in the room when she opened her eyes. She thought she had heard a noise, but now it was quiet. It hadn't been Sam—Ellie was alone in the room. Then she heard it again—*tap, tap, tap!* She turned her head toward the window beside her bed and immediately spotted the source of the disturbance. She rolled onto her side for a better view.

"Are you back, you idiot bird?" Outside the window a male bluebird ran back and forth along the sill, pausing now and then to peck at his arch-nemesis, an improbably identical-looking bluebird he believed to be intent on taking over his territory. *Tap, tap, tap!* She shook her head in disappointment. "I thought we agreed on this back in the spring—that's just your reflection. Talk about being a birdbrain!"

She flopped onto her back and stared up at the ceiling. When she had first awakened, she had been filled with a sense of wistful happiness. The feeling was tied to something in her dream, but, as was usually the case, when she tried to recall the details, she found they had faded away in the daylight. She closed her eyes and concentrated. She thought maybe Aaron had been in the dream. And something about… a giant *calendar*? That made no sense.

The dual distractions of the bluebird at her window and trying to recall the ephemeral images from her dream initially kept the events of the day before from reoccupying her mind, but not for long. As soon as her thoughts turned to Aaron, she felt a great sense of hopelessness crash down on her all over again.

Her phone buzzed on the desk beside her.

Aaron—Are we still on for this morning?

Huh? For a second, she was confused. Then she remembered what he meant and groaned. They had all agreed days ago to meet this morning for breakfast at the Atomic City Café. Then she realized where Sam must be. No doubt she had left early to hook up with Ryan, probably so they could bike in together.

Ellie—You still want to?
Aaron—Yes. Things will be different after we tell them.
Ellie—Yeah, okay. See you there.
Aaron—

This ought to be fun, she thought sourly. She didn't feel like putting on a happy face for Sam and Ryan, but if Aaron still wanted to give it a go, she would not let him down. The clock on her phone said she had less than half an hour to get showered, dressed, and make the hike to the café.

"Better get crackin'!" she muttered, then reluctantly forced herself to slide out from under the covers.

At nine-thirty they were standing in line, waiting patiently to place their orders. Ellie tried to imagine how she would be feeling if it were forty-eight hours ago and did her best to project that. Even so, she noticed Sam watching her, a thoughtful expression on her face. She tried to project a little harder.

"Isn't it weird how the best place for coffee in this town is in the middle of the university?" Ryan said.

"That'll be handy starting in the fall," Sam said.

"Starbuck's isn't *bad*," Aaron said.

"Yeah, but it's Starbuck's," Ellie said.

"Still, the one at Smith's has that amazing view," Aaron said.

"*Mmm*," Ryan said, conceding the point.

"Lily's is pretty good," Sam said.

"Yeah, but it's...." he said.

"You're right—it is," she agreed.

"But the chocolates there are *really* good," Ellie said. Remembering Aaron's delight over the truffles finally brought a genuine smile to her face. Okay, maybe she could do this.

"Diamond Dee's? *Meh*," Aaron said.

"Great sandwiches, so-so coffee," Ryan agreed.

"The co-op's good, but it's so far out on the other end of town it might as well be on another planet," Ellie said.

"And, so, here we are," Ryan concluded. "You know, I still think you two should open your own place. 'Sam 'n' Ellie's Café.' I heard the coffee shop business in the medical center is up for sale. Could it be any more perfect?"

"Yeah, if my name were 'Ella,' for instance."

"There's such a thing as being too on point," Aaron said.

Ellie wasn't sure if the comment was directed at her or Ryan, but Ryan had already moved on from the name and was now working on marketing his oft-proposed, *Salmonella*-themed restaurant.

"'Now offering convenient, on-site stomach pumping!'"

Sam rolled her eyes. "That wasn't funny the first fifty times."

Finally, they reached the register and placed their orders for assorted coffee drinks, breakfast sandwiches, and pastries. After another short wait, they carried their breakfasts to a nearby table, sat down, and dug in.

"How you can come here and not get an apple empanada," Aaron said, his voice garbled by a mouthful of pastry, "is totally beyond me."

"*Mmm!* If you'd ever tried the Breakfast Melt, you'd understand." Sam held her sandwich up for him to inspect. He peered dubiously at the egg topped with not only bacon but two kinds of cheese, all layered between slices of buttery sourdough toast.

"That's just wrong in so many ways," he said, then sighed. "It does smell delicious, though."

"You should be glad it's not a green chili BLT," Ellie said, not bothering to explain the cryptic comment. Sam bumped her with her shoulder and laughed. The carefree joy in that laugh was almost too much for Ellie to bear, but the change in topic gave her something to say. She waited until Aaron had swallowed his next bite before asking her question. "By the way, you never told me how you liked that coffee truffle. Good?"

He smiled at her. "Oh, yeah... *Wow!* Does the 'Church of Chocolate' or whatever accept converts?"

To Ellie's relief, they finished eating in silence. At the end of the meal, Sam and Ryan stood and gathered everyone's plates and trash. They were going to hike the Rendija Ridge Trail, a relatively short but challenging loop north of the residential section of town. With monsoon season already into its second week, they wanted to be off the trail and back in town before any afternoon thunderstorms rolled through, although on this route it was lightning, not flash floods, that provided cause for concern. They were eager to get started, but before they left, Ryan took a moment to pass on some information.

"Whatever you two are cooking up, it looks like next week would be a good time for it. Seems like half the departments have something going on out of town for some conference or other."

"'Tis the season," Sam said. Work at the LAB customarily slowed to a crawl for a few weeks each summer while families took vacations and project heads ventured out of town in search of additional funding.

Ellie nodded. "Mom and Dad leave early tomorrow on a little Wednesday-through-Sunday golfing vacay. Not work-related, but they'll be gone." She caught Sam smirking at her. "Of course, you already knew that."

"My mom's in Washington talking to JPL, NASA, a few other groups. She'll be away until the middle of next week. Dad's...." Aaron had to clear his throat before he could continue. "The most important thing is that Dad's leaving for Denver today, along with some of his staff. Then they're off to Seattle for a few more days. No clue about who they're meeting with, but I know they won't be back until late on Monday. We can't count on ever having a time when the shack will have fewer eyes on it."

"That's not next week, guys. That's this weekend," Sam said.

"*That* figures," Ryan said. The others waited for him to elaborate. "Well, come on—has there ever been a more perfect time for a party?"

Ellie and Aaron's eyes met. "Trust me," she said. "We'd rather be partying."

After Sam and Ryan had pedaled away toward the Rendija trailhead, Ellie and Aaron crossed over Diamond, walked past the high school, and picked up a trail that dropped into Pueblo Canyon. The day was too hot to enjoy sitting in the sun's full glare, but the shady ravine would be a comfortable place in which to discuss their upcoming plans and sufficiently remote to do so in complete privacy. It wasn't until they reached the trail that either of them spoke.

"Okay, so *that* was horrible," she said at last.

"No. It was okay. I wanted to have one last 'normal' time with them, you know?"

She nodded. "I get it. I think Sam knew something was up, though. She kept giving me this look like she was trying to see inside my skull."

The trail gently descended to a formation called the Pueblo Bench, a wide, level ledge halfway down that surrounded an even deeper part of the canyon. After a few hundred yards, they left the trail and soon found a boulder near the edge that provided them a view both across the canyon and to its bottom. Once seated side by side on its smooth top, she laid her left hand on his leg. He rested his hand on top of hers and squeezed. To her delight, his touch caused that high-static prickle to crawl over her whole body again. *This is so much better than the café!* She was about to say as much, but he spoke first.

"I have to say something. Before we get into anything else." He turned his face away from her and looked across the canyon for a moment. She waited silently for him to continue. When he faced her again, she could see his eyes glistening. "I need to be done." He sniffed once and coughed once before continuing. "I know I said we'd give it another day, and if you can come up with a different idea I'll hear you out. And I hope that you can. But it's too hard pretending that we're ever going to somehow solve this thing so we all walk away from it and always coming up empty. We tried, and that's all we can do. But all of the emotional back and forth? I'm sorry, but for me it's been five days. I can't keep it up. I need to accept that this plan is it and start dealing with it."

She considered this. She remembered when her grandfather was at the end of his fight with cancer three years ago. Each new treatment came with its own promise of hope, just as each failure delivered another crushing disappointment. At some point, it became a relief to give up fighting and accept the inevitable end. At least, that is how he had explained it to her and Sam.

She realized something else, too, a thought she could barely admit to herself, never would to Aaron. His words brought her an enormous sense of relief, the feeling that the obligation to carry out an impossible task had been lifted from her. It was a surprisingly physical sensation, like a tight band had been removed from around her chest, and for the first time in more than a day, she could truly breathe. It was the guilt that came on the heels of the relief that stayed her tongue, and she promised herself she wouldn't quit working on alternatives, despite what he said.

She gave his hand a firm squeeze. "I understand." It was hard to speak, and she knew they were both on the verge of breaking down. Several minutes ticked by before either of them could continue.

"So, when do we tell *them*?" Aaron said.

"*Do* we tell them? And if so, how *much* do we tell them?"

"I think we have to. And all of it. If we're going to rely on their help, the plan has to make sense to them. Especially with Sam. You know that if she senses that anything is off, that we're holding something back, she'll bail and take Ryan with her."

"Do we absolutely need them?"

He understood she wasn't arguing but simply making sure they analyzed their idea from every possible angle. "'*Absolutely?* Maybe not, but it's far safer to have two teams of two rather than us splitting up and each going solo. It's too important that we don't fail." He paused to hone his argument to its sharpest edge. "That's also why I believe they have to know everything —and agree to it—before we go. They have to be every bit as committed as we are, just as willing to do whatever it takes. For them to feel that way, they have to know it all."

Ellie shook her head slowly, still not entirely convinced. "All I know is how *I* feel. It's going to be hard enough for *me* to go through with this. It might be easier for them if they don't have that burden to deal with. You know how Ryan is. 'How about those Yankees?' It would be a game to him. And Sam would follow his lead, just play along with whatever he did. God— this is so *hard!*"

"I know. I see your point. If we tell them, we may lose them. And if we *don't* tell them? What's the downside then?"

"They may not push as hard? I don't know." Then she confessed what was truly bothering her. "I guess what worries me most is that they'll hate me forever." She barely got the words out before beginning to cry.

He let go of her hand, put his arm around her, and pulled her close to him. She put her head on his shoulder and let the tears flood from her eyes. She wept quietly for a few minutes, then sat back up, sniffling.

"But it's going to end the same way regardless," Aaron said. "What if we told only Ryan? It's not like he and I are BFFs, exactly."

She was surprised to discover he felt that way. "He likes you a lot more than you seem to think. But no. Afterward, Sam would hate both me *and* Ryan. I can't do that to them."

"We don't have a lot of time left to make a decision," he said. "In the end, you'll be the one who has to deal with the fallout. We've looked at all the possibilities—I'll go along with whatever you decide."

"*Jerk!*" She bumped him with her shoulder. "Don't put this all on me!" Although she was mostly feigning her irritation, the nudge was nearly hard enough to tumble him off the end of the rock.

"Fine, fine!" he said, sitting upright again. "Okay, we'll tell them tomorrow morning." She scowled at him but said nothing. "Seriously. I'm just now realizing that you're the one who'll have to deal with things after- ward—alone. You should be the one to choose what we do. And when."

"Life sucks!" She picked up a small rock and chucked it over the cliff. As it left her hand, she remembered that there could be hikers on the trail below. "*Whoops!*" She leaned forward and peered over the edge. Relieved at not seeing anyone, she sat up, placed her hands behind her, and leaned back onto them. "But you're right. We should tell them all of it."

After further discussion, they agreed that putting off the unpleasant conversation would only make the anxiety worse. She texted Sam and asked if they could get together later in the evening. She suggested the small park by the lodge—this was not a discussion she wanted to be forced to relive every time she walked through their living room. Plus, her mom and dad would be at the house packing for their trip. Both of these reasons made home a less-than-ideal setting for what was sure to be an emotional—and ideally a secret—conversation. They agreed to meet in the park at seven.

Next, she sent a text to her mom asking if it was okay if she skipped dinner at home tonight. She knew she wouldn't have much appetite, and sitting at the table pushing her food around the plate would raise questions she couldn't answer. She promised to be home early enough to say goodbye. To her great relief, the message that came a few minutes later told her that was fine. She pocketed her phone and sat forward, arms crossed and resting on her knees.

They discussed how to present their plan to Sam and Ryan, and by then it was *their* plan. They decided that he would give them the outline, then he and Ellie would jointly deal with any questions or objections. As they talked, he reached across the space between them and put his hand on hers. She turned hers over so they were touching palm to palm and laced her fingers through his.

"I guess the way you told me would be best," she said. "Keep it linear. Start with the background, explain how central your dad is to the project, then move on to the story about your grandfather. Ideally, we'd like them to see the end for themselves before you get there. Especially Sam. They don't need every detail as long as they get enough for them to connect the dots."

"And if they don't?"

"It's fine if we have to spell it out for them, but it's better if they can jump ahead of you at the very end. If they think of the answer before you tell them, it'll feel more like it's their own idea. That shouldn't be a problem, though. They're not dummies."

The strategy session over, they sat quietly for a time, admiring their surroundings. They spotted the occasional hiker or two on the far side of the canyon, and once several mountain bikes chattered close by on the trail behind them. Otherwise, their whole world was just each other, the sound of wind in the trees, and the resinous scent of pine sap carried on the heat of the day. She turned her face toward him and let her eyes roam across his features. His expression was warm but sad, too.

He shook his head. "You know, for two, dare I say, incredibly smart people, this may be a very dumb thing to do." He raised their joined hands between them to make the object of his point clear. She'd had the same thought several times over the past twenty-four hours but hadn't reached a definitive conclusion. Now she thought she had. She gripped his hand a little tighter, looked him in the eyes, and smiled.

"*Incredibly* smart, definitely. 'Top five,' in fact. But not *infinitely* smart."

"Meaning?" He couldn't help but smile back.

"Meaning if we were infinitely smart, maybe we'd see that this is the wisest thing we've ever done."

He thought about that. Suddenly his smile got brighter.

"Any good theory *must* take the uncertainty factor into account."

It wasn't long before Ellie began to feel restless. Faced with almost seven hours to kill before the rendezvous with Sam and Ryan, she was starting to regret making it so late. She considered texting again to move the meeting forward, but decided against it—if her time with Aaron was winding down, she wanted to make the most of every remaining minute. In her mind, that didn't mean just sitting on some rock in the woods all day.

"So... If you could do anything you wanted today, what would that be?"

"Anything?"

"Anything at all. I mean anything here in town, obviously."

"*Hmm*...." He gazed at her, his eyes narrowed to slits.

Abruptly aware of her question's unintended undertones, she felt sweat dampen her palms. She studied his face and wondered what she would do if he were thinking what she thought he might be thinking. These were, after all, his final few days. And Aaron, despite being Aaron, was still an eighteen-year-old male. But no, he wouldn't say *that*. Would he? Now she wished she'd spent *more* time talking to Sam about boys!

"What?" he said.

She puffed out the breath she hadn't been aware of holding. "What *what?*"

"You had a funny look on your face."

"I was just… thinking," she said, struggling to keep her expression neutral.

"Uh-huh." He flashed her a mischievous smile. "Well, *I* was thinking you… me… a darkened room….."

She swallowed hard and felt heat rise in her cheeks. Her mind whirled as she tried to figure out what to do, and it was a second before she realized she must have misheard something he'd just said.

"*Huh?!*"

"*Dinosaurs,*" he repeated, still wearing that playful smile.

Confusion rendered her momentarily speechless, but when she belatedly put all the pieces together—darkened room, flickering light, dinosaurs—she burst out laughing. "You want to see *Fallen Kingdom?!*"

"What were you expecting me to say?"

"Hah, hah. Are you serious? A *movie?*" She was relieved, mostly, but couldn't deny she also felt the teensiest bit insulted.

"We used to go to movies all the time when we were kids. Then it somehow became just Ryan and Sam's thing. I'd like to do that again."

"Is *that* the movie you'd like to see, though? The whole 'science running amok and threatening to destroy humankind' theme isn't a little too, as you put it, 'on point?'"

"I think it's either that or *Boundaries*, but when you put it that way…."

"I just so happen to know that they're still running *Incredibles* 2 as a matinée. I mean, if you want to relive old times…. And if going to movies is really what you want to do, we have plenty of time to see both."

"Let's do *Incredibles* and decide after," he said. "I get what you mean, but still—*dinosaurs!*"

She looked into his smiling face, captivated by what she saw there—a formidable intelligence and an innocent, childlike wonder combined in a precise way that was uniquely *Aaron*. Warmth radiated all through her, and she felt like crying yet again, only this time out of happiness. *Why did it take me so long to see it?*

Aaron stood and held out a hand. She took it and let him pull her up.

"Oh, and this time?" he said. "It's my treat."

33

Instead of going directly downtown, they first hiked back to Ellie's house. She excused herself and slipped into her room to change from her shorts into jeans, in anticipation not only of the overly air-conditioned theater, but of the evening's chill later on. Even in June, the air cooled quickly after sunset, and there was no way to know how long the talk with Sam and Ryan would take. After a moment's consideration, she also pulled a light jacket from her closet and tied its arms around her waist.

In the kitchen, she poured a glass of water, drank half, then handed the remainder to Aaron. She explored the drawers and cupboards in a fruitless search for munchies they could smuggle into the theater. Although she had come to appreciate her parents' life-long efforts to instill good eating habits in her and Sam, sometimes junk food was the only way to go. She pulled a promising-looking bag from a cupboard by the fridge, hoping it contained the mini-pretzels they had shared a few days earlier. It did not. *Kale chips… really?!* She replaced them on the shelf and abandoned the hunt. Finally, she scratched out a quick note telling her mom she'd be home by eight-thirty—nine at the latest—then they were gone.

They backtracked their way down to the bench and, following the same path she had taken to the library the previous morning, came out of the canyon in the parking lot at the aquatic center. Once they reached the street, they could see the movie theater near the top of the hill, not quite a quarter mile away.

Ellie recognized the boy behind the ticket booth's window from several classes, but she couldn't remember ever talking to him. *Mike? Mark?* As they slowly inched toward the front of the line, she could see his eyes flit first from her and Aaron, then back to his current customers at the window, an ill-concealed look of amusement on his face. The sight of either of them out on a date—perhaps especially with each other—was evidently as astonishing as seeing a Sasquatch riding Nessie's back through the middle of town. She looked at Aaron, but he seemed oblivious to the scrutiny.

Whatever! She turned her attention to the "Coming Soon" posters hanging on the walls.

Aaron stepped up to the window and slid a twenty under the glass. "Two for *Incredibles*, please."

"'Incredible' it is!" The boy was still eyeing them like they were a carnival sideshow attraction. He tore two tickets in half and slid the stubs and four dollar bills back through the window. "Enjoy the movie."

The smirk on his—*Matt!* she suddenly remembered—face made her livid. She opened her mouth to tell Matt in precise and colorful detail where he could shove that smirk, but Aaron quickly wrapped an arm around her waist and guided her away before she could say a word.

"Come on," he said, nudging her toward the concession area. "He's so not worth it. Pick out a snack."

The feeling of his side pressed to hers, the warmth of his hand resting on her hip, instantly dispelled her irritation. She smiled at him. "You're right," she said, then turned her attention to the candy-filled display case. "You choose. I like pretty much anything red."

After leaving the theater, they crested the hill and walked the rest of the way into town. As they passed the library, Ellie couldn't help but cast a sidelong glance at the spot near the playground where her life had so radically changed only the day before. She used to love coming to the library. Today she was sure she would be perfectly happy if she never entered it again.

Aaron, guessing the direction of her thoughts, pointed at the park on the opposite side of the street. "Hey—look over there."

She dragged her attention away from the library and gazed across the lawn to the pond beyond. The fountain tossed up a fine, white spray that glittered diamond-like in the late afternoon sun.

"That day you told us what you suspected about the shack? That's still the most amazing moment I can remember. I get impressed all over again every time I think about it." Doubt furrowed her brow. "I'm serious. I could tell how nervous you were, but you laid it all out there anyway. You knew the idea sounded totally ridiculous, but also that the evidence was on your side, so you went for it. That took guts."

"Thanks, but I don't know…. Back then, it was just this amazing discovery. It was exciting imagining such a thing might actually exist. Now, though...."

Before she could go any further down that particular road, he changed the subject. "Speaking of guts, mine is empty. Wanna get a sandwich or something?"

She considered the idea. Except for the popcorn and the pack of Twizzlers they had shared at the movie, she had eaten nothing since that morning at the café. She still didn't feel hungry, but she decided she should have something. "Maybe something small?"

"I know!" he said, as if the thought had just occurred to him. "Let's go to that Old Adobe place and get a few appetizers to split. How's that sound?"

She smiled inwardly, remembering Sam's spot-on description of his idea of a perfect first date. *A do-over? Well, why not?*

"Excellent," she said, then made a silent promise to stay positive despite her grief.

To Ellie's relief, the hostess who seated them did not seem to have any opinion regarding the two of them being together. Wearing a polite smile, she led them to a small table pressed up against one of the brightly painted half-walls that broke up the interior in a way that was meant to make the large, wide-open space feel more intimate. Before settling onto the wooden chair, Ellie removed her phone from her rear pocket and laid it along the wall at the midpoint of the table. The hostess handed them menus, informed them their server would be with them momentarily, then turned and left.

Ellie picked up her menu and gazed across the table at Aaron. "This is nice. I can't remember the last time I was here. It used to be anytime someone came to visit us we'd all come here for dinner." She frowned. "I guess people are done visiting."

"Spring of freshman year. When I won the Science Fair. That's the last time I was here." He looked around the room. "Except it wasn't *here* here. It was at their old place."

"I've been here once since the move, so that means it hasn't been *too* long." *Yes, keep it light,* she thought. "So, what did you think of the movie?"

He quoted Mr. Incredible. "'Suit up. It might get weird.' That's my new motto. Covers a lot of situations." They laughed quietly. "I thought it was good. I like Violet. She's a little less dark in this one."

"Ooh, crushin' on a cartoon babe, huh?" she teased.

He raised his hands in a placating gesture. "Now, now… no need to get jealous. What about you?"

She chose to misinterpret the question. "Oh, I'd *totally* date her!" They laughed again. "I liked it. Every time I see one of those movies, I can't believe how much better the animation keeps getting. I enjoyed the story, too, but did you notice that early scene with the light patterns under the pool and the mist hanging in the air?"

"Yeah, that was amazing. I liked that bit toward the end when they're sitting in the snow, too."

A woman Ellie guessed to be in her forties arrived, placed two glasses of water on the table, and pulled an order pad from her apron pocket. "Anything else to drink?" She waited, pen poised on pad.

"Do you have a 2010 Château Lafite-Rothschild?" Aaron said, his expression perfectly deadpan.

Their server did not miss a beat. "Do you have a 1997 driver's license?"

"*Touché.*" To Ellie, he said, "Iced tea?" She nodded. "Two iced teas, please. 2018 is fine."

"Cute!" She recorded their order, amusement twitching the corners of her mouth. She smiled at him before leaving to get their tea. "I'll be right back, wise guy."

As soon as her back was turned, she laughed again. "'*Château Lafite-Rothschild,*'" she said, mimicking his high school-French accent. "Where'd you pull that from?"

He smiled and shrugged. "It just popped into my head. I have no idea what it is."

He opened the menu flat on the table and began scanning the list. "Seriously, though—since we won't be splurging on wine, get whatever you want."

She read down the list of appetizers and salads offered during the transitional hours between lunch and dinner services. The restaurant's aromas and the enticing descriptions of the menu items worked together to stimulate her lower brain functions, and suddenly the idea of eating seemed appealing.

They started with an order of fried mozzarella and vegetables served with an assortment of dipping sauces. They followed that with fish and chips, which Aaron remembered enjoying the last time he ate there. Ellie was amazed to discover she had an appetite after all, and by the end of the first dish, she was enjoying not merely the food but the whole experience.

During the meal, she got him to share more of his memories from New York. He had little to say about his former classmates, but he recalled other aspects of his life there with great fondness. He had enjoyed the Museum of Natural History—because, of course, dinosaurs!—but he had especially loved visiting the Hayden Planetarium. There he became fascinated not only by the science of astronomy but by the technology that made the science possible. For three consecutive birthdays, the one present he asked for was to spend the day there. Between visits, he read all he could about telescopes, probes, and landers, captivated by the notion of doing research in places hundreds of millions of miles away.

She had always known how much he loved astronomy. They had spent many summer and autumn nights stargazing on the big deck behind Ryan's house. Sometimes he had even brought his telescope along so they could look at the planets. Now she knew where that interest had started.

He began listening to Neil deGrasse Tyson's podcast StarTalk when he was ten. He didn't care that nearly everyone he told found this immensely amusing. Those programs gave him his first taste of a world where people talked the way he heard his own voice in his head. It was a revelation to hear people from many different backgrounds discussing complicated ideas without feeling the need to dumb them down. Even more exciting was the way Tyson and his guests explored abstract scientific concepts with the same enthusiasm with which most people he knew discussed the most recent Yankees game or the latest episode of *Breaking Bad*. It was a world he could not wait to become a part of.

With sudden insight, Ellie realized that his hesitant speech, his frequent 'ums' and 'ahs,' were the result of a constantly running, real-time, Aaron-to-normal-humanoid translation algorithm, one that was always searching for, and often failing to find, a simpler way of expressing his thoughts. She thought about how his speech sounded smoother and more natural on the rare occasions they were alone together, like now, and as they had been Thursday on top of the mountain. That he felt no need to filter his thoughts around her was the highest compliment anyone had ever given her.

She was so absorbed in his story that she almost asked if he thought he might study astronomy or astrophysics in college, maybe even minor in one of the subjects. She caught herself in time and covered her upset by trying to tease more ketchup out of the bottle.

"I wish I could go there with you," she said instead. "To the planetarium in New York, I mean. It won't be there yet when we go."

"No, you're right." He considered that for a moment. "That's bizarre! It's like Paris without the Eiffel Tower."

She laughed. "More like Geneva without the collider, I think, but I know what you mean." She pointed at her plate. "Take some of these fries. I'm done."

But at that point, the server returned, and Aaron decided that he, too, was finished. She placed the bill on the table and left with their plates. He reached for the bill with one hand and his wallet with the other.

"Thanks," she said. "This was nice. I'm going to the…." She pointed toward the back of the restaurant where a sign said *Restrooms* in blocky sky-blue letters. "Will you take my coat with you?"

"Sure," he said.

Minutes later, Ellie met him at the front of the restaurant and he handed her the jacket, which she again tied around her waist. He opened the door and held it for her, but she suddenly stopped short and frantically started patting her pockets.

"Oh, wait! My phone!" She left him standing by the hostess station and returned at a trot to their table. The table had yet to be bussed, and her phone was where she had left it, pushed up against the wall but mostly concealed by her crumpled napkin. It was no wonder he hadn't seen it. As she slid it toward her, she knocked the check folder onto her chair, spilling its contents across the seat. She scooped everything up—the bill, a pen, and the cash—intending only to replace it all on the table, but what she saw made her pause. Confused, she studied the check and saw that the total came to thirty-nine eighty-five. She also noticed that Aaron had scribbled a big "Thanks!" across the bottom. But why had he left four twenties to cover a forty-dollar tab?

As she stared at the cash, her first thought was that he had made a mistake, had meant to leave two fives as a tip instead of the two extra twenties. She was on the verge of taking the bill and money to the front with her and scolding him for his poor math skills or inattention, but still, she hesitated. He simply didn't make mistakes like that.

Then the answer came to her and her breath caught in her chest. Her vision blurred by sudden tears, she clumsily placed the money back in the folder and laid it in the middle of the table. Aaron, she realized, knew his money would soon be of no use to him and so had chosen to pass some of what little he had on to someone else. It was a small thing, a random act of kindness. Would it even mean anything in a few days after everything changed? She decided that didn't matter. The gesture had been made, and all she could do was love him for it.

She wiped her eyes with her napkin, put on what she hoped was a natural-looking expression, and returned to find him still waiting patiently by the door. She waggled her phone at him. "Found it!"

"I was about to come help look."

"I got a text from Mom. Had to let her know when I'd be home. Guess she didn't find my note."

Why she didn't just admit she'd seen the money, tell him how wonderful she thought that was, she couldn't say. She sensed, though, that it should remain his secret, even if it meant telling a white lie to keep it that way. She also knew they needed to be gone before their waitress returned to their table and discovered the overly generous tip. Otherwise, the situation "might get weird."

"C'mon," she said. She smiled at him and took him by the arm. "What do you say we blow this taco stand?"

"If that means 'leave,' I'm in favor."

Out on the sidewalk, she led him away from the front of the restaurant as quickly as she could, still concerned the waitress would spoil their clean getaway. Once they rounded the corner at the end of the building, she slowed her pace.

"We still have almost two hours," she said. "What would you like to do next?"

"How about we get a couple more of those chocolates and take them over to the patio outside Starbuck's?"

"You're sure you don't want another of those espresso brownies?" she teased.

He glared at her in mock anger. "You've ruined them for me, thank you very much!"

"Another soul saved! That sounds like a great idea."

They retraced their path back to Central Avenue and walked half a block to Wolf's. They pushed through the glass door and stood again in front of the tall, glass display case.

"We call ourselves 'Chocolatarians,' by the way. It's not the 'Church of Chocolate.'" She smiled at him, making sure he understood that she was joking.

"Huh? Ahh, like Unitarians... got it." He smiled back.

"See anything you want to try?"

"I have no idea. Just pick out your favorites."

She did.

At Starbuck's, Ellie chose the same table they had used the week before. She spread the white paper bag flat on the table and lined up the chocolates on top of it. There were four this time, all truffles. The only repeat was the Chocolate Decadence, to which she had added a Hazelnut, a Black Forest, and an Amaretto. She had barely finished laying out the truffles before Aaron arrived bearing two lattes.

"Here you go," he said, handing her one of the drinks. "And look—spill-proof lids. So, cheers!" He rapped his paper cup solidly against hers. He didn't expect the twin jets of milky foam that shot up through the sipping holes in the lids, and he almost dropped his cup in surprise.

Ellie laughed. "Cheers!" she echoed, and took a drink.

She described each of the chocolates and watched as he sampled them one by one. Taking pleasure from his enjoyment, she was reminded of something she had once read, although she couldn't remember the source. *Food sometimes tastes better in the mouths of others.* It had been meant metaphorically but now proved true for literal food, too.

"That one with the cocoa on top… that's still my favorite," he said when the last truffle was gone.

"I guess that makes you a purist," she said. "Chocolate and nothing but the chocolate."

"Occam's Law of Chocolate—the simplest truffle is the best."

Although she smiled at the jest, she could feel her melancholy mood from earlier in the day threatening to return. For a while they sat quietly, nursing their coffees and staring off toward an unseen Santa Fe. A jumble of thoughts swirled through her mind making her feel fidgety, and every now and then she stole a glance at him from the corner of her eye. She couldn't reconcile his apparent composure with the storm of emotions she could barely manage to keep in control.

"You want to ask me something," he finally said. "Just go ahead."

She hung her head, embarrassed by having been read so easily. "Sorry. I get this image…. You know the cartoon where the character opens the door, and outside it's like a total blizzard with swirling snow and a howling wind that sounds like a freight train? And it blows the door in and he can barely get it closed again?"

Aaron took over describing the scene. "But then he manages to slam it shut and it's instantly calm again. Yeah, I know what you mean."

"Whenever I think about what we're doing or try to imagine what this must be like for you, it's like that. In my head, I mean. It's like opening that door. No thoughts at all, just a howling storm. But here we are, eating chocolate and going to a movie—how is that… how can you…? *Oh, I don't know!*" She was frustrated by being unable to express herself any more clearly.

He considered her question for what felt like minutes. "If you want to look at it that way, then you could say there are *two* doors in my mind. And if I think about our plan, what it's going to mean for me… if I open *that* door, then yeah, it's like you said. But if I concentrate on what might happen to you, to Sam and Ryan, to everything we know if we did nothing? What lies on the other side of that door is much, much worse. It's like *The Lady, or the Tiger*, except with one regular tiger and another, even bigger tiger. At least by picking the first door, the lady gets to live without having to worry about what's behind the second door." He gave her a wan smile. "We hope."

"*It's not fair!!!*" she yelled, her pain and anger finally finding a voice. People at nearby tables stared momentarily in their direction before resuming their conversations. "It's not fair," she repeated more quietly. She felt a lone tear meander down her cheek, but she ignored it. She looked at him, trying to sense what was going on behind his glasses.

"No. It's not." He extended his hand across the table to her. She took it and squeezed it tightly, willing herself not to cry.

"Come on," he said. "We'd better go."

"*No!*" she said, her tone firm. Being contrary felt surprisingly good, and she tried it again. "No! Uh-uh! Not happenin'!" That *did* feel good!

Without letting go of her hand, he rose and walked to her side of the table. He offered her his other hand, and she reluctantly took it and let him pull her to her feet. They stood facing each other, their noses mere inches apart.

"It's not fair," he repeated, "but it's what we have to do."

"I know," she said, her voice barely a whisper. "I know."

They were halfway to the meeting place, walking slowly, when Aaron broke the silence. "I have imagined it, you know. Not today, when you asked, but other times."

"When I asked what?"

"What I would do if I could do anything I wanted. You're very pretty when you blush, by the way. You don't do it very often."

"Thanks, I guess." It was the first time he had paid her a compliment without couching it in corniness, and it was on her blushing skills? But now she knew exactly what he meant.

"You have? You've thought about it?" *Great.* Now *she* was thinking about it, and she tried hard not to blush again as a rapid-fire sequence of vividly sensual images flashed unbidden through her mind. Finding herself unable to meet his eyes, she dropped her gaze to the pavement and watched as first one foot and then the other popped rhythmically in and out of the lower edge of her field of vision.

"Well, *yeah!* I think you're… I mean you're *really…!* And I've never, um, you know…. But I know you've never even thought of me as a boyfriend before, let alone as a… as something more. But bad timing aside, I can't imagine anything more morbid than, you know, doing *that* under these circumstances. I wouldn't want your first time to be like that. And if you did say yes, I wouldn't want to wonder if it was only because...." He shrugged, clearly feeling under no obligation to complete even a single thought. "Does that make any sense?"

She was pretty sure she understood what he was trying to say, despite his complete inability to actually say it. She nodded.

"Anyway, I thought… I don't know why, but I thought I should tell you that."

"*Hoo-boy,*" she muttered. She continued looking at the ground as she considered what he'd said. *Morbid,* she decided, was precisely the right word. *Depressing* worked, too. On the other hand, it pleased her to learn he might not rank her below velociraptors after all.

"Of course, I realize I am making certain assumptions here."

She peeked up at him from the corner of her eye. "Really? What assumptions?"

"I said 'first time,' but maybe it would be your twentieth time, or fiftieth." He was grinning now, and he gave her a playful jab with his elbow. "Or *hundredth! Hmm?* Am I getting warm?"

Now she was smiling too, amused by the complete absurdity of the suggestion. She knew he was trying to cheer her up, and she decided to let it work. "Stop it," she tittered.

"What, too low? Help me out—are we talking three digits or four?"

She wrapped his left arm with both of hers and pulled him to her, laughing.

"Surely not five!" He sounded mortified. "When would you have had time to study?!"

She leaned her head against his shoulder, still smiling. "Sorry—my one rule is that I don't kiss and tell."

"Yes, and where would we be without rules? Total chaos, that's where."

34

They arrived at the park with ten minutes to spare and sat side by side on the same bench they had shared the day before. However, Ellie was too full of nervous energy to remain seated for long. Almost at once, she got back to her feet and started pacing around the bench in a tight oval.

After a dozen or so laps, Aaron rose and placed himself in her path, forcing her either to stop or run into him. He took her upper arm gently in one hand and led her at a more leisurely pace toward the rear of the lodge. "How about we try straight for a few minutes."

When they reached the near corner of the building, they turned around and started back toward the bench. He gave her arm a brief squeeze, then let go of it. When he spoke, he was very solemn.

"After we talk to those two, well, like the man said, 'it might get weird,' so I want to say this now, while it's on my mind. I know spending the afternoon that way—trying to be cheerful and pretending everything was normal —I know that was hard, believe me. But thank you. It means a lot to me."

She tried to smile but couldn't quite get it to happen. "I know," she managed to say. "Me, too." She took his hand and squeezed.

Sam's voice called out to them from across the lawn.

"Hey, guys!"

They looked up, startled to find that she and Ryan were just a dozen yards away. They hadn't seen them coming.

"Hey," Ellie replied.

Ryan carried a sports drink in one hand and an open, snack-sized bag of chips in the other. They both walked over to the bench, sat on top of its back, and planted their feet on the seat's wooden slats. Neither Ellie nor Aaron spoke even after the two had situated themselves for the big presentation.

"So," Ryan eventually prompted. "What's the brain trust finally come up with?"

"Well...." Ellie said, then waited for Aaron to take the lead as planned.

"It's, um...." Aaron said.

Ellie could tell he was feeling far less confident about sharing their idea than he had been a few short hours earlier. She gave him an encouraging smile.

"You're not going to like it," he said.

"You're really not," Ellie agreed, looking apologetic.

"Enough with the 'Deep Thought' crap," Ryan said. "Let's have it!"

Ellie heard the agitation in his voice and realized he already suspected he wasn't going to like their idea

"Neither of you should consider a career in marketing," Sam advised. She tossed a chip into her mouth and chomped on it noisily. "Just sayin'."

Ellie was familiar with this affected air of nonchalance and knew Sam was experiencing the same misgivings as Ryan. "Just thought we should get that out of the way up front," she said, then nodded at Aaron. "Go ahead." Still, he hesitated, unable to get started. She hissed at him through clenched teeth. "Do it like we talked about. You know, ease into it."

He cleared his throat, but there was another long pause before he finally spoke. "So, the plan is this—we need to wreck my grandparent's marriage."

Ellie buried her face in her palm, shook her head, and sighed. *Or we can do it* this *way!*

Sam squinted at him, confused. "Aren't they, like... *dead?*"

"Okay, here's the thing...."

.   .   .

Aaron started over, this time laying out the plan the way they had initially agreed. As Ellie studied Sam and Ryan's reactions, she began to appreciate just how brilliant Aaron's opening statement had been. Whether it had been the result of conscious design or a sudden burst of inspiration, she now understood that the comment, flatly absurd on the face of it, had planted a seed in their minds. The rest of his explanation now worked like sunlight and water, slowly bringing that seed to blossom. Although he often seemed uncomfortable dealing with people, especially ones his own age, she was starting to recognize that he had unrevealed depths.

Aaron finished explaining how his father's work was central to the shack's creation, how the files he had snuck out of the lab all pointed to him as the device's sole architect. Ellie knew the next part was the delicate one. She slowly drifted to one side of the group to a spot from which she could observe Sam and Ryan less conspicuously. They remained completely silent, the food and drink forgotten, but every now and then, one of them would slowly nod in agreement—or at least in understanding—as Aaron continued to lay out the dots. Finally, as the sun started to slide behind the mountains, he went into his wrap-up.

"So, if we can prevent them from meeting on that one specific day, at that one specific time, the problem just disappears. Or, to be more precise, never appears in the first place. At least that's the theory." He looked at Ellie. She nodded and gave him a small smile, then they waited for what they expected to be an impassioned reaction.

Ryan understood right away. He looked at Sam, who seemed to be waiting for more, then at Ellie and Aaron. Ellie saw a savage light in his eyes, noted muscles clenching along his jaw, and realized it might be the first time she'd ever seen him mad.

"So that's it?! *That's* the plan?!" He practically spat the words out.

Confused, Sam's eyes ricocheted from one person to the next. "What? What did I miss? Why are you...?"

Ryan cut her off. His rising anger gave his words a harsh, bitter tone. "We've seen this movie, Sam. A couple of times!" He slid off the table to stand practically nose to nose with Aaron. "One of us isn't coming back. Right, *A-Ron*? Are you supposed to be Gandolf, or is this more like the *Dark Knight Rises*? No, wait—knowing you, I bet this is a Spock thing. 'The needs of the many,' blah, blah, blah.... *Huh?!*" When Aaron remained silent, Ryan raised his hands to chest height and gave him a rough shove. "*Answer me, man!*"

Aaron staggered back a step to maintain his balance, but he continued to meet Ryan's furious glare without flinching. Ellie tensed, ready to step in between them if Ryan raised his hands again. *How ironic.*

"Ryan, stop it!" Sam said. She grabbed his arm and pulled him away from Aaron. "Just tell me what's...." Her voice trailed off. "Hold on... *what?!*"

Ellie watched Sam's focus go inward as she replayed the past several moments. She recognized the instant she deciphered Ryan's movie references, connected the last dot, and finally understood the ramifications of Aaron's plan.

"No!" Sam cried. "Ellie, *no!*" She dropped from the bench, ran to her sister, and grasped her firmly by the shoulders. She stared pleadingly into her eyes, her anguished expression as intense as her grip. "You can't seriously be thinking of doing this! You *can't!*"

Hearing in Sam's pleading tone all the distress and heartbreak she had been holding in check for the past day and a half, Ellie struggled hard to remain composed. She took hold of Sam's wrists and pried the clutching fingers from her shoulders. She pressed Sam's hands together between her own and spoke as soothingly as she could.

"We don't *want* to, Sam, but we have no choice. We have no other plan and we are running out of time." She laughed mirthlessly at that. *Irony, indeed!*

Sam refused to accept that argument. She turned to Aaron, still pleading. "Talk to your dad—make him see how dangerous that thing is!"

"It wouldn't matter. Too many people know the science now. The genie is out of the bottle... Pandora's box has been opened... pick your metaphor. We can no longer solve the problem here, now." He shook his head sadly. "Besides, I'm sure he already knows."

"Come on. " Ellie guided Sam back toward the bench. "Let's sit down."

As the discussion progressed, both Ryan's anger and Sam's anguish gradually diminished. Neither could deny the magnitude of the threat posed by the shack, nor could they offer a different solution. Ultimately, all their main objections came down to a simple question of morality, at least in Sam's mind.

"But if we *do* do this, aren't we doing the exact thing we'd be doing this to prevent others from doing?"

Ryan blinked. "Well put! I think."

"'Playing God,' you mean?" Ellie said. They were ready for this objection. "Aaron?"

"So, yeah," he said, agreeing with Sam's fundamental point. "We are going back intending to make changes, to alter people's lives. But there are two things to bear in mind. First is the *why* of it. It's not for any personal gain. Obviously," he added, a not-very-oblique reference to their plan's ultimate impact on him. Sam dropped her gaze to the ground. "Our entire goal is to make the fewest alterations possible. You know I'm an only child. So's my dad. I don't know what I might discover or achieve in the future, but going by statistics, I don't believe that future generations will be any worse off because I'm no longer around. And anyway, who's to say I don't get run over by a truck next Thursday?" He let them consider that for a moment before he went on.

"What I believe most is that it's very unlikely any of us have a future if that machine is allowed to exist. How do we know that what we're living right now isn't already the result of changes made by someone using that device? I don't believe that's the case, but we've seen how this works—I wouldn't, would I? They don't even have to be trying to make changes. As Ellie pointed out, all they have to do is screw up. Like I did dropping that camera." He paused before making his final point.

"The other thing is this—if this plan works, it's all over. Yes, we'll make some one or two changes, and there'll almost certainly be some side effects we can't even guess at. But the threat the shack poses will be over. Gone like it was never there to begin with."

"But there's a third thing," Ryan said. "When it comes to playing God, that is. In some way, we'll be killing you. Not to mention dear old Dad. That will be on us."

Aaron shook his head emphatically, unwilling to concede the point. "It's *my* plan. *My* decision. Help or don't help, but this is going to happen either way. I'll do it alone if I have to." He paused as if mulling over a new thought before continuing in a calmer tone. "Look, what we need to focus on is the greater good, on everything we're protecting. I'm just...." He abruptly stopped again, struck by a sudden realization.

Ryan looked at him, his eyebrows raised. "Yes?"

"Okay, so maybe it is sorta the 'Spock thing,'" Aaron admitted.

"'Future generations,'" Sam said, quoting his phrase back at him. "So what about your children? Or theirs? What might *they* achieve? And don't they have the right to exist? You just said we don't know what the long-term effects of doing this will be."

"Aaron has already decided he's never going to have kids," Ellie said, and before Sam could get angry over her flippant response, she pressed on, holding a hand up traffic-cop fashion. "You're right. You are absolutely right. We *don't* know. Not for certain. But that's the future, and it hasn't been written yet. We're free to make whatever choices we want about that. It all comes down to choosing to sacrifice the uncertain possibilities of an unknowable future to protect the 'now' we *do* know. The worst you can say is that we're doing one small, bad thing to stop a much, much bigger bad thing from happening."

Sam and Ryan looked at each other for a long moment.

"Sacrifice," Ryan repeated. He his head slowly, trying to process everything that had been said. "Yeah, I don't know, man. This is—I don't know what I was expecting, but it sure as hell wasn't this! It's obvious you two have talked about this and have come to terms with it, but it's a lot to be hit with all at once. We need to talk this through, just the two of us." He paused and looked at Sam to see if she had anything to add. When she remained silent, he turned back to Aaron. "You're absolutely sure? No other way?"

Aaron answered with a single nod. "I'm sure. Listen. I know how this will sound, but I need you—all three of you—to understand something. Last week, when I first started to realize what the plan was likely to be.... No, let me say it this way.

"I don't believe we're alive for some grand purpose, like there's something we're each 'meant' to do. But I do believe we each have certain strengths, things we're especially good at, and that by doing those things, maybe we can make a difference. You know, have some kind of impact on the world. When I imagine how much damage the shack could cause, I know that nothing I might one day accomplish could ever be more important, have more of an impact, than being part of destroying it."

Ellie, openly weeping once again, moved to stand close beside him. She held his left hand tightly in both of hers and laid her head on his shoulder as he continued explaining.

"So, anyway, when I figured out this has to be the plan, I also knew that this is my 'thing,' what *I* can do to make a difference. It's not like I *want* to do this… who would? But I feel like I *have* to. If we decided to do nothing, go along like the shack doesn't exist, how could we ever live with the constant fear of what it could do? I truly believe we need to do this, and that it's best if we do it together."

Ryan let out a long, shuddering sigh. "Okay. We're going to take a walk. When we get back, we'll let you know what we've decided." He slid off the bench and held his hand out to Sam. She took it and stood beside him.

"Fair enough," Aaron said.

Sam and Ryan started to walk away. Feeling a sudden surge of resolve, Ellie called out across the growing distance between them.

"Sam!" Sam stopped and turned to face her. "This is the path." Their eyes locked and held for a long moment, then Sam nodded and walked away. Ellie watched them until they disappeared into the evening gloom.

"So now we wait," Aaron said.

"So now we wait."

"What did you mean, 'this is the path?'"

"It's something Sam said to me a while ago. That we needed to be ready to recognize the path when it showed itself."

"Wow. That's uncharacteristically Zen of her."

"I know, right? You don't expect it, then, all of a sudden and from outta nowhere, she pops up and puts one straight into the bull's eye. Like with her 'quantum collapse' thing. Isn't there some quote about not 'hiding your light under a basket?' That's what she does, I think."

"*Bushel*," he said, "and it's Biblical, but maybe it means a bushel basket, so I guess you're close enough. That part of the book isn't in my wheelhouse."

"Ah," was all she could say.

At first, they wandered around the small park, walking shoulder to shoulder, comfortable in the new sense of intimacy between them. Aaron finally spoke, clearly reluctant to say what was on his mind.

"You could stay behind, you know."

"Huh? What do you mean?" She was genuinely confused.

"Stay here, in this time. Not come back with us."

"But you said all four of us should go. You said...."

"I said four was better than two. Three is still better than two. It would work." He paused, still hesitant to spell it out. "It's just that if you stayed here...."

Then she understood, and it was her turn to interrupt. "If I stay here, then I'll forget! *That's* what you're saying!" She was stunned, not only that he would suggest it, but because not for a single instant had that idea crossed her mind. She refused to consider it now. "*No!* Absolutely not! How could you even... how...?" But her throat had become too tight for her to finish the question. She could only stand there, staring at the ground, willing herself not to break down again.

"Hey, hey, it's okay." He placed his hands on her shoulders and spoke softly into her hair. "I'm not saying that's what I want. I thought you should have the choice, that's all. I'm sure they would go along with that." He jerked his head in the direction Sam and Ryan had gone.

To live without the pain of losing Aaron at the price of having never known him? In her mind, there was no decision to be made. She tilted her head back to look up into his face and locked her eyes on his. "Well, just so there's no question about what I want, I choose *this!*"

She reached up, placed a hand behind his head, and gently guided it down until their lips met. She couldn't have said how long the kiss lasted, but she knew there was no possible way it could have been even remotely as long as it seemed. When they finally parted she felt dizzy, and for a second she thought she actually might pass out. She rested her head on his shoulder and he slipped his arms around her.

"*Wow!*" he said. "A few more of those, and I won't want to go through with this myself!"

She raised her head to look at him. "Excuse me? I'd like to think the one would be enough." They both laughed and the tension of the moment eased. "Seriously," she began, and gave him a quick peck on the lips. "I can't begin to imagine what it's going to be like—the actual *doing* of it, then not having you here—but I'll be beside you all the way."

She leaned forward and laid her head against him. A few moments ticked by, and then she spoke again, her voice muffled from having her face pressed to his shoulder. "Remember what I said about chocolate the other day at the store?"

"Mm-hmm."

She snuggled even more tightly against him. "I take it back."

35

W hile they waited for Sam and Ryan to return, the last glimmer of twilight slowly faded from the sky. The temperature had been falling for the last hour, and Ellie was glad she'd thought to bring the jacket. She and Aaron sat close together on the bench, holding hands. For a while, they distracted themselves with trivial talk about movies and TV shows. Aaron especially enjoyed picking out every inaccuracy of any sci-fi title Ellie cared to name.

"But that's not fair," she countered after one particularly brutal critique. "That movie isn't actually science fiction. It's barely even science *fantasy*!"

"Hey, all I'm saying is that all of your brain is active all of the time! It's not like parts of it are sitting around idle, just hanging out and waiting to give you telekinesis, or ESP, or something."

"Are you saying if there were a drug you could take that would boost your brainpower by even a little, say ten or fifteen percent, that you wouldn't be tempted to try it?"

"My brain gets me into enough trouble the way it is."

He had meant this humorously, but the offhand reminder of the seriousness of their situation abruptly killed the light mood they had managed to create. Ellie laughed, but it was a bitter sound.

"You know what's stupid? Whenever I try to come up with something reassuring to say, the first thing I always think of is, 'We'll get through this.' How dumb is that? *I'm* the one who could use the brain boost."

He stood to face her, took hold of her hands, and pulled her to her feet. "You know what helps me? Knowing that *you'll* get through this."

"Stop it. You're going to get me crying again."

"It's true, though. And that's all the consolation I need." Still holding her hands, he looked into her glistening hazel eyes. "That and maybe another kiss."

He leaned forward and had no more than touched his lips to hers when they were interrupted by the sound of Ryan's voice.

"I see you two have come a long way in the past, what...?" He made a show of consulting his still-bare wrist. "...hour, or so?"

Startled, they jumped away from each other to see Ryan and Sam entering the glow of lamplight surrounding the bench. Ellie imagined they looked comically guilty. Aaron, especially embarrassed to have been caught *in flagrante* by Sam in particular, tried adopting a casual tone, a man-of-the-world insouciance. Instead, he managed only to sound like he was babbling.

"You know, *carpe diem*, and all...." That his face was bright red did not help at all to sell the pretense.

"Yep, ya gotta seize that carp!" Ellie agreed. She discovered, to her surprise, that she didn't feel even the slightest bit embarrassed.

"Relax," Sam said as she walked to stand in front of Aaron. "It's not like you were caught, oh, I don't know, sneaking top-secret documents out of a high-security LAB facility or something."

"Umm, yeah, right," he nervously agreed.

"No," she continued, her tone still mild, "this is far, *far* worse." Then she thrust a finger at his face, and her voice was abruptly harsh. "You were *kissing my sister!*"

Stunned by the unexpected intensity of her accusation, he responded out of reflex. "I'm sorry, I... I...."

Ellie, reading Sam's intentions perfectly from the beginning, played along. She, too, turned on Aaron, fists planted firmly on her hips. "Hold on!" she cried. "You're *sorry* you kissed me?" She sounded every bit as angry as Sam.

"No, I.... *No!*"

Sam cranked up the pressure. "So, you're *not* sorry!"

His eyes bounced from one angry expression to the other. "Yes... I mean *no*... I mean...."

"I have just one thing to say to you," Sam said, her voice pitched in tones that could shatter granite. *"It's about time!"*

Aaron threw his arms up in surrender. *"Okay, okay!* Wait, *what?!"*

Sam and Ellie laughed, finally letting him in on the joke. Baffled, Aaron looked to Ryan for an explanation, but he merely smiled and shrugged.

"Take that as a warning. You never want to get on the wrong side of these two. And hey, listen," he went on, sounding more serious. "I'm sorry. You know, about earlier."

Before Aaron could respond, Sam surprised him yet again by wrapping him in a warm, friendly hug that pinned his arms to his sides. "I'm glad you two have finally figured it out," she said, and gently patted his back. She winked at Ellie over his shoulder before she stepped away to stand beside Ryan.

Ellie recognized the incongruous interlude of forced levity for what it was—what their father would have called "whistling past the graveyard." She studied Sam and Ryan's faces and noted signs of stress and pain in both. Sam's eyes were red, her face flushed from recent weeping. Ryan, who always seemed to vibrate with an excess of energy, stood utterly still. Everyone knew the question, and judging by Sam's "kissing my sister" bit, Ellie figured she already knew the answer. Still, she waited for one of the others to speak.

"Ellie," Sam said, "I said before that I trust you, and I do. Both of you. We talked it through, and while neither of us can imagine having to make such a decision, you guys *did*, and, well, that says a lot. We also know that if we said 'no,' you two would try it on your own, and I...."

Ryan cut her off, unable to bear drawing the exchange out even a second longer. His words came out high and reedy through a tight throat. "We're in."

Ellie had never seen his expression so cold, so controlled, and she understood he was fighting hard to keep it together. She knew exactly how he felt.

"Look," he continued, "I know there are plans to make, details to work out, but, to be honest, we're wiped. Can we pick this back up tomorrow?"

As he spoke, he swiped his hand through his hair, a gesture of fatigue, and now he stood there, palm clasping the back of his neck, waiting.

Aaron responded with a nod.

"Let's go." Ryan slid his arm around Sam's waist, and they retreated the way they had come.

"So now it's real," she said.

"So now it's real."

Ellie assumed Sam and Ryan would head for her house, so she and Aaron began walking toward his. She wanted to give them as much extra time and privacy as possible while they began coming to terms with the commitment they had just made. More than that, though, she wanted more time alone with Aaron.

At first, they strolled silently, hand in hand, occasionally exchanging shy smiles. They talked in general terms about how they might execute their newly adopted plan, but Ellie's thoughts were too focused on Aaron, on the still-unfamiliar sensation of his fingers entwined with hers, to concentrate on anything else. She squeezed his hand tighter as they approached the edge of his front yard.

"It's funny, you know? I used to get so pissed off when I had to watch those two doing their little 'lovebirds' act. All the whispering, the touches, her silly giggles and his dopey grins—that drove me *nuts!*"

"You don't say." His tone was desert-dry. "Remember our last hike out onto the mesa? When we found the shack? I was pretty sure that day was going to end with me helping you bury their bodies."

She laughed, remembering the dark mood she had been in when that outing started. "Yeah. It was this close for a while," she joked, holding up her thumb and forefinger. A very fine hair might have fit between them— barely. "But like I was saying, it's funny because it never once occurred to me that I felt that way because I was envious."

"And now?"

Having reached the front of his house, they stopped, and Ellie turned to face him. "And now I'm *so* much older," kiss "and wiser," kiss "and too busy doing *this* to care!"

The next kiss was longer, and by the end of it, Ellie could feel a familiar, gentle heat suffusing her body. Over Aaron's shoulder, she could see the glow from a light he had left on in the entry, and she felt its pull as strongly as would any moth. This was far from the first time she had experienced the warm rush of arousal, but it was the first time those urges had a defined target, let alone one so close. The raw intensity of those feelings scared her, and she did her best to push them aside. She leaned her head against his shoulder and sighed. "I'd better go. I told Mom I'd be back early enough to say goodbye before their trip."

He nodded. "About tomorrow—text me with the time? And I'll let you know if I come up with any ideas about exactly how we're going to do this."

"Yeah. Let's say by lunch at the latest, but I bet it will be before then. I'll let you know as early as I can." She took his hand, her eyes once again brimming with tears. "This is so hard."

"I know. I'm sorry."

"Me, too."

She let go of his hand and watched him walk across the lawn toward the empty house. He opened the door and stepped in, then turned to face her. Backlit from the light in the hall, his expression was lost in shadow, but she saw him give a little wave and heard a soft, "Goodnight."

"Goodnight," she said, then the door closed.

She stared at the house until the hallway light went off, then started trudging home.

She arrived twenty-five minutes later and found Sam sitting on her bed, reading. When Sam lowered the magazine to her lap, Ellie could see her eyes were puffy, her cheeks splotched with patches of red, and she knew Sam had been crying again.

"Hey," she said, softly closing the door. "I told Mom and Dad to have a good trip. They said they'd be gone by the time we got up."

Sam made no reply, and Ellie began peeling off her clothes to get ready for bed. It was still early, but she was exhausted. It wasn't until she popped her head through the collar of her nightshirt that she finally noticed Sam had not gone back to reading but was continuing to watch her closely.

"*What?!*" The word came out sounding more irritated than she felt. "Sorry. What?" she repeated more mildly.

Sam stretched an arm out and patted the mattress beside her thigh. "Come here," she said, her voice gentle.

Ellie expelled an exasperated sigh but walked across the room to stand beside the bed, arms crossed in front of her, one eyebrow raised.

Sam patted the bed again. "Sit. Please?" She scooted toward the bed's opposite side to give Ellie more room.

The last time Ellie had heeded those words, things hadn't turned out so well, but hearing the tenderness in Sam's tone, she let go of her irritation, uncrossed her arms, and sat. "Okay, I'm sitting. What's up?"

Sam brushed her fingertips through Ellie's short hair, traced a line up and over her left ear, and let her hand come to rest on her shoulder. "When did you guys come up with this plan of yours?"

Ellie shook her head, indicating Sam had gotten it wrong. "Not *my* idea. You heard him—he came up with this all on his own. He told me yesterday morning."

"So you've known for, like, *two days?*" Ellie nodded. "I can't believe you've been able to deal at all. I'd be a total mess. I sort of am, actually. But why didn't you say something last night? Am I right in assuming you weren't really asleep when I came in?"

Ellie heard no hint of accusation in Sam's voice, but some other emotion suffused her tone, one harder to define. She remembered how she had felt after hearing Sam's story about Kyle's attack and thought she understood the emotion even though she couldn't put a name to it. She lowered her head and answered softly.

"Yeah, you are. Mostly because we weren't completely sure yet. I hoped that today we could come up with something else. Then we had to figure out how to explain it all to you two so that you'd agree to help. We didn't want to try it alone or, worse, wind up having you guys working against us. Plus...." She continued staring down at Sam's quilt. "Do you remember Carmela?"

"You mean the girl in Lawrence. The one with the...?" Sam grabbed a handful of hair at the top of her head and gave it a sharp upward tug.

Ellie smiled weakly. "That's the one. When she was getting ready to leave home and go to Washington, she knew she could be killed by the people hired by the mill owners to stop the strike. *And* she knew she was doing it so she could go back to work in a mill where she also could die. I mean, she'd already gone through the whole"—she mimicked Sam's hair-tugging gesture—"thing, and that was bad enough. When I was researching her, I wondered if I would be strong enough or brave enough to make the same kinds of decisions she made. Then all this shack stuff happened, and it's Aaron who's had to decide, and I...." She turned to look out the window and sniffed back tears.

"And you...?" Sam prompted, but Ellie shook her head.

"It hurts too much to think about it. I couldn't bear to say anything. I was afraid that if I...." Her voice failed her, and now tears ran freely down her cheeks.

Sam guided Ellie's head to her shoulder, wrapped her arms around her, and softly stroked her back as her body shook with sobs. "Oh, El, I am so, *so* sorry," she said, and rocked her gently.

After a few minutes, Ellie became still. Not really wanting to, she pulled herself out of the comfort of Sam's embrace. "*This!*" she said. "*This* is what I was afraid of. I can't fall apart now—he needs me. And we *have* to do this, Sam. We *have* to."

"And what do *you* need, Ellie?"

She considered this for a long, silent moment. "Right now... just to get through this," she whispered. "Then we'll see."

She stood and started toward her bed. Suddenly overcome by the love implicit in Sam's expression of concern, she turned back, leaned down, and kissed her on the cheek. "Thanks, Sis. I love you, too."

36

Defying her every expectation, Ellie did not lay awake the entire night. Exhausted by the events of the past two days, she dropped into sleep more quickly than she had dared hope. Even the sounds of her parents' early-morning departure didn't disturb her, and when she woke, she discovered she had slept soundly for almost nine hours.

Padding from the bathroom down the hall to the kitchen, she discovered Sam and, to her mild surprise, Ryan seated at the dinette table, hunched over bowls of granola. It was unusual for him to be at their house so early, and she wondered how much less frazzled she'd have to be before she could summon the energy needed to feel self-conscious standing before him wearing nothing but her nightshirt and ankle socks.

Her minimal outfit did not go unnoticed by Ryan. When she entered the room, the first thing he did was jab his spoon squarely toward her chest. "Cute!"

Puzzled, she gripped the front of her shirt with both hands, pulled it away from her body, and craned her neck to peer down at it. The design on this one was simply a side view of a Holstein, each of whose black markings was a crude approximation of the Greek letter π.

Ryan grinned at her. "'Cow pie'—I like it!"

"Thanks," she said, smiling back. She was surprised to discover that being declared cute mere minutes after tumbling out of bed, even by Ryan, was a decidedly pleasant way to start the day. At the counter, she poured cereal into the bowl Sam had put out for her, added a minimal amount of milk, and took a spot at the table.

As soon as Ellie sat, Sam sprang from her seat and crossed to the sink, where she tipped the remainder of the morning's coffee into a mug. She returned to her chair and set the steaming brew in front of Ellie. "Can't forget the most important food group!"

Ellie froze, her spoon halfway between bowl and mouth. Her gaze darted back and forth between the two pairs of eyes regarding her with unusual intensity. "What?" she said, realizing it sounded like an echo from the night before.

Ryan, speech impeded by the need to swallow, merely raised his hands in a *don't look at me* gesture. Sam shook her head emphatically.

"Not a thing," she said.

"Sam texted me last night, said we should be ready to hook up sometime this morning," Ryan said, finally explaining his presence at the breakfast table.

Ellie considered this as she chewed, nodding slowly. "Yeah. About that… Well, first, thanks for the coffee." She lifted her mug in a toast to Sam, taking extra care not to spill any.

"No problem."

Ellie glanced up at the clock on the microwave oven. "How does eleven o'clock sound? Here at eleven unless that doesn't work for him. That good for you?"

They both nodded. Sam stood, placed their dishes in the washer, then returned to the table. "Mr. *Cow Pie* and I are going to take a walk while you, you know, maybe put some clothes on? Text me if anything changes."

Ellie gave her a thumbs-up. Ryan slid out from behind the table, and as they made their way toward the front door, Ellie heard Sam's voice, something she couldn't quite make out, followed by Ryan saying, "What?! It *was* cute!" Then the door closed with a firm thud.

She recalled a similar moment from a day that seemed to have happened roughly forever ago. This time, instead of feeling irritated, she simply smiled to herself. She glanced again at the front of her shirt. "Cow pie!"

Back in her room, she found several messages from Aaron waiting for her on her phone. Together they formed a rough sketch of how they would go about trying to breach the shack a second time, and what they would need to do if they actually made it to Brooklyn. He had included a pair of links to locations in Google Maps, so she put aside her phone in favor of reading his texts on her MacBook. One address was where Aaron's grandfather had lived. The other turned out to be Aaron's best guess about where they would find the tailor shop. The basics of the plan were simple enough —find the apartment, find the newsstand, and keep his grandparents from meeting. Nevertheless, she read through everything a second time before crossing the hall to shower.

Aaron arrived at a quarter to eleven, and Ellie walked with him to the middle of the back yard to confer privately for a few minutes. While she thought he looked better than he had on Monday, he still seemed tired, and there was a distant, hollow quality to his expression that worried her.

"Are you okay? Did you get any sleep?"

"I... yeah, some. My mind gets going, latches onto something, and sometimes it's hard to get it to let go, you know?"

She nodded, feeling guilty for having slept so soundly. "Is this still our one and only plan?"

He seemed to give the question serious consideration, and for a moment she dared hope that his ever-active mind had come up with a new idea. But then he frowned and gave her a single firm nod.

"Yes. I still believe this is the best shot we have."

"Well... crap." She sighed and looked down at the dry grass. "I think Sam was mad at me last night for not telling her sooner. No, not *mad* exactly, but.... I don't know, upset with me somehow." She still couldn't find words to describe the complicated mix of emotions she believed she and her sister had each recently experienced. She looked up to see Aaron shaking his head. "What?"

"No, I'm sure she wasn't mad. You two have always shared everything. She knows how hard this is for you and understands that sharing will make it easier for you to deal with it. She wants to help, that's all, but she can't if you aren't letting her in."

"How and when did you become so wise in the ways of women?"

"*People*," he corrected. "I watch, I listen...." He shrugged. "I don't always 'get' them, but sometimes I do."

She heard loneliness in his voice and thought about how much time he must have spent watching and listening to her. And to Sam, too, it seemed.

She reached out and placed a hand on his cheek. "I wish you had said something a long time ago." Again she noted signs of stress. "Are you sure you're okay?"

He shrugged again and looked away toward the house, refusing to meet her eyes. Instead of answering, he gestured toward the door. "Can we just, uh...?"

"Sure," she said quickly. "Let's go in."

They joined Sam and Ryan, who were waiting quietly, albeit apprehensively, at the table. Ellie could see Ryan's left knee rapidly bobbing with nervous energy. Her MacBook rested in the middle of the table, topped by a few small sheets of heavy paper Aaron had brought. Ellie took a seat beside Sam, but Aaron remained on his feet. She decided to launch straight into it.

"Okay. So, the first thing we need to accomplish is getting back inside the shack. They might have put cameras up by now, or some kind of trip-wires, or they might actually have guards out there watching it. We haven't dared go out to check on it since May because, well, because *duh!* there might be sensors or people guarding it. And we *know* they've been working on it. So this time, we're not all going to approach it at once, just in case." She looked at Aaron, and he took over the explanation.

"We'll go after hours when the fewest number of people are likely to be at Dad's lab. Once we reach the general area of the shack, you and Sam will move up first while Ellie and I hang back. If you can get the door open without anyone bursting out of the bushes and nabbing you, we'll run in and join you. If not, we'll wait a bit and try it again after they haul you away. I'm assuming that if they catch somebody trying to break in, they'll think, 'case closed,' and won't expect someone else to be coming along right behind."

"And if we do get caught? What will happen to us?" Sam wanted to know.

"If Ellie and I are successful, then it's hard to say. You'd have become part of the altered timeline at that point. You'll probably be in there," he gestured toward the living room, "watching a movie with no idea that any of what we've done over the past month ever happened. If we're not.... I still don't know what to tell you. If it makes you feel any better, I don't believe it will be an issue. We're smart. If we're also careful, all four of us oughta make it into the shack. Plus, it's been a month and a half since the last time we were out there. If anybody is guarding it, odds are they're starting to get sloppy by now."

"Gotta love an optimist," Ryan said. "But you're right. My dad calls it 'surveillance fatigue.'"

"And once we're back in Brooklyn—what then?" Sam said.

"Okay. I know my grandfather's old address, I know approximately where the tailor shop was, and I know he used to get in shortly before it opened at eight. Once we find out where the shack will let us land, we'll select an arrival time early enough that we can be sure that two of us—that will be Ellie and me—can get to his apartment before he leaves in the morning. We'll follow him to the newsstand, staying as close to him as we can. You two will already be there on the lookout for Judith. What we actually do, though? We'll have to make that up on the spot. Anything we can come up with to keep them from meeting, that's what we'll go with. Shouldn't be too hard."

He took the papers from the laptop, turned them over, and spread them out on the table, revealing them to be old photographs of a man and a woman. Ellie, Sam, and Ryan leaned forward to get a better look.

"These are the earliest pictures I could find of my grandparents." He tapped a black-and-white photo of a man who looked to be in his mid-forties, dressed in a suit jacket and tie. His jaw was clean-shaven, but he sported a dark, bushy mustache. "Granddad will be easy since we know what door he'll be coming out of."

He pointed to the other portrait. This one was of a woman of roughly the same age, meaning it must have been eight to ten years more recent. Also, it was in color. A third photo, also in color, showed the two of them together. They looked older, and Ellie assumed it had been taken on an anniversary.

Aaron tapped the top edge of the picture of just the woman. "This is Judith, my grandmother, in 1950, or so." He flipped it over to see the back, then laid it on the table again. "Looks like they didn't believe in putting dates on any of these. She's going to be a lot harder to pick out. Aside from being about five-four, blonde, very pretty, and what you see here, I don't have anything else on her. I don't even know for sure which direction she'll be coming from. Plus, it will be early morning in winter, so she'll no doubt be wearing a heavy coat. And probably a hat."

"Odds are she'd be wearing a hat anyway," Sam noted. "Most ladies did back then. Guys, too, for that matter."

"Since you brought that up," Aaron said, "we have a little assignment for you. One right up your alley. Or, ah, 'runway,' might be better. We were hoping you could put together four outfits from today's stuff that wouldn't raise any eyebrows in New York in December, 1941. Emphasis on December —it'll be cold."

Caught off guard by this suggestion, Ellie cast him a quizzical look, but he kept his attention fixed on Sam. They had not discussed this idea, but she thought maybe it did make sense. Dealing with the costumes in Lawrence had been a bit of a pain, and if it meant avoiding any more close encounters with garter belts, corsets, girdles, or whatever else the forties might have in store for them, she was all for it. She decided to go along with the idea.

"Yeah. We don't want to waste time sorting through the clothes in the shack. Plus, they weren't made for people our age." That was true enough.

Sam considered this a moment. "So, let's see… That means calf-length, belted dresses for us, shoes that will allow for running, if necessary, heavy coats…. You boys could get away with off-the-rack Levi's and button-up shirts, but I'll see what else we can come up with." She gave them a nod. "Sure, I can do that."

"No jeans for us?" Ellie said, hoping it could be that easy.

"In Santa Fe—you know, anywhere out here—that might be fine. In Brooklyn, though, eyebrows would raise. Not exactly typical even for the guys. Sorry."

"Make sure you cut off every tag," Aaron said. "Just in case." Sam nodded.

"Ooh, yeah—good catch!" Ellie said.

"I bet that since the U.S. has just declared war," Ryan said, "people will have too many other things on their minds to worry about how we're dressed." He shook his head in wonder. "Man, this is bizarre! My grandfather fought in the Pacific. To be in New York the day that all started? It's, well… *bizarre!*"

Ellie pulled her MacBook toward her and flipped it open. Firefox still showed a Google Maps view of Brooklyn, with the two addresses marked with pins. Sam and Ryan stood to peer at the screen from over her shoulder. To give them a better view, she tilted the screen back and pushed the computer farther away from her.

"All right, back to the plan. Here's where we're going to be. You don't need to memorize everything, but you should have a general sense of the area in case we get separated." She sketched out a small circle on the touchpad, and on the screen, the black arrow began to orbit a large area of green.

"This is Prospect Park," she explained. "I'm guessing we'll be starting from somewhere in here." She dragged the arrow northeast on the map. "This is Crown Heights. Daniel lives on Park Place, somewhere in this area, assuming the street numbers were the same back then." She ran the cursor back and forth between Nostrand and New York Avenues. "This is the eight-hundred block, right Aaron?" He nodded.

Ellie shifted in her seat, accidentally brushing her fingers down along the trackpad as she moved. This caused the view of the map to zoom out and left Brooklyn occupying a tiny portion of her screen. The rest was filled with a seemingly infinite tangle of streets, avenues, and alleys, a lab rat's nightmare vision of a maze. Seeing the map this way made her aware of how large the city truly was, and she suddenly felt much less sure of the possibility of their success. The others were also staring at the screen, and she guessed they were experiencing similar doubts. She hastily zoomed back in on the area immediately surrounding Prospect Park.

"Okay, yes, it is a big freakin' city, but we only have to worry about one short stretch of this one street and one newsstand. We can totally do this! I know this doesn't actually mean anything, but after being in Lawrence and running into Carmela in a crowd of fifteen thousand people, I feel like we're somehow destined to run into these two, as well." She saw Aaron staring at her as if she had just declared that the Earth was flat or that evil spirits caused diseases. "Oh, I'm not willing to leave this up to fate," she hastened to add. "You know better than that. I'm saying I'm feeling hopeful—that's all."

"'Gotta love an optimist,'" Aaron echoed, then he wrapped up the plan. "Once we've managed to keep them apart and they've both gone their separate ways, we'll head back to the shack and, uh, come back here."

They all stared at the screen and let the obvious question—*What happens then?*—remain unasked.

After a few silent seconds, Sam spoke. "When?"

"Tomorrow evening," Ellie said. "If anything goes wrong, that still gives us Friday or Saturday as a back-up. We want to be out at the shack somewhere between seven and eight o'clock, which means leaving here between five and six. We figure that with most of the senior staff gone, this is our best opportunity. Even if they did install any new security measures around or on the device itself, this will be the time when the fewest number of people will be paying any attention."

Sam placed her hand on her stomach. "I am so not looking forward to that horrible feeling again. *Oof!* I get queasy just thinking about it."

"My guess is that's some kind of, ah, 'temporal motion sickness,'" Aaron said, as if naming the problem would make it easier to deal with.

"You mean, like when you try to read in the car?" Ryan said.

"Yeah, when your eyes and your inner ears are getting mixed signals and you wind up feeling kinda barfy. In this case, it could be a reaction to being ripped out of our natural time. Maybe it won't be as bad this time since we're not going back as far."

"I still think that machine does something to us during the trip," Ellie said.

He shrugged. "No way we're ever going to know for sure."

"Well, whatever it is, I'm not going to be downing a big dinner before we go," Sam said.

"So, what do Aaron and I need to do about clothes?" Ryan said. "You said blue jeans would be okay?"

Sam nodded. "Yeah, I want to get started on this right away. So for you guys, let's go with basic jeans, cotton tee-shirts, and long-sleeved, button-up shirts. For your feet? Dark, cotton socks and leather shoes—not sneakers! Not dressy shoes, either, but something like work boots would be best. Ooh! Ryan! Your Red Wings would be perfect."

"I have an old pair of those, too. They might fit you, A-Ron."

"I'll give 'em a try," he said.

"How does that sound to you guys?" Sam said. "Okay so far?"

Aaron and Ryan both nodded.

"Good. I figure jackets will be harder. They can't be Gore-Tex or any other modern material. Wool would be best...." She looked at Ryan. "Does your dad still have that vintage Yankees jacket? The one with the funky leather sleeves?"

"Probably. Don't know why he wouldn't."

"I could list a bunch of reasons, but that might do… as a last resort. Do you have anything you think might work, Aaron?"

"I'll look, but I'm not sure. Would something *all* leather be okay? Dad had an old leather coat he used to wear. It was pretty plain. I have a wool sport coat, but I'm sure it's too small now."

She waggled her head. "Maybe. Here's the thing—if it *is* old, it shouldn't *look* old. Remember, it would be brand-new back then."

Ellie had to admire the ease with which Sam was handling outfitting an expedition into another century. She knew if she had to do it, it would take her hours on the internet, and they'd still all end up looking like a troop of circus clowns.

"Let's do this," Sam said. "You two go home and gather up all the things that might be possibilities. Ellie and I will go downtown to the consignment shop and see if they have anything that will work for us. We'll also look for jackets for you two, plus anything else we may want to have along. Like hats, for instance."

"See if you can find me one with earflaps," Ryan said. "They're so 'cool.'"

"I can't believe you're still jealous about that hat," Aaron said.

Sam laughed. "Can you be back here in two hours?" she said.

Aaron nodded.

"No problem," Ryan said.

"Ellie?"

"Let's say we meet back here at two-thirty," she said, adding an extra twenty minutes of padding into the schedule.

"Bring anything you think might work, and we'll sort it out then," Sam said.

"A-Ron, you walked?" Aaron said.

"No, I've got my bike."

"Perfect. Let's go to my place first, and we'll hit your house on the way back. Sound good?"

Ellie saw a dark expression flicker across Aaron's face as though this suggestion irritated him, but then he gave Ryan a friendly smile.

"Sure. Sounds great."

Ellie and Sam followed the boys out the front door. They stood shoulder to shoulder on the front stoop, waiting in silence as they retrieved their bikes from alongside the garage, walked them to the street, and started pedaling away.

"Don't forget the boots for Aaron," Sam called after them.

Ryan acknowledged her with a wave over his head.

37

Ellie and Sam watched until the boys turned left at the end of the cul-de-sac and disappeared around the corner.

"Take the bikes?" Ellie said.

"Probably a good idea. I don't know how much time we'll need—better safe than sorry."

"I meant as opposed to the car."

"Ah. No, the bikes are good. If we do run late, I can text Ryan."

Ellie walked through the house to the door that led to the garage. She opened it, reached in, and pressed the button that opened the roll-up door. She called to Sam over the loud rumble.

"I need to get some shoes, and I'll be right back," she said.

"And get two packs, too," Sam shouted back. "The bigger ones. We'll need them for the clothes."

Sam had their bikes waiting outside when Ellie reemerged through the front door.

"Thanks," she said. She handed off one of the empty backpacks before shouldering her own. She gave each tire a quick squeeze to check the pressure, then they were on their way.

To avoid being drenched with sweat when they arrived at the shop to try on clothes, they maintained a moderate pace. Once they reached Central

Avenue, they turned off the busy street as soon as they could. They took a left onto Rose and entered a residential area. It was a slightly longer route, but now they could safely pedal side by side and talk. Riding on the outside, Ellie repeatedly checked her mirror for cars coming up on them from behind.

"How's Aaron doing?" Sam said.

"Okay, I guess."

"You *guess?*"

"I've tried to ask him a couple of times, but he changes the subject."

"Well, if that's the case, then my guess is that your guess is wrong."

Ellie was still mulling over Sam's comment when they arrived at the small shopping center that housed the consignment shop. They locked their bikes to a rack near the corner and started walking toward the middle of the block.

"I've been trying to work something out," Sam said. "I still can't wrap my head around all this 'timeline' stuff. Here's the thing—if everything goes according to plan tomorrow, we'll never have needed to buy these clothes today, right?"

"Right. Won't have happened."

"But for us, it will still have happened. I'll remember doing this."

Ellie nodded.

"So, when we get done, will I have the money back or not? It's not that I mind spending the money," she added quickly. "I'm just trying to figure this all out, that's all. Seriously… it hurts my brain."

"Then do what I do—don't think about it!"

Sam studied Ellie closely, but she kept looking straight ahead, ignoring the stare.

"*Ha!* You don't really know, do you?"

They reached the entrance to the shop, and Ellie was spared having to answer. What Sam had said was true. Ellie didn't know, not for sure. She had a few guesses, though, and felt it was best if she kept those guesses to herself.

Sam pulled the door open, and a bell attached to the door jingled cheerily as they entered. A young woman Sam remembered as having graduated a few years earlier greeted them from behind a glass display case. Instead of a cash register, the sales area was equipped with an iPad fitted with a credit card reader. The iPad was supported by an articulated bracket anchored to the case.

"Hello."

They returned the greeting with a pair of waves and walked to the counter. Ellie's eyes drifted over the offering of costume jewelry and small accessories while Sam explained what they needed.

"Hi," she said in a cheery tone. "You're… *Katherine?*"

"Close. It's Kaitlyn." She squinted at Sam. "Do I know you?"

"Samantha Henderson. Sam. I was a few years behind you in school. This is my sister, Ellie. I remember you went by 'Kate' at the time. I always assumed it was short for Katherine."

"Nope. Kaitlyn."

"Got it! So, Kaitlyn, we're trying to do a forties-themed party with our boyfriends, and I'm hoping you might have something we could use. At least something we could alter to get close enough." Sam went on, listing their needs in greater detail. "We need two plain dresses, vintage A-line, if you know what I mean, shoes… I don't guess you'd have any period stockings....

To Ellie, who had looked up from the case when she heard Sam refer to Aaron as her "boyfriend," Kaitlyn's expression did not hold much promise. Her mouth drew to one side in a little pucker, and her eyes shifted up and left as she conducted an inventory from memory.

"You know, we don't really *do* vintage," Kaitlyn said with evident regret. "We try to take in only what...." Her words trailed off as a thought took shape in her mind, a process that seemed to occur in slow motion. "Now, wait just one *second!*"

As instructed, they waited patiently.

Kaitlyn leaned across the counter and spoke in a soft, conspiratorial whisper, asking what she plainly thought was a rhetorical question. "You all know about Mrs. Pavlova, right?"

"Mm-mm," Sam said, shaking her head.

"Doesn't ring a bell," Ellie said. She was barely able to stifle a yelp after Sam's heel came down sharply on the bridge of her left foot.

"*Really?!*" Kaitlyn sounded quite beyond surprised by their ignorance. "I thought everybody knew her. She's lived in Los Alamos since, like, forever. Well, up until last week."

"What happened last week?" Ellie said.

"She died, of course," Kaitlyn said, then she made a noise that sounded oddly like a chuckle.

Ellie glanced at Sam with an expression meant to suggest she had serious doubts about the vertical range of Kaitlyn's mental elevator.

"And this helps us how, exactly?" Sam said, ignoring her sister's look.

"So, Mrs. Pavlova was going on a hundred, right?"

"Until last week," Ellie agreed brightly, then quickly sidestepped to avoid another jab from Sam's foot.

"Right! So her family brought all her clothes to us. She must have kept everything she ever wore, 'cause there was *tons* of boxes. I mean *tons*! Anyway, Shirley—that's Shirley Deavers... she's the owner?—and me took everything out and hung it up on racks in the back so we could go through it all. I noticed some of it looked old. Like, old-fashioned?"

Ellie did the math. If Mrs. Pavlova had been in her late nineties last week, she would have been in her late teens in 1941. If she truly had kept everything, they had reason to hope.

"Kaitlyn," Sam said, "I don't know how to put this delicately, but was Mrs. Pavlova—would you say she was a large woman?"

"Oh, yeah!" Kaitlyn said with that same peculiar chuckle. "Not *super* big, but she must have been around one-eighty, maybe one-ninety."

Ellie's heart sank. *So close!*

"But that's now," Kaitlyn added. "Lookin' at some of her old stuff? She must've been skinny as a stick back when she was younger."

Ellie and Sam exchanged excited looks. Sam reached down and pulled her wallet from her pack. She opened it and made a show of examining the stack of bills it contained. Ellie was sure they were mostly ones and fives but managed to maintain what she hoped was a passable poker face.

"So, um, Kate... is there any way we could take a look at Mrs. Pavlova's clothes?"

Kaitlyn stared at Sam's thumb flipping across the top edges of the money. "I don't see any reason why not."

Kaitlyn led them through a door at the rear of the shop into a space nearly equal in square footage to the sales floor itself. The opposite wall was outfitted with a metal roll-up door intended to accommodate loading or unloading large trucks, and to its left there was a regular, people-sized door. Along the right-hand wall were two sewing machines, an ironing board, and a large steamer, its thick, gray hose hanging limply over a shiny metal hook. Pushed up against the left wall and extending two-thirds of the way across the wide floor sat rack upon rack of clothing on hangers.

"Wow! You weren't kidding when you said tons," Sam said.

"Took us *hours* to unpack in all. It was exhausting!" She sounded worn out all over again just talking about it.

"The older clothes you mentioned—are they sorta together or all mixed up with the other stuff?

"The boxes were packed with stuff that went together. Like, had the same style? We took it out and put it straight on the racks, so it should all be together."

"Kate, you are wonderful!"

Kaitlyn beamed.

"Ellie, you know what we're looking for?"

"Dresses with belts, sorta poofy up top."

"Not *poofy*, exactly. Lapels or ruffles, maybe, but tailored."

"Gotcha."

Sam turned back to Kaitlyn. "Is there a best place to start?"

Kaitlyn pointed at the least accessible racks of clothing. "I think all the old stuff's up against the wall."

Working from opposite ends of the long racks, Ellie and Sam began rolling them one by one across the receiving room floor. After less than three minutes, only the final two remained in place. They pulled the next-to-last rack out partway to create two narrow aisles, but before they could start inspecting the clothes, they heard the jingle of the bell on the front door. Kaitlyn looked at them uncertainly.

"Don't worry about us, Katie," Sam said and placed a hand lightly on the woman's arm. "We'll be fine."

Kaitlyn hesitated. "You sure?"

Sam gave her a reassuring smile. "Absolutely! Go take care of your customer."

Kaitlyn smiled back, then returned to the sales floor.

"I thought she'd *never* leave," Ellie quipped.

Sam was already inspecting the items on the racks. She flipped past a couple of the dresses, evaluating them at a glance until she found some from the correct period. "This stuff is *good*. Looks like these three will have what we need." She waved her hand at the trio of racks they had separated from the others.

Ellie picked the end of the rack opposite Sam, and they began working their way toward the middle. The racks made a metallic ringing sound as they slid the hangers along the metal crossbars one by one, stopping every now and then to give a potential dress further consideration.

Zing, zing, zing, zing—pause—*zing, zing, zing*….

When either of them came across a dress they thought might work, they hung it facing outward from the top of another item's hanger.

"There aren't any coats," Ellie said when they were only a dozen or so dresses apart.

Zing, zing, zing….

"Coats are over there." Sam indicated the other racks with a slight tilt of her head. Sure enough, the last of the three racks held almost nothing but coats. "I'm worried about *shoes*."

"There are some boxes by the door we came through," Ellie said. "Could be shoes are in there."

Ellie let Sam inspect the final few dresses, then they both stepped back to appraise the five possibilities. Each was unique, but even Ellie could tell they were all of a style. She pointed at them. "See the shoulders? They're poofy."

"*Padded*. Anyway, I thought you meant the whole bodice. Here—come stand over here." Sam motioned Ellie toward her as she slid one of the heavier dresses off its hanger and held it by its shoulder seams. "Turn around." Ellie turned and felt Sam's fingers on her shoulders as she held the dress against her back. "Length is good, shoulders look good… it should be warm enough… Turn back around." Ellie spun on her toe, and Sam held the dress up for her to see. "What do you think?"

Ellie didn't have an opinion. "Like, is it okay? I think it's fine if you do."

"I do." Sam handed Ellie the dress, then passed her the empty hanger.

"Why don't you hang that on the back of the door so we don't lose track of it. Hold on—put this one with it. And this one, just in case." She passed her two more dresses.

"Okay… now for the coats!"

By the time Ellie returned from the door, Sam was already holding a coat out to her.

"Check that one out." She selected a second coat for herself and began shrugging into it.

"This fits almost perfectly," Ellie said.

"Mine, too. That old bell ringer must have been just our size."

Ellie smiled at her. "When we were shifting the racks around, did you see anything for the guys?"

"No, it looked like it was all her stuff."

"I guess we can check out front."

As if on cue, the bell over the front door rang again. Sam extended her hand to Ellie.

"Here—give me your coat." Ellie slipped it off her shoulders and handed it over as Kaitlyn reappeared through the door.

"Kate! Perfect timing," Sam said. She flashed her a warm smile and held the two coats up for her to see. "Ellie and I have found some things to try on. But first, we have a question."

"Yes?"

"Did Mrs. Pavlova's family bring only the things on these racks, or were there any other items? Shoes, for instance, or hats, gloves, that sort of thing?"

Kaitlyn pointed toward the boxes Ellie had noticed. There were four of them, large, stacked in pairs on either side of the door.

"In there," she said. "She had lots of shoes, but not many hats."

"Great! Do you mind if Ellie looks through those boxes while you and I talk about something else?"

Kaitlyn shrugged. "Sure."

"Thanks," Sam said, still smiling with all the radiance of a supernova. She looked at Ellie and nodded toward the boxes. Ellie walked over and pulled down the upper box to the right of the door. "Oxfords—they'll be leather, sturdy-looking, with about a one-and-a-half-inch heel. Or Mary Janes. Know what I mean?"

Ellie nodded. "Yep. Got it."

Sam turned her attention back to Kaitlyn. "When you unpacked all this, did you and Shirley make any kind of inventory? Or did you hang it up, and that was it?"

"We just unpacked it and hung it. This all came in yesterday afternoon. By the time we got it on the racks and broke down all the boxes, it was long after closing time. Then Shirley left right away 'cause she had to go home and get ready to leave town for a few days, so we didn't make any inventory."

"Mm-hmm... mm-hmm...." Sam nodded thoughtfully as Kaitlyn spoke. "And with Shirley gone, you're the boss?"

Kaitlyn answered slowly while she considered this. "I guess that's right." Her sudden smile made it clear she liked that idea.

"Well, Katie, here's what I was thinking...."

As Ellie examined the contents of the four boxes, she kept part of her attention on the deal Sam was making with their new bestest friend "Katie." The gist was that since Shirley didn't know what was back here, she couldn't miss any of it, could she? This was especially true for the older clothes, which Shirley would most likely pass on to someone else. Or perhaps even toss. Sam then reminded Katie that they only needed the clothes for a day or two. Aside from the party, they had no use for them.

As Ellie progressed from one box to the next, she set aside any items she thought Sam would want to see. Awaiting inspection so far were four pairs of shoes, none of which she thought was remotely appealing, and three hats. The hats were better. Two were berets, and the third was a different kind that flipped up around the back and had a short brim.

While Sam and Kaitlyn continued to negotiate, Ellie tried on the shoes. She found two pairs that fit comfortably enough that she figured she could wear them for a few hours without problems. And if they fit her, they'd work for Sam, too. She placed the shoes with the other items she had piled together, then quickly sifted through the contents of the final box.

From what she overheard, she gathered that Kaitlyn had agreed to 'rent' them the outfits for thirty-five dollars—to be paid to her directly—with the understanding that everything would be returned to the shop by noon Monday at the latest, long before Shirley was due back. Although this was a fraction of what the clothing would sell for, it was many times the commission Kaitlyn would earn on a sale. As a bonus, if Shirley decided to keep the clothes, Kaitlyn still stood to earn the commission in the future.

"There's one more thing," Sam said. She stepped across the room and picked out what Ellie thought was a rather ugly, multi-colored coat from among the ones she had looked through minutes earlier. She returned to where Kaitlyn stood and held it out in front of her.

"This is a Bonnie Cashin, probably from the early sixties. The leather trim is in good shape, all the clasps work.... You might want to tell Shirley that she could get a thousand for it on eBay. Maybe more." As she spoke, she looked meaningfully into Kaitlyn's eyes. "You understand what I'm saying, Kate?"

Kaitlyn might have been a bit of a ditz, but she was far from dumb. She took the coat from Sam's hands, held it high by its shoulders, and began nodding slowly, a loving expression on her face. She looked up from the coat and cast a loving gaze over rack upon rack of similar vintage clothing.

"Oh, I gotcha, all right!"

Ellie knew right then they could have anything else in the store they wanted for that same thirty-five dollars.

As Ellie waited outside the shop's single small dressing room, she thought about Sam's earlier question regarding the money. That led to a question of her own concerning the clothes they were renting. Sam was right—with Aaron absent from the timeline, there would be no reason for them to have come into the consignment shop. Yet they would still be wearing these clothes when they returned, wouldn't they? Or would they suddenly be standing in the middle of the forest in only their underwear? She wondered how far Aaron's influence extended beyond his direct actions. How far, in other words, did his personal ripples spread?

After they exchanged places and Ellie closed the curtain, Sam lingered outside and spoke through it, passing on the gist of Ryan's most recent messages. He was reasonably confident the boys were both set, although if a jacket suitable for him caught her eye, they should pick it up. Aaron was pretty sure he had a heavy wool sweater at home that looked like some photos they had seen online, but he would also take a coat if she found one.

Ellie kicked off her shoes, slipped out of her shorts, and pulled her tee over her head. She removed the dress from its hanger and, with a little effort, shimmied it down into place. Unlike her Lawrence dress, this one closed in the front, and it took her mere seconds to get it buttoned. She twisted back and forth in front of the mirror to check the look, smoothing any wrinkles with her palms. She marveled at how well it fit. It was snug going on, but once in place, it acted like a second skin, conforming comfortably to her body no matter how she moved. She wasn't sure what to make of the padded shoulders, but she found the overall cut flattering. She placed the beret on her head, adjusted the angle, and smiled approvingly at her reflection. Maybe Sam was on to something after all.

She knew Sam was going through the shop's meager offering of men's clothing, searching for anything Ryan and Aaron could use. She didn't know how that search was going, but it looked like she and Sam were set to go at the drop of a hat. *Or 'beret!'* she amended. She was pleased by how easily this part of the plan had gone. After this, it would just be a matter of killing time until tomorrow evening when….

For the second time in her life, she experienced the sensation of her blood running cold. She suddenly knew with absolute certainty something she should have realized far earlier. Instantly, her mood plummeted from relative optimism into deep despair. *"No, no, no,"* she moaned softly as her reflection blurred. Long minutes later, Ellie heard Sam's voice through the fabric.

"Hey, how's it going in there?" Sam waited, but Ellie didn't reply. "El?" Sam peeked through the curtain to see Ellie looking back at her, tears streaking her cheeks. "Too tight? Hate the color?" she asked in a feeble attempt to lighten the mood.

Ellie shook her head.

"Sorry. What is it, El?" Sam slipped through the curtain and, taking hold of Ellie's hands, guided her back to a low stool in the corner. Ellie sat and hung her head low, sobbing. Sam knelt in front of her, then reached out to brush the hair from her damp face with her fingertips.

Ellie couldn't answer. She clasped her hands so tightly in her lap that her knuckles were pale from the effort of trying literally—albeit unsuccessfully —to hold it together. She began to sob even harder.

Sam stood and, placing a hand tenderly on Ellie's head, pulled her toward her until her cheek rested against her stomach. She stroked her hair while giving her time to cry it out. Whatever *it* was. When she felt Ellie squirming within her embrace, she hunkered back down, placed her hands on her knees, and looked up into her eyes.

Ellie wiped her face with one of her sleeves and sniffed loudly. "I'm such an idiot. I should have known it this morning."

"Known *what?*"

"He's going to want to do it tonight. Sam... I'm not ready!"

"He who? Do what? You mean *Aaron?*"

Ellie nodded. She drew in a deep breath, held it a moment, then let it out in a ragged sigh. "I lied earlier. I mean, no, he hasn't come right out and said it, but I know it's been hard for him the last few days. He's tried not to show it, but...." She shook her head. "It just now came to me that once we have the clothes ready to go, there won't be anything left to do. He's not going to want to sit around for another day thinking about... you know." She sniffed again and swiped the other sleeve across her face.

"I've tried to imagine what it must be like for him," Sam said. "If I try to picture not seeing you or Mom and Dad ever again, not being with Ryan or not ever growing up—I go blank. It's like my mind won't let me go there." She sniffed back a few tears of her own. "The only thing worse would be if it was you instead of Aaron. I couldn't deal with that at all."

"I know. I've thought about that, too."

"What are you going to do?"

"I can't make him wait another day if he doesn't want to. That wouldn't be fair."

Sam nodded in reluctant agreement. "Okay. When we get back, I'll give Ryan a heads-up, let him know what you're thinking. He doesn't have anything going on tonight. With his dad or anything. We thought we'd be hanging out with you two."

As if the decision had already been made, Ellie rose to her feet. Sam stood with her, and they silently appraised the fit of Ellie's dress in the full-length mirror.

"Looks good," Sam said.

"Doesn't really matter. We'd have to take it anyway."

Sam looked at the reflection of Ellie's eyes, not understanding. Ellie held her arms out in front of her and gave Sam a crooked smile.

"I got snot all over the sleeves."

Once convinced that Ellie was okay, Sam left the dressing room to settle up with Kaitlyn. Ellie began packing her outfit. She folded her wool coat lengthwise and rolled it up, starting at the bottom. When she had compressed it as much as she could, she jammed it to the bottom of her pack. The shoes went in on top of the coat. She hung the beret on a wall hook for the moment—that would go in last.

While unbuttoning her dress, she puzzled again over Aaron's desire to have their costumes assembled before they went to Brooklyn. After all, if the shack's designers could put together enough appropriate clothing for as many as six people going to 1912, they could easily handle 1941. Maybe it was his way of keeping everyone busy and distracted until it was time to go. What else were they going to do—throw Ryan's party, pretend to be oblivious to what was about to happen? That would be morbid beyond words.

She stretched her arms over her back and clawed at the dress, trying to work it up and off her shoulders, but she found it hard to get a grip on the taut fabric. It seemed tighter coming off than going on. She figured there must be some kind of trick to working these things and made a mental note to ask Sam later. Meanwhile, her mind jumped to something Aaron had said the night the two of them had shared the plan with Sam and Ryan, an event that seemed ages ago. He'd suggested she stay behind and become a part of the altered timeline. Okay, so not literally *suggested*, she corrected herself. He had merely mentioned the idea as an option. She managed to get the collar over her head and began tugging at the fabric a little further down.

Another image flashed through her mind. It was the look Aaron had on his face when Ryan suggested they go to his house to look for clothes. For just an instant, he had seemed irked by the idea. What had passed through his head just then?

Busy and distracted! With a fresh burst of insight, she thought she had solved the puzzle of the clothes.

"*Crap, crap, crap!*" she exclaimed into the heavy folds of the dress. It seemed impossible that mere seconds ago she had been feeling sorry for Aaron. Now she wanted to wring his neck!

"*Ohh!* That lying, manipulative, deceitful... Sam!" she yelled, trying to get her attention, but her voice was muffled by the layers of cloth wrapped about her head. "*Sam!*" she called again, this time louder.

"Yes?" When Sam pulled the curtains wide, Ellie was bent over at the waist and clutching feebly at her back, still trying to wriggle out of the dress. As a result, Sam found herself addressing Ellie's rear end. "*Whoops!*" She quickly glanced behind her, but the store was still empty of other customers. She pulled the curtains tight around her neck so only her head was visible from Ellie's side. "*Now* what?"

Ellie, finally free from the tight grip of the dress, stood up straight and turned around to face her. "Get Ryan on the phone and find out if Aaron is still with him!"

Sam bristled at Ellie's peremptory tone. "Why don't you...?"

"Please—find out!" She yanked the cuffs over her wrists and pulled the sleeves off her arms.

Sam rolled her eyes, then slipped in through the curtain and relayed the latest message from Ryan, watching as Ellie pulled her tee on over her head. "He's not. He texted me a few minutes ago. He said they were done with the clothes, and Aaron was riding home alone to get the sweater, that they would both see us back at the house. Look, why don't you tell me what's...."

"Get him on the phone! There's something I need to know right away!"

The intense urgency in Ellie's voice tempered Sam's resentment over feeling ordered around. She heaved a frustrated sigh but stopped resisting. "All right, hang on." She pulled her phone from her pocket and unlocked it.

While Sam worked on reaching Ryan, Ellie stepped into her shorts, pulled them over her hips, and fastened them. She made a half-hearted attempt at folding the dress before giving up and roughly cramming it and the beret into her pack on top of the shoes. After assuring herself that she had everything, she pulled the flap over the top of the pack and fastened it.

While waiting for Ryan to answer, Sam finally managed to ask one of her many questions. "Why don't you just call Aaron?"

Ellie stood up, pack in hand, and looked at Sam. "Because he won't answer."

"What do you mean he won't—wait—I've got Ryan. Hey, Ryan. Ellie needs to ask you something." She passed Ellie her phone.

"Ryan—hey, hold on a sec." She lowered the phone and spoke to Sam. "Are you done with Kaitlyn?" Sam nodded. "All right. Grab your stuff and let's go. *Now!*" She slid one strap of her pack onto her left shoulder, pushed through the curtain, and trotted toward the front of the store as she replaced the phone to her ear. "Sorry. Listen, was Aaron wearing the clothes for tomorrow when he left your house?"

"Yeah. Well, some of it. The shoes, a jacket I had... he said he wanted Sam to see them to make sure they were okay. I'm about to leave for your place. What's up?"

"*No!* Your dad's car is there, right?"

"Yeah. He's..."

"Good! You need to get out to the Rim trailhead as fast as you can! We're on our way, too, but we're on bikes. If you make it there before us, find Aaron and stop him. Knock him down and sit on him if you have to. Got that?" Ellie rushed past the sales counter without so much as a sideways glance at Kaitlyn and pushed through the shop's door, Sam hard on her heels.

Ryan didn't hesitate long enough to ask even a single question. "Got it!"

"*Go!*" She pressed the hang-up button and jammed the phone into Sam's hands as soon as they were both outside. Ellie turned left and broke into a run toward their bikes. Sam trotted after her.

"*What is going on?!* Why did you tell him to sit on Aaron?"

Ellie didn't answer. Instead, she kneeled at her bike and dialed in the lock's four-digit combination. She jerked the cable through the spokes of both rear wheels, quickly coiled it, and stowed it in the small pack attached to the rear of the bike's saddle. Only then did she respond.

"Because I was wrong before. He doesn't want to leave tonight—he wants to leave *now!*"

Stunned, Sam's hands froze halfway to her bike. "That doesn't make any sense!"

But Ellie was already pedaling as fast as she could down Central Avenue.

38

Sam threw her leg over the bike and pedaled hard to catch up. At the next block, Ellie was forced to slow for a car pulling out of a parking lot, and Sam was able to close the gap. By the time she pulled alongside her sister, she was breathing heavily.

"That doesn't make any sense," she repeated. "How would he know if we're ready or not?"

"It doesn't matter. He's not planning on us going with him," she said, then she sped off again.

They were lucky at the next intersection and barely had to slow as they negotiated the tight right-left wiggle onto East Road. East was busy at almost any time of the day, but even with its usual traffic and no designated bike lane, Ellie knew they would make better time on it than on Rim Trail. Beyond the edge of town, the shoulder widened enough to allow Sam to ride beside Ellie, and she called out over the roar of a passing truck.

"Ellie, what's going on?"

"Remember the night we told you about Aaron's plan?"

"Um, yeah—that was *last* night."

"*Really?!* Wow! When you and Ryan went off alone to talk it over, he pointed out that I could stay behind. He thought it might be easier for me if

I forgot about him along with the rest of the world. Except for you and Ryan, that is. You two would still have to go and help him out."

"I assume you told him exactly where he could file that idea?"

"In so many words. And this morning? That thing about you getting us set up with clothes? That was all him. He said 'we,' but we'd never discussed it. I went along with him at the time because I figured he must have a good reason. I made up the parts about not wanting to take the time and the clothes in the shack being intended for older people, but I guess it sounded good."

"I bought it."

"I didn't. Not really. We can get there as early as we want—time's not an issue when you have a time machine. And who cares what the clothes look like? Well, *you* maybe, but in terms of the plan, I mean."

Sam looked up from the road and gave Ellie a wry smile. "I'm not *that* bad!"

"Later on, I figured it was just meant to be something for us to do instead of sitting around feeling all depressed. I was wondering about that in the shop, planning to ask him later, but then it hit me—getting the clothes ready now *doesn't* make sense. No—what he wanted was to split us all up so he could make a run for the shack."

"But why? I thought he needed all of us."

Ellie shook her head. "I'm not sure. Maybe he thinks he's doing us a favor. I'm hoping we get to ask him."

When they were still almost a mile from the trailhead, a bright blue, two-door Jeep Wrangler honked as it roared past them. They recognized the car by its "Semper Fi" spare tire cover and the heavy-duty mountain bike rack protruding from the trailer hitch. When Ellie saw its brake lights come on and the vehicle start drifting onto the shoulder, she waved her hand forward, urging Ryan to keep going rather than stop to get them. The next second he was back on the blacktop and speeding away.

They turned into the Rim Trail parking area three minutes later, soaked with sweat. Aaron's bike leaned unlocked against the trail map signpost. They piled their bikes on top of his and dropped their packs onto the dirt below the sign. The Jeep was parked sloppily across two spaces, and Ryan had bailed out of it so quickly that he'd left the driver's door hanging open.

Ellie headed straight for the trail, but Sam stopped to lean in through the open door and check for keys. Finding the ignition switch empty, she closed the door and started after Ellie at a trot.

When Ellie turned right onto the narrow strip of blacktop, the first thing she saw was Ryan walking back the trail toward her, alone. She assumed at once that he had missed Aaron, and her pulse skyrocketed. Then, when she reached a curve in the path and could see beyond him, she spotted a figure seated on a park bench twenty yards farther on. He was leaning forward, forearms on his thighs, staring at the ground. Sam caught up to her then, and they broke into a jog. When they reached Ryan, he spread his arms wide to bring them to a stop.

"He's okay," he said at once. "I mean, I think he's pretty messed up, but he's not *hurt*. I found him just sitting there, almost like he was waiting for me. How did you know?"

"Sam'll tell you. What did he say?"

"Not much. Except that he wants to talk to you." He shifted his eyes to Sam. "Alone."

"You guys wait here. We'll be back in a minute."

She covered the remaining distance at a fast walk. Aaron didn't look up as she approached. She walked past him and sat on his far side, throwing her left leg over the metal bench and straddling it so she could look directly at him. In the background, she could see Ryan talking to Sam, who was looking in their direction. She couldn't hear what he was saying.

"Hey." It was all she could think of to say. During the frantic bicycle ride, she had pictured herself running up to him, shaking him by his shirtfront, and shouting, *What were you doing, you selfish jackass?!* But the intense, physical exertion had burned away most of her anger, and what remained she had under control.

"Hate me?" He spoke so softly that she barely heard him.

"No. I want to pummel you senseless with one of my ugly, new oxfords, but no, I don't hate you."

He responded with one short exhalation through his nose, a breathy snort that might have been a laugh. "I wouldn't blame you, you know. That was cruel."

"Yes," she agreed. "It was."

She could feel a whisper of her earlier anger returning, and she took a slow, deep breath. "Why you wanted to do it—I think I get that. But that's not the way this is going to work. Look at them." She pointed at Sam and Ryan. When he failed to respond, she repeated herself more sharply. *"Look!"*

He twisted his neck to glance their way, then returned his attention to the pavement.

"Those are your friends over there. A big part of who we are today—Sam, Ryan... me—a lot of that comes from knowing *you*. Six years—that's more than a third of my life! You are *literally* part of us. You don't have the right to take that away."

He nodded his head slowly.

"*And* you tried to play us all for fools," she added. "Not the best way to treat your friends."

Ellie noticed Sam and Ryan were both looking in their direction. Now Sam was doing most of the talking, and she assumed she was filling him in on the events at the consignment shop.

Aaron nodded again. "I know." His voice was still a raspy whisper. "Believe me, I know."

"So why didn't you go? All you needed was to be two minutes ahead of us, and you would have made it."

He answered while still staring vacantly at the ground between his feet. "Because of exactly what you just said. If I succeeded, I would be changing your history. Changing you. I said the only thing that lets me get through this is knowing you'll be okay, and maybe you would be, but you wouldn't be *you* anymore. The Ellie I know would be *gone!* And not just you, but Sam and Ryan, too. Once I got that, I couldn't go through with it. Also, I wasn't one hundred percent sure I could handle everything by myself." He shrugged. "Like I said—it's too important to risk messing it up."

She glanced at the pack in the gravel between his feet. She assumed it contained the sweater and the rest of his outfit. "What was the plan?"

"Whatever it took, I guess. I figured I'd come up with something." He made another of the maybe-laugh sounds. "Not *much* of a plan, I know."

They sat quietly for a moment. She looked across the canyon, hating the fact that the shack was sitting out in that beautiful, rugged landscape. She imagined what it must have been like for him to consider carrying out the plan on his own. She had thought it selfish for him to make the decision he could most easily accept, but was it? Now she wasn't as sure. He had been assuming an enormous responsibility. And what about his decision *not* to go? She thought she understood that, now, too.

"There's something else, isn't there? Another reason you didn't go."

With what seemed like an enormous effort, Aaron pulled his gaze from the pavement to look at her for the first time since she had sat down. She saw his lips tremble as he tried to speak, and the misery in his expression tore at her heart.

"I don't want to be forgotten." This was all he could manage before the fragile composure he'd been able to maintain finally crumbled, and he began to cry.

She leaned forward and put her arms around him, drawing him tightly against her. "You won't be." She cradled his head against her shoulder and brushed her fingers through his hair. "I will *never* forget you—I promise."

She held him that way awhile, rocking slowly from side to side. She recalled Ryan's outburst when she and Aaron shared the details of their plan. *Last night,* she reminded herself—everything was suddenly moving so *fast!* She remembered how she had felt in the dressing room when she was positive Aaron would want to leave a day early. How ultimately that had seemed like not such a bad idea. Now Aaron's having a meltdown of his own. *Perhaps we do need to do this sooner rather than later.*

She kissed the top of his head, then spoke softly into his hair. "Hey. You ready to deal with the others?"

He pulled away from her and sat up. His eyes were swollen but dry, and the red flush on his nose and cheeks was fading. Lying pressed up against her shoulder had knocked his glasses askew. She reached out, pinched them carefully at the hinges, and straightened them.

"There. That's better. Can I call them over?"

He nodded, and Ellie waved a hand over her head. Sam noticed, said something to Ryan, and they started walking toward them.

"Is Ryan going to punch me?"

"He probably wants to, but nah, he won't. Now Sam, on the other hand...."

Aaron's head snapped up and looked first at the approaching Sam, then Ellie, his eyes wide with apprehension. She laughed.

"I'm kidding," she assured him. "Nobody's punching anybody."

Sam and Ryan stopped beside the bench but remained standing, looking down at them.

"What's this about punching people?" Ryan said.

"He was wondering exactly how mad you are."

"Look, man, nobody here is in any position to be mad at you. Not with what you're going through."

"Ellie said she wanted to beat me with her shoe."

Ellie was relieved to hear more of the usual Aaron coming through in his voice.

"Well, Ellie is a girl," Ryan said. "Girls say things like that."

Sam grinned at this and gave Ryan a nudge with her shoulder.

"We do," Ellie confirmed. "And *sometimes* we're just kidding."

Now even Aaron smiled. "Look… I'm sorry. You guys really are the best, you know."

39

"So... what now?" Sam said.

Ellie kept her eyes on Aaron as she answered. "We should go back to our place. We'll figure it out there."

"We can load the bikes onto the rack," Ryan said. "Unless you two need more of a workout."

"Oh, I'm good!" Sam said.

Ellie stood and offered a hand to Aaron. He took it, grabbed his pack with the other, and rose from the bench. Hand in hand, they followed Sam and Ryan back to the parking lot. They stood back and let Ryan load the bikes by himself. He had long ago mastered the intricacies of intermeshing multiple sets of pedals and handlebars into such a tight space, and any attempts to help only slowed him down. While he worked on the loading, Sam pulled the passenger seat forward and allowed Ellie and Aaron to climb into the back. Sam sat up front with her pack between her knees.

Ryan got in and closed his door. "We ready?"

"We're set," Ellie said.

He started the engine, pulled the vehicle through a tight arc toward the exit, then turned west onto East. Ellie kept a tight grip on Aaron's hand during the entire fifteen-minute ride home. Once everyone had wriggled back out of the vehicle's tight interior, Aaron, pack dangling from one hand, started toward the front door. Ellie waited with Sam and Ryan until they could talk without him overhearing.

"Did she tell you we might do this thing today?"

"Yeah. I can make that work. What was *that* all about?"

She turned and saw Aaron standing by the front door, staring at nothing in particular. She shook her head. "He thought he was doing the right thing. Didn't want to put us through what we're going to do. Didn't want us to feel guilty, I guess. About him. About his dad." She looked back at Ryan. "Do you have your stuff? Your clothes?"

"No. I changed again after Aaron left. Then when you called, I bolted straight for the door. Should I go get it?"

She nodded. "Yeah, you guys should go do that. I need a few minutes alone with him anyway. Did he think to mention a watch to you? This whole plan is all about timing. It would be good if we had something." She also didn't want to risk returning late to discover the shack had left for home without them, but she decided not to mention that.

"He did. We found my granddad's pocket watch in Dad's desk. It seems to be working okay. I'll bring it."

Sam gave Ellie's upper arm a comforting squeeze. "We'll be right back." Then she smiled. "And, hey… go easy on him."

Ellie assured them Aaron would still be breathing when they returned.

Aaron's eyes tracked her approach down the long walk from the driveway, but he avoided meeting her gaze. She stepped past him and pushed the door open.

"Come on," she said, not looking back.

She led him through the house, detouring to her room to place her pack at the foot of her bed before they made their way to the kitchen. She took four large glasses from the cabinet and began filling them at the fridge. She handed two to Aaron, then elbowed her way through the screen door, holding it open with her toe as he followed her outside. They each placed one of the glasses on the table and sat.

"We may not want to eat before we go, but we should make sure we drink up. It might help."

He regarded her for a long moment, then hung his head. "So, you figured out Plan B, too."

"Before the other thing, actually. It occurred to me how horrible it would feel to hang out for another whole day with nothing to do but dwell on what was coming. At first, I thought the business with the clothes was just to keep all our minds off *that*."

His head drooped even more. "I'm...."

She interrupted before he could complete the apology. "It's over. Forget about it."

He exhaled loudly. "Do they know, too?"

"They went to get Ryan's stuff. They'll be back in a few minutes, I suppose."

"I thought I could make it through another day. I want to so badly, but it's... it's like I'm being ripped apart inside."

"I get it. At least a little. I've been bursting into tears so often I feel like a freakin' lawn sprinkler! Sam says I should blame you. Says you screwed up my hormones."

"I'm...." Again he started to apologize, and again she cut him off.

"I was kidding, you dope!"

She rose from her chair and turned to stand in front of him. She took the glass from his grip, set it on the table, and offered him her hands. He took them and allowed himself to be pulled up from the chair. She wrapped her arms around his back, pulled him close, and leaned her head against his shoulder. He responded by placing his arms around her waist. She started to move in a gentle swaying motion, and he joined her in a slow dance without music.

Without relaxing her grip, she leaned back enough to look into his eyes. "What time we have is this—these few hours. It's not enough, I know, but it's all there is. Let's not waste it all regretting there isn't more."

He returned her gaze without any hesitation or self-consciousness. She could see him considering her words, making decisions.

He nodded. "You're right. And I keep asking myself how much time *would* be enough. I don't think there's a good answer to that question."

"Like I said—wise? *Priceless*."

They heard the rumble of a car engine from the front of the house, the crunch of gravel as it pulled in along the curb, then silence.

"Sound like our partners in crime have returned," she said. She leaned forward and briefly touched her lips to his, wishing she could think of something—*anything*—to say.

When Sam and Ryan joined them behind the house, Ellie indicated the glasses of water and repeated her idea that being well-hydrated might lessen the side effects of using the shack. When everyone had taken a seat, she voiced an obvious observation.

"You came back in the Jeep."

"It was just easier. Your bikes were still on the rack. Three bikes, two riders…. Dad said I could keep it for the evening. The bikes are outside along the garage now, by the way."

He took a long drink, then looked at Aaron and Ellie. "So, we're doing this?" he said.

Ellie nodded slowly. "Yes. Tonight."

Sam pointed across the back yard toward the southwest. Ellie followed her finger to the undulating crest of the Jemez Mountains.

"From Ryan's place, you can see it's already getting super dark on the horizon. I checked the forecast on our way back. Looks like some pretty rough weather is on its way."

"I saw that, too," Aaron said. "If we time it right, that could be to our advantage."

"How so?" Ellie said.

"Only idiots would be out on the mesa in the middle of a thunderstorm. Present company excluded, of course. And if they did bother to add any remote monitoring devices, they'd have to be wireless with lots of relays. Lightning's basically nature's own EMP, right? It'll interfere with their signals at the very least, and it might even knock them completely offline for a while."

"What about the shack, though?" Ryan said. "Any chance the lightning would affect it?"

Aaron shook his head. "I'm sure that in order for it to function where it does, in some dimension *between* spacetimes, it's so isolated from its environment that it wouldn't be bothered by something as comparatively minor as lightning."

"When is the storm supposed to be here?" Ellie said.

Sam looked up from her phone. "Looks like sometime between seven and eight."

Ellie looked at Aaron. "So the original timeline still works?"

He ran the scenario through his mind, then nodded. "We get to the shack around seven forty-five, eight, use the weather for cover.... Yeah, that should work."

"So that gives us...." Ryan held up a finger and made a show of pulling a dull, silver pocket watch from his jeans pocket. It was a J.W. Benson, made in London in the 1930s, and had come to America with his grandfather. Unlike Ellie's digital camera, it wouldn't cause any problems even if they lost it in the middle of Madison Avenue. He thumbed it open and read the time. "...right around two hours."

"I'm glad you finally have a watch again," Ellie said.

He gave his head a slow, sad shake. "The other one didn't make it."

"I hate to say it, given what's coming, but I could stand to eat something," Sam said.

"The flip is more than three hours away," Ellie said. "We should be okay if we don't overdo it."

"Just don't eat anything you'd regret tasting a second time," Ryan said.

"*Eww!* You can be really gross, *Mister Collins*, you know that?"

"*Mmmm!* How about some yummy tuna salad?" Ellie said.

"With pickles," Aaron added.

"On pumpernickel!" Ryan piled on even more ickiness.

"*Ugh!*" Sam said. "That's disgusting. But at least I'm not hungry anymore."

Ellie stood and picked up the two emptiest glasses. "Come on, Sam. Let's see what we've got inside."

They returned to the table five minutes later. Sam carried a plate of snacks they hoped wouldn't cause them problems later on—a sliced pear, two peeled and sectioned oranges, a jar of almond butter, and some sliced bread —and Ellie brought the refilled water glasses. They caught Aaron and Ryan in mid-conversation, Aaron attempting to clarify some technical detail.

"No! It's *way* more complex than that!" Aaron's voice all but bubbled with excitement.

"What did we miss?" Sam said. Instead of returning to her own chair, she plopped herself crosswise on Ryan's lap, letting her feet dangle over one of the chair's arms. She wrapped her arms around his shoulders and leaned against him while he answered.

"He was explaining how we mere mortals cannot grasp the subtle intricacies of the engineering that went into designing the shack."

"No, no, no!" Aaron said, quick to deny he had implied even a hint of intellectual superiority. "All I said is that it's natural for people to simplify the challenges involved. They think, 'Oh, it's just about getting the shack to disappear from the present and reappear someplace else at a different time.'"

"'*Just!*'" Ellie said. "'Cause *that's* no big deal."

"Well, isn't it?" Sam said.

Ryan rolled his eyes. "Thanks for backing me up there, fellow mere mortal."

"I'm being serious. *Isn't* it?" she pressed.

"Kinda, yeah, but it's...." Aaron took a second to compose a response before trying to explain. "Okay, where were you five seconds ago?"

"I was sitting right here." She answered him as if she thought he was trying to be ridiculous. Ellie began to understand what he was getting at and grinned.

"No, you weren't. You were over there." He pointed away from the house. "Maybe the middle of the back yard. Probably somewhere out in the canyon."

"Huh? I don't get it."

He stood up and faced her.

"As we're sitting here, the Earth is rotating, right? So every second, even if we're sitting still, we've moved to someplace new." He turned in place once, slowly, while keeping his eyes on Sam as much as possible. "At the same time, it's orbiting the sun." He walked in a small circle, rotating several more times as he went. "And the solar system is orbiting around the center of the galaxy, and on top of that, the whole universe is expanding."

He back-stepped across the lawn away from her, spreading his arms wide as he went to illustrate the concept of expansion. When he thought he had made his point, he walked back to the table and sat down.

"You see? It's more than merely knowing where on Earth Brooklyn is relative to where we are now. That thing has to be able to calculate—within *millimeters*—where a specific landing spot in Brooklyn was on an Earth that in 1941 was billions upon billions of miles from here!"

Sam, who hated math as much as Ellie loathed writing, was silent as she thought about this.

"'Billions and billions,'" Ryan said.

Until that very moment, Ellie had thought *anyone* could do a passable Sagan. Now she realized she had been wrong. She also realized that this was the most relaxed and animated she had seen Aaron for nearly a week. She didn't know what had changed his mood, but she was grateful for it.

"It's an unbelievably complex calculation," Aaron said, "and the ability to solve it is built into that thing out there. It has to be using quantum computers. Unless somebody has discovered a new method for calculating the relationship between two specific points across all that space/time, quantum computing is the only way it could be done. *That's* the part I hate to see go."

"So, how did this come up?" Ellie said.

"I asked him if there was anything he regretted about destroying the shack," Ryan said. He smiled at her, just the slightest curving of his lips, and winked. She smiled back and gave him a single nod of thanks.

Aaron continued, sounding more serious. "But that's weird, too, you know? They don't exist yet. Not in a working form like that, anyway. And the neural interface, the graphene batteries... All that tech is decades ahead of anything I've read about. Even the wall panels would be a stretch. It's all being worked on, sure, but right now it's just vaporware. I guess *somebody* can keep a secret."

They considered this for a moment, but no one had anything to add.

"If you're going to eat, you should do it pretty soon," Sam reminded them. She waved her hand at the plate of food, such as it was. "There's more inside, but we should keep it to this to be safe."

Ryan looked over the meager offerings and was clearly unimpressed. "Yeah—we wouldn't want to go and get all, you know, *not hungry*."

"Hey!" Sam said. "It's entirely up to you. Just be sure not to hurl all over *me!*"

"I make no promises. But I am going to need my arms back if I'm going to feed myself."

"Sorry," she said, sounding anything but. "Too comfy."

He reached for the tray with his less-encumbered left hand, awkwardly laid a slice of pear on a piece of dry bread, and raised it high as if making a toast. "Let us feast!"

Ellie thought the ninety minutes that followed passed far too quickly, but she was relieved to see that everyone, including Aaron, seemed to be making the most of the time. Ryan's party idea might have worked out after all. She still had a question pecking at the back of her brain, hesitated on the verge of not asking it, then took the plunge.

"Okay, so—is there any chance Sam and I will wind up naked when we get back here?"

Ryan started to respond, but Sam quickly cupped a hand over his mouth. "What do you mean?!" she said, sounding alarmed.

"It's like your question about the money." Ellie turned to face Aaron. "When we get back, we won't have needed to get those clothes from the consignment shop, right? So, what's going to happen to them? Will they just... *poof?*"

Ryan, still muzzled, made mumbling sounds and waggled his eyebrows at Sam. She pulled her hand from his mouth and gave his chest a playful slap. "Behave, you!"

"Should we maybe wear the stuff in the shack, instead?" Ellie said.

Aaron answered without hesitation. "You're asking if the reason you went to the shop in the first place—me—will influence what happens after? Do you think it would be different if you guys had bought the clothes at the beginning of May, before we even found the shack?"

She hadn't looked at it like that. "Umm... maybe?"

Aaron shook his head. "No, I don't think we need to account for inten-tionality. If *I* had gone there and bought everything, it might be a different story, but it was you two. Besides, whatever happens to the shack will be exactly what happens to whatever is *inside* it. You'll be better off with the clothes you bought."

She thought he seemed awfully sure of his answer. Her eyes went wide as comprehension blossomed in her mind. "So *that's* why you suggested we get the clothes!" Realizing their errand hadn't been entirely a deception brought her a surprisingly large sense of relief.

He nodded. "One of the reasons, yes. The original one. But you were right about the other," he admitted.

Finally taking pity on Ryan, Sam got up from his lap, gathered the dishes, and carried everything back into the kitchen. There were a few clunks and bangs as she put everything in the dishwasher, followed by some softer sounds as she seemed to conduct a search through various cupboards. Ellie could see her moving around the darkened space through the window above the sink, but couldn't tell what she was doing. Then Sam disappeared from view for a moment before returning to the patio half a minute later.

"Did you notice the time?" Ellie said.

"Just after five-thirty."

"You guys need to put your New York stuff on. Sam and I need to get ready for the hike." She looked at Aaron. "You have everything you need?"

He nodded. "I have a sweater and a jacket in my pack. I'll show them to Sam."

Ryan stood and stomped his feet a few times, trying to get some feeling back into them. "Okay, boys and girls, let's go get ready!"

"You guys can change in the bathroom if you want," Ellie said. "Or wherever, really," she amended, remembering they had the entire house to themselves.

"And then we should *all* use the bathroom," Sam said as they filed indoors. "I, for one, would rather not find out what New York public toilets were like in 1941. In *December.*"

Ellie was in total agreement. "*Brrr!*"

40

At six o'clock they squeezed back into the Jeep, and fifteen minutes later they were parked at the trailhead. Ellie watched the clouds rolling in from the southwest, blown along by a strong, high-altitude wind. Far out along the distant horizon, the sky was nearly black, and despite the early hour, the day was growing unusually dim. At ground level, however, it was eerily calm, as if the entire rest of the world, everything except themselves, had been muted. It felt like a *very* big storm was on its way. She decided they would likely be okay for the hour and a half it would take to reach the shack. She wasn't as optimistic about the return trip.

Ellie and Sam wore shorts and trail shoes suitable for the rough terrain, but each carried a backpack that contained their Brooklyn outfits, plus the woolen coats. They had both opted to wear light-colored camisoles on the hike. Being plain cotton and freshly de-labeled, they could safely leave them on under their dresses. Aaron and Ryan could appear on the streets of Brooklyn dressed as they were without raising any questions—or eyebrows—but Ryan also carried a pack stuffed with two medium-weight jackets.

After locking the Jeep, Ryan turned to face his companions. "Are we forgetting anything? Caution? Prudence? Common sense?"

Ellie's smile was grim. "How about 'all of the above?' But I think we're good, yeah?"

Aaron nodded in confirmation.

"All right, then. Let's do this," Ryan said.

They paused at the spot on the rim trail where the path down began and looked both directions for anyone who might witness their illegal descent. Seeing no one, they left the pavement and made their way as quickly as possible over the edge and out of sight. They retraced their usual route along the bottom of the wash, and when they reached the start of the first steep climb, Ellie and Aaron led the way. Within twenty minutes of setting out, they were peering down at the skinny ribbon of blacktop that ended at the nuclear research lab.

As Ellie crouched beside a thick tree trunk, watching and waiting, she abruptly saw how the unnatural gloom of the storm gave them an advantage. They would be less noticeable as they moved through the low scrub that sided the road, but any car traveling along that road would likely have its lights on. It would be more easily visible to them, and from much farther away. *Score one for the good guys!*

A few seconds later, Sam and Ryan caught up and knelt beside them. "See anybody?"

"One car went by when we first got here, heading out. Since then, nothing," Aaron said.

"Yeah, we saw it. So we keep going?"

"From now on, you two go first," Ellie said. "Once you're into the culvert and the coast is clear, Aaron and I will follow you."

"Don't stop until you get to the bottom of the next wash. We'll meet up there," Aaron said.

"Shouldn't you two be the ones to go first?" Sam said. "I mean, if only one pair of us makes it through, shouldn't it be you?"

"Yes," Ellie said. "But remember—you two are sort of like bait for this first part, right? You're going first so that if anyone gets caught, it's you two." She gave Sam an apologetic smile.

"Oh, right. Thanks!"

"Ready, Sam?" Ryan said.

"Cast away, chum."

Ryan winked and fired a finger pistol at her, acknowledging the clever double pun.

"You're clear," Aaron said. "Go."

Ellie watched Ryan and Sam set a quick pace toward the road. They maintained a half-crouch as they traversed the sixty yards to the mouth of the culvert. Although they had made this crossing many times in the past, and usually in broad daylight, she repeatedly found herself holding her breath during the half-minute it took for the pair to disappear below the road. Once they had, she relaxed and dried her damp palms on her shorts. She heard Aaron start a brisk ten-count.

"Ready?" he said when he finished.

She scanned the road again and still saw nothing. "Let's go."

Instinctively mimicking the postures of Sam and Ryan, they headed off through the low brush, moving as fast as they could while being careful to avoid sideswiping a prickly pear pad or spearing a leg on the needle-sharp point of a yucca leaf. Ellie reached the culvert first and ducked inside with Aaron close behind. The corrugated pipe was almost five feet in diameter, but years worth of accumulated sediment raised the floor by more than a foot. This meant they had to duck-walk their way through, negotiating a poorly lit obstacle course of rocks and debris along the way, but at least there was no standing water to make progress even harder.

They reached the far end, and Ellie was about to step out of the culvert when Aaron grabbed the back of her shorts and pulled her to a stop. The unexpected sensation of his fingertips under her waistband caused goose-bumps to break out over her entire body.

"*Wait!*" he hissed.

She dropped back into a crouch and waited, instantly as still as a field mouse that has spotted a circling hawk. After a second, she heard the sound of a vehicle getting closer at great speed. Suddenly the noise was directly overhead, extremely loud. She guessed it was an SUV or small truck fitted with oversized, knobby, off-road tires. Only they could produce that much of a racket. The next instant the sound was receding, its pitch dropping along with its volume as the vehicle roared away from them. They waited a few moments longer to be sure the noise wasn't covering up the sound of a second car, but fifteen seconds later the area was completely silent.

"Okay," he said, at last releasing his grip on her shorts. "Go ahead."

Ellie emerged from the confines of the tunnel but remained hunkered low until the ditch delivered them into another grove of trees. Picking her way carefully through a mix of road gravel, plant debris, and litter, she continued down the drainage bed until she reached the bottom, Aaron no more than a step or two behind her the whole way.

Breathing hard from her efforts, Ellie scanned down the wash for Sam and Ryan. At first she saw nothing, but a second later she made out the figure of Sam, partially obscured by juniper branches, waving her arms over her head. She and Ryan had hiked much farther than she expected. Ellie caught Aaron's eye, nodded in Sam's direction, and they started making their way along the arroyo's rocky bottom.

"You must have great ears!" Ellie said, surprised that her own extremely acute sense of hearing had failed her.

"They're symmetrical if nothing else," he said.

"Seriously—I did *not* hear that guy coming."

"I didn't hear it either. I had my hand on the wall—I felt the vibrations, that's all."

"'That's all,' he says—like that isn't way cooler!" Just then they reached Sam and Ryan.

"Problem?" Ryan said.

"Not with Aaron's 'spidey sense,' there isn't," Ellie said.

"A truck or something came by," Aaron explained. "We had to wait it out in the tunnel for a few seconds—no big deal."

"Should be easy from here on out," Ryan said. "Until we get close, anyway. Ready?"

"Lead on," Ellie said, and she dropped in behind Sam as they resumed the trek through the woods.

An hour later they guessed they were within a quarter-mile of the shack—the area looked very different under the dark sky. The wind was an issue now, too. Its intensity had been growing for the past half-hour, and what started as a needle-ruffling breeze was now causing the entire top of the forest to sway. Lightning flashed off to their west at random intervals, followed seconds later by the rumble of thunder.

Ellie couldn't remember another storm ever making the day so dark so early. She looked up into the sky, and for a moment she felt the same prickling feeling on the back of her neck she had experienced when they returned to the shack outside of Methuen. Was the universe somehow aware of what they were doing? If so, it was pissed! *Hey! We're on your side… I swear!*

They stopped to confer one last time before making their final approach to the shack. Although the center of the approaching storm was still a comfortable distance away, the nonstop roar of the wind meant they had to yell to make themselves heard.

"So much for stealth," Sam shouted.

"Don't sweat it too much," Aaron said. "Our voices won't carry far in all this racket. Plus, it's blowing toward us."

"How much farther?" she said.

"Not very," Ellie said. She waved everyone toward her until their heads were practically touching. "We need to start taking it very slowly. You guys will continue to go first. Move up a dozen yards or so, look around for any guards, then move ahead again if you think the way is clear. Aaron and I will continue to stay pretty far back. When you reach the shack, hang out in front of it for about twenty, thirty seconds. Just stand there. If anybody is around, you two showing up should bring them out of hiding."

"After half a minute, get to work on the door," Aaron said. "At that point, we'll come running as fast as we can. We'll want to get it open, get in, and get it locked as quickly as we can."

"Last chance to bail," Ellie said. "I mean it."

Ryan and Sam exchanged brief, solemn looks.

"We're in all the way," he said. "Ready, Sam?" She nodded.

"Good luck!" Ellie said.

Ellie and Aaron crouched low behind a dense cluster of Gambel oaks, watching Sam and Ryan advance thirty to forty feet at a time, find a new hiding place, then scan the area for sentries before moving forward again. When they were almost out of sight, Ellie rose and began to follow with Aaron close on her left.

Now hiding behind an enormous ponderosa stump, peering intently through the woods in front of them, Aaron leaned close to Ellie's ear. "After this, you should consider becoming a Ranger. Or a SEAL."

"I bet SEALs don't feel like throwing up like I do right now. I'm not cut out for covert ops."

"See anything?"

She shook her head. "Nope. Let's go."

It was another ten minutes of hide-run-hide before they finally glimpsed the triangular profile of the shack's roof rising out of the gloom ahead of them. They peeked around either side of a large boulder, and their low vantage point meant they were straining to see through a tangle of under-growth they usually would be looking over. They could see the two figures slinking through the trees ahead of them just well enough to tell they had stopped at the edge of the clearing surrounding the shack. Ellie guessed they were using their former picnic tree for cover while taking one last look around before making the final dash. The ferocity of the wind had momen-tarily slackened, and now they could talk at an almost normal volume.

"This is their last stop," Aaron said. "Let's close it up a little, then get ready to run."

They inched forward, covering almost half the remaining distance before stopping to kneel behind a scrawny juniper. Ahead of them, now much easier to see, Sam and Ryan vaulted the log and trotted past the end of the shack. They reached its far side, stopped close to the door, and scanned the forest. As near to thirty seconds later as Ellie could tell, Ryan turned to the wall and began probing for the trigger that revealed the door control. Sam stood with her back to his, alert to any sign of unwelcome company.

"Come on!" Ellie said. They sprang up and began sprinting toward the shack. They dodged low-hanging branches, jumped over rocks and small shrubs, and somehow avoided catching a toe on a protruding root as they ate up the distance between them and the door. They were halfway there when a brilliant, staccato flash lit up the forest. Ellie, disoriented by the sudden strobe effect, stumbled. Unbalanced by the extra weight riding high on her shoulders, she barely managed to stay on her feet. The lightning was followed not two seconds later by an intense crash of thunder. The storm was much closer now—it would be on top of them in minutes.

Ryan was still pulling the door open when they broke out of the trees and into the clearing. They barely slowed as they leaped through the widening gap and into the dim, sterile interior of the shack, Sam and Ryan tight behind them. Aaron helped Ryan swing the door closed, and the handle *snicked* up into the locked position. When the seats began descending from the ceiling, they knew they had done it.

"*Hoo-rah!*" exclaimed Ryan. He held a fist up toward smiling Sam, and she gave it a solid bump with her own.

Ellie's eyes were on Aaron, watching his reaction.

"Hoo-rah," he echoed flatly, and the celebratory mood instantly evaporated. He shrugged. "Sorry. Really—we did good."

"We sure done did," Ellie agreed.

"No, *I'm* sorry," Ryan said. He looked embarrassed. "I kinda forgot for a minute, that's all."

"No worries. Honestly? Five seconds ago, I was feeling the same way."

"At any rate," Ellie said, "we shouldn't be counting our chickens until we get this coop outta here."

She moved around to the control panel. The others moved up to stand close beside her, peering over her shoulders as she began entering their destination data. None of them had seen this part of it on their first time out, and they were curious. She explained each step as she quickly went through the process of preparing the shack for travel.

"First, I'll pick the destination." She scrolled to the east coast of the U.S., then zoomed in tight on Brooklyn. Prospect Park filled most of the lower left side of the screen, while the right side was crisscrossed by a haphazard grid of city streets intersecting at various angles.

"Next, I'll set the time." They watched as she deftly slid the controls to December 8, 1941, then adjusted the time to 11:30z.

"What's the 'z' mean?" Sam said.

"'Zulu time,'" three voices answered in unison.

Sam sighed. "Okay, so it was just me then."

"This whole thing is based on Greenwich Mean, or 'Zulu,' Time," Ellie said. "That'll make it six-thirty in the morning. We can change that in a minute if we need to because this is kinda the tricky part. It won't allow you to pop up in the middle of a street or anyplace else so visible. Or, you know, convenient. That's why we ended up in a forest outside of Methuen last time. Let's see what happens if I...." She pushed the "Auto Optimize" button and, after a moment, was rewarded with not one but three options, all within the confines of Prospect Park.

"That's exactly what I was hoping." She selected the option closest to the park's east side, and the crosshair marker slid to the chosen location where it changed from a pulsing red to solid green.

"Six-thirty still work?" she said with a glance toward Aaron. He nodded.

"All right then. Last, I'll pick stations one through four, same as last time, and... *voilà!*" With a flourish, she tapped INITIALIZE, and four chairs hummed to life behind them.

"That's it. Go get yourselves settled in, and we'll get out of here," she said. "And 'now,'" she muttered to herself.

While Ellie stood at the controls, waiting for the others to take their places, a recurring fantasy of the past few days played itself out in her mind. In it, the four of them would pick some interesting place and date and, upon arriving there, completely destroy all traces of the shack. After, they would blend into the population and spend the rest of their lives there, Aaron safe from the very consequences he was facing today. Or just she and Aaron would go, disappearing into a long-ago when the telephone or maybe AM radio was the most modern technology. That didn't in any way solve the basic problem posed by this terrible device—another one would quickly take its place—but it would relieve them of any responsibility of handling it themselves. She recognized the fantasy for what it was—the coward's way out.

But as she watched Sam pull on her helmet, a new possibility flashed into her mind. What if she and Aaron went back to a time around the turn of the century, as far back as they could go? They could destroy the shack, bury the pieces, and find a place to live. They could get a small house far out in the country to minimize the possibility of changing the timeline, and he could safely live out almost an entire lifetime, all the way until December 8, 1941. *Half* a lifetime, anyway. All they needed to do was make sure they were in Brooklyn on that all-important morning to carry out their current plan, only in their fifties instead of in their teens. She froze, hand poised over the control panel, transfixed by this new idea. She had never made it as far as imagining spending the rest of her life with him in such a scenario. Would they be partners? Friends? More than friends?

Her mind was suddenly filled with a beautiful image, startling in its rich and vivid detail. *Is this a memory?* She and Aaron were standing on a front porch somewhere lush and green, waiting for dawn to roll over the horizon. She knew they had grown older together and that she was happy. So... not a memory. Yet it was. It was the memory of a *dream*. She realized she had come up with this exact plan days before—in her sleep! *Could that idea truly work?*

She wished she had more time to think it through, to talk it over with Aaron. Now it was too late! An inner voice wailed within her mind, full of outrage and regret. *No! It's not fair!* She bowed her head and clenched her eyes tightly shut against the emotional turmoil while she considered what they should do. If they bailed now, could they even be lucky enough to manage a third successful break-in? Not likely. The decision was obvious. They had no choice but to go ahead with the plan. The sound of Sam calling to her as if from a great distance finally brought her back to the moment.

"Ellie! Earth to Ellie! Are you still with us?"

"Yeah, sorry. I was just... um, thinking." She was shaking all over, and even her own voice sounded far away. She waggled her head to clear it. "Never mind. Ten seconds," she said, then pressed EXECUTE.

She took her place in station one and hurried to get herself ready. Aaron turned his head toward her as far as the helmet allowed and spoke quietly.

"Thinking what, exactly?"

"I'll tell you later."

"Promise?"

"No. Get ready—there's only a second or two before...."

She realized at once she had been off by a second or two. She felt the helmet's rows of studs tighten against her scalp, sensed paralysis lock her body rigid, then the darkness returned and pulled her under.

41

They waited to recover from the worst of the 'temporal motion sickness' before easing themselves out of their seats. As before, four compartments clicked open along one wall, different ones this time, but presumably still offering them each a variety of costume options. Ryan began pushing them closed but hesitated when he noticed Aaron looking in his direction.

"You want to see if you got another 'cool' hat?"

"Seriously—you need to let that go. But since you mentioned it, I'll take a look."

Ryan stepped aside and let him inspect the contents of his cubbyhole.

"Ryan," Ellie said, "why don't you check outside—make sure we're alone. And make sure your watch is set to the right time. It's on the screen, toward the top."

Ryan called for the exterior view to be displayed, but at the early hour it was too dark to see anything under the trees. The wall with the door showed an area of almost pure black. The only discernible details appeared high on the walls and around the perimeter of the ceiling, where the upper branches of distant trees were silhouetted against a sky that still offered little light.

Hoping the shack was equipped with some form of night vision, he asked the computer for an enhanced image, but there was no change. Finally, he gave up and switched off the external view. Then, to make adjusting to the outside darkness quicker, he asked for the interior lighting to be dimmed to half its current brightness. He consulted the display panel, made a slight adjustment on the watch, and checked that it was fully wound. He turned away from the panel just as Aaron closed the hatch.

"What, no hat?"

Aaron shook his head. "If you thought the *last* one was bad...."

Meanwhile, Ellie and Sam put on their dresses, slid their hiking shorts off from underneath, and changed shoes. Ellie checked the mission clock and saw they had a little more than six hours to carry out their plan. A few passes through her hair with a brush Sam had packed erased the worst effects of the windstorm, and then they were ready to go. She placed her beret on her head and turned to face Sam.

"How's that?"

Sam gave the hat a minor adjustment. "Perfect!"

Ellie nodded to Ryan. He pulled on the door handle, waited as the seats and control panels moved back into hiding, then canceled the "set password" routine. Once the door finally unlatched, he placed his shoulder against it and shoved.

Outside, they found themselves standing in the middle of a dense cluster of cedars that blocked any view of the park. They stayed hidden behind the trees for a minute, pulling in deep, restorative breaths and puffing billowy white clouds out into the frigid December morning.

Ellie moved cautiously to the edge of the line of trees, scanned the area around them, and was happy not to see a single person. Considering it was still twenty minutes before sunrise, she wasn't much surprised. By the time she slipped back to the others, the last of her nausea had passed.

"We seem to be alone," she reported. She leaned her shoulder against the door and pushed. Ryan reached out to help, and a second later, they heard the solid sound of the lock sliding home.

"That was definitely easier on an emptier stomach," Aaron said.

Ryan agreed, but only up to a point. "Except for the whole 'empty stomach' part. I'm starved!"

"Are you *joking?!*" Sam said. "You just ate!"

"Well, *barely!*"

"And to be fair," Aaron said, "That won't be for almost eighty years."

Ryan pointed at him in a double-handed *what he said* gesture.

"No, it was just—*ohhh*...." She groaned. "Please don't do that." This time she used both middle fingers to massage her temples.

Ellie chuckled. "That was *mean!*" Aaron grinned back at her.

"Whatever," Sam said. "But I guess it's a good thing at least one of us was thinking ahead." She extracted four paper towel-wrapped parcels from her deep coat pockets. "Ta-da! Clif Bars!" Ellie opened her mouth, but Sam cut her off before she could speak. "Don't worry—I left all the wrappers at home." She passed the bars around.

"All I was going to say was, 'best sister *ever!*'"

"What are they?" Aaron said. "I mean, what flavors?"

"There were two Blueberry Crisps, one Trail Mix, and one... something else. I don't remember. Of course now...." Sam looked at the irregular, brown rectangles in their hands and saw that they were practically identical.

Ryan's enthusiasm was undimmed. "Yum! Mystery munchies!" He raised his bar to his nose and gave it an exploratory sniff. "Yep—still a mystery." He bit off a hearty chunk and mumbled around the first, gooey mouthful. "And... still a mystery."

"The finest in 'oat cuisine!'" Aaron said.

As they downed their snacks, Ellie concentrated on orienting herself to their location within the park. Although they'd had the luxury of planning their route in advance this time, there was still the matter of setting off in the right direction. Until they were sure which direction that was, the crude map drawn on her hand wouldn't help them much.

They had studied 3D views of the city and tried to memorize landmarks that had been around since at least the late thirties. Crown Heights was due east of the park's northern end. She knew that the site she had chosen from the three the computer had offered was in a section of the park called The Ravine, and that the closest exit from the park was southeast of them. It occurred to her that she could have gotten the exact direction from the display in the shack, but she wasn't overly concerned. As on their first trip, they needed to head toward the sunrise, and that, now mere minutes away, would not be hard to find. She pointed toward what she was pretty confident was the southeast.

"This way." She started off through the underbrush with Aaron on her heels.

Before they followed, Ryan caught Sam's eye. *"The Voyage Hom*e, right?" She smiled and nodded. "One... two... three...."

"'Everybody remember where we parked!'" they quoted in unison, then dropped into line behind Aaron.

Their chosen route rose gently, and very soon they reached one of the many small trails that wound through this densely wooded section of the park. Ellie veered slightly south, leading them toward the brightest spot she could see. "Let's get out from under these trees so we can figure out where we are."

Ryan held up the remaining half of his Clif Bar, eyeing it speculatively. "So, why don't these things disappear if they weren't invented until the nineties or whenever?"

"What do you mean?" Aaron said.

"I mean the photos in those books changed after we got back from Lawrence, right? So why would these things stick around in the past if they won't even be thought of for another fifty years?"

"I have no idea," Sam said, "but you'd better be glad. Otherwise, we'd all be walking around in just our skin right now."

"Not that I have a problem with it," Ryan said, "but you two seem oddly obsessed with being naked."

Ellie caught Sam's eye. "But that's not true, Sam. Remember? Our clothes are from this time. Except for suddenly going commando, we'd be fine. It would just be *them*." She pointed at Ryan and Aaron, whose clothes were entirely of twenty-first-century origin.

Sam laughed. "At least Ryan would have his pocket watch to cover himself with!" She held a hand up, thumb and forefinger two inches apart, indicating the watch's diminutive diameter.

"Har, har, har," he said.

Aaron was ready with an answer. "I thought about this a while ago. Shortly after we... or rather I should say after *Ellie* correctly identified our 'unicorn' back there." She gave him a grateful smile. "At first, I assumed that the Lawrence clothing we had worn all dated to the early nineteen hundreds.

Then I realized that didn't have to be the case, even though I bet much of it did."

He went quiet and looked at Ellie, giving her the chance to see the answer for herself. It took her only a second, and then she spoke with certainty.

"No. They would have known it didn't matter—because of the shack itself. This whole thing wouldn't work if it vanished shortly after it went back. After the first successful test, they would have known. So, we were right to begin with—the costumes are strictly for blending in. And besides, if that weren't the case, *we* would disappear, too."

"Seems kinda strange trying so hard to blend in if they were planning on changing history, anyway," Sam said.

"Whatever their plans were, I think they would have tried to be as careful, as, ah, 'surgical' as possible," Aaron said. "Hence that herd of historians. They would have wanted to make very precise, very specific changes, not random ones."

"I get it," Sam said. "I guess it makes sense about the clothes and the bars and stuff, though. To us, it's all still history, whether it's happened yet or not."

"What she said," Ryan agreed.

Ellie remembered an idea that had occurred to her after Aaron had first revealed his plan to her. "Actually, I bet a lot of those researchers were genealogists. After all, history is made by people. The one thing they would absolutely have to avoid is exactly what we're doing—anything that would prevent the shack from being made. That means knowing the entire family tree of everyone vital to the project."

Aaron nodded slowly as he realized she had nailed it. He smiled at her. "I told you—you're good."

The bright spot Ellie had seen turned out to be an opening in the trees, a long cut over a road near the park's east edge. Across the road, a tall, wrought-iron gate blocked a road leading to a large, dome-roofed building beyond.

"That's the zoo over there?" Sam said.

"Yep. And we need to get around it. It'll be better if we go to the right. Shorter." She studied the smudged lines on the palm of her left hand. "Once we're out of the park, we can get on a street that'll take us straight up to Park Place."

They crossed the empty road, found another footpath, and started making their way toward the muted sound of traffic. As the minutes passed, a somber mood fell over the group, and Ellie became aware of Sam and Ryan casting furtive glances at Aaron. He noticed too, and he picked up his pace to walk alongside her. He spoke softly so only she would hear.

"I feel like they're already sitting shiva." She took his hand but said nothing. "Remember how you said Carmela could have been hurt or killed when she was trying to sneak out of Lawrence? I don't feel like I'm doing anything different."

"I know." Her reply came out as a croak. Again she remembered wondering if she could make the same decisions Carmela had made. *But this is different—Carmela was in danger only if things* didn't *go according to plan.* She coughed to clear her throat. "I know. But I still hate it."

After walking for a few minutes more, they exited the park and found themselves at an intersection where the city streets diverged at odd angles. Ellie glanced again at the map on her palm. "That's the botanical garden across the street, so this must be Flatbush. We're in the right place. We want to cross here and then take the second street over."

When she looked up from her hand, she saw nobody was paying her any attention. During their entire time in Lawrence, they had believed they were in a simulated environment. Now that they knew their surroundings were real, they couldn't help but be captivated by the sight of the city rising all around them. Sam and Ryan were openly gawking, grinning in delighted wonder at the brick buildings, the—to them—antique cars humming by on cobblestone streets, and even the few people already out on the sidewalks. She not only let them have their moment, but joined them in appreciating their unique situation. Aaron, too, was absorbed in the cityscape that surrounded them, but his expression was blank.

"New York City, 1941," Ryan said. "America has entered the last World War. Next up, women in the workplace, the Tuskegee Airmen, a massive industrial build-up—the atom bomb, of course. Then the whole Cold War thing, McCarthyism, and civil rights protests. The moon landing! But also some truly important things, too, like the Beatles, hula hoops, and pet rocks. I wonder who would believe us if we told them what was about to happen."

"Aaron said we were probably the first to use the shack," Ellie said, then paused while a Plymouth taxi motored noisily past them. "After that, they were busy figuring out why they'd had a big power drain, so it's very likely this is only its second manned trip. If that's true, then we are the only four people in the world who have experienced the past this way."

"You know what's bizarre?" Sam said. "Everything is in color!" She laughed. "I mean, *duh*, but all the photos, the news footage, all you ever see is black and white, gray people dressed in more shades of gray. Or color pictures so funky-looking they seem more fake than the black-and-whites. This all looks so... *normal*."

"You said almost the same thing about Lawrence, remember?" Ellie pointed out.

"God, I would love to see Times Square, Central Park...." Sam continued.

"You know, I have to say...." Ryan began, but Aaron cut him off.

"No! You don't. Let's go." A gap opened in the light, early-morning traffic, and Aaron stepped off the curb onto Flatbush Avenue. His terse tone shattered the momentary mood of innocent wonder and reminded everyone of the seriousness of their task.

"Come on," Ellie said, then hurried across the street after him. She walked double-time to catch up, then took his hand.

"Hey, what's up?" She turned to study his face as they neared the next intersection.

"He was going to say that maybe we should scrap the plan, that we instead go back and let this thing keep on being. And yeah, I know he wasn't serious—I *know* that—but part of me kind of agrees with him. Look around!" Although he had meant it rhetorically, she swept her gaze across the buildings lining the street. "This is incredible! If I were smart enough to work out the theories Dad did, *I* probably would have made that thing!"

Crossing Washington Avenue, she glanced back to make sure Sam and Ryan were still close behind them. As they stepped off the cobblestones and onto the sidewalk, she squeezed his hand. "Yeah, it's definitely your kind of gadget. But you have to be even smarter to understand that it has to be... *erased*, I guess is the word."

He sighed. "I agree with that, too. Not the being smarter part, but yeah—it does have to go."

"But that's not all, is it? Just the thought of having a different option makes it harder to keep going, right?" She saw different emotions play across his face before he brought himself under control.

"I thought this would all be easier to deal with once we got started." His voice came out raspy through a tight throat. He took a deep breath, shuddered as he blew it back out. He looked into her eyes. "It's not."

"No. It's not," she agreed. At the next corner, they veered left and started up Franklin Avenue. Ellie stopped and turned around to face Ryan. "It's eleven blocks up to Park Place. How are we doing for time?"

Ryan retrieved the watch from a jacket pocket and flipped open the cover. "It says six forty-five. Give or take a couple, probably."

She turned to Aaron. "We're still good?"

"Should be. Maximum twenty minutes to Park, another five or so to find the shop, then another ten to get to the apartment. We ought to have at least fifteen minutes to spare. Probably more."

Nevertheless, when the four resumed walking up Franklin, it was at a considerably quicker pace. Ellie occasionally overheard bits of Sam and Ryan's conversation behind her. It was largely unintelligible, but they seemed to be commenting on whatever caught their attention along the way. Aaron, however, was silent.

42

Seven blocks farther up Franklin, they waited on a corner to cross Eastern Parkway. Like Flatbush, Eastern was a four-lane road and carried much more traffic than the side street they were on. The cars, trucks, and other vehicles that rumbled by on the uneven road mostly seemed strange to their eyes. They did recognize a few, ones familiar from old movies or, occasionally, from having seen them on the road in their own time.

"It smells funny here," Sam said.

"Leaded gas," Aaron explained at once. "No catalytic converters, no emissions standards. We went to a vintage car show in Santa Fe a few years back. The exhaust from the cars there smelled exactly like this."

Ryan made an exaggerated shrug. "And here *I* was going to say 'clown farts.' Shows how much I know."

Sam nudged his ribs with her elbow. "Don't be gross."

Finally, the traffic light changed, and they crossed the street at a trot. On the far side, they resumed a normal walking pace, and soon the sounds from the busy thoroughfare behind them began to fade. When it was quiet again, Aaron reviewed the next steps of the plan.

"Okay, the first thing we'll do is go left on Park Place and find the shop.

Once we do, we'll head the other way toward my grandfather's building. Somewhere in between has to be the newsstand." They were approaching Saint John's Place, a neighborhood street with almost no traffic. "You two will stay near the newsstand and be on the lookout for Judith. Ellie and I will go hang out in front of Grandpa's apartment and wait for him to leave."

"So," Sam said, "when we see you coming, we'll know she's about to appear, then we keep them from running into each other."

"Maybe, maybe not. She could already be standing there talking to the stand's owner, or she might be reading the headlines, same as Grandpa. Or, yeah, she could show up at the last second. And she could be coming from either direction. What I'm saying is that we can't make any assumptions. Stay alert and be ready for anything."

"Got it," Ryan said.

"Afterward, we'll hang out for a little while, make sure he makes it to the shop and that she doesn't show up again for some reason. Then we'll head back to the park," Aaron said.

"We had a little more than six hours from when we got here until we have to leave," Ellie said. "After we're done, we'd like to spend a little of that time, you know, together, walking around the park or whatever before we leave here."

Aaron stared at her, his expression stern. "Unless our new addition to the landscape is starting to draw attention. In that case, we go as soon as we can. Right?"

Ellie stared back. She felt a strong urge to be defiant again, but knew he was correct. Finally, she dropped her gaze to the sidewalk and nodded sullenly. "Yeah. Right."

They reached Park Place, turned left, and found the shop not quite halfway down the block. At the early hour, the interior was still dark and empty. They stood on the sidewalk before the large, plate-glass windows and peered up at the building. The wooden frames around the windows were deep green, and the name "Nathan's" was written across the glass, painted in gold with a black shadow effect. Near the bottom of each window, smaller, unornamented text read, "Custom Clothier—Nathan Kleid, Proprietor."

"This is it?" Ryan said.

Aaron nodded. "This is it." He stared at the store for a moment longer, his expression somber. "Okay, let's head back the other way."

After crossing Franklin, they soon became aware of a voice shouting in the near distance. When they were close enough to understand the words, it sounded so much like a cliché they could hardly believe it was genuine.

"Extra! Extra! Japan attacks Hawaii! Extra! Read all about it!" the voice cried. A small wooden stall occupied part of the sidewalk. It displayed an assortment of newspapers and magazines along its front. Inside, standing behind a nearly chest-high counter, a man took coins from customers eager to get details of the air raid. The shouts came from a young boy, presumably the man's son.

"Sneak attack on Pearl Harbor! Extra!"

"I think we've found the newsstand," Ryan said.

"I would say so," Aaron agreed. "You two good to hang out here for a while?"

Sam nodded. "We're okay. We'll wander up and down the street while we look for her. Or sit over there." She pointed to a low brick wall in front of a row house.

Ryan indicated the newsstand with a jerk of his head. "I wish I'd been able to find some cash older than 2004. I'd love to get one of those papers."

"You've got the photo?" Aaron asked him. "The one of Judith?"

Ryan nodded and pulled the picture from a jacket pocket. "Got it."

"What's the time?" Ellie said.

Ryan passed the photo to Sam and consulted his watch again. "Eight past seven."

"Okay," Aaron said. "We're going to go find my grandfather. Expect us in half an hour. Maybe less."

"Roger that!"

Ellie and Aaron left the newsstand behind them and continued on their way east down Park Place.

"How is it an 'extra' if it's only seven o'clock in the morning?" she said.

"Maybe it's just something they said. Or could be they're left over from yesterday evening."

Soon, Bedford Avenue was also behind them, and they were nearing Rogers. The buildings lining both sides of the street were similar to each other, differing mostly in the details. They were all either brick, limestone, or stucco—or occasionally some combination of the three. Each was four stories tall, with the lowest floor half underground. The intricately detailed façades were seldom flat, and many had turret-like features, either rounded or three-sided, on the corners, and these were set all around with small windows. The doorways were large and ornate, sometimes framed by carved panels, other times topped with arched windows set into pale stone deeply etched with diverging lines that looked like rays from a setting sun. The buildings at intersections usually housed businesses, at least on the ground floor, and these had a completely different style from the residences that formed the rest of the blocks.

"It's only a block and a half from here," Aaron said, his voice sounding tight and unsteady.

Ellie found that unsurprising. She couldn't imagine how he must be feeling, but her own jangling nerves made her anxious and jittery, as if she were severely over-caffeinated. They crossed Rogers, still making good time. A few minutes later, they heard a now-familiar cry coming from further up the street, and Aaron cried out in dismay.

"*Oh, no!*"

He broke into a run, and Ellie fell in behind him. At the corner of the block, on the opposite side of the street, sat another newsstand, nearly identical to the one behind them. Another young boy waved papers at the people passing by, many of whom paused to buy one.

"Extra! America attacked! Read all about it!"

They stopped directly across from the newsstand and stared at it. Aaron shook his head in disbelief. "Two of these things in four blocks! They're almost as bad as Starbuck's!"

"What do you want to do?"

"I don't know!" He sounded alarmingly frantic. "I don't... I don't.... Would he stop here or at the other one?"

"Wouldn't he stop at the first one he came to?"

She watched his eyes dart first right, down the street, then left to the newsstand, then back to the right again, the whole while muttering the same words over and over.

"Oh, man... oh, man...."

She could almost see his mental gears billowing out massive clouds of dark, acrid smoke as his mind veered toward hysteria. She turned her back to him, scrunched her eyes closed, and tried to ignore his panicky mantra.

"Okay, brain, think!" She took a quick, deep breath, then opened her eyes and looked around. The sidewalks were by no means busy, but already there were more than a few people walking in either direction along both sides of the street. Daniel could arrive at any second. She sensed that earlier feeling of futility threatening to overwhelm her, knew she couldn't let that happen. In the end, their choices were few.

"Hang on a second. Aaron... Aaron—*listen!*" Giving his arm a firm yank finally got his attention, sparing him an old-fashioned slap across the face. "Here are the options—one, I can wait and be on the lookout for Judith while you go wait for your grandfather to come out of his door. If Judith doesn't show up here, we follow him, just as we planned. Two, I can run and bring Sam and Ryan back to this newsstand, then meet up with you at your granddad's. At the very least, I should go tell them what's up. They need to know they might have to handle that stand on their own."

He closed his eyes and lowered his head. She waited as he played out the various scenarios in his mind. After a few seconds, he opened his eyes.

"Yes, go," he said, "but tell them to stay there. You're probably right that Daniel and Judith meet here, but we can't assume that, and they need to know what's going on. Judith *has* to be coming from that direction—it's all neighborhood this far east. Tell them if they see her, they need to stay with her. I'll move down the next block a little and watch for Daniel coming out of his apartment. Get back here as quick as you can, okay?"

She nodded once, then turned and started running back along Park Place, the blocky heels of her oxfords clunking noisily on the sidewalk. She imagined she could feel his eyes on her back as she zigged-zagged her way between other pedestrians, and hoped he could keep it together long enough to make this work.

Within seconds she was across Rogers and making good time until she reached Bedford. There was too much traffic now to risk crossing against the signal, and she had to wait for what seemed an eternity for the light to change. Standing on the curb, poised to sprint the final block, she became aware of distant sirens. The racket was coming from somewhere ahead of her and getting louder. Then the light changed, the last few cars cleared the intersection, and she was off again.

She spotted Sam and Ryan while she was still over fifty yards away. They were sitting on the wall holding the photo between them. Anytime a woman approached, they looked at her, then at the photo, then back at the woman. Ellie was almost upon them before they noticed her. They both stood as she came to a stop in front of them.

"What's wrong?!" Sam said, and it was clear from her pale expression that she'd already concluded the worst.

Ellie was panting hard following the nearly half-mile run but knew she couldn't waste any time recovering. She pointed at Ryan and spoke between gasps. "You—keep looking for Judith!"

He immediately went back to scanning the passing faces, and Ellie pulled Sam aside. The approaching sirens were getting so loud that she leaned in close to be sure Sam could hear her over the din.

"There's a little problem."

"I got that. Where's Aaron? Is he okay?!"

Ellie raised a hand to calm her. "Physically, yes, but there's another newsstand back there." She pointed over her shoulder and drew in a deep breath, trying to will her heart to stop pounding so fast. "Not even a block from Daniel's apartment. So now we need to cover both of them, and he's freaking out a little." She reconsidered that. "A lot, actually. You two are supposed to watch for Judith here and follow her if she shows up. We'll find Daniel and follow him while also looking out for Judith down there. With luck, you'll see us coming before you see her, but my gut says they met—are going to meet... whatever—at the other one. Got that?"

"Got it."

"Then I need to get back there. Good luck."

Ellie spun around, but before she could dash off, Sam stopped her with a warning.

"Hey! Be careful in those shoes. Trip and break something here, and the problems will *really* begin."

Ellie's face blanched as she realized just how right Sam was. She nodded, then started rushing back toward Aaron, but only as fast as the continuing echo of Sam's admonition would allow her to go. She had only covered a block when she was forced to come to a complete stop at Bedford again.

What are the odds?

By now, the sirens are practically on top of her, the sound so piecing it hurt her ears. She looked over her shoulder to see a mini convoy of emergency vehicles coming up from behind. There were two patrol cars, two fire trucks, one an enormous hook-and-ladder truck, and an ambulance, all threading their way through traffic that had few places to go but which was doing its best to yield to them. Even with their red lights flashing and sirens wailing, the driver of the lead police car was laying on his horn for all he was worth. Finally, a gap opened up all the way to the intersection and the line of wailing vehicles surged forward.

Taking advantage of the rolling roadblock, Ellie zigzagged through the haphazard snarl of vehicles stopped on Belford, this time taking extra care on the cobblestones. By the time she reached the far sidewalk, the line of emergency vehicles was already racing away from her down Park Place with a long string of traffic trailing close behind.

The sirens and flashing lights faded into the distance just as she saw Aaron. She knew instantly something was very wrong. He sat on a limestone stoop across from the newsstand, but he wasn't watching it. He wasn't watching anything. He was hunched forward, elbows on knees, his face buried in his palms. She sprinted the final distance and knelt beside him.

"Aaron, what is it? What happened?"

He didn't look up at her. He merely shook his head, which he kept cradled in his hands. She sat beside him and laid an arm on his back. For a moment, she merely sat quietly, gazing across the street at the people passing by the newsstand. When he remained silent, she leaned forward and spoke softly into his ear.

"Hey, what is it? Talk to me."

Another long moment passed before he sat up and turned to face her, his expression a mask of stunned disbelief. He opened his mouth, but at first, no words came out. "I blew it," he managed at last. "They're gone. They were here, just like we thought. But now? All this planning, all this.... We had one chance. One! And *I blew it!*" His anguished lament, rising to a shout at the end, drew reproving looks from the people nearest them.

Ellie forced herself to speak mildly. "Hey. Easy. Just stay calm and tell me what happened." She couldn't imagine what had gone wrong.

"You left, and I was about to cross the street. Then I realized I could see much more from over here. You know, a wider view of the other sidewalk. Of course, I didn't see either of them. Then I heard those sirens coming, and I could tell they stopped further up the street. I couldn't see anything when I stood up to look, but I figured whatever was going on, at least it was happening up there, and that was good. Then the sirens started getting closer, and fast. I turned back toward the newsstand, and there he was, suddenly, like he had just *beamed in* or something, walking up the sidewalk. For a second—a *second*—I froze. I just stood there, gawking at him! I couldn't believe it was actually my grandfather coming at me.

"So I head for the street, but that's when the cop cars and fire trucks get here. And *then* a car further down the block starts to pull out from the curb. Guy must be completely deaf! Everybody comes to a complete stop until he gets back into his spot, but now that giant fire truck is parked directly in front of me. I run down the street to cross in front of it, but then they all take off again, and I'm still stuck on this side, seeing everything over there happen through gaps between the trucks. Then a woman comes up behind him while he's got his nose in the newspaper, and *bam!* Just like in the story, he backs right into her. Now there are all these other cars stacked up behind the ambulance, so I *still* can't get across! All I can do is watch them walk away... *together!* What could I do at that point?"

"Nothing." She tried to sound calm and soothing, but she knew nothing she could say would make him feel the slightest bit better. "There wasn't a thing you could do."

He groaned. "I don't know.... There *had* to be."

"Look, right now that doesn't matter. What we have to do is go back and tell Sam and Ryan what's happened." She wasn't sure that was necessarily true, but she wanted to get Aaron out of his puddle of self-pity and get his brain working on what to do next. She stood up and offered him her hand. "Come on. Let's go."

They began making their way to where the others waited. Except for the one instance when she had to call out to keep him from wandering into the crosswalk against the light—at Bedford, of course—they walked in silence. Finally, they reached Franklin and could see Sam and Ryan on the far side. They were stationed at opposite ends of the newsstand, but they rushed to the corner when they saw Aaron's expression and understood something had gone terribly wrong.

Ellie and Aaron crossed the street and headed for the low wall where Sam and Ryan had been sitting earlier. Aaron sat and stared at the ground, looking utterly defeated. Sam and Ryan got there a second later, looked at Aaron, then turned to Ellie for an explanation. She merely shook her head.

"So that *was* them," Sam said. "We thought so. They came through almost ten minutes ago."

"But we never saw her go by us," Ryan said. "What happened?"

"It was those fire trucks," Ellie said. "They trapped him on the wrong side of the street at just the wrong moment. It was right before I got back. He saw the whole thing happen but couldn't do anything to stop it." Then she realized something she should have thought of earlier. "Oh, *crap!* The other newsstand is on *that* side of the street." She pointed across Park Place. "She probably went by over there. I should have told you to watch both sides."

Aaron shook his head slowly back and forth as if trying to deny her description of the events to himself.

"Hey," Ryan said, "it happens. 'No plan survives its first contact with the enemy,' as my dad would say."

"Great," Sam said. "Fine. Good to know, I guess, but how does that help us now?"

Aaron looked up at them, raised one hand as if drawing their attention to a point he was going to make, then let it fall back into his lap without saying a word. Ellie sat, put an arm around him, and rested a hand on his shoulder.

"Can't we just go back home and then come back here again?" Sam said. "I mean, now we know exactly what's going to happen."

"Yeah!" Ryan said. "Let's call this a dry run."

Aaron shook his head again, this time more emphatically. "No, that won't work. After we got back, it would probably take the batteries at least half a day to recharge. And once anyone in Dad's lab saw the power had dropped again, they'd send somebody to check it out. But first, they'd cut the power." He shook his head again. "That means if we didn't make it out of the shack in seconds, we'd probably wind up sealed inside."

Everyone pondered that for a moment.

"Well, *that* sucks," Ryan said.

They thought some more, and it wasn't long before Sam floated a new idea. "Okay, so what if we didn't go back home but went here at six-thirty again, instead? Landed in one of those other places in the park."

"Still won't work," Aaron said. "If it did, I'd have seen the other us doing what I screwed up."

"Or maybe we don't try because we're assuming it won't work only *because* you didn't see your future self," Ryan pointed out. "That's circular reasoning! We have to...."

"*Stop! Stop!*" Sam was rubbing her eyes hard with the knuckles of both index fingers, trying to stave off a major migraine.

"Hey, guys," Ellie said into the momentary silence. "Aaron's right. None of those kinds of ideas will work. There's no way to choose a new destination from this end. All you can do is hit *return*. Whatever we do next, it has to be done here. Now."

Out of reasonable ideas, Ryan jumped straight to the straw-clutching options. "So what're we supposed to do... *kidnap him?!*"

There were no immediate objections. Suddenly that didn't seem like such an absurd idea.

"Hold on a sec," Ellie said. "What happens after they meet at the newsstand? You said they go to lunch or something, right?"

Aaron nodded. "Yes. They meet for lunch, but I don't know when and I don't know where."

"That's not a problem," Sam said. "As long as there isn't a back door out of the shop, we'll just wait here until he comes out at lunchtime and follow him. I assume it won't be far. Walking distance."

"But how do we work with that?" Ellie said.

Sam and Ryan looked at each other. "You think, maybe...." he began.

" *...The Parent Trap,* but in reverse?" she finished uncertainly.

"Might work," he said.

Aaron leaned forward, buried his face in his hands again, and moaned. "Oh, God, no—not movie plots! We are so screwed!"

"Parent Trap!" Ellie chirped. "I've seen that!"

43

For the next twenty minutes, Ellie, Sam, and Ryan discussed as many ways to break up the newly-formed couple as they could contrive. When some of their ideas strayed into the realm of the absurd, they could not help but laugh, and Aaron's mood slowly improved as he was drawn into the conversation. Once they had refined their best idea as much as possible, Ryan summed up their plan.

"So it's really *Parent Trap* with a dash of *Raiders of the Lost Ark* thrown in," he concluded, while Sam nodded her enthusiastic agreement.

Even Aaron sounded mostly convinced. "This could work," he said. "These are pretty conservative people we're talking about. There's still the other problem, though."

Sam and Ryan spoke in unison. "What other problem?"

"Time is not on our side," Ellie said.

They shook their heads, not seeing the point.

"Lunch isn't for a few hours yet," Aaron explained. "We got here at six-thirty, so six hours later is twelve-thirty. We have to do whatever we're going to do and be back at the shack by twelve-twenty at the absolute latest."

"So, if he goes to lunch early or if they've picked a place to eat that's someplace near the park, great," Ellie said.

Sam now understood the problem. "But if they've agreed to meet later on, or at someplace ten blocks in the other direction...."

"We'd be out of luck, yes," Ellie finished.

Aaron threw his hands in the air. "As I said—totally screwed!" He took a second to calm himself. "But, from what I know of the story, Grandma is here in Brooklyn today on some specific errand, so I assume she didn't plan on being here very long. And I know she was too far east when she got lost and ran into my grandfather, so if they're going to meet up after she's done, I'm guessing it will be to the west of here, somewhere in the middle, which means closer to the north end of the park." He held up both hands, fingers crossed. "Besides, *something* has to go right today."

"'Gotta love an optimist,'" Ellie said. "Meanwhile, we keep an eye on Daniel, make sure he doesn't slip on us. That's at least three hours to kill. How about this—Aaron and I will stay here for now and watch the shop. Why don't you two go for a walk around the city? When you come back, we'll take a turn. Sound good?"

Sam and Ryan looked at each other and exchanged nods. "Sure," Ryan said. "I'd love to see more. It's not as if we'll ever have another chance."

"As long as it's okay to split up," Sam added.

Aaron looked up and gave her a lopsided smile. "Yeah. But don't get hit by a truck or anything. And don't go too far and get lost. And don't...."

Ellie cut him off. "Just be back in ninety minutes."

Together the four of them crossed the street. After Sam and Ryan disappeared around the corner on Franklin, Ellie and Aaron moved further down the block until they found a place to wait almost directly across from Nathan's. They sat facing each other at an angle that allowed them to steal looks through the shop's large front windows without obviously staring.

"How much have you thought about the actual engineering of the shack?" she said. "The technology involved."

"A little," he said, then laughed softly. "Okay, a lot. Do you have something in particular in mind?"

"Yeah. I get how we can come back for an hour, or six hours, or whatever, and return at the same instant we left. Not *technically* how, exactly, but I get the general idea. In theory, we could be gone years and still get back at that same instant. But that implies that the time it takes to *get* somewhere—the actual transition from one time to another—that could also take almost any amount of time, too, couldn't it?"

The question surprised him. It was one aspect of the shack he had not considered, and he took a moment to do so before answering. "Within limits, I guess. It couldn't take so long we'd dehydrate during that time, and the air supply must be limited, but up to a point, yeah. Why?"

"It was the thing with Ryan when we went to Lawrence that got me wondering. He was hit hard, in the middle of his chest—with a *baseball bat* —but he came back without so much as a bruise. I've been wondering if the shack somehow healed him on the way home. And if it did, how much time would that have taken? I think that thing can do a lot more than monitor our heartbeat and breathing. You saw the display—it knows our genders!"

"It could be those hand pads. There's all kinds of info they could get by analyzing sweat, for instance. And that little hole between the wrist studs? Those suits I saw might plug in there, but that's also a good injection site. That is where they put IVs, after all. Did Ryan have any red marks on his wrists after the last time?"

"I don't know. Neither of them said anything about that." She tried to recall watching Ryan that day at the park, then later in Diamond Dee's. In memory, she saw him rub his chest but couldn't recall seeing the underside of either wrist. That probably didn't matter, though. If the device was capable of healing some pretty serious blunt force trauma, it could easily handle repairing a few tiny puncture marks.

"But what if someone went someplace where there was, I don't know— typhoid or something. Or where there was some other disease we don't have to deal with anymore, something we don't normally vaccinate against? Could it vaccinate a person on the way?"

He shook his head. "From what I could see when I was with Dad, there was a lot of research going on. My guess is that every detail of these trips would be planned out way in advance. There'd be plenty of time to deal with issues like that beforehand. And enough time for vaccinations to kick in on the way *would* be too long."

"Okay, so what if someone picked up a bug they didn't plan for? They couldn't bring back some disease and let it loose."

"They could have a quarantine protocol ready in case that happened. It's just as likely, though, if it really can monitor people that closely and *can* tell if someone's infected, that it could be designed to, ah, 'sterilize' the interior instead."

She gaped at him, incredulous. "What, you mean kill the infected person? Get rid of the body somehow?"

He stared back, his gaze flat and cold. Her eyes went even wider when she realized his true meaning.

"No... you mean kill *everybody* inside!"

"I have come to believe these are not very nice people we're talking about," he said.

"Including your dad?"

"It's one of the things that makes this whole plan a little easier to live with. So to speak."

She couldn't tell if he was answering her question or merely elaborating on his own comment. She wondered how she'd handle discovering her father was some kind of mad scientist whose creation threatened the entire world. How had the children of the original Los Alamos scientists regarded their parents' work once its true nature was revealed? She found it hard to imagine, mostly because she couldn't conceive of any way in which her dad's research, which involved using bioluminescence to detect waterborne toxins, could ever be used to hurt anyone.

"It's those nerve induction studs *I* keep thinking about," Aaron said.

Ellie remembered how fixated on them he had been back in May, but at that time, she'd been too consumed by her own concerns to give much thought to his. "What do you mean?"

"Why? We were right about *what* they do—they hijack our nervous systems. But *why?*"

"Your best guess?"

He turned to face her directly. "I have one, but I doubt you want to hear it."

"I already don't like any of this. How much worse could it be?"

"We've been assuming that, whatever the precise nature of the time shifting effect really is, its impact on living organisms is pretty extreme, right?" Ellie nodded. "But that's *living* organisms. It's possible that the shack essentially 'kills' us before the flip, then jumpstarts us immediately after. It would probably be for no more than a second or two, but who knows?"

Ellie felt a knot form in her stomach. "Okay, so *that* much worse. Sorry I asked."

"I'm not saying that's definitely what happens, only that it could be."

She checked on Daniel while she ran the idea through her mind, saw he was still at work behind a high counter. Was it true that they'd all died three times in the past month? *Four* times for Ryan, she corrected. The notion was almost too preposterous to accept. Yet here they were, sitting in Prospect Park in 1941. A month ago, she would have found *that* impossible to believe. So, yeah—who knows? Even so, the idea didn't feel right. She believed she was consciously aware during every moment of the transition.

She chose to drop the subject, and they sat quietly for a while, mostly because she couldn't figure out what else to say. Talking about the future was pointless and painful, talking about the past was maudlin and painful, and talking about the present was just plain painful.

"Not many people going in and out over there," she said at last.

"It's Monday. And it's early. It'll get busier."

"I bet Sam would love it, but I'd feel funny going someplace to have my clothes made, having somebody measure me. I want to walk in, grab something from the rack, and go."

"It's not all that uncommon, even today. Well, you know… *our* today. But clothes aren't your thing, are they? Most people would prefer to go to Apple or BestBuy, take computers straight off the shelf, and walk out with them tucked under their arms. But I'm guessing you went online and specced out your MacBook to make it just the way you wanted it, didn't you?"

"You got me. Still, a computer is a lot less personal than clothes."

"A lot of people might argue with that, too," he said.

A familiar voice called from a distance. "Hey!"

They looked up and were startled to see Sam and Ryan coming up the block. Sam backed up her 'hey' with a wave. Ellie returned the gesture, even though they were now only a few feet apart. "You guys weren't gone very long. Everything okay?"

"Everything is a-okay," Ryan said. "Hunky-dory, copacetic, and five by five. We decided to cut our walking tour short and give you two a little extra time."

"Since you won't have time in the park afterward," Sam added.

Ellie felt like giving them both the biggest of hugs but controlled herself.

"Nothing to report here," Aaron said. "Two people in and out since you left. Both pick-ups. Daniel is sitting near the back on the right."

"We'll take over the watch," Ryan said. "And speaking of, you'd better have this." He handed his pocket watch to Aaron.

"Thanks," Aaron said, sliding it into his jeans pocket. "We won't be gone long."

They started walking west, the direction from which Sam and Ryan had come. After a couple of steps, Ellie looked over her shoulder and saw that Sam and Ryan were still watching them.

Thank you, she mouthed. Sam jabbed her thumb toward Ryan, who waved his hand in a dismissive, *don't-worry-about-it* gesture.

Ellie smiled at him. *He really is the best!*

Ellie and Aaron wandered aimlessly at first, paying attention to their surroundings only enough to avoid becoming disoriented. They talked very little as they walked, content with holding hands and enjoying the feeling of being close. Ellie soon decided she was not especially impressed by Brooklyn, except for how its size contrasted with tiny Los Alamos. She was interested in neither the cars nor the clothing, and she figured the city itself probably wasn't too different from how it was in their own time. And here, unlike in Lawrence Common, there was no major event to witness.

She studied the people they passed, still looking for some reaction to the attack on Pearl Harbor and still surprised to find none. Aside from the newsstand kids hawking their papers, that was. She figured they all had heard about the attack the day before, so perhaps the initial shock had worn off, or maybe it was because Japan seemed so very far away. The reaction might be a little stronger in a few more days when Germany and the fighting in Europe became part of the equation.

"Nobody seems too bothered by the attack yesterday," she said.

"We don't actually declare war until this afternoon, but I bet there are already lines at recruiting stations. If we were by the shipyard, we'd see things happening, for sure. This is just a neighborhood." He was quiet for a moment before adding, "Could be why Nathan's was so slow, though."

It eventually occurred to them to return to the park and scout out in advance the shortest route back to the shack. From Washington, they discovered, they could cut across the museum grounds or through the botanical garden with no trouble, then reenter the park where they had come out earlier. Their best bet, though, would be to use the park's main northern entrance, which is what they did now.

They walked through the park far enough to see the shack's roof rising under a stand of bare maple trees. They sat on a park bench a hundred yards away and watched. A few people wandered past, thinly spaced along the many footpaths, but none of them ventured near the shack. In fact, no one seemed even to notice it. The morning was not bitterly cold, but it was uncomfortable enough to keep most people from wanting to linger outdoors. Ellie now saw how being here in winter worked to their advantage—the place would undoubtedly be crawling with people in the middle of summer.

"That's good," she said. "Nobody seems to care it's there."

"Let's hope it stays that way."

"Do you think it's like that old myth about Cook's ship and the native Australians?"

"You mean what… that they can't *see it?*"

"No, not that, I guess. More like how you see something abnormal and then tell yourself stuff to rationalize it. Like, 'that shack certainly couldn't have materialized out of thin air last night—it must be that I just never noticed it there before.' Mind games for one—that sort of thing."

"It's possible, I guess."

She briefly entertained the idea of going into the shack for a while. It would be warm there, and they would be free from the intrusive looks of strangers. She also knew that would risk calling attention to its presence, but she so badly wanted to feel him holding her one last time that she almost didn't care. She turned to find him studying her face, and she blushed as though he had read her mind.

"Are you ready?" he said.

"What, to go?"

"No—to tell me what knocked your brain off its rails back in the shack. Right before you hit the button."

His expression told her he wouldn't let her say no, and she sighed.

"Okay, fine. After all our planning, I finally got a better idea—right at that second! At least, maybe it's better. But we were already committed to this one, so I wasn't sure I should even say anything. Certainly not right *then*. But now, sitting here with you like this, well...."

"Let me guess. It's the one where you and I go back to nineteen-oh-something, trash the shack, and spend all the time between then and this morning together," he said.

For a second, Ellie was too stunned to speak. All she could do was stare at him, mouth hanging open like a fool's. Then she cocked her arm back and slugged him, hard, on the shoulder. "You mean, awful, horrid *beast!*" she exclaimed. "How long ago did you come up with that?"

"First of all, *ow!* And second, about three days ago. It was a logical variation on this plan, but it has one major flaw, which I'm sure you would have seen if you'd had more time to play with it."

"Which *is?!*" She snapped, still upset.

"Time, ironically. Specifically, too much of it. Every day of every month of every year for almost *four decades* would be yet another chance for something to happen to one or both of us. I could get drafted and be killed in France, or you could die in childbirth. The train we'd be riding to get here today could derail, and we'd *both* die in the crash. TB, yellow fever, polio.... All the ways we could fail to make it to this place on this critical date are too numerous to list."

Realizing he was right, she hung her head and sighed. "Okay, I get it. And, yeah, I suppose I would have thought of that eventually."

"I know. And to be fair, I didn't mention it to you for the same reason you didn't want to tell me."

"Sorry I punched you."

They stood and began to make their way out of the park.

"But hold on—that's what you were thinking about earlier, isn't it?" She remembered his reaction after she pointed out that it was harder to carry out the plan if they thought there were other options. "And this morning, in the back yard. I asked if this was still our one and only plan, and you thought about it before you said yes."

He nodded slowly. "It's been hard not to at least fantasize about going that route, but it's still the wrong choice."

Her brain belatedly caught up to something he had said some seconds before. "Wait... *childbirth?!*"

He kept his focus fixed straight ahead as he answered. "It was just an example."

A big grin spread across her face. "You know, one of the problems with being so fair-skinned is that you turn *really* red when you blush!"

But his mind was already somewhere else. "I can't believe we're betting being able to pull this whole thing off on a harebrained plan based on one of their movies."

"I agree that when you put it that way, it does sound sorta desperate. But as Ryan says, you can't go wrong with a classic. What's the time?"

He took out the watch and flipped it open.

"Oh, wow! It's almost eleven already. We'd better get back."

Quickening their pace, they continued along the parkway until they reached Classon Avenue, where they turned left. Striding briskly, they made it back to Nathan's just after eleven-thirty. Sam and Ryan sat on the low, stone wall, staring across the street into the shop. They exchanged a few short comments, and even without hearing the words, Ellie could tell they were nearly panicking. Sam wrung her hands in her lap, and Ryan repeatedly wiped his palms up and down his thighs. As soon as he saw them approaching, he slid off the wall and bounded forward.

"Where've you guys *been?!* I'm sweating bullets here—he's put away his needle and thread and is practically reaching for his coat!"

They turned to face the shop at the same time Sam called out, "Here he comes!"

A bell jingled as the front door opened, and Daniel Siskin emerged from the shop. He turned left onto the sidewalk and pulled on a hat while he walked. They matched his pace but stayed on their own side of the street.

"*Whew!*" Aaron said. "Something *is* going right!"

Sam couldn't see the source of his evident relief. "What do you mean?"

"I was half terrified he'd hail a cab, and we'd lose him for good."

"So, who says he won't?" she pressed.

"This street's one-way going east, so if he got into a cab, he'd be going that way." He jabbed a thumb over his shoulder. "He wouldn't start off walking west if he wanted to do that."

"I actually *did* know that one," Ryan said. Sam responded with a major eye roll.

"But since he started out walking this direction, he's most likely going to walk all the way," Aaron said.

"Unless he picks up a cab at the cross street," Ellie pointed out.

Aaron again held up two pairs of crossed fingers.

At the end of the block, Daniel made no attempt to hail a cab but merely turned left onto Classon and kept striding along at a steady, determined pace. They crossed Park Place and followed. Now on the same side of the street, they momentarily slowed to let him get a little further ahead.

"I don't remember passing any places to eat along here," Ellie said.

Daniel walked one short block south, then made a right onto Sterling Place. They made the same turn a few seconds later.

"The good news is he is definitely heading closer to the park," Aaron said.

This observation was followed by a loud rumble from Ryan's midsection.

"Speaking of eating...." He placed his hand on his stomach and gave Sam a pleading look.

"Sorry. All out of snacks."

At the intersection with Washington Avenue, Daniel crossed Sterling, then Washington, and headed toward a small diner on the opposite corner from where they stood watching. A small sign hanging inside the window to the right of the door said, "Tom's." The place was already beginning to draw a lunchtime crowd. Daniele pulled the door open and disappeared inside.

"*Ding-ding-ding!*" Ellie said. "Time?"

Aaron waited for Ryan to answer until realizing he still had the watch. He opened it and read the time. "Eleven thirty-eight. We are cutting this *very* close, guys." He closed the watch and returned it to Ryan. Then, without a word, he turned and plodded up the sidewalk away from them.

Ryan pocketed the watch. "You ladies up for this?"

Sam gave a confident nod in reply, but Ellie's attention remained fixed on

Aaron. He had taken a seat on a short flight of concrete steps that led up to an apartment building. He put his elbows on his knees, rested his chin in his hands, and stared at the pavement. Pain spread through her chest, and she raised her hand and rubbed a spot over her heart, an unconscious echo of Ryan's gesture of weeks before. Eventually, she heard her name being called and turned back to face a pair of quizzical expressions.

"*Hmm?*"

"I said, do you know what you're going to do?" Ryan repeated.

Ellie nodded absently, and her answer was vague. "Yeah. I'm... yeah...." She noticed Sam was watching her disapprovingly and avoided meeting her stare.

"*Whatever* you do," Ryan said, "make it quick!"

Sam continued to frown at Ellie, but instead of addressing her directly, she shifted her attention to Ryan. She smiled, her manner abruptly seductive, and she practically purred in response to his innocent comment. "Well, *Mister Collins*, I'm fairly positive you've never said *that* before!" She playfully tapped him on the tip of his nose and gave him a coquettish wink. Then she turned her smile on Ellie. "Ready, Sis?"

44

Sam spun away without waiting for an answer and started across the intersection.

"*Huh?!*" Ellie gaped at Sam's departing back, shocked by this bizarre and totally inappropriate turn in her behavior. With everything Aaron was going through, something she thought Sam wholly understood, this was hardly the time to be flirting! Confusion slowed her reaction, and she was seconds late following Sam into the street. By the time she caught up to her at the curb along Washington, Ellie was far past being merely confused—she was furious! When she turned to confront Sam, she could see Ryan staring at them from across the street. He, too, had clearly been bewildered by Sam's actions.

"What the hell was *that* about?! You have no...!"

Sam cut her off before she could get a good rant going. "That was about you paying attention to something other than Aaron for five minutes. *Snap out of it!*"

Ah! Grasping Sam's intent instantly quenched Ellie's anger, and she tried to calm herself. "All right, I get your point. But *look* at him." She pointed to where Aaron still hunched on the concrete stoop. "He's...."

"Listen—you said you didn't want to let him down. Okay, then the last thing he needs is for you to get so freaked out by how he's feeling that we go in there and screw this up." Sam fixed her with a steely look. "This is it, right? Our last chance? We do this now, or else we go home in failure. *Or* we decide to stay until we get it right, which means getting *stuck* back here, and that, let me assure you, is definitely not happening! You need to *focus*, got it?"

Ellie said nothing because there was nothing to say. Sam was correct, of course. After a moment, she nodded, but Sam continued to glare at her.

"Yes, I got it! Jeez!"

"Good!" Sam's next words were gentler. "Hey, I know this is hard, okay? And I'm sorry, but I needed your head back in the game."

"Actually, that wasn't half as bad as Mom talking about Dad running around campus naked," Ellie muttered, but the passing traffic drowned her words.

"What was that?"

"I said you're right. And thank you." She took a deep breath and tried to push her concern for Aaron to the back of her mind so she could concentrate fully on the upcoming encounter.

On the far side of Washington, a lone figure hustled to beat the changing light across Sterling, then she headed for the diner's door. Sam saw her and pointed across the street.

"That's Judith. We're on in less than a minute. You know your job?"

"Yep! I work on her. Make her feel like a home-wrecker and a total sleaze."

"You got it. There's the light—let's go!"

Daniel and Judith were just settling into their seats when Ellie and Sam bounded noisily through the door. All eyes turned their way at the sudden commotion. They raced through the diner to stand beside their table, and Sam, exuding the same self-confidence she had displayed when dealing with the men in Washington Mill, began pleading with Daniel in a voice loud enough for everyone in the diner to hear.

"Father! Oh, thank God we found you!" she cried.

"There you are, Papa!" Ellie added, trying to sound as though they'd been searching for hours.

"What?! *Who?!*" Daniel was so stunned he couldn't form a complete sentence. So far, so good.

"Nathan said we would find you here," Sam said. "You have to come home! Something *terrible* has happened, and Mama needs you now!"

"'*Mama?!*'" Judith echoed. "Daniel, who are these girls?!"

Daniel spread his hands on the table, palms up, and lifted his shoulders in a shrug meant to convey complete ignorance on his part. Before he could raise a verbal protest, Ellie turned on Judith.

"Who are *we*? Who are *you?!*" She redirected her outrage at Daniel. "Is this another 'special client,' Papa? You *promised!* 'Never again!' you told Mama. And here we find you with this... this... no, I can't even say the word!" She laid the back of her hand across her forehead and looked away as if the whole situation was just too, too much!

Having gathered enough of his wits to speak, Daniel leaned across the table toward Judith and spread his arms wide atop its green Formica surface.

"Judith. Honestly, I have no idea who these girls are! I assure you, I am not...."

Sam cut him off. "*No idea?!*" She drew herself up as tall as she could, planted her fists on her hips, and tapped her foot loudly on the checkerboard-like floor. "No idea about your own *daughters?*" She turned to Judith and stabbed a finger at her face. "And I assume you had no idea that—did you say 'Daniel'? Is *that* what he told you?—that he has a wife and four children at home?"

Aghast, Judith mouthed a silent, "*Four?!*"

"Are you truly that naïve?" Sam went on, her voice dripping with sarcasm and disdain. She grabbed Daniel's hand and began tugging on it as though trying to drag him to the door. "You have to come now. We need to go home," she said. "Mama *needs* you!" But Daniel remained frozen in his seat, literally too stunned to move.

Ellie felt a surge of sympathy for this man whose life they were disrupting, but with great effort, she managed to push her guilt aside. Sam was right—this plan had to work! Arms tightly crossed, she glared fiercely at Judith with what she hoped was an expression of deepest loathing mingled with intense hatred. "*Jezebel!*" she snapped, her voice heaped with scorn. Sam gave her a surprised double-take at her use of the epithet, but Ellie ignored the look. "I guess *some* women simply have no shame!"

Judith had finally heard enough. She nearly toppled her chair as she sprang to her feet, casting a look of utter disgust at the still-seated, still-dazed Daniel. For a moment her mouth worked, but no words came out. Then she whirled around and stormed out of the diner.

Daniel could do no more than sputter helplessly as she left. "But... but...."

Ellie and Sam remained at the table, ready to stall Daniel if he attempted to follow Judith, but he made no such move. He watched mutely as she slammed through the door and disappeared from his life. Then he turned to face his two "daughters," his stare intense and piercing, as though he believed that if only he tried hard enough, it was possible he might actually remember who these two girls were. Finally, he gave up, let out a loud, dispirited sigh, and slumped back in his chair. He looked up, desperate for an explanation.

"Please tell me," he begged. "Who *are* you?"

Ellie leaned forward and whispered close to his ear. "Your grandson Aaron sends his regards—and his regrets." Struck by another pang of remorse, she kissed him lightly on his cheek. "And we're sorry, too."

Sam, meanwhile, smiled brightly and gave a quick wave to the diner's other patrons, nearly all of whom had been observing their performance with an air of detached amusement. Ellie straightened, and together they made a hasty exit.

"Oh, God," Ellie groaned as soon as they reached the sidewalk. "I think I'm going to be sick."

"Nonsense! You were great! But what was that last bit about? What did you whisper to him?"

"I told him his grandson said hi."

Sam looked worried. "Umm... was that a good idea?"

Ellie shrugged. "I wanted to rattle him as much as possible, and I thought that was bizarre enough to keep him sitting there for a while."

Sam twisted to look over her shoulder. Sure enough, Daniel was still frozen in place at his table, staring through the window into the sky. "It definitely seems to have worked."

Ryan was waiting on the opposite corner, grinning and shaking his head and amazement. "Less than three minutes!" he exclaimed. "You two are *good!*" He held his arms out, and Sam rushed into them.

"You know, Ellie might have an Oscar somewhere in her future." Sam sounded proud. "It was her giving Judith the ol' evil eye that finally did it."

"Honestly? I can't believe you were able to do it at all. I never really thought…"

"Keep an eye on the restaurant," Ellie interrupted, walking briskly past them.

Aaron stood when he saw her coming. She stopped directly in front of him, and they faced each other.

"You did good," he said. "Whatever you said in there, she burst through the door and headed down the street without looking back even once. I doubt she'll ever cross the East River again."

Ellie managed the barest hint of a smile. "We did put on quite the show. I hope that wasn't your grandfather's favorite lunch place. He might find eating there a little awkward from now on."

"He's not my granddad anymore." Ellie thought he had never sounded sadder. "Now he's just… some guy."

His head drooped, and he stared at the ground. She stepped forward until their toes almost touched and took hold of his hands.

"Stupid question, I know, but how do you feel?"

"Very strange. I don't know if it's all in my head or what, but I feel—I don't know… kinda… *floaty?* It's like I'm dreaming all of this, but I don't want to wake up because I know that it's this *dream* that's real and that waking up is really going to sleep, but for good."

Sam and Ryan joined them at the stoop.

"We've got a little time to spare, but we should get going," Ryan said, holding up the watch. "He's still sitting in there, and she's long gone. I don't think she's coming back, and it doesn't look like he'll be going after her. Looks like we did it!"

"There's one way to find out," Aaron said. "Let's go."

He abruptly turned and strode off at a rapid pace. Ellie trotted after him, and Sam and Ryan fell in behind. Aaron had already crossed Washington and was walking down Sterling so fast that Ellie had to jog to close the gap. They were halfway down the block before she was able to catch up and take his hand.

"Hey, slow down! What's up? Ryan said we have enough time."

"Maybe," he said, and he did slow slightly. "But what if there's someone back there? By the shack. We might need every extra second to get inside. And besides, I feel like...."

She studied his face carefully while waiting to see if he would finish the thought. She tried to imagine what he must be feeling, knowing that the final few minutes of his all-too-short existence were ticking inexorably away. She squeezed his hand and leaned close to him. When he remained silent, she said the one thing that came to her, even though she knew it wasn't true. "It's okay."

After a left turn onto Underhill, they quickly covered the three short blocks from there to Eastern Parkway. They crossed the wide road and skirted past the front of a library that looked so new that Ellie could only assume it hadn't been open very long. They broke into a trot to catch the next signal, but missed it by seconds. After another minute, they crossed Flatbush Avenue and arrived on its far side at the base of a tall column topped with a huge bronze eagle, the park entrance directly ahead of them.

"We should take the road we crossed this morning, not the footpath," Ellie said. "It'll be quicker." She led them across the plaza and past the trail she and Aaron had used earlier, then turned toward the park where the narrow, blacktop lane emerged from the trees. Spread out single-file along the road's edge and walking fast enough to make conversation difficult, nobody bothered to speak again until they were once more near the zoo, the shack close by on the slope below them.

"We're almost there," Aaron said. "If we veer off here, we should be heading straight for it." He pointed southwest into the grove of bare trees.

They crossed the road and started down the first footpath they found. Where the trail branched, they took first a right fork and then a left as they gradually descended through the wood. After making a second left, Sam caught a glimpse of the shack.

"Over there—I see it!" she cried, pointing through the trees. Ryan grabbed her wrist and jerked her hand back down to her side. "*Whoops!* Sorry."

Ellie peered toward where Sam had pointed until she spotted the roofline protruding above the grove of cedar trees. They were coming in from a slightly different angle than she and Aaron had when they scouted the area earlier, but they had found it. All they had left to do was close the remaining gap without drawing the least bit of attention.

"Okay, let's go," Aaron said, "but keep it quiet."

They stopped where the path drew closest to the shack and scanned the entire area. They were about to step off the trail when a lone figure, walking a different trail on the shack's far side, cleared its corner and emerged into view. Ellie assumed he must have been standing for a time on the side directly opposite from them, no doubt perplexed by its sudden appearance under the trees. As they waited, he halted, turned to face the shack again, and stared intently at it for another long moment. Then he shook his head and walked away. The loud *whoosh* of a collective sigh of relief broke the silence when he at last disappeared around a bend in the trail.

"That was close!" Sam said.

"Let's go," Ellie said, and she began leading them into the undergrowth.

Moments later, they were safely shielded behind the screen of cedars, invisible to anyone on the path. Aaron stood next to the shack with Ellie close at his side, facing Sam and Ryan. They returned his steady look uncomfortably, their glances barely connecting before sliding off to the forest beyond. Ellie felt miserable, all too aware of the grief the next few minutes would bring.

Aaron did something then that Ellie did not expect, something she would remember with perfect clarity for the rest of her life. In spite of the horror about to unfold, he tilted his head back and cast his gaze across the canopy of brightly lit branches arching high overhead. He drew in a long, deep breath and held it, eyes closed, as if savoring the earthy, autumnal aroma of the fallen leaves. And then... he *smiled*. Ellie watched in wonder. She thought he looked liberated, somehow, as if suddenly freed from a life spent suffering under some invisible weight. He nodded once to himself before, still smiling faintly, he returned his focus to Sam and Ryan.

"Listen—if what I think is going to happen when we get back happens, there isn't going to be any time for goodbyes. Or thank yous. I know this was a lot to put on you, but there's no one else we could have counted on to help us see it through. I meant it when I said you guys are the best. I have one last thing to ask, though." He slipped his arm around Ellie's waist and drew her close before he went on. "Please, make sure she's okay, all right?"

Sam rushed to his side and wrapped her arms around him, sandwiching him between herself and Ellie. Tears streamed from her eyes as she fought to get words out past a lump in her throat. "Of course, we will." It was all she could manage. She sniffed loudly, let go of him, and withdrew a few steps. Ellie likewise disengaged from his side, making room for Ryan.

Ryan took a half-step forward, and from two feet apart, they eyed each other without expression. "To be honest, Aaron, I never believed we'd be able to pull this off. It's like I told Sam… I figured we'd get here and find out it literally wasn't possible. The whole 'paradox' thing and all. I thought that's what this morning's miss was all about."

He paused and silently regarded Aaron for a moment. "Listen. I know I've occasionally, or often—or, to be honest, pretty much constantly—given you a hard time, but all props to you, man. I know *I* couldn't do this. I'm going to miss you."

"Thanks," Aaron said, his expression solemn. "I appreciate that." He took a step forward and offered Ryan his hand.

Appalled, Ellie and Sam stared at them, unable to believe the pathetic display of macho stoicism playing out before them. But before either could say a word, Ryan closed the gap between him and Aaron.

"No way that's going to cut it, bro." Like Sam, he wrapped Aaron in a tight hug. Surprised, it was a second before Aaron responded and placed his arms on Ryan's back. When Ryan stepped away, his eyes were brimming with tears he made no attempt to hide.

"Don't worry about Ellie," he assured him. "We got her."

Aaron nodded in thanks, then turned toward the shack. "We better get going." After a few misses, he found the spot that revealed the scanner. But when he placed his hand on the glass surface, it produced only the faintest flicker of a red outline, then nothing.

Ryan frowned. "'Houston, we have a problem!'"

Sam gasped and went pale.

"No, it's…. I think it's okay," Aaron said. He moved back a step. "Ellie, you try it."

Eyeing him quizzically, she stepped up and placed her hand on the scanner. The red outline immediately appeared, then changed promptly to green when the device recognized her palm print. She looked back at Aaron, but he was staring off through the trees, refusing to meet her gaze. Her eyes widened in alarm as she began to suspect what was happening.

No, not already! Fighting back a rising sense of anxiety, she carefully keyed in her entry code and heard the lock disengage. "Okay. We're in. Come on, Aaron."

Ryan and Sam tugged the door open, followed Ellie and Aaron inside, then pulled the door closed after them. Accompanied by the now-familiar sequence of clunks and hums, the interior began to reconfigure. Ryan stood by the control panel, waiting for it to lock into place. After a soft click, the panel lit up and offered its display of data. Ryan located the MISSION CLOCK readout.

"Twelve minutes," he said.

Across the small space, Sam pushed the storage compartments closed after they again opened unnecessarily. When Ryan looked up from the display, he saw Ellie and Aaron remained where they had stopped upon entering the shack. They stood facing each other, much as they had across the street from the diner, aware only of each other. Their hands were joined between them, the tops of their heads touching. Ryan gave Sam a nod, motioning for her to join him at the opposite side of the room.

"We'll be, you know, over there," she said, then walked around to the far side of the seats.

Ellie found that looking at Aaron made it impossible for her to speak. Instead, she stared at their joined hands and spoke into the tiny, intimate space between them, her voice barely a whisper.

"Aaron Alden Siskin, you are the smartest, gentlest, *bravest* person I know. It's not fair that it took so long for me to figure that out."

"Lauren Emilia Henderson, you are the most intelligent, most confident, most *complicated* girl I've ever met. And I've known that from the first day I met you." They joined each other in a quiet, tear-filled laugh. "I'm glad that if I got to love someone, it was you."

She finally summoned enough resolve to look into his eyes, but had to blink away tears before she could see him clearly. "I guess I've never actually said it, but I do, too, you know. I do love you."

She placed her hands behind his neck and drew him into a deep kiss. Aaron responded by wrapping his arms around her and pulling her tightly against him. Eyes closed, clasped in his embrace, she again felt the moment expand until it became timeless. As long as the kiss lasted, her universe consisted solely of the taste of his mouth, his body's warmth, and the solid pounding within her chest.

"Hey. We have to go now."

She was surprised to realize he was whispering into her ear—she had not been aware of the kiss ending. He was still holding her close, though, and she wished she could stay wrapped in his arms forever.

"I know." She took a step back and swiped a knuckle across each eye. Behind her, she could hear Sam and Ryan settling into place. She walked around to the console, and as Aaron took his seat, she checked the display.

"Everybody ready?" she said.

"Yes," Sam said, so quietly Ellie barely heard her.

"Go," Ryan said.

She looked over her shoulder at Aaron. He gave her a weak smile, then nodded once.

"Ten seconds," she said. She quickly wiped the side of her hand across her eyes and pressed `Return—Execute`. She found she could not return Aaron's smile, but she surprised him with one last, brief kiss before taking her seat.

"Love you. Always."

She sat and lowered the helmet onto her head, then slid her feet into place. As she lowered her hands onto the gel pads, she remembered their long-ago discussion about Schrödinger's cat and their individual roles in creating reality. Overcome by a powerful, irrational idea, she clamped her eyes shut.

It won't happen if I don't look! She thought this with all the fierce determination she could muster. *I'm not going to look! It won't happen…*

Then the shack took her over, once more severing her brain's connection to the rest of her body. For the fourth and final time, she felt the gut-churning tilt of the shack as it wrenched them out of one time and back into another.

45

'm not going to look! The thought was still running through Ellie's mind when her normal awareness returned. Overwhelmed by panic and dread, she barely noticed the few, transient seconds of nausea. A wave of panic gripped her mind, and she kept her eyes shut tight against what she feared she might see. A split second later, the shack itself disappeared from around and, more consequentially, from under them. Ellie, Sam, and Ryan crashed awkwardly onto the forest floor.

Ellie's heels struck the thin cushion of pine straw, and she fell backward onto the dirt. She heard Sam cry out—"Aaron!"—and knew then that he was gone. Eyes still closed, she rolled onto her side, curled herself into a tight ball, and began to keen.

"No... no... no...!" She wailed the word over and over, fiercely denying her new reality, one that would never again include Aaron. Unable to face this, her conscious mind retreated into the safety of a tiny, dark room deep in her brain, slammed the door, and locked it.

Her senses, however, continued feeding her raw, unfiltered data. She was aware of many sounds, but they ceased to have any personal relevance. Above a tempestuous howl, she heard people moving close by.

"Are you okay?" a voice said, shouting to be heard above the ambient roar.

"I'm—actually, I'm fine!" a different voice called back, sounding surprised. "I don't feel sick at all. You?"

"I'm good. Let's get her up. We have to go. Now, before this storm cuts loose!"

Why are those people yelling? Why is everything so loud?

She felt someone kneel behind her, then heard something unintelligible spoken close to her ear.

Just let me lie here! That wasn't too much to ask, was it?

With a flash—a literal flash—all of the loud sounds made sense. Her vision flared an intense, bloody red as the brilliance of a lightning bolt blazed through her closed eyelids. At the same instant, a deafening thunderclap exploded directly overhead.

That one was close, she thought impassively. *Yep, we probably oughta go inside.*

The thunder rolled away into the distance, but the howl of the wind remained. Curious about the storm, Ellie forced her eyes open and found she was looking at a face only a few inches from her own. She thought it was a pretty face. Familiar, too. *That's funny—she looks like me!* She recognized distress in the girl's wide-eyed expression, but she was incapable of connecting the emotion to anything to do with her.

A second later, she felt herself being pulled to her feet under the combined efforts of those others. Now standing, her head lolled back and she stared straight up into the night sky. Low, scudding clouds, faintly illuminated by stray light from distant LAB buildings, provided a hazy background against which she could see the dark tops of pine trees whipping violently in the wind. Perversely, she found the effect hypnotically soothing. She began swaying in rhythm with the trees, entranced by the movement.

She was distantly aware of someone pulling on her arms, but she resisted any efforts to get her moving. She was content to remain where she was, spellbound by the fierce motion and primal sounds swirling around her. Her mind, witnessing everything from deep within its warm, safe bunker, registered the storm as something remote, a phenomenon to observe, and not as a source of any real threat.

"It's no use," one of the voices said. "You're going to have to carry her!"

Must be that pretty girl. Why would a girl be out there in a storm like that?

"You get the packs. I've got her!"

There was another simultaneous flash/crash of lightning and thunder.

"Go! You start! I'll break an ankle if I don't change out of these shoes. I'll catch up in a second."

Ellie felt her feet leave the ground, and for an instant she thought she was falling. She forced her eyes to focus again, and this time it was Aaron's face she saw looking at her from mere inches away. He cradled her tenderly, one arm under her thighs, the other supporting her back.

"I need you to help me," he said. "Put your arms around my neck."

She smiled and silently complied, wrapping her arms around him and snuggling her cheek against his shoulder.

I thought you were gone. Why did I think that?

It was her last coherent thought of the night.

46

Following the events in Brooklyn, Ellie's mood plummeted. To Sam, it seemed as though her normally buoyant spirit had become trapped at the bottom of some dark hole, pinned there by the weight of her all-consuming grief and self-recrimination. She soothed her fractured feelings as best she could, occasionally holding her at night until she eventually drifted into a fitful sleep. After, Sam would return to her own bed only to find rest often eluded her. She, too, was haunted by guilt over losing Aaron, and by her memories of the night she and Ryan had brought her nearly catatonic sister out of the forest.

They didn't make it far before he had to switch to carrying Ellie on his back. They covered most of the path this way, but they were forced to make her walk up and down the steep sides of the ravines. Ryan couldn't handle the extra weight and still have any hope of keeping his footing on the loose, rugged terrain.

Sam realized almost at once that her dress getting hung up in the under-brush was slowing them down at least as much as Ryan struggling to carry Ellie, so when they stopped to rest before attempting the first descent, she changed into her shorts. She also swapped Ellie's slick-soled oxfords for her trail shoes.

Full night descended on the mesa with nearly half of the hike remaining, and the darkness slowed them even further. At no point during the planning had anyone thought to bring a flashlight. The result was that a usually easy, ninety-minute walk stretched out to over three hours of intense exertion.

Still, the night could have been much, much worse. When the rain finally came, it stayed far to the south, and they suffered no more than a few brief, cold sprinkles. More importantly, the washes stayed dry. This allowed them to remain at the bottom after their second descent and thereby skirt around the end of the mesa with the nuclear lab. It added nearly a mile to their route, but that was still easier than navigating Ellie safely up and back down yet another set of steep slopes, not to mention negotiating the difficult detour around the snag of uprooted trees.

It wasn't until they were starting the final scramble up to Rim Trail that Sam remembered they had not pedaled to the trailhead as originally planned. The Jeep, not their bikes, waited for them in the parking lot. Once they got Ellie to the top of this final climb, the rest would be easy.

This realization gave her a fresh burst of energy. With Ryan supporting her from behind and Sam guiding her from the front, they patiently talked her through each separate footstep. Fifteen minutes later they were at the top, standing on smooth, level pavement with only a few hundred very easy feet remaining.

They gently eased Ellie onto the front passenger seat, tilted it back, and strapped her in. Sam squeezed through the driver's door and rode home in the rear, leaning forward to steady Ellie's head. Ellie occasionally mumbled what sounded like complete, rambling sentences, but her words were unintelligible. Otherwise, they passed the short drive in silence.

Ryan carried Ellie into the bedroom, then left while Sam removed her shoes and socks, stripped off her Brooklyn dress, and tucked her into bed. She remained there for a short time, one hand resting lightly on Ellie's hip, watching her breaths come and go at slow, even intervals. But even though her eyes remained closed, Sam was not sure she was sleeping.

She found an exhausted Ryan waiting for her in the kitchen, leaning heavily against the counter. With a soft grunt, he straightened and held out his arms. She stepped into his embrace and, finally free of the overriding need to care for her sister, released her pain and sorrow in a torrent of tears. He held her and gently stroked her hair until her crying eventually ceased.

After a long time, she backed away and wiped her eyes with the heels of both hands. "C'mon. Let's go sit outside."

They stepped out to the patio, leaving the door open so Sam could listen for any sound from the bedroom. The storm had moved off to the east, and the sky was now calm and filled with stars. They sat side by side at the table, Ryan's arm draped over Sam's shoulder, pulling her close to him. Not yet capable of transforming the raw experiences of the past few hours into meaningful words, they sat in weary silence and let the day's events percolate in the back of their minds.

After nearly an hour, Sam sat up straight in her seat. "I should go in. Make sure she's okay."

"And what about you?"

"*Hmm?*"

"Are *you* okay?"

"I guess so. I miss him. I mean, I'm *going* to miss him once this all sinks in. Right now, none of it even feels real. But I believe we needed to do what we did. At least, I know *they* thought that." She glanced through the screen door. "So, I guess I'm okay."

"Yeah, same here. I guess."

She walked him to the front door and kissed him. "Thanks for… well, everything you did tonight."

Ryan smiled. "I'd say 'no problem,' but I suspect tomorrow it will be. Don't expect me to be very limber, is what I'm saying. Or even remotely mobile, probably."

She slumped against the door jamb and watched while he got into the Jeep and drove away. As he turned the left at the end of their street, he stuck his arm out the window and waved. She knew he couldn't see her, but she waved back anyway, then closed and locked the door.

On her way down the hall, she imagined how good a hot shower would feel, but by the time she had undressed, she found she simply didn't have the energy. Instead, she opened the closet and, working as quietly as she could, lowered a dusty cardboard box from the overhead shelf. Digging through its contents, she eventually found what she was looking for, set it aside, and returned the box to the shelf. Although it had been many years since they last used the tiny nightlight, when she plugged it in and turned it on, it lit up at once, bathing the room with a warm, comforting glow.

Their parents returned from vacation to find a daughter who was withdrawn and sullen, eating little and talking less. Sam did her best to ease their concerns, explaining vaguely about "boy problems." In private, she pleaded with Ellie to try harder to put on a brave face whenever they were around. Still, there was no concealing the fact that something was deeply wrong.

"Look," Sam reassured them one evening, "she'll be fine. She just really misses Aaron, that's all." She realized her mistake at once, but it was too late.

Her parents stared at her, visibly confused. "Who's Aaron, honey?" her mom said.

"Oh, he was a boy she liked. He moved away at the end of the school year."

That slip finally enabled Sam to understand what was driving Ellie's grief. Aaron hadn't died, exactly. She thought that might have been easier. Instead, his brave sacrifice had erased all knowledge of his existence from everyone's minds but their own. To everybody else, Aaron, that awkward, brilliant, beautiful boy, had simply never been. Ellie wasn't mourning just her personal loss—she was missing him on behalf of the whole world.

The incident was also a sharp reminder that they were now strangers to their own pasts. So far, almost everything about this new timeline seemed to be the same, but she guessed that many of their most recent memories no longer matched everyone else's. Aaron's absence from their lives undoubtedly meant they'd developed a completely different network of friendships over the past six years. She was happy she was out of high school and would soon be in an entirely new social environment at the university. She would have to warn Ellie, though. Who knows? She might even have a boyfriend somewhere in town.

To deal with the information gap, Sam and Ryan decided that each of them would, under the guise of idle curiosity, quiz the other's parents for answers to some of their basic questions. In this way, they learned, among many other things, that Sam's family had not visited Williamsburg before they moved west, but had gone to Busch Gardens instead. Sam's grades were somewhat better than in the old timeline, while Ellie's had suffered, although only slightly. Sam guessed that not having Aaron around to impress was the most likely reason. Ellie was still a straight-A student, of course, but somewhere closer to the middle of the range.

Sam sometimes thought back to the night they had discussed Aaron's idea for destroying the shack. Afterward, Ellie had cried on her shoulder and told her it was *he* who was making the tough decisions. Sam remained convinced that her sister's role had been the harder one to play, but she kept that opinion to herself. She knew Ellie would never see it that way.

Only two things made Ellie smile since the day she lost Aaron. The first was her discovery of four unfamiliar science fiction novels on her bookshelf, all written by someone named D. Hakham. Recognizing neither the name nor the titles, she tilted the leftmost one off the shelf and examined it. *The Messengers* was a first-edition print of a book published in 1948. She had no memory of it. The spine was creased from having been read many times, but that meant nothing. It was seventy years old and had undoubtedly been owned by multiple people over those many decades.

According to the jacket blurb, the book told the story of a man whose fate was forever changed following the brief but impactful intrusion into his life by two mysterious young girls from another time. The rear cover displayed a black-and-white photograph of a face she found, to her amazement, she *did* recognize. D. Hakham was the *nom de plume* of none other than Daniel Siskin.

Hakham's biography explained that he was often haunted by feelings that he was not living the life he had been meant to, and that he sometimes had dreams or visions of a different reality in which he had a wife and son. He started writing the visions down as they came, and later he decided to turn them into stories. Over time the stories became a series of best-selling books. She glanced at the spines of his other two books and noticed that they were all recent reprints, not first editions.

She returned her attention to the book in her hands. She still felt guilty about how she and Sam had disrupted the man's life and was genuinely pleased he had found something positive in his altered future. *Good for him!*

She opened the front cover and saw a handwritten note on the title page. "Happy 15th! Love, Dad" *Well, hey—happy birthday to me!* She was almost sure the book *she* had unwrapped that year had been *Seven Brief Lessons on Physics,* and she was already looking forward to digging into this series. She flipped forward a few more pages, and when she reached the dedication page and read, "For 'Aaron,'" her smile evaporated. She closed the book and, with an unsteady hand, slid it back into place on the shelf.

The other bright spot came later in the summer when she read a brief online article about a young activist in Sweden staging a solo protest—a 'school strike,' she called it—outside her country's parliament building, urging lawmakers to act more quickly in the face of the rapidly changing climate. The link to the article had come in an email from Ellie's mom. Or so it initially seemed. Her mom replied to her note of thanks with a confused denial. When Ellie double-checked the sender's address, she found it was an exact match to her mom's, down to every dot and underscore. She enjoyed the article, wherever it had come from, and the mystery of its origin only added to her pleasure. The girl's passion and courage reminded her of Carmela, and it pleased her to learn that such spirit and courage were alive and well in her own generation. She was skeptical of the idea of skipping school, though. *Sure, the environment is important, but let's not go all crazy!*

She continued to spend most of her days isolated in her room or robotically doing her chores, but now and then she passed hours at a time sitting on the patio outside of Starbuck's, silently gazing toward the spot where a certain weathered shack no longer stood. She kept a small hardbound journal with her at all times, and frequently paused to jot down short notes.

After several weeks, she approached Sam and Ryan with a request. She found them stretched out on the lounge chairs in the back yard. She crossed the lawn, now browning in places, and stood at their feet.

"I need you guys to do something with me," she said. "I have to go back out there. To where the shack was, I mean, and I don't think I can do it alone."

Caught off guard, they merely stared up at her. She pressed on, responding to the mix of concern and confusion on their faces.

"I know this sounds wacko, but I feel like that place is, I don't know... *pulling* on me, or something. It's only because Aaron and I spent so much time together working on the shack problem that I ever truly got to know him. And then, for the thing that brought us together to be the same thing that took him away—how ironic is *that?!* I need to go back and see that it's really gone, that all of this was worth it. I need...."

She tried to say more but the words caught in her throat. Although her eyes brimmed with tears, she didn't cry. In fact, she hadn't cried even once since their return.

Ryan looked at Sam and gave the slightest shrug—*it's your call.* Sam stood and drew her sister into her arms.

"Of course, we'll go. Just say when."

"Tomorrow? Please?"

At ten the following morning, they were already scrambling up from the bottom of the second arroyo, which was still damp in places from the previous afternoon's storm. They spoke very little as they made their way through the fractured mesa's sparse forest, just enough to confirm now and then that they were heading in the right direction. Ellie plodded along in silence. Despite them all being there at her own request, she seemed to be forcing herself past a deep reluctance to return.

After an hour and a half, they reached a familiar-looking spot amid a stand of ponderosa pines. They scanned the area, but without the rough, wooden structure, it was hard to be sure they were in the correct place. Where they stood was not the barren, lifeless zone they remembered. There were no large trees in the space, but the undergrowth was the same there as it was everywhere around it. After scanning their surroundings for a few moments, Ryan pointed to the left.

"There. That's the fallen tree we sat on while we ate lunch the first time we were here."

He led Sam to the large trunk and they sat, giving Ellie some privacy and solitude at the center of what had previously been a clearing. They watched her move slowly about the area, shifting back and forth as if searching for a particular spot. At last, she stopped and stared into the trees. A moment later, she called back to them over her shoulder.

"Remember that first day? You could stand right here and see that line through the forest where they had run the power over from the LAB. Now it's gone." She remembered Aaron's words. "Like it was never there to begin with."

She walked to where the shack had stood, rotated slowly through one complete turn, then sat on the dry needles. When she stretched her arms behind her to lean back, her left hand encountered a small, unnaturally smooth stone. She glanced around to see something so coated in dust and grime, it took her a long second to realize what it was. Not a stone. A camera. *Her* camera! She picked it up and examined it, wiping away the accumulated layer of reddish dirt as she turned it over in her hands. It had spent almost ten weeks alternately baked by the summer sun and drenched by seasonal afternoon downpours. It was filthy and extremely weathered, but she slid the power switch to the "on" position anyway. She expected nothing to happen and was not disappointed when nothing did. Even if the battery still held any charge, the electronics were sure to have been ruined by the weather.

Ha! My camera died of exposure!

She noticed that the narrow, nylon wrist strap was frayed in places. It had been gnawed on, probably by a squirrel or some other small rodent after traces of salt from Aaron's sweat.

That thought abruptly brought back the full emotional weight of his absence, but instead of being overcome by grief, she felt the gears of her logic module fully engage for the first time since returning from Brooklyn. It couldn't be *his* sweat on that strap, could it? And how did the camera wind up here in the first place? She thought back to the day of the discovery, remembering how they had all sat together on the log and eaten their sandwiches while staring at the strange building. Remembering, remembering....

She stood up quickly, any previous reason for being there forgotten in the wake of sudden comprehension. She turned to face the others, her expression animated by rising excitement.

"We need to go back!" She held the ruined device out for them to see. They stared at it in confusion.

"Huh?" Ryan said.

"Now," Ellie said.

"But we just...." Sam began, but Ellie was already gone, taking long, purposeful strides back up the trail.

"Come on, slowpokes!"

She led the way during the entire return hike. Fueled by her eagerness to get to her computer, the trip back took fifteen minutes less than the hike out. Sam and Ryan repeatedly asked about the camera, what she thought it meant, what she hoped to find. "We'll see," was all she would say on the matter, but they both suspected she already had a pretty good idea.

Once home, Ellie led them to her desk and opened her MacBook. Sam and Ryan hopped up to perch side by side on the edge of her bed. As her computer came out of its slumber, she extracted the SD card from the camera and slid it into the slot on the computer's side. Then she pivoted on her chair to face them.

"Okay," she said. "What's the big, obvious problem here?"

"You mean if Aaron dropped the camera into a canal in Massachusetts in 1912, how did it wind up back here?" Ryan said. "That problem?"

"*Ding-ding-ding!* So, remember what we did the first time we were out there, the day we found the shack." Two nods indicated they were with her. "After we ate, he wanted to get a group shot of all four of us. Remember how he didn't have the camera because it was in my pack, and how *I* was the one who set the timer for the picture?" She got two more nods. "After, I picked it up from the log, walked back, and handed it to Aaron so he could look at the picture."

"Then *he* took it back to Lawrence in his pocket—only he didn't," Ryan said. "Because he couldn't have. It's been sitting there since day one." He closed his eyes and groaned. "Oh, man, that's...." His voice trailed off, and he shook his head as if trying to clear it of some repellent image.

Sam looked at Ryan. "What?" Back at her sister. "*What?!*"

"Think about it, Sam. The way things are now, everything we remember doing—the four of us, I mean—that all really did happen. But also it *didn't*, because nothing we did with Aaron is *real* anymore. We remember taking that hike, but if we did, he wasn't with us. Except, obviously, he was. He's like the cat in that experiment. He both is and isn't a part of our past, all at the same time."

Ellie was pretty sure Aaron would like that idea. She saw Ryan smile and nod as if sharing the same thought.

Sam, however, was still not satisfied. "I don't see how that answers the question about the camera."

"Okay, so I said I handed it to Aaron, but after we changed things...." She couldn't go on. She knew what disturbing image had flashed through Ryan's head moments ago—she had experienced it herself out on the mesa. She had seen herself giving the camera to a smiling Aaron who was already fading from existence, saw it pass through his insubstantial hand to land unnoticed in the pine straw. The knowledge that it hadn't happened that way, that the actual truth was undoubtedly far more complicated, made the vision no less painful.

Ryan picked up the explanation from where Ellie had faltered. "It's like he wasn't *there*, you know? It's like she just... dropped it on the ground and walked away from it."

"No," Sam protested, "it's not like that at all! Where you found that today would have been in the middle of the shack—he couldn't have been standing there. Plus, 'as things are now,'" she hooked air quotes in front of her, "we wouldn't have found anything there for him—for you, whatever—to take a picture *of*. Oh, my head!"

"Look at the strap." Ellie held the camera up. "Something's been chewing on it. Squirrel, porcupine—who knows? Whatever it was, it dragged it around a bit, that's all."

Sam was still unwilling to concede the point. "But.... But I...."

"I know. I get it. It feels like we're dealing less in physics than in metaphysics sometimes, but I think I'm right. Anyway," she said, turning in her chair to face her desk, "I'm almost certain I'm right about *this*, and that'll tell us a lot."

The display on her MacBook was dark again, but after she tapped on the space bar, they saw the tiny image of a photo storage card had appeared on the screen. She right-clicked on the card icon and selected "Get Info" from the pop-up menu. The Info panel showed the sixteen-gigabyte card to be almost full. She nodded to herself, remembering that she had noticed the card had been nearly maxed out on that morning in May. She double-clicked on the card, and its contents were instantly displayed in a new window. Instead of row after row of images, they saw a solitary JPG icon.

"Look at that," she said. "Fourteen point two gigs of data on the card, but only one readable file."

She positioned the cursor over it and clicked once. She believed she knew what they were about to see, was equally certain that seeing it was going to hurt. Before losing her nerve, she drew a deep breath and tapped the space bar. The file that instantly opened in Preview filled the screen.

She had been right. It did hurt, and her hand rose to clutch at the center of her chest. It was the group photo from that day, but now there were three people in the photo, not four, and instead of a weathered, wooden shack behind them, there was merely endless, open forest. Ryan and Sam were posed toward the left side of the frame, arms around each other's waists. Ellie stood alone to the right, leaning in awkwardly with her arm extended toward them as if saying *behold—my sister and her boyfriend!* She knew the reason for her odd pose. Standing next to Aaron, she had placed her palm in the small of his back and tilted toward him. The empty spot where he had been tore at her heart.

"There he is." She gestured toward the gap between them on the screen. Her eyes were wet, and her voice was raspy. "That's Aaron. That's all that's left of him now—just that space between us." Then, for the first time since Aaron had vanished from their lives, she wept.

Sam worried about her sister a little less after that. Even so, when Ellie disappeared a week later without a word, she and Ryan scoured the residential mesa in search of her, covering both the neighborhood streets and the canyon trails. They eventually found her several hours later, sitting on the low curb along 41st Street, staring at the house where Aaron and his family had lived. They took seats on either side of her and joined her in silent contemplation of the modest, two-story home.

Ellie finally spoke. "He used to say if his house were any closer to school, he could have homeroom in his driveway. But like that would be a *good* thing. He was such a *dork!*"

Her voice was tight with sadness, but it also carried a hint of laughter, and Sam knew then that she was finally on the mend.

"I can't argue with that," Ryan said, and Sam thought he sounded as relieved as she felt. "But it's a little weird to sit here staring through their front window all afternoon. If we keep this up much longer, somebody might decide to call the cops."

"Won't happen," Ellie said. "The house is empty. Has been for a long time, by the looks of it. I thought maybe his mom would be here, but *nobody* is. It's as if someone forgot to tell the real estate agent six years ago that they weren't coming. I think *that's* a little weird."

"I can't argue with that, either. Still...."

Ellie's gaze went wide and vacant, and her voice became breathy. "It's like it's waiting for them," she rasped. "For *him!*" She saw Sam and Ryan exchange worried glances. "*Wooo...!*" She stretched the sound out, giving it a wavering, haunted-house timbre. Her theatrics were rewarded with a huge eye-roll from Sam, who realized she'd just been had.

Ellie's smile brimmed with love, and when she spoke again it was in her normal voice. "Don't worry. I'm not nuts. And I'm not waiting for him, either, any more than that house is. He wouldn't want that. He did what he did to ensure that I—that *all* of us—would have a future we could count on. I'm not going to waste that." She continued to smile, even as her cheeks were streaked by fresh tears.

"Is that everything?" Sam said.

Ellie dropped her gaze to the pavement. She sniffed and took a few long seconds to compose herself before answering. "At first, I was scared I wouldn't be able to keep a promise. One that I made to him. When we got back, I was terrified that, despite what Aaron and I believed would happen, our memories of him would start to fade, that they'd eventually disappear like everybody else's. I was determined not to let that happen. But it's been weeks, and I still remember everything. And so do you." She looked left at Sam, then right at Ryan. They each nodded in turn. "So I think I'm... okay."

Sam stood up, brushed off the seat of her shorts, and extended her hand to her sister. "Come on, Ellie. It's time to go home."

EPILOGUE

Over the weeks that followed finding the camera, Ellie's wounded heart slowly continued to heal. She still missed Aaron terribly, of course, but nearly every day was easier to get through than the last. She discovered, much to her frustration, that even admitting she was feeling better sometimes made her feel worse again. Recovery, she concluded, was a fine line to walk.

One thing she knew for sure—she was no longer the same person she had been in early May. Acknowledging her latent feelings for Aaron, opening herself to receive his love—"paying attention to what was going on around her," in other words—had changed her. She couldn't deny that the change had brought her pain, but now she felt more balanced, closer to those she loved than ever before. She decided, all things considered, that it was a fair trade.

Occasionally, when she was lost in thought, she would feel the touch of Aaron's hand or the tingly sensation of his lips against hers, and the sense of loss would threaten to overwhelm her all over again. Sometimes he came to her in dreams, and they would talk. The dreams felt intensely real while she was in them, but the content of their conversations largely eluded her once she woke. Even though she could never recall their words, his midnight visits made her feel like he was somehow still with her, and she took great comfort from them.

At other times she could only marvel at how utterly gone he was from the minds of everyone else. Except for Sam and Ryan, naturally. They, too, remembered, and both had their own struggles dealing with the aftermath of their decisions. No one else had even a clue.

The questions raised by such a total erasure gave the analytical part of her mind something to focus on and helped keep her lingering grief pushed to the periphery of her awareness. While devising their plan, they had considered its potential impact on their personal futures, but Aaron had been touching many other people's lives for years. What was different for them? And what other consequences had there been? Trying to discover all of the effects his absence from their past had made on their new present was a welcome distraction.

"Catharsis through analysis," she told herself.

"Dealing by not feeling," Sam said.

"Go with whatever works," was Ryan's advice.

Eventually, the new school year started, and the demands of classes and social distractions began to wear away the remaining raw edges. Sam and Ryan settled easily into their new environment, adjusting quickly to the less structured pattern of their university schedules. Ellie was happy to learn Sam had signed up for one early class, and on most Monday and Wednesday mornings they still walked in together, just like old times. Ryan occasionally waited for them where the far end of the canyon trail met the pavement, but that was okay with her. She had come to appreciate him as a part of her own life as much as for being part of Sam's.

She even saw him at the high school from time to time. Shortly after the school year started, Ryan assumed a volunteer position as an assistant coach with his old swim team. She was startled the first time she encountered him in a hallway at the end of the school day. Unaware of his new job, she froze in her tracks, terrified for one intense, panicky moment that she had somehow slid back in time. Now she looked forward to their occasional random encounters.

Of all the changes she noticed after the Brooklyn incident, what bothered her most was that the plaque listing the winners of the annual science fair now displayed someone else's name for 2015. To her delight, she eventually learned she was not the only one disturbed by this alteration.

One evening, after swim practice had run late, Ryan found himself alone in the lobby. He used the tip of his house key to scratch an asterisk after the new name there. Sam told Ellie about this the next day, leading a few hours later to a bewildered Ryan finding himself unexpectedly crushed in her grateful embrace. Ellie never knew if anyone else ever noticed the minor defacement, but she made a point to look at it on her way in every day.

On a bright Monday morning in early September, Sam and Ryan walked along Diamond Drive on their way to the university. Ellie trudged behind, staring absently at their heels as they struck the concrete in a complex, syncopated rhythm. As they walked up the hill toward the front of the high school, she noticed a car pull into the drop-off area thirty yards ahead of them. It was a white Volvo, one of the XC models, its back end covered in bumper stickers. It looked very much like the one Aaron's mother used to drive, although this one was much newer. The front passenger door swung open, and a sneaker-shod foot emerged and touched down on the sidewalk. They were closer now, and she could hear the woman at the wheel speaking to the exiting figure before he could complete his escape.

"All the paperwork is done. Find the Guidance Office, and someone will show you where to go for your first class. I talked with a Mrs. Johnson on Friday, so she'll know who you are. Okay?" There was a brief, muffled response. "Then out you go. Have a good first day!"

"'Kay, Mom," the boy replied, this time loud enough for them to hear. "I'll see you at home."

Ellie watched as he emerged from the car, rump-first, leaning in to retrieve his backpack from the footwell. He stood and straightened, then stepped back to close the door. The car pulled away, and for a moment he remained in place, looking around as if getting his bearings. She thought he might be trying to figure out exactly where the front door was along the school's sprawling exterior. Then he swung his pack onto his shoulder, and his gaze shifted briefly in their direction.

Ellie became aware of several things simultaneously. First were the boy's spiky blond hair and his glasses, not round and wire-rimmed, but a more stylish, rectangular shape. Next was the 'I Grok Spock' button pinned to the top center of his bright purple backpack. The last was the warning voice of Sam shouting, "Ellie, stop!" after she dropped her own pack onto the side-walk and began sprinting toward him. The Volvo had driven out of sight by the time she reached him, flung her arms around his torso, and pressed her face against his neck.

"Aaron! Aaron! I can't believe it! How...?" Tears of purest joy streamed down her cheeks, and her voice was so choked with emotion that her words were unintelligible. *"How?!"*

Aaron stood frozen in place, his eyes wide, arms held out from his sides. His entire posture could have been a comical illustration for a dictionary definition of *bewilderment*.

"Umm.... Hi?"

Ryan and Sam arrived the next second.

"Yeah, she's a hugger," Ryan said, offering him his hand. "'Aaron,' is it?"

Sam tugged gently on Ellie's shoulder. She awkwardly detached herself from the startled boy and took a step back. Sam set her abandoned pack at her feet.

"I'm sorry," Ellie said, dabbing at her eyes. "I was just so surprised."

"Not half as surprised as me! I'd heard this is a friendly town, but, um... *wow!*" He realized Ryan still had his arm extended. He took the hand and shook it. "Yes, Aaron. Aaron Weisskopf."

"Weisskopf," Ryan repeated. He shot a glance at Sam and Ellie. *"That's* different. Hi. Ryan Collins."

"You guys wanna hear something weird?" Aaron said.

Ryan nodded. "We're good with weird. We and weird go way back. Shoot."

"Right after I stepped out of the car, I had the most amazingly strong feeling of *déjà vu*. Like, *scary* strong." He regarded them briefly, looking each one in the eye. "I know I don't, obviously. I mean, I *can't*. But I have to ask—do I *know* you?"

"No, you don't. I'm Sam." She stepped forward and shook hands with him. "Maybe that was the universe telling you you're exactly where you're supposed to be." She waved her hand at the manically grinning Ellie. "This is my sister, Ellie. She *really* likes it when new students transfer in. I'm sure she'd be happy to show you to the Guidance Office."

Ellie, nearly bursting from happiness and about a billion questions, did not trust herself to speak. Instead, she nodded vigorously and beamed at Aaron—*her* Aaron!—at his familiar smile, his glowing cap of short, white hair. But she was already noticing subtle differences, too. Hit blindside with this bizarre, first-day reception at his new school, he seemed neither awkward nor uncomfortable. He was taking the odd situation in stride, and appeared only mildly puzzled at most. He exuded an air of relaxed self-confidence, an easy-going outwardness that she found at once disconcerting—coming from Aaron—and *very* appealing.

"That was your mom dropping you off?" Sam said.

"Yeah. She just got a job here heading up her own research project." Ellie heard the familiar undertone of pride in his voice and smiled.

"Let me guess," Ryan said. He struck a thoughtful pose, stroked his chin, gazed skyward, and appeared to consult the ether for a moment. "I'm gonna go with… 'energy from algae,' something along those lines." He looked back at Aaron. "How'd I do?"

Startled, Aaron came to a dead stop and gaped at him. "How did you…? That's supposed to be a secret, at least for now."

Ryan brushed his index finger along the side of his nose, a gesture lifted from *The Sting*. He gave Aaron a cryptic smile but made no other reply.

"*Okay*…." Aaron said. "You do look a little like a young Redford, you know."

Ryan grinned at Sam. "I *like* this guy!"

Without a signal, they turned as one and resumed walking toward the high school's entrance.

"Your dad's at the LAB, too?" Sam said.

"My *dad?!*" At first, Aaron seemed shocked by the suggestion, then he laughed. "God, no! He's a guitarist. Solo jazz mostly, a little classical…. At least that's what he used to do, back in New York. I guess now he'll try to find a gig in Santa Fe or something."

Sam and Ryan smiled at the strangeness of hearing the word "gig" come out of Aaron's mouth. There was a lot to learn about this new version.

When they reached the end of the sidewalk that led to the high school, Aaron turned to go down it.

"You know, I would have guessed you'd be over there with us," Sam said, pointing across the street to the university campus. Ryan gave her a cautioning look. She got the message and tossed Aaron an indifferent shrug. "I mean, you look older, that's all."

"Where I went to kindergarten, I could have started a year sooner because of when my birthday is—exactly on the borderline. My mom didn't like the idea, so...." He spread his arms as if to say *ta-da—here I am!* "Now, everyone automatically assumes I failed a year." He cupped one hand to his mouth and called loudly in the direction in which his mother had driven off. *"Thanks, Mom!"*

"I think your mom is *brilliant!*" Ellie gushed, not caring that she sounded like a babbling idiot.

"Ellie!" Sam ran her thumb and forefinger along her lips as if zipping them shut. She leaned in close and hissed into Ellie's ear. *"Chill!"* She turned back to Aaron. "You know, after you get past her totally freaking you out, I bet you'll like her. Go on. You guys better get inside before the bell."

Sam indicated the school with a nod, then started toward the pedestrian overpass with Ryan. Ellie waved, then she and Aaron turned and headed for the main entrance.

"I like your button," she said. "The one on your backpack." She was amazed enough by Aaron's sudden reappearance in the world, but that something as insignificant as that goofy button had somehow likewise survived the—the what... the *reset?*—seemed nothing short of miraculous.

"Really?" He looked wary, as though he thought she might be teasing him.

She nodded. *"Really* really!"

"Thanks. My dad gave that to me. A *long* time ago."

His dad! Sudden understanding flared in Ellie's mind, as bright as the lightning that had streaked above the mesa the night they destroyed the shack. All at once, she knew the answer to her biggest question. *How could Aaron possibly be back?* Because of his *dad!* His *real* dad, the 'guy' who once before had given the very same Spock pin to his girlfriend, who, years later, then passed it on to their son. Had the old Aaron ever suspected? If he had, would he have told her?

A shout from behind them brought them to a halt.

"Yo, guys! Hold on a sec!"

They turned around to see Ryan waving from the steps of the overpass. They backtracked a few paces to hear him better.

"Hey, Aaron! The high school has this science fair thing at the end of each year. It's a pretty big deal, this being the town it is. You might want to think about that." He shrugged. "Just sayin'." With a final wave, he turned away and climbed the rest of the steps to where Sam waited. Ellie and Aaron turned around and resumed walking to the entrance.

"Well, I suppose I could. You know, I've always...."

Aaron continued talking, but Ellie did not hear a word that followed any more than she felt the sidewalk beneath her feet. The final remnants of her pain and guilt had dropped away, and she glided along as if on a cloud. As more answers clicked into place within her mind, she understood this was not the same boy she had known—a different childhood guaranteed that. She knew he was not *her* Aaron. She also knew they might never share the same feelings. But that was a worry for another day. Somehow he was back, and this gave her both hope and a place to start. Today that was all that mattered.

So far this year, she had traveled into history—twice. She had helped destroy a secret and dangerous time-machine project, almost certainly securing the future of mankind in the process. She'd even been on a date! But that was the past. Now, for the first time in months, she was looking forward to whatever the future might bring.

Who knows? In time, anything is possible.

ACKNOWLEDGMENTS

I want to acknowledge the brave men, women, and—most especially—the children who worked in mills and factories a hundred years ago and struggled to improve working conditions for everyone in this country. All those alive today owe them a debt of gratitude for the sacrifices they made.

Thanks go out to the following people for their help in making *Benders* better than I could ever have made it on my own:

Sandy
Mia
Audrey
Olivia
Pablo
Christopher

Finally, my apologies to anyone annoyed by how I have manipulated the wonderful city of Los Alamos to suit my own, purely selfish purposes. I have visited it several times and consider it a true gem cradled in a magnificent setting. However, I needed the forests on the lower plateau to be slightly more "tree-ish," and for UNM-LA to be a four-year institution, so in my story, they are. But remember—first impressions are often deceiving, and some of these alterations, along with a few name changes (including *Starbuck's*), may not be what they seem but subtle hints of things to come.

Stay tuned! — D M S